W9-DCA-520 5289

WITHDRAWN

NEWARK PUBLIC LIBRARY

NEWARK, OHIO

GAYLORD M

WILD WINDS

Also by Janelle Taylor
in Large Print:

Anything For Love
Destiny Mine
Promise Me Forever
Defiant Hearts

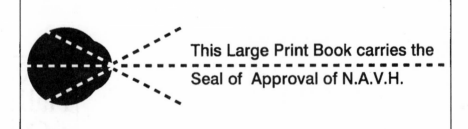

This Large Print Book carries the
Seal of Approval of N.A.V.H.

WILD WINDS

Janelle Taylor

G.K. Hall & Co. • Thorndike, Maine

Published in 1998 by arrangement with Kensington, an imprint of Kensington Publishing Corporation.

G.K. Hall Large Print Romance Series.

The text of this Large Print edition is unabridged. Other aspects of the book may vary from the original edition.

Set in 16 pt. Plantin by Al Chase.

Printed in the United States on permanent paper.

Library of Congress Cataloging in Publication Data

Taylor, Janelle.
    Wild winds / Janelle Taylor
        p.   cm.
    ISBN 0-7838-0303-6 (lg. print : hc : alk. paper)
    1. Large type books. 2. Frontier and pioneer life — West (U.S.)
— Fiction. 3. Women detectives — West (U.S.) — Fiction.
4. Cheyenne Indians — Fiction. 5. West (U.S.) — Fiction.
I. Title.
[PS3570.A934W55 1998]
813'.54—dc21   98-26446

Michael and Melanie Taylor,
thanks for the excellent and time-saving
research help!

Richard Megginson,
who, during the writing of this novel,
rescued me three times when my old computer
"died" and my new system crashed twice;
thanks!

ACKNOWLEDGMENTS TO:

Karen Roberts
at the Yuma County Historical Society

The marvelous staff at the
Yuma Territorial Prison State Park

The Yuma Daily Sun
for many helpful articles

The staff at the Yuma Visitor's Bureau

Early Yuma
by Sidney Brinckerhoff and Rosalie Crowe,
© 1976 by the Yuma County Historical Society

Prison Centennial 1876–1976
by Cliff Trafzer and Steve George,
© 1980 by the Yuma County Historical
Society, Rio Colorado Press.

The Tombstone Tourism Association
and
many kind people at Chambers of Commerce,
Tourist Bureaus, museums, libraries,
and historical sites in Tucson, Prescott, and
New Mexico who aided my research.

Chapter One

Wilcox, Arizona Territory
Friday, April 13, 1883

Margaret Anne Malone gaped at her stepfather in disbelief. "Did I understand you correctly, sir: you want me to help your son escape from the Yuma Territorial Prison?"

"That's right, Maggie," answered Newl Carver, his expression solemn. "You're the only one who can save his life and prove his innocence. Having you come to visit us at this frightful time is nothing short of a miracle, a godsend, the answer to our prayers."

Maggie suppressed a smile at Newl's choice of words. As the owner and manager of the Paradise Club in Tucson, an establishment that dealt in "sins of the flesh" — drinking, gambling, and prostitution — he was not a man she could easily imagine praying. Yet, how could this man be a bad person when he had swept her mother off her feet in less than a month and enticed Catherine to his home in Tucson where they, according to her mother's letters, had been blissfully happy for the last two years? She forced her mind back to the matter at hand. "I work helping to put men behind bars, sir, so why would you ask

7

me of all people to break one out of prison, even though he's your son? Besides, I doubt it's possible for a single person — or even a gang of men — to carry out such a . . . scheme."

"Thank you for not saying it's *crazy*. I have no choice but to try. He's my only child, Maggie. I'm desperate. If the man he's convicted of wounding dies, Ben will be hanged for murder the next morning. I swear to you: Ben didn't shoot or rob anybody. He's been incarcerated for four weeks and his chances for survival grow slimmer every day, every hour — even if that bank teller recovers. Yuma Prison isn't called the Hellhole of the West without good reason. He's forced to work like a slave under the desert sun, from the time it rises until it sets. Those cells have iron gates for doors, so they're infested with all kinds of creatures and bugs; and there's nothing solid to keep out the bad weather. He has to sleep on an iron bunk stacked three high. He's cramped in with five brutal men at night and is around hundreds of them during the day."

Newl took a breath. "Shortly after he got there, he was attacked and beaten and, to make matters worse, those malicious guards punished *him* for the trouble by tossing him into that notorious Dark Cell for three days. I've heard about that place. It's nothing more than a cave chiseled out of a rock hill with one tiny hole in the top. Ben was chained inside a cage that's only five feet high, so standing was impossible; and he was given just bread and water once a day. It lacks any kind of sanitation and it's only cleaned out every four months, so you can imagine the stench and filth. It's said some inmates have gone mad or gotten deathly ill while locked in there. Ben told me a few of the guards think it's funny to drop snakes and scorpions down the air hole to terrorize and punish the unlucky captive. One way or another, my son won't survive such perils and hardships long enough to serve his sentence or earn a pardon. You have to get him out so he can hide in safety while you prove his innocence."

Maggie had never met her stepbrother but she felt sorry he had to endure such torments. Still, he shouldn't have broken the law. She tried to sound sympathetic, "Since Ben was tried and convicted, sir, the authorities must be certain he's guilty, which I'm sure is difficult for you to believe."

"He was convicted because the two witnesses at his trial were either mistaken or outright lied about him. I *know* he isn't guilty."

"Pardon me for asking, sir, but how can you be sure he's innocent?"

"Because Ben was with me on a hunting trip, not robbing a bank in Prescott. I swore to that in court with my hand on a Bible, but the judge and jury didn't believe me because I'm his father and because nobody saw us together to corroborate my testimony. If he had been tried in Tucson where everybody knows the two of us, this travesty of justice wouldn't have occurred. People there know I'm an honest and honorable man."

"If the witnesses were wrong or lying, sir, how do you expect me to expose that? I wouldn't be able to convince them they're mistaken; and they surely wouldn't admit they lied intentionally, if that's the case."

"You're a detective. You can rescue Ben and obtain the truth. You're highly skilled at what you do according to what Catherine has told me."

Maggie glanced at her mother who looked younger than her forty-two years and was elegantly dressed in the latest fashion from back East. But the blue gaze which matched the color of her own eyes revealed tension and fear. She noted how her mother allowed Newl to do the talking, never concurring or disagreeing with his shocking request. Even so, she knew that Catherine Malone Carver was a strong, courageous, and intelligent woman; she'd had to be to sell the family's Texas ranch after Jed Malone's death, move to St. Louis alone, buy a new home, and open a dress shop which she turned into a profitable enterprise. Yet, to prevent Maggie from quitting school in her final year and returning home to comfort and help her, Catherine had kept her father's death a secret for months. Maggie had found the action angering and deceitful at first, but she had come to understand her mother's motive and had forgiven her. Was her mother part of a deception now? A deception based on the good intention to help the man she loved? Maggie sighed.

Having an independent and adventurous streak, Maggie had helped her mother for a year before she went to work for a St. Louis lawyer. In the two years she worked for the man, she carried out many investigations for him, and one day had been approached and then hired by a detective agency whose owner was impressed by her skills. For the last two years, she had handled cases from St. Louis to Denver, to Kansas City, and recently in Sante Fe. Being so close to Tucson, she had decided to visit her mother and stepfather. She hadn't visited earlier in order to give the newlyweds privacy to begin their new life together, and because she was so involved with her challenging work. Now, Newl Carver was asking her to not only risk destroying her job and reputation, he was also asking her to risk imprisonment and possibly her life to free his son. She didn't know Ben Carver, who was four months older than she was, but her mother had written and said only good things about him.

After those jumbled thoughts raced through her mind, Maggie took a deep breath and said, "I can work on his case for you, sir, but I can't get him out of prison or I'll wind up serving time with him."

"You have to try something, Maggie, anything. If not, Ben won't live long enough for you to get him exonerated or pardoned. He can hide out with a close friend of mine in Sante Fe. If you can't clear his name within two months, Ben will turn himself in and never tell anyone you helped

11

him escape. Do this enormous favor for us, and I'll pay any price you set."

"Money isn't a consideration. As I said, it's impossible, especially with Yuma Prison involved. I've heard it's built atop a steep rock bluff, has walls that are eighteen feet high and eight feet thick, and has guard towers on all sides, one manned by a Gatling gun. It's bound by rivers on two sides and has deserts and mountains in all directions. True?"

"Yes, but you have an advantage that would help you pull it off."

"I don't understand your meaning, sir. What advantage?"

"Do you still correspond with your roommate from boarding school, Miss Abigail Mercer?"

"Yes, but what does Abby have to do with this matter?"

"Have you heard from her since January?"

"Probably, but I've been away from St. Louis for months, so I haven't been home to get my mail. Which is also why I didn't know about Ben's troubles, as I'm sure Mother wrote to me about them." As Catherine nodded her head, Maggie repeated, "Why did you ask about Abby?"

"Her father became a Yuma Prison commissioner in January, so the Mercers are living there now. You could conceal your true reason for going there under the guise of a visit to your best friend. With her father employed by the prison, you can find clever ways to extract needed information and can obtain access to the prison to study those inhuman conditions yourself."

"How do you know about me and Abby?" Maggie asked, truly puzzled.

"Catherine told me she was your best friend after we read an article in the *Arizona Sentinel* about Mercer's appointment. I take the Yuma paper so I can keep up with the news there, especially what's written about the prison."

"Knowing the Mercers still doesn't give me a way to get Ben out."

"That's why I said your timing is a godsend: Ben's working on road detail outside the prison walls, at least for now."

"But he'll be guarded, maybe even wearing leg irons. Surely you aren't asking me to disarm the guards in daylight and ride off with him?"

"Certainly not. For your safety, nobody can be told you have a connection to us. Everybody in Tucson knows I have only one child, Ben. Since we've only visited in St. Louis and you've never been to Tucson, nobody there knows who you are if the Law comes to question us later. There's no reason why Miss Margaret Anne Malone of St. Louis — guest of a prison commissioner and best friend to his daughter — should fall under suspicion for planning and carrying out Ben Carver's escape."

"But Abby knows all about me. I wrote and told her two years ago that Mother remarried: I told her your name. As soon as Ben escapes, the Yuma paper will be flooded with facts about him.

13

She would surely realize something is wrong when the son of Newl Carver of Tucson escapes while I'm in town for a surprise visit."

"If you confided in her, would she betray you to the authorities?"

"No, she wouldn't betray me, but I can't make her an accessory to a crime. Abby's like a sister to me, so it wouldn't be right to involve her in any way."

"When the truth comes out and an innocent man is saved and the guilty are exposed and punished, you two will be heroines."

"What we'll be is hauled off to jail if we're exposed during or after the escape, whether or not Ben remains silent or turns himself in later."

"You're a brave and clever woman, Maggie, I'm certain you'll make this plan work."

"I fear I lack your confidence in me in this particular matter, sir. I can't imagine how I could get him away unnoticed and unharmed."

"Don't worry, my dear. I brought along everything you'll need: a copy of his trial, articles about the crime, maps and sketches of Yuma and the prison, and the inmates' daily schedule. I also included other items you'll need to pass along to him: boots, 'civilian' clothes, money, a weapon."

Maggie glanced at the bulging satchel Newl had placed on the floor. "How did you get all of this together so fast?"

"I prepared myself in advance for the time I would find the right man to rescue my son. But the right man turns out to be a beautiful and talented young woman, my stepdaughter. Ben's stepsister."

"Thanks for your faith in me." *This idea is insane, Maggie, so tell him absolutely no and leave before he figures out a way to ensnare you in it! Don't be deluded by grandiose visions of heroics and righting thwarted justice. It's stupid and illegal, so don't get involved! Besides, it's an impossible task, isn't it?*

"I'll confess I already have a detective working on Ben's case, but he's accomplished nothing useful in weeks. I doubt he's doing more than collecting the high salary I'm paying him. You aren't my second choice, Maggie, I just was reluctant to drag you into this perilous situation."

She smiled her gratitude before asking the questions that raced through her mind. "Why would those witnesses lie? What made them think the culprit was Ben? Prescott is a long way from Tucson, so do they know Ben Carver? If so, how?"

"One of them is an old rival of mine," Newl explained, "so he would do anything to hurt me. Years ago we butted heads over where the territory capital would be located. It was Prescott from '64–67; but Tucson snatched away that honor and kept it until '77 when it was moved back to Prescott. I don't have to tell you how important it is to a town's survival in this wild territory to be the capital. I was one of the main forces that got it moved and held in Tucson for those ten years. By the same token, he was one

15

of the main forces that helped take it away from us. Needless to say, he knows me and my son well. He claimed one of the five robbers' masks slipped down during the holdup and they recognized Ben before he could replace it. Hogwash! If Ben was a criminal and knew they could identify him, he would have killed them to protect himself. As for the teller who was wounded, he never saw that alleged mask incident. The other witness married my self-appointed enemy shortly after the trial ended, so that should explain her motive. I swear to you, Maggie: Ben was hunting with me that day, not committing crimes in Prescott. The other men you want to locate and put behind bars are Pete Barber and Slim Jones. Find them and their accomplices, and force the truth out of them. Save my son for me, please, my dear, I'm begging you. If I'm forced to watch my only child hang and for a crime he didn't commit, it will kill me, Maggie, simply kill me."

While in New Mexico, Maggie had heard of Pete Barber and Slim Jones and knew they were trouble, big trouble. As she watched her stepfather dry his misty eyes with a handkerchief as her mother tried to comfort him, she wondered if she should at least pretend to consider his urgent request rather than saying an emphatic no. What if, she reasoned, Newl was right? What if Ben Carver was innocent? What if Ben's life was in jeopardy? What if she could save him, prove his innocence, and bring the guilty parties to justice? Maybe this visit's timing wasn't a coincidence; maybe it was a propitious omen; maybe a divine force had guided her there to right a terrible wrong. *Watch it, Maggie, you're getting sucked into this whirlpool and may drown!*

"I'm scared and I'm desperate, Maggie," Newl continued, "and becoming more so with each hour that passes. I've taken every legal step I could find to get Ben out of this horrendous predicament, but nothing has worked. And Ben's lawyer has used every loophole and trick he could think of, to no avail. That detective is stumped, too. I don't want to hire a gang of outlaws to ride into Yuma to free him because innocent people could get injured or slain and that would make matters worse for Ben. If you don't help us, Maggie, my son will suffer terribly and maybe die. At least go to Yuma and check out the situation for yourself, see if it's possible to engineer a rescue without endangering yourself. Whatever you decide, I won't hold it against you. But one way or another, I'm getting my son out while he's still alive."

Against her better judgment, Maggie told herself there was no harm in going to Yuma to analyze the situation. Surely that was kinder than refusing outright to do anything useful. Once she got there, perhaps she would find or think of something that might at least get Ben's case reopened. And she'd see Abby. She pushed long strands of light-brown hair with golden streaks behind her ears and focused her blue gaze on Newl. She had gone into her line of work to face challenges, to experience stimulating adventures, and to uphold the law, so what better way, she reasoned, to achieve those goals than by agreeing to her stepfather's request? After she looked the area over, if an escape didn't appear just and feasible, she wouldn't make the attempt. Besides, if she handled this, she could prevent the violence and bloodshed that would surely result from Newl's alternate plan. "Give me a few minutes to study the things you brought along and to think about this matter from all angles; then I'll give you my answer."

Newl gave her a quick hug. "That's fine. Catherine and I will sit quietly on the bed while you use the table and chair. Ben will love you forever for rescuing him, Maggie, and so will I. You won't regret helping us; I swear it. If anything goes wrong, I'll use every dollar and breath I have to rescue you."

Maggie's quick mind scoffed, *If your money, power, and energies have failed to help your son, what makes you think you can use them to save me?* Yet, she said, "Thank you, but I hope it won't be necessary."

Catherine worried aloud as she grasped her daughter's hand and gave it an affectionate squeeze, "I know you're highly skilled in your work, Maggie, but don't take any risks." She was so proud of her daughter, but she lived in constant dread of being informed Maggie had been killed or injured badly in the course of an investigation. What she wanted most was for Maggie

18

to meet a good man, get married, have children, and be safe, and preferrably close by in Tucson. She urged in a strained voice, "If no safe opportunity arises, please don't attempt a rescue. Like Newl, I would die if anything happened to my only child, my beloved daughter."

The women embraced for a minute. Afterward, Maggie gazed into Catherine's tear-filled blue eyes and said, "Don't worry, Mother, if I can't pull this off without endangering myself, I won't try it."

"You promise?"

"Yes, Mother, I promise. Now, relax while I go over this material." *Please, God, help me find at least one useful clue to save us all from certain jeopardy and misery.*

Hawk Reynolds slipped out of a window to the room next to the one he had watched Newl Carver and his wife enter earlier that evening. While awaiting the cover of darkness, he had paced the floor and wondered what was going on in there. He had been informed by a friend in Tucson who worked at the Paradise Club that Carver was secretly seeking somebody to bust his son out of Yuma Prison. He had been en route to hire on for that job when he saw the couple arrive in town shortly after he did. He trailed them to this hotel and registered in the room next door. He suspected — from the satchel Carver had brought along, probably loaded with money, and from Carver's covert actions — that

19

Carver had found a man to do the dirty task for him, a position Hawk needed desperately if he was going to obtain his revenge. Not *if*, he told himself, but *when*. Those bastards were going to pay for what they had done to him and his family! Even if he had to eliminate his competition.

When night had fallen, Hawk sneaked along the porch roof to reach his target, his bare feet moving soundlessly on the shingles. He had removed anything that might make a noise, and knew his black garments masked his presence. Those were precautions partly learned from his mother's people, the Cheyenne, and partly from experience in his line of work. He was relieved the two rooms were located at the rear of the hotel and his had been available. He was also fortunate that the recent new moon was still little more than a dark ball in the sky and helped obscure his actions. He saw ivory lace curtains fluttering in a steady breeze. He halted, pressed his back against the building, and listened.

Newl reiterated their plan to make certain it was clear, "Catherine and I will leave in the morning, and we'll have no further contact here since we can't risk any of us being seen together even in Wilcox. She'll get off the train in Tucson and return home while I continue on to Yuma and tell Ben the good news. You'll leave Monday afternoon; that will put you in Yuma Tuesday evening, after I've returned home so we won't be there at the same time. I'll take care of your horse while you rescue Ben." He paused before asking Maggie, "Do you have everything you'll need?"

"I think so. I'll keep you informed of my location and progress using the code we discussed earlier. Tell your son to do whatever is necessary to stay out of trouble with the other prisoners and with the guards. If he gets himself tossed into the Dark Cell again or taken off road work, there'll be no way I can get to him."

"Don't worry, he'll do anything you tell him; I promise."

"After this is over, Maggie, you and Ben can return home and settle down here." As Catherine hugged her daughter, she whispered in her ear, "Take care of yourself. I love you."

Maggie hugged her mother and whispered in return, "I'll be careful, and I'll be seeing you again soon, for a long and quiet visit. I love you." She looked at her stepfather and said, "Good-bye, Newl."

Newl sent her a wry smile. "I know I haven't given you any choice in this matter, but I'll make it worth your while after it's settled."

"I've told you I'm not doing this for money; as you said, I have no choice but to give it my best effort. Besides, I have a feeling Ben would do it for me."

"Yes, Maggie, he would. Good-bye and good luck."

"I'll need more than simple luck to pull off a jailbreak from Yuma Prison without getting me and Ben in worse trouble. Good-bye, and I'll send you a report soon, hopefully a good one." *But I doubt it.*

Hawk was astonished by what he overheard. He was astounded that Newl Carver would hire a female for such a daring and perilous job. He wasn't convinced even he, with all of his skills and training, could pull off a break at Yuma Prison, and was certain a mere woman couldn't do so. From what they had said, he hadn't learned why she was taking such an awesome risk. It didn't sound as though she was Ben's sweetheart or as if she really believed it when she said, "Ben would do it for me." He wondered if she was a criminal whom Carver was forcing to do his dirty work, since she had said money wasn't her motivation and she had "no choice." Yet, they were on a first-name basis, as if they knew each other well. Who and what was this Maggie? What kind of "job" did she do that would qualify her to be considered for such a feat? Why was she willing to risk her life and freedom to help the Carvers? Perhaps answers to those questions had been given before his arrival, or during those whispered words between the women that he couldn't overhear.

After the couple left, the woman bolted the door, then she approached the window, took a deep breath of fresh air, and closed and locked it. Before he could sneak a peep inside, the drapes were drawn. With caution, he crept back to his room. Somehow, he resolved, he had to get a look at her, but make certain she didn't notice him. At least he knew her schedule and plans, so he wouldn't have to risk exposing himself to glean those facts. If he shadowed this mysterious woman and she miraculously succeeded, Ben would be on the loose to lead him to his cohorts. Then the last three members of that gang would be within his reach; and they would all pay dearly just as the other two had! Plus, if she succeeded, Ben would surely trust and confide in her faster than the sorry bastard would in him! If not, he would wrangle the facts he needed out of Ben, and there would be nothing Maggie could say or do to stop him from exacting his revenge.

He told himself he wouldn't feel bad about using her in any way necessary to get to Ben Carver, Pete Barber, and Slim Jones, even though she was a female and his mother and grand-mother had taught him to respect and defend women. Since she had an unknown connection to Ben and was about to commit a serious felony for him, she deserved whatever misfortune fell upon her head.

For all he knew, this Maggie could be a mem-ber of Barber's gang. During his travels, he had run into several highly skilled and daring female outlaws, females who often disguised themselves as men while committing crimes. For certain, she was in for the biggest trouble of her life if that was true or she tried to interfere with his plans! Maybe she owed Ben a favor for getting her out of peril in the past and she was trying to repay that debt. Perhaps Barber or Jones had asked or was forcing her to get their cohort out of prison.

No matter her motive or identity, if she failed in her task, he had a valuable ace up his sleeve to make sure *he* didn't . . .

Maggie changed into a nightgown, doused the oil lamp, and got into bed. It wasn't late, but she was tired. The train ride from Sante Fe had been noisy, bumpy and hot. And now, she had a heavy burden on her shoulders. She should have guessed that something was amiss when her mother responded to her telegram with such a confusing and mysterious message, saying to meet them at this hotel in Wilcox, a railroad town eighty-one miles southeast of Tucson.

What have I gotten myself into? This reckless action could cost me everything. How can I possibly carry off such a crazy scheme?

Even as she posed that last question to herself, Maggie's adventurous and keen mind was spinning with clever ideas. She felt excited, frightened, reluctant and eager, all at once.

As she lay in darkness and deliberated the just-as-dark situation, Maggie realized the important question was not if she could do it but if she *should* do it. If Ben was innocent, shouldn't she try to save him? If she refused and he was hanged or died in the prison, Newl would never forgive her, no matter what he had said earlier.

That resentment and bitterness could wreak havoc on their family life, trapping her mother between her husband and daughter.

Her mother had to believe that Newl's urgent request was the right and only thing to do. If not, Catherine would have somehow let Maggie know. There was no way Catherine Malone Carver would endanger her only daughter's life and freedom just to please or to prevent displeasing her husband of two years.

Go to Yuma on schedule and study the situation at close range, Maggie told herself, *then make your decision to either retreat or advance. Right now, get to sleep; you need the rest and a clear head for tomorrow.*

On Sunday night, Maggie lay in the darkness once more with thoughts of her impending actions racing through her head. All preparations had been made and all precautions had been taken to accomplish them.

Yesterday, her mother and stepfather had left Wilcox, taking her beloved roan with them to be stabled in Tucson during their separation. She had purchased her train ticket to Yuma, along with one for Ben from that town to Sante Fe; that one would appear to be for her return trip if somehow seen in her possession. She had sent excess belongings with her mother to allow room in the secret compartment under a false bottom in her trunk for the items she must deliver to Ben. She had telegraphed Abby to ask if she could visit her this week, and Abby had returned a quick and enthusiastic response. She had written a page of explanations and instructions for Ben to carry out following his escape, which she would conceal with the other items somewhere near the prison, in case Newl lacked the privacy to reveal their plan to him. Later, she would write Ben a note giving their location and find a way to pass it to him. She had made sure to sign her name and identify herself as his stepsister to avoid any extra confusion on his part.

She had attended an Easter service at a small church this morning, and had eaten her meals downstairs at the least busiest hours; otherwise, she had kept to her room yesterday and today to study Ben's case and to avoid calling attention to herself, though she now had a credible explanation for being in Wilcox while en route to the Mercers.

Tomorrow, she would bathe, dress, and eat before boarding the one-o'clock train to Yuma. She was fortunate that one of the newer styled cars had a sleeper compartment available so she would have privacy and rest along the way. The thirty-hour journey had many stops and a pace that was slower than a stagecoach's swift run between waystations.

Heaven, help me if I'm exposed. As for my unknown stepbrother, if I discover he's guilty after I bust him out, I'll do whatever is necessary to track him down and send him back where he belongs!

It wasn't too late to change her mind, Maggie told herself, but she knew she couldn't do so. Ready or not, she would be on her way soon.

Chapter Two

Maggie knew the sun would be setting around seven o'clock, her arrival time, but it would remain light enough to see outside for an hour or so beyond that time. Despite the train's open windows, the air rushing inside the cars was hot and dry, the temperature still lingering above the mid-eighties. While eating in the dining area provided in this more costly hotel car, she had learned that it rarely rained in Yuma, but when it stormed, usually it was a harrowing and powerful assault with fierce thunder and lightning and strong winds. That, along with excess water from either or both of the nearby rivers, could create a dangerous flood that threatened to wash away the low-lying town.

She used a handkerchief to collect the perspiration gathered on her flushed face and hoped her blue day dress wasn't getting wet and stained with the salty moisture. Her light-brown hair was secured with a matching ribbon at the nape of her neck, but that style did little to help cool her. She longed for a bath, a refreshing drink, for the rolling motion and noise of the train to cease. It had been two and a half years since she had seen Abby. Maggie could hardly wait to see her friend again and her elation steadily increased.

As Maggie's thoughts roamed in many directions, she studied the arduous landscape which had remained almost the same since leaving the Maricopa Wells station, almost since pulling away from Tucson. At times, it had been thick with mesquite, palo verde, acacia, desert willow, white sage, creosote bushes, ocotillo with its lovely red blooms, prickly pear, and other varieties of cacti and wildflowers. On occasion, the saguaros had been so abundant that it looked like a vast forest of them. Their sizes and shapes were fascinating, and for a while, she had played a mental game of imagining the things those shapes reminded her of.

She had sighted kestrels capturing mice, doves nesting on the huge arms of those mammoth plants, great horned owls sitting atop lofty cacti limbs, and hawks circling overhead. She had been told the rattlesnakes, venomous gila monsters, scorpions, and tarantulas had to escape the blazing sun during the day while awaiting nightfall to seek their prey.

She journeyed through a near circle of distant and dark mountains and seemingly endless stretch of rugged desert where the sandy ground was nearly barren except for a sprinkling of low scrubs. For certain, there was no way a rider — a fleeing convict — could conceal himself on that terrain.

Then the tracks drifted closer to the Gila River and the Muggins, Gila, and Laguna mountains where the greenery returned in abundance. Maggie paid keen attention to the remaining stops and topography along the Southern Pacific route. In particular, she made mental notes about the sidings at Adonde and Dome where the steam engine halted for water and where a few passengers either boarded or deboarded or goods were unloaded. Either site would be an ideal location for Ben to sneak onto the train; hopefully he would go unrecognized in the disguise and civilian clothing she would conceal for him. She noted the distances and terrain her stepbrother must cover in order to reach those areas. Newl had told her that Ben was familiar with this section, so it would be up to him to make it this far either walking, using the Gila River, or riding a stolen horse. There was no safe way she could purchase a mount and hide it for him to use, not without casting suspicion on herself if their relationship was discovered and she was investigated.

Soon, Yuma loomed ahead in the lowlands at the confluence of the Gila and Colorado rivers, a long stone's throw from the California border beyond the swift flowing Colorado River. The town appeared larger than she had imagined from Newl's description and the sketches he had provided. Mountain ranges, varying in heights and widths, were visible in every direction. With fertile valleys located eastward and southwestward, the many hues of green and abundant water were welcome sights following those dry and drab ones left behind. Even so, the treacherous Sonoran Desert was wildly beautiful in its spring glory.

As the train slowed to a near crawl to work its way down Madison Avenue toward the river and railroad station, Maggie's gaze was glued to the steep bluff and high adobe walls of the Yuma Territorial Prison atop it, its many guard towers silhouetted against a brilliant sunset. Her fingers absently touched the Remington derringer in her dress pocket, as if it could protect her from the tingle of danger that swept over her. She took a deep breath and swallowed with difficulty, her throat suddenly gone dry and tight.

She jumped and almost squealed when the train's whistle sounded to let townfolk and passengers know they had arrived and would be stopping soon. *Relax, Maggie, you haven't done anything wrong yet, and you may not honor Newl's request after you have a look around. For now, don't think about anything except your reunion with Abby and her parents.*

The train halted, and Maggie finger-checked her dress and hair, then headed for the doorway. Before she could descend the last step to the ground, Abby rushed forward to greet her with a shriek of her name, an affectionate hug, and a kiss on the cheek.

"Finally you're here! I've hardly been able to contain myself since I heard from you on Saturday. I'm so glad you came, and I've missed you."

"I've missed you, too, and you look wonderful,

absolutely wonderful," Maggie told the green-eyed blonde who was almost bubbling with exhilaration.

"So do you, my dearest friend. What are you doing in this area of the country? Have you been to see your mother?"

Maggie answered in a hurry to get that hazardous topic behind them. She hoped Abby hadn't reminded her parents — especially her father — that her mother lived in Tucson and was married to Newl Carver, as she didn't want that last name fresh in Mr. Mercer's mind when Ben Carver from Tucson escaped soon. "I just completed an assignment in Sante Fe, and since I was so close, I decided to visit you. When I telegraphed you from Wilcox, Mother was away on a trip, so I'll visit with her another time. I hope this surprise is all right."

"Of course it is; any time is fine with me. What were you doing in Sante Fe? Another secret and dangerous job for your agency? I so love receiving your letters and reports of your exciting adventures. I'm envious of you for having such stimulating experiences. You must tell me all about your travels and daring deeds during your visit," Abby coaxed, her green eyes twinkling.

Tom Mercer and his wife joined them. "Abigail, dear, give Margaret Anne a chance to catch her breath before you flood her with questions," he teased as Lucy Mercer gave Maggie a welcoming hug.

"Yes, Father; it's just that I'm so happy to see

her. It's been so long since she visited us in Virginia and so much has happened to both of us since that time. Letters aren't the same as being face-to-face, so we have plenty of catching up to do, right, Maggie?"

Tom smiled at his daughter, then at their nodding guest. "It's good to see you again, Margaret Anne, and you look lovely. Welcome to Yuma."

"Thank you, sir, and it's delightful to see you and Mrs. Mercer again. Do you like living in Yuma? It's so different from the South."

"It's small and distant and the weather can be a real bear but we're getting accustomed to it. We'll give you the grand tour tomorrow. Presently we're staying at a local hotel because our house is being repaired from damage by a recent earthquake; they have them here on occasion."

"I'm sorry, sir, I guess I came at an inconvenient time. I can return home tomorrow and visit again later if that's best for you."

Tom shook his head. "If you don't mind staying at the hotel, your timing is fine with us, and my daughter would be heartbroken if you left so soon. In fact, I've already rented you a room close to our suite. If one can call two rooms a suite. It's where the owner lived until he built a new home recently, so I guess our timing was perfect. Lucy, dear, why don't you take Margaret Anne and Abigail to the carriage while I see to her baggage? It's being unloaded now."

"Come along, young ladies," the older woman said with a smile.

Abby looped her elbow through Maggie's and guided her toward their waiting carriage where a passing gentleman halted to assist Mrs. Mercer into the front seat and then two friends into the back one.

As she sat sideways in the carriage, the easier to converse, Lucy said, "We're so happy to see you, Margaret Anne, and so glad you came to visit us. With so few things of interest here for a proper young lady, Abigail can use a good diversion. We waited for your arrival before we dined tonight, as we were sure you'd be hungry and looking forward to a good meal."

"Yes, ma'am, I am. How long have you been staying at the hotel and when will your house repairs be finished?"

"We've been there for a week and expect the work to require another week or so. That earthquake shattered a chimney, broke windows, and caused a wall to crumble. The delays have to do with having to wait for the same size adobe bricks to be made and replaced and waiting for those size windows to arrive from back East. After the repairs are completed, the men have plastering, painting, and cleaning up debris to do. Frankly," Lucy confided with a playful grin, "I'm enjoying the holiday from routine chores. No cooking, washing dishes, scrubbing floors, doing laundry, or other housework tasks for a while. I feel like a princess, but, alas, it won't be for much longer."

Maggie and Abby shared gay laughter, at

34

Lucy's dramatic expression and tone. It was as if the passage of time instantly vanished and they were young schoolgirls having fun again.

Shortly, Tom Mercer joined them and they departed.

Hawk observed the intriguing scene but stayed out of his quarry's sight, just as he had aboard the train. He wished he could overhear the conversation, but the distance between them was too great and he dared not move closer. It was apparent that Maggie was well acquainted with the newest prison commissioner and his family, so he wondered if she would seek help from them with her daring and dangerous plan. If so, would they comply? If not, would they try to talk her out of committing a serious crime, or expose her if she carried it out? How did those four people know each other? His questions seemed endless. Mercer's appointment had to be a coincidence because it had taken place before Ben's crime. He didn't like or trust the many unknowns that were cropping up in this situation and intruding on his personal plans. He should learn all he could about Tom Mercer and Miss Margaret Anne "Maggie" Malone, and fast.

He collected his belongings, saddle, and horse before he trailed them to the Palace Hotel, located next to the Yuma Exchange Saloon and Corral where he stabled his black mustang. As the animal began to drink from the water trough, Hawk stroked its dark neck several times, and the creature responded by nuzzling his master's hand. He waited until the owner brought Diablo's feed and the horse was eating before he left the stable.

After the Mercers and Maggie were seated in the restaurant section, he tried to register at the hotel, but no room was available. Though his complaining belly rumbled with hunger, Hawk refused to appease it. He wanted more time to observe those people, especially the female whom he had followed from Wilcox. As he spied on them through a front window, he pretended to rest while leaning against a porch post and staying in the shadows.

As they ate supper, Maggie encouraged Abby's father to tell her about Yuma, because the more she learned, the better prepared she would be for her task ahead. She learned that three events had spurred settlement at the Yuma Crossing: the California gold strike, the successful navigation of steamships on the Colorado to as far northward as Utah for transporting goods and people inland, and the Gadsden Purchase of land from Mexico.

The town covered an area of about six blocks in length and about four to five blocks in width. It contained many various businesses and shops. Most of the structures were built of adobe or of willow and mud, and the majority of them were one story and with flat roofs. The main street was wide, and dusty from desert sand and traffic.

Yet, the surrounding areas featured mountains, fertile valleys, two rivers, the Gila floodplain, the Sonoran Desert, and the enormous sand dunes in California.

Tom related more details about the town. "There's a railroad drawbridge over the Colorado River and plenty of people love to ride it for amusement when a steamer passes going up-river," he told them. "Until the Southern Pacific arrived from California in '77 and crossed south-ern Arizona in '81, goods and supplies were brought upriver by steamers from the Gulf; we still have two to three coming and going every month. I suppose that might slow down after the Atlantic & Pacific Railroad completes its route across the northern section from New Mexico to Flagstaff and on into California. At the pace they're going, they should reach the river and border in a few months. Until that happens, those captains can still earn big money by delivering goods to towns along its banks and for those located inland, especially the territorial capital and those mining settlements. Arizona is proving to have an abundant supply of gold, silver, cop-per, and other needed ores."

As Tom halted to enjoy his food for a while, Maggie suppressed a smile of relief as she added another angle to her impending plan after she learned about the steamers and railroad in Prescott's direction.

"We don't have a traffic bridge on the Colo-rado, so anybody crossing her has to use the ferry or a boat," he continued his informative narrative. "On a bluff on the other side is Fort Yuma, but I hear the government is planning to close it down this summer. I suppose because it's served its original purpose, which was to keep peace between the local Indians — mainly the Quechans and Mohaves — and emigrants using the Crossing. The quartermaster depot on this side of the river will be shutting down, too, since it's used for storing and passing along supplies to forts in this area, with the railroad routed through here, it's no longer needed. Since we have the main rail line here, the town will continue to grow and prosper without Fort Yuma and steamships."

So, Maggie reasoned, with the fort scaling down and closing soon, it probably wasn't heavily manned and gunned and therefore wouldn't present an obstacle to her task. Nor would the local Indians who were at peace. The only serious Indian trouble she knew about was with the Apaches in the southeastern section, but General Crook was dealing with them by chasing and keeping them across the Mexican border.

"We'll have to take Margaret Anne by the Chinese Gardens," Lucy said. "They're so beautiful and fragrant, I'm sure she would enjoy seeing them." She explained to Maggie, "The Chinese and their gardens provide us with many of our fruits and vegetables. Because Yuma's climate is good most of the year, we have fresh produce even during winter. We even have a bee keeper near town for buying honey, and an ice company here."

"I suppose we aren't as rustic as we appear to travelers," Tom added, "and we certainly get plenty of those with two passenger and four freight trains coming through daily."

"So, you do like it here in Yuma," Maggie assumed aloud.

Tom smiled and nodded as he finished chewing his meat, then sipped some coffee. "Yes, but Mother Nature can be harsh with us at times. Yuma has occasional floods, earthquakes — from what I've been told, several big ones in the last few years — and whirlwinds that can pick up heavy objects and sling them around like feathers. Actually, it's most pleasant here, especially during winter. January and February weren't bad at all."

"It's nice, dear, if we make allowances for the dust and heat," Lucy teased.

Tom sent his wife a smile. "I'm afraid that comes with the package, my dear."

Though her insides quivered with tension, Maggie tried to appear normal as she queried, "How did you obtain your current position on the prison commission?" From the corners of her eyes, she saw Abby give her an odd glance. Maggie assumed her friend had written her those facts and must be wondering why she appeared ignorant of them. She also assumed that Abby must be wondering why, if she hadn't received that informative letter, how did she know they were in Yuma? The slip had been made, so Maggie decided it was best to ignore it.

"I grew weary and bored with the mercantile business back home in Virginia, so I sold out to my partner to hire on at a local prison as assistant superintendent," Tom began his explanation. "But when the prison was relocated and a new one was built, another man was appointed to my place as a political favor. I heard about the Yuma Prison expansion and made inquiries about the superintendent's position, but it was already filled. However, I was asked to join the commission because of my business experience and problems here. Charges of fraud and corruption and misuse of funds for personal gain were leveled against certain members of the current board, so I was asked to investigate and resolve them. Those accused are some of Yuma's first and most prominent citizens, so I have to be careful what I say and do until the situation is settled. I'm hoping to become the next superintendent; with rumors circulating about Vander Meeden's harsh behavior with some of the prisoners, he might not be around much longer."

So, Maggie deduced, Newl hadn't lied about trouble at the prison. "That means you hope to become a permanent resident of Yuma?" she asked.

"If things work out in my favor, yes. Until that decision is made, we won't build a home here; we're currently renting a house."

That news dismayed Maggie, as she could

jeopardize his chances and possibly endanger his freedom and life if she was exposed later and their friendship was revealed and he fell under suspicion as an accomplice. She realized that if she couldn't carry out her plan without jeopardizing Abby's father, Ben would have to remain in prison. Then, the best she could do for her stepbrother was try to prove his innocence and hope he stayed alive long enough for her to accomplish that feat. She suppressed a sigh and turned her attention back to Abby's father. "Do you like working with prisoners?" she asked.

"I don't deal with the inmates much; I just handle orders for supplies and construction, oversee certain jobs, take care of the records, and make reports to Governor Tritle and the legislature. Currently, I'm trying to track down missing construction supplies and clarify some questionable expenses. We're also in the midst of making improvements, repairs, and additions; the convicts do most of the labor, as it should be if they're going to be punished and reformed. At present, we have over a hundred men confined there for various crimes."

"I saw the prison during our entrance to town; it's an awesome sight."

"It covers more than eight acres on an ideal location," Abby's father revealed. "It's had few escapes because the surrounding terrain is almost impossible to cross. No man could get over those eighteen-foot-high walls, and the cells are lined with iron grates under the plaster. Besides that, it has plenty of well-armed guard towers, and it's impossible for an escapee to go unnoticed in striped prison garb. If an inmate happens to get loose, he isn't free very long; there are Quechan braves who hire on to bring them back dead or alive. It's said those Quechans can 'track a bee in a blizzard' and used to be fierce warriors, so I wouldn't want one coming after me. Only a few men who've walked through that Sallyport have made successful escapes," he said before finishing his dried apple pie.

So, there's an important fact you failed to reveal to me, Newl, because I'm sure you know about those Indian trackers. If what Mr. Mercer says about their skills is true, they could present a serious problem for me and Ben. "What do the prisoners do there?"

"Some work in the stone quarry, adobe yard, and blacksmith shop on the premises. Some do the gardening, cooking, and other such chores. Others help with local road construction and repairs, mainly after harsh weather has damaged them. During their off time, they can make crafts like canes, ornaments, belts, and hat bands to sell at a bazaar held on the premises about every four months; the prison gets a third of any money they're paid. It's to their advantage to do their work and behave themselves because that shaves time off of their sentences. Anybody can tour the prison with permission and by paying twenty-five cents, but I'll give you a free tour during your visit."

"That sounds fascinating, sir, thank you." *It's*

42

time to change the topic. "What about you, Abby? Have you made lots of new friends here?"

"Not many. Most of the females are either years younger or older than I am, and the few my age are married with families. It seems as if the people here have more sons than daughters."

"Oh?" Maggie hinted.

"I remember that mischievous grin, Maggie. Yes, I do have several suitors, but nothing serious to date; and Mother and Father are checking them out with magnifying glasses. I'll tell you all about them later."

"Speaking of time, young ladies, I'm sure the kitchen help is more than ready to clean this table and complete their chores for the day. If you're finished with your desserts, I think we should leave."

"Yes, Father. I'll help Maggie get settled in and spend the night —"

"Hold on, my dear," Lucy interrupted. "I'm sure Margaret Anne is exhausted after her long trip, so you two can visit and talk tomorrow while you help her unpack and settle in. Besides, the only room available had a single bed, which would be too crowded for two people, and I'm sure you would keep her awake half the night by chattering away."

"You know me too well, Mother," Abby teased amidst laughter as the four stood to depart.

They all embraced Maggie and kissed her cheek before she bolted her door and went inside. She leaned against the wooden jamb and drew a quiet breath of relief. *So far, so good, but wait until you have to tell Abby the shocking truth tomorrow . . .*

After watching Maggie and the Mercers ascend the stairs, Hawk Reynolds headed for the Colorado Hotel on Gila Street, one block away and near the base of Prison Hill. For a moment, he was tempted to visit one of the many local saloons for a relaxing drink of strong whiskey, but decided he was weary enough to get to sleep without one, despite the fact his head was spinning with questions and alternative plans if Margaret Anne Malone's failed to succeed, and he presumed it would. Besides, he wasn't in the mood for talking to strangers, and certain men in saloons always wanted to converse with others to distract themselves from their loneliness and troubles.

After he registered and got a bite to eat just before the kitchen closed for the night, he went to his room on the front of the hotel. He tossed his saddlebags, weapons, and hat onto the bed, then walked to the window and leaned his shoulder against the frame. He crossed one booted ankle over the other and ran his fingers through hair as dark as a moonless night. His golden brown gaze stared at the other hotel as if it were trying to penetrate its walls.

He furtively had observed Margaret Anne Malone for days, having gleaned her name from the hotel registry in Wilcox. Her speech, behav-

44

ior, and dress bespoke a proper lady; she sounded educated, well mannered, and well bred. She had a smile as bright as the sun and her eyes were as blue as a clear summer day, their gaze most expressive when she smiled or talked, he had learned that from an up-close study with his fieldglasses. She stood at a little over five and a half feet tall, and had a body saloon girls would envy and men desire. Her hair color, except for scattered golden streaks, reminded him of a doe's hide in early spring. Unless tied back with a ribbon, it flowed over her shoulders and down her back like strands of Chinese silk in Chang's store in San Antonio. Her skin looked smooth, flawless, neither pale nor darkly tanned; and her facial features were perfect. In fact, she was beautiful, angelic, and enormously tempting.

So, he reasoned, why was a seemingly proper lady entangled with scum like Ben Carver and about to commit a criminal and hazardous act for him? What powerful or misguided hold did Newl or Ben Carver have over her? How could a woman alone free Ben from Yuma Prison? Yet, if she wasn't confident she could do it, she wouldn't be there, unless she truly had "no choice" but to try. In all honesty, he didn't know whether to feel sorry for her or to detest her.

Blast it all, she was a complete and intriguing contradiction!

If he concluded she was being coerced, should he approach her and try to change her mind before she got into a swift river over her head?

No, because that could jeopardize his own plans. Maybe beneath that pretty and genteel facade she was as bad as the targets he was pursuing. Should he expose her to either Sheriff Tyner or Superintendent Vander Meeden and get her out of the way so he could carry out Ben's escape? No, that could get Ben trapped inside those walls under heavy guard. Should he join forces with her? No, at least not yet, because a relaxed and trusting Ben with her at his side would lead him straight to Barber and Jones. It was best if he waited until after she succeeded or failed before he took action.

Hawk moved his belongings to a chair. He shucked his dusty boots, stripped off his clothes, and lay down. He stared into the darkness for a few minutes before closing his eyes. The instant he did, her lovely image was almost as visible to him as if she were standing before him in person. Her name — Mag . . . gie Ma . . . lone — kept coming and going inside his head like the gentle waves at low tide on a Texas beach.

When he realized his naked body was becoming aroused, he rolled to his stomach and forced her from his thoughts. *Don't go messing with my head, woman, because it won't do you any good. You've sided with Carver, so that makes you one of my enemies.* He resolved that nothing and no one would stand in the way of him meting out his revenge and justice.

As the two women unpacked Maggie's baggage

on Wednesday morning, they talked about old times at boarding school and Abby's current suitors.

"Before I know it, you'll be married and having babies," Maggie said. "We're twenty-three. I suppose it's about time for settling down — at least for you. Aunt Maggie, that has a nice ring to it."

"I see," Abby laughed, "you want me to try on this marriage garment first. If it fits, you'll get yourself one, too. Right?"

"Perhaps, after I get tired of my work."

"I have to find the right man for a husband," Abby said thoughtfully. "Two of my beaux are handsome, from well-to-do families here in town, and I like them. One in particular; he's calling on me Sunday after church, so you can give me your impression of him. As for you, Maggie girl, if you don't stop gallivanting around the country and endangering yourself, you'll never find a proper husband and you might get yourself killed. I couldn't bear losing you."

"Don't worry about me, Abby; few of my jobs are life-threatening. I mostly do investigations undercover for fraud or corruption, or I track down missing people, mainly runaway daughters who want to marry men their parents don't approve of or who want to work instead of marry or they've gotten themselves into trouble and are trying to avoid a scandal."

"Speaking of fraud and corruption," Abby said, "didn't you receive my long letter about our move to Yuma and Father's appointment to the board of prison commissioners?"

Maggie thought it was best to travel slowly with her revelations. "I didn't get your letter; it's probably waiting for me at home in St. Louis."

Abby sat on the bed and laid aside the dress she was holding. "Then how did you know we were living here?"

Maggie stopped removing things from her trunk and faced Abby. "Mother and Newl told me last Friday in Wilcox."

"I don't understand; I thought you said your mother was out of town on a trip."

"That was true, she was in Wilcox, not at home in Tucson."

"What's going on, Maggie? Why the secrecy and deception?"

Maggie went to sit beside her friend and looked her in the eye. "I had no choice but to answer as I did because you asked me in front of your parents. It has to do with a secret job for Newl."

"What kind of job? Is it dangerous?"

"Yes, it concerns my stepbrother, Ben. We still haven't met, but he's in serious trouble and desperately needs my help."

"He lives or works in Yuma?"

"In a way, yes to both."

"And?" Abby coaxed her to continue and end her confusion.

"Let me see . . . How shall I explain this crazy matter to you?"

"As Mr. Graves used to say, 'Just spit out the

answer, young lady; it isn't going to bite your lip.' We've never had problems talking about anything before, Maggie, so what's wrong?"

She took a deep breath and confessed, "I'm caught in a terrible predicament. If I don't do this job, Ben could die; but if I do it, I could involve you and your family in a hazardous situation."

"You can tell me anything, Maggie. Why did you really come here?"

"To bust Ben out of the Yuma Prison."

Chapter Three

Maggie watched Abby's green eyes enlarge and her lips part with astonishment. "I know, it's a crime," Maggie put her reaction into words. "It's perilous and maybe impossible. But if I don't rescue him, he could be hanged or killed soon by one of the other inmates. Newl claims he's innocent and was wrongly convicted and imprisoned. After I free him and he's safe in hiding, I'm going to Prescott to investigate the case and the witnesses against him. Newl claims they're enemies of his and they lied about Ben." When Abby remained silent, just staring at her in disbelief, Maggie revealed the other details Newl had told her.

"You can't be serious; the chances of breaking him out are nil," Abby said after listening to Maggie. "Wait until you tour that place and you'll see what I mean. Father is taking us as soon as we finish unpacking your things."

"As I told you, Abby, Ben's now on work detail outside the prison walls. Somehow I have to get a message to him and figure out a way for him to elude the guards while I distract them. The only thing that has me worried is getting your father into trouble if it's revealed I'm Ben's stepsister and I'm friendly with your family."

"Even if your wild scheme works, Maggie, no one will believe you — a mere woman and a proper lady — plotted and carried out his escape. They'll think the timing was coincidental."

"Are you sure? I don't want to imperil any of you."

"I'm positive, but still you must forget this crazy idea because it won't work. Not without help anyway."

"I can't hire anybody to help me commit a crime. There's no one I could trust with such information."

"I was referring to me, silly. Maybe I could —"

"No, Abby, I can't let you get involved."

"I'm already involved because I know about your plan. I could help you distract the guards while you slip a message to Ben and he sneaks away. If your stepbrother is innocent and he's in immediate jeopardy, I agree we have to help him. Besides, think how exciting this will be. Have you ever pulled off a job as risky, and seemingly impossible as this?"

"Yes, but I did it alone; I didn't risk anyone else's life. I would simply die if anything bad happened to you or to your family."

"It won't, if you let me become your partner."

Abby's green eyes sparkled and her face glowed. Maggie didn't know why her friend had done an about-face in the last few minutes, still,

Maggie wasn't sure her involvement was such a good idea. "The minute Ben Carver is free, your parents might connect me to him. That could evoke suspicions about me, and they'll wonder if I told you, and if I did, why didn't you tell them?"

"No, Maggie, it won't, I'm sure of that. Now, the first thing we have to do is get a good look at the prison and where that gang is working. Let's hurry and finish unpacking so we can begin our adventure. We haven't gotten into mischief since our school days; this will be so much fun. Life has been almost boring here in Yuma. It's so good to be together again. Just think, we'll be heroines soon."

"If we do this deed, Abby, we can't ever tell anyone about it; don't forget, whether Ben is guilty or innocent, aiding a jailbreak is a crime."

"What if he is guilty?"

"If I make that discovery during my investigation, I'll see to it that Ben is returned to prison." She took a deep breath before continuing. "I'll let you help me on several conditions. First, don't do or say anything to cause suspicion, especially toward yourself and your parents; secondly, don't veer from my instructions in the slightest; thirdly, you keep this episode a secret forever. Agreed?"

Abby hugged her, grinned, and responded, "Agreed."

"Then you're my partner," Maggie said, though she knew she would allow Abby to take only a small role in the impending drama.

As they headed up the dirt road to Prison Hill, Maggie sat on the left side of the carriage to observe the work gang and terrain. As they passed the laboring convicts at a slow pace, the men paused to look up at them but the guards shouted in haste for them to get busy again. Their black-and-gray striped uniforms were dusty and wrinkled, and their expressions revealed their misery in the heat. Guards, to whom Tom spoke as each was encountered, were spaced out along the road's edge with rifles or shotguns at the ready to discourage trouble or flight. To the captives' rear were thick and green scrubs and trees, ample cover to conceal a man if he could get to them.

From the photographs Newl had shown her, Maggie easily picked her stepbrother out of the large group that was filling in ruts, removing debris, strengthening the road's bank with many layers of heavy rocks, and filling in washes on the gradually elevating slope. At twenty-four, Ben Carver was a good-looking man, but Maggie couldn't be caught inspecting him, so she averted her gaze from his direction.

Tom halted the carriage near the Sallyport, a huge adobe arch with strap-iron gates and a free-standing guardhouse. Outside the walls were the guards' quarters, superintendent's residence, stable, and other structures. The main guard tower — an enormous roofed platform — had been built over a circular rock water reservoir. Shovels and picks not in use were leaned against the wall to the left of the Sallyport, "to prevent men from taking them inside and using them as weapons," Tom told them.

Maggie noted how breezy it was at that height. She saw the steep drop to the Gila River along one side, and a similar one to the Colorado on another — both impassable for escapes. Yet, the view of the mountains, fertile valley, town, rivers, and Fort Yuma was breathtaking.

Tom spoke with Fred Fredley, the turnkey and yardmaster, for a few minutes before the gate was unlocked and they passed through the wide arch into the first of three yards. Tom told them the walls — built by the inmates of adobe bricks they also made there — were eighteen feet high, eight feet thick at the base, tapering to five feet. Some of the thirteen guards employed there walked or stood on the wall while on duty. In addition, there were six lofty guard towers constructed at the corners and middle of two sides, one of them armed with a Gatling gun.

Before they toured the site, they were introduced to Superintendent C.V. Meeden, an odd and gruff man who was heading to his office in a nearby structure and made it apparent he didn't want to be detained longer than necessary, even by a board commissioner.

For almost two hours, they strolled around, looking at the kitchen and mess hall where "trusties" worked, the granite quarry, adobe yard, bathrooms, machine shop, farm, and a small hospital.

Tom showed them the convicts' cells; some were excavated out of solid rock hills, or built into the interior walls, or located in separate blocks with two rows facing each other with a wide corridor between them and with sturdy strap-iron barriers with gates at each end.

Six men were confined at night in what, Maggie noted, were cramped and smelly quarters with bad ventilation, though their interiors were surprisingly cool when compared to the exterior heat. Tom told her the rooms were lined with iron bands beneath the whitewashed plaster to prevent men from digging out; the floor, of course, was impassable granite. To discourage bedbugs, the bunks were made of impenetrable iron rather than wood. There was a chest with six drawers for the men to share, and a single chamber pot which was emptied once a day and attracted numerous insects. Dead roaches, scorpions, and other unknown bugs lay here and there, victims of the soles of irate prisoners' shoes. The only doors were iron grates, so they couldn't keep out bad weather and pests.

Maggie gazed into one cell and imagined Ben confined there, cut off from family and friends, locked away for years under such terrible conditions. She shuddered when she thought of herself enduring such a harsh existence.

When Maggie asked Tom about the large iron ring secured to the floor between the two three-bunk-high furnishings, he revealed it was a mild form for punishment for minor infractions: the other five men were chained to it along with the offender, a ploy used to discourage misconduct or face the wrath of one's cellmates.

"Needless to say, my dear, after such an experience, the culprit will try to stay out of trouble the next time," Tom affirmed. "The inmates work six days a week, with Sundays off. They also get time taken off their sentences for good conduct and good work, so it's up to them to behave and do their duties."

"Father, please show Maggie the Dark Cell."

Tom guided the three women to where a chamber had been blasted out of a rock hill. They passed through one portal with a solid door, walked down a short corridor and stepped past an iron grate door. "We shouldn't go any farther," Tom advised, "because it's a filthy place."

As Tom related almost the same description Newl had given to her, Maggie eyed the dim interior of the rough-walled cave. She imagined Ben locked in the low strap-iron cage, naked, given bread and water once a day. The air was so stale, musty, and heavy with stench from human waste that she nearly retched. If a man wasn't put in the center cage, he was limited to either standing, walking, or sitting on the hard rock floor. She had seen jails and prisons before, but nothing like this one.

"Close the door for a minute, Father, and let her see how dark and scary it is in here," Abby coaxed.

"Only for a minute, Abigail," Tom relented with reluctance.

Lucy departed before Tom shoved the door shut after he gave the two young women a warning about not venturing farther into the chamber.

Maggie was astonished by how dark it was after the sunlight was taken away, and at how the smell worsened without the air flow between the ceiling shaft and exterior door. She couldn't see her hand before her face, and her breathing was hindered. Her pulse quickened, and panic welled within her. "Spending several days and nights in here must be horrible, especially if the guards truly drop snakes or scorpions or filthy cockroaches down the air shaft like Ben told Newl," Maggie whispered. "If we aren't careful, my friend, we could spend time in here."

"Don't worry; this is the first and last time we'll step in this place."

The two young women had to shield their eyes from the bright light when Tom opened the door until their gazes adjusted to it.

"Come along, my dears; we need to leave because the men will be returning soon for the midday meal. I don't want to subject you ladies to their stares and the offensive sight of them. I'll take you back to the hotel, we'll eat, then I'll return to work while you three look around the town and shop."

From a concealed position near the base of the bluff, Hawk watched the carriage slowly make its way down the dusty slope. Mr. and Mrs. Mercer occupied the front seat, while the two young women sat in the back one while they laughed and chatted. He noticed that Maggie didn't even glance toward the work gang, of which Ben Carver was a member, but Ben — who kept laboring with his shovel — cocked his head in such a way as to observe Maggie without the guard's awareness. Using fieldglasses, Hawk obtained a close-up view of Ben's expression as his enemy ogled Maggie. Hawk felt his body stiffen with anger at Ben's lustful grin and matching gleam in those green eyes. As his own gaze returned to Maggie, he wondered if she had changed her mind about her impending mission after a close-up study of the prison.

As the carriage passed near his hiding place, his tawny gaze roved Margaret Anne Malone from head to feet. What his grandmother would call a "high-styling hat," made from straw with a wide brim and very little adornment, covered much of her light-brown hair. Today, her shiny locks were secured away from her neck and shoulders, no doubt to help keep her cool. Her dress had a full skirt and gathered into a downward point at her waist where a row of tiny buttons ended. Its sleeves were long, despite the desert heat, probably to avoid sunburn on her delicate flesh. It was a simple and practical garment, yet, lovely and feminine, like the woman herself. The most striking thing about her attire was its bluebell color, which matched her beautiful eyes and flattered her skin tone.

He had met some beautiful and tempting females before, but he couldn't think of a single one who compared with his forbidden target.

His body seemed to experience a crazy itch and warmth from her radiance and he was glad when she moved out of his sight. Maybe it was a good thing he hadn't joined forces with her; she would make it most difficult to concentrate on his work and avenging his lost loved ones.

After eating at a nice restaurant on Main Street, Tom left the three women to tour the town while he tended to prison business.

At a slow pace, Lucy guided the carriage up and down the streets while Abby pointed out the sights and certain people to Maggie. They paused at the Chinese Gardens on Gila Street but didn't get out to look around since many people were working there and they lacked a male escort. On Madison Avenue, Maggie saw the large one-story courthouse, many homes, and the Quartermaster Depot near the river.

As a steamship approached the swing drawbridge, Abby tugged at her mother's arm and asked if they could ride it. Lucy was reluctant to give her permission until a soldier standing nearby overheard the request and offered to escort and protect the two ladies during the adventure.

After walking them to a safe position and cautioning them to hold on for balance, the bridge began to move out of the steamer's watery path. A river breeze tugged at their hair and clothing, evoking laughter from both women. The current was swift, but the ship was powerful and its captain skilled. During the entire event, the soldier behind them didn't utter a single word, as if he were either too shy or too enthralled by them to speak.

After the bridge was in place again, the two women thanked the man, whose cheeks rosed slightly as he smiled and nodded his return gratitude before assisting them into the carriage.

They halted again for a while at the west end of Main to watch a ferry work its way across the river carrying a flat-bedded wagon along with several people.

At that point, Maggie realized that without a road bridge it would take soldiers from Fort Yuma in California a long time to reach this side of the bank if they were summoned for an emergency. Hopefully Ben would be long gone or well hidden before help arrived on the scene. Her only concerns now were the guards and Indians.

As the ride continued, Maggie saw many kinds of businesses, shops, homes, animal pens, and rough fences. Though Yuma lacked the social amenities of a large town or city like St. Louis, it was better and safer than many of the western locations she had visited.

During their outing, Lucy halted four other times to introduce Maggie to certain people: Sheriff and Tax Collector Andy Tyner, two members of the prison board who were local businessmen, and the commanding officer from the nearby fort. She saw a variety of people who lived or worked near the town: farmers, Mexican ranchers, railroad men, cowboys, and a few Quechan Indians at the outskirts of town.

Since she could come into unwanted contact with those Indians, she queried Abby about them. The ones she saw were tall and muscular with a proud demeanor and Abby revealed, didn't hang around the town or the fort waiting for government subsidies. It was clear those past warriors had made honorable peace and weren't disrespected or disliked by the local residents. She was relieved when Abby told her that the ones who hired on as trackers lived and did other work around the fort, across the time-consuming river.

During those hours of sightseeing, Maggie was always aware of the high bluff where the prison stood and her stepbrother was incarcerated.

By the time the tour ended, the women were hot, dusty, and weary. Lucy returned the carriage to the stable owner before they headed to the hotel so they could bathe and rest before dinner.

On Thursday, April nineteenth, Maggie's menses began shortly after breakfast. She was prepared with clean and thick cloths for the monthly event which always came on schedule and flowed lightly for only three days. Though it rarely troubled her, Lucy Mercer advised her to stay out of the heat and take it easy for that first day.

For a while, Maggie stayed with Lucy and Abby in the Mercers' "suite," which consisted of a nice sitting room and a bedroom with two beds. The large second room contained a curtained-off area for bathing and dressing and a white chamber pot with red trim. Maggie was told it lacked a kitchen because the owner and his wife had cooked and eaten downstairs in their restaurant. She was also told the couple had built a small adobe home to the hotel's rear shortly before the birth of their baby, who was now two months old. The owner's old lodgings had been kept as a "suite" for wealthy travelers passing through or visiting Yuma, or for renting to locals during times of need, as was the case with the Mercers.

As the three sewed and chatted, Lucy asked about Maggie's mother.

Abby responded for her so Maggie would know what she had told her parents about Catherine. "Maggie told me her mother is doing fine in Tucson and is blissfully happy in her marriage. She and her husband are away on a trip so Maggie plans to go see them later this summer. I'm sure they're all looking forward to a visit because they haven't been together since last spring." Abby laughed and said, "Maggie and I have teased each other about becoming spinsters if we don't find husbands soon. Of course, my dear friend stays too busy and on the road to have enough time to get to know any man well enough to consider him as a suitor."

"Is your work dangerous, my dear?" Lucy asked her guest.

Maggie noticed that Abby avoided revealing Newl's whole name and Catherine's new married name and how Abby cleverly changed the subject. "Not often, ma'am. A few people I investigate become angry with me for snooping and reporting their foul deeds, but only a couple have tried to harm me. I was fortunate to receive training in how to recognize and thwart such threats; and I become more skilled and experienced with each case."

"I can't imagine having my daughter traipsing around alone and placing herself in possible jeopardy, although Abigail does show a wild streak ever so often. Thankfully she's curbed her mischievous impulses before they got her into deep trouble or caused us embarrassment. I recall receiving letters about some of the foolish pranks you two pulled at boarding school."

"But they were never serious or dangerous ones, Mother. Besides, we're grown now and those days are far behind us. Right, Maggie?"

Maggie nodded agreement. "I know I try my best to stay out of trouble and harm's way, and I'm sure Abby does, too."

"I must confess, Margaret Anne, though it sounds biased, Abigail is a fine young lady and we're so proud of her. Of you, too, my dear. Actually, I must also confess that your work and travels sound exciting and rewarding."

"See, Maggie," Abby jested, "that's where I

get my wild streak from; my dear mother is a closet adventuress. I've seen her reading action novels and daydreaming about their contents. She particularly enjoys those *Little Nell* dime novels about a daring heroine who has all kinds of adventures in the Wild West."

"You mustn't tease me, Abigail, or tell your father that little secret."

The three women laughed before they began discussing the books they had read and the ones they liked best.

Following the midday meal, Maggie and Abby went to her room to visit while Lucy took a nap to rid herself of a headache. Before doing so, Abby scolded her mother in a gentle tone about needing to remedy the reason for those occasional headaches: sewing or reading too long without using glasses to prevent straining her eyes.

In Maggie's room, Abby whispered, "I don't know why Mother won't admit she needs spectacles. I suppose she thinks they'll make her look or feel old, but that isn't true."

"I guess she's like everyone else, she has to deal with her feelings in her own time and way. Once she realizes how many lines she's creating on her face with squinting, she'll rush to the doctor's office and demand a pair that very day."

"If she can see well enough to detect the wrinkles," Abby said with a grin.

"Abigail Mercer, you're a naughty girl," Maggie teased.

"What I said is true, but I would never make fun of my mother with a mean spirit. I love her dearly and respect her greatly."

"I feel the same way about my mother. That's why I know I'm doing the right thing in this matter. If she disagreed with Newl or thought I would be in terrible danger, she would have insisted I not take on this job, no matter how much she loves Newl and wants to please him."

"Knowing your mother, I'm certain you're right about her. So, what's our plan to extricate Ben? He appeared well guarded on the road. There's no way you can get close to him to pass along a message, and you certainly can't risk calling attention to yourself by visiting him before his escape."

"I have an idea that might work with your assistance," Maggie began, then explained it to Abby, who smiled and nodded agreement.

The two friends discussed their venture some more, then Abby posed a question she had been wondering about. "You told Mother and implied to Father that your work isn't dangerous, Maggie, but that isn't totally true, is it? At least not all of the time, right?"

"I don't want to worry them, so I colored the truth a little bit. I have to do the same with Mother or she would live in constant fear of me getting slain or seriously injured. I've had a few close calls, but I handled them without being harmed. The worst time was when I was investigating a bank teller in Denver who was pocketing deposits. The owner suspected him but couldn't accuse him without proof, and the man was too clever to get caught redhanded. I went to work there and snared him in the process of secreting money into a slit on the inside of his coat. He drew a weapon on me and the owner to make his escape, but I used a few moves another agent had taught me and disabled him. I not only received my salary but I also got a bonus for saving the owner's life."

"That's wonderful! What were you doing in Sante Fe recently?"

Maggie sent her a playful grin. "Would you believe I was pretending to be a dancehall singer, wearing colorful face paints and dressing in gaudy and risqué gowns and entertaining leering strangers?"

"You didn't?" Abby saw her nod and grin. "Tell me every detail."

"I was sent there to catch a bartender in the act of watering down the establishment's whiskey, then selling the leftovers to men who peddled it to Indians, which is a crime that earns a man six months to a year in prison. Since the owner was the one who hired me on the sly through my agency, he told the manager I was an entertainer 'downstairs only,' if you grasp my meaning."

"I heard you sing back in school and in church choirs, so I know you gave more than a credible performance. How did you entrap him?"

"I hid in the backroom on the day a shipment

of whiskey arrived, watched him pour a third from each bottle, refill them with water, then let his cohorts collect it after we closed. I trailed them to their camp and observed their meeting the next day with the Indians. I overheard their names and plans, so I reported them to the owner and my agency."

"You spied on them all night?" Abby watched her nod. "You stayed out there all alone?" Abby saw her nod again. "What if you'd been seen and captured? They would have murdered you, and probably done worse things before doing so. Were you scared?"

"I was careful. I wore dark clothing, covered my hair with a black scarf and sooted my face so I would blend into the shadows. My horse is well trained, intelligent, and loyal, so she wouldn't make any noise to give me away. Mother and Newl are keeping Blaze for me until I finish my work for Ben. As for being scared, a good dose of fear is wise and healthy, under such circumstances, it keeps one alert and alive."

"Tell me about some of your other adventures; you've had so many."

For the next hour, Maggie complied, pausing here and there to sip water or to let Abby make comments or ask questions.

"I would be terrified and I would probably make mistakes and get hurt, but I envy you for your skills, courage, intelligence, and stimulating work," Abby confessed. "I'm glad you'll let me have a tiny sample of what it's like to do something wild and wonderful. I promise, no matter how scared I get, I won't disappoint you."

Maggie hugged her and said, "I do love and miss you so, dear Abby. I'm almost glad this happened so it could reunite us for a while; isn't that awful of me?"

"Only a tiny bit. Besides, you can tell me anything and I would never betray you."

"I know; that's why I told you about Ben and my plans. Now, you do some of the talking for a change; tell me more about your many suitors."

After Abby responded in colorful detail, she asked, "You will take time off from your busy job to come to my wedding, won't you?"

"Of course, I will. As soon as you've decided on a husband and set a date, let me know. But I think I can already guess which man it will be. Every time you say Matthew Lawrence's name or talk about him, your eyes glow and you end each sentence with a dreamy sigh."

"He is handsome and wonderful, Maggie, and I quiver with desire just thinking about him. If he takes my elbow or accidentally touches me or just smiles at me or I hear his voice, I almost melt like butter in the sun. I do hope he feels the same way about me, but until I know for certain, I must keep my feelings for him concealed. I would simply die if I revealed them and he rejected me. When you meet him on Sunday, put those keen instincts and observations to work to see what you think. No matter how it hurts me, tell me the truth about your impression."

"I promise, because I wouldn't want you chasing a dream."

"Mother and Father will be so happy when I marry and give them grandchildren, but they haven't pressured me to take those steps because they want me to marry only for love, not to avoid spinsterhood."

"I wish my father were alive. I still miss him and our ranch terribly. He taught me many things I know and use in my work: riding, tracking, self-defense, shooting. But he never tried to make a son of me; he was always proud to have a daughter, and one who loved to shadow him. He was a good and strong man, and I loved and respected him greatly. He was so different from Newl, but I don't begrudge Mother her happiness. I'm sure she was lonely after Father died, and I'm sure that move to St. Louis was scary and difficult. I suppose that's what helped her endure Father's loss. Until Newl came into the scene, it was just the two of us. I don't even have grandparents; they were all gathered at Mother's home when the Union swept through Virginia and blasted the house, killing everybody inside. It was fortunate for me that Mother was away helping to tend the wounded and Father was away fighting and I was attending a makeshift school that awful day or none of us would have survived. That's why Father moved us to Fort Worth and started ranching, to make a fresh start far away. You're fortunate to have both sets of your grandparents back in Virginia."

"You're right, I am lucky. It's almost strange, Maggie, but I recall little about that ghastly war, and I'm glad of that. It's also strange that you and I wound up at the same boarding school when we were both born in Virginia. You know that's why the headmistress had us room together: two southern girls attending a fancy northern school. Remember how some of those little Yankees teased us spitefully about our accents and lost cause?"

"Yes, and I remember how we played mischievous pranks on the worst of our offenders. We would have been yanked out of school by our parents or tossed out by the headmistress if they only knew one-tenth of the wild things we did there."

"I can close my eyes and envision Evelyn's face when she opened her desktop that morning and found it filled with spiders and bugs." Abby laughed at the memory. "I thought she would scream her head off before the teacher calmed her down."

As they sat on the bed facing each other, Maggie added, "Or when we put that warty toad in Mary's shoe and she almost squished it. She cried like a baby and refused to wear those shoes again."

After suppressing her giggles, Abby reminded, "Or when we hid Mr. Zimmer's lessons and he had to reschedule class to redo them. His face was red as a beet and he could hardly speak without sputtering. We were lucky we didn't get caught and punished. Even if or when they suspected us, they could never prove we did those devilish things. We were so daring and stealthy in those days."

"We had some wild and wonderful times repaying those mean Yanks, didn't we? Mercy, how we and our lives have changed. Just think, Abby, by this time next year, you'll probably be married and having a baby."

"Have you ever met a man who made you feel the way I do now?"

Maggie shrugged. "Not really. I've been out for nice evenings with handsome, well-mannered, educated, and even wealthy men, but none of them made my heart race and my body surge with desire. When I meet a man who does, believe me, I'll grab him fast and —"

A knock on the door interrupted Maggie.

"It's time to get ready for supper, girls," Lucy said. "I thought I should come over because I was certain you two had lost track of time."

Abby laughed and replied. "As always, Mother, you're right. We were reminiscing about old times and having so much fun. I'll come freshen up while Maggie does the same."

Long after midnight, Maggie took the next step in her plan. She was attired in a black shirt and pants, and had a strip of black cloth secured around her hair to prevent reflections on the golden strands. She had darkened her hands and face by rubbing charcoal on them. Barefoot, she crept to the back door of the hotel where she

71

donned men's shoes; if prints were found by those Indian trackers, they would imply a male cohort. Her gaze scanned every direction several times and she listened for any sound that would indicate somebody was nearby, though it appeared as if the entire town was asleep.

From her trip on the train, her tour of Yuma, and from window observations, Maggie was certain she knew where every animal was located so she could avoid startling one in passing and have it sound an alarm to its owner. She sneaked to the end of the block on Main Street, worked her way down First, turned left on Gila at the Colorado Hotel, and located the site she had chosen for hiding the items for Ben. From the progress the convicts had made and by the pace they were laboring, Maggie surmised the gang would be in that area while she and Abby were present to distract the nearest guard in order for her to make contact with him.

After she made it back to her room safely, Maggie exhaled in relief. She had removed the coverlet from the bed and hung it over the drapes earlier and laid one of her dresses at the bottom of the hallway door to make sure no light was visible from her room during her preparations to leave; once again, she spread out the dress at the door. She lit a candle, returned the clothing and shoes and charcoal container to the hidden compartment in her trunk, and used a special cream to take off the charcoal. She spread a silky lotion from France on her face and hands to soften and moisturize them following their abuse. She donned a cotton nightgown and checked the room for any oversights. Finding none, she blew out the candle, laid the dress over a chair, replaced the coverlet, and climbed into bed.

Maggie told her trembling body to relax and her anxious mind to calm. She had completed her first major challenge, but it remained to be seen if she could carry out the second and third.

Hawk tossed and turned on his bed, unable to sleep for thinking about Margaret Anne Malone and the many challenges looming ahead of him. He hadn't seen Maggie all day and wondered why she had stayed inside the hotel. Maybe she was sick, or running scared, or simply didn't want to expose an intense interest in the prison and town. He tried to imagine how she could engineer Ben's escape, but no theories came to mind. There was no way she could get a drop on the guards; they stood too spaced out along the road's edge; all it would require was one warning shot for the Gatling gun and sharpshooters on the wall to open fire on her and her target. It would be foolish for Ben to just take off running, because he couldn't get far on foot, in prison garb and with so much firepower to thwart that effort. And for certain, she couldn't bust him out from the inside; no attempted escape from the inside had ever succeeded. He also doubted she could bribe any of the guards or Meeden for assistance.

If you do have a cunning idea to use, woman, you best get busy with it. If you don't have him out by Sunday, you're out of luck and I take over from there.

Hawk wondered if Maggie was only duping the Carvers with a pretense of trying to free Ben and soon would tell Newl it was impossible. Or perhaps Maggie only came to scrutinize the area, come up with a clever plan, and others would arrive soon to carry it out for her. From now on, Hawk resolved, he couldn't let her out of his sight or Ben could be gone in a flash; and he himself would be right back where he was before Maggie Malone entered the scene, trying to locate and punish those three vicious bastards.

Friday morning, Abby told her mother that she and Maggie were going for a walk and would return before mealtime. Lucy nodded and returned to her sewing. Both young women knew that Tom wouldn't be a problem because he had left for Los Angeles yesterday morning to question the owner of Perry, Woodworth, and Company about a missing prepaid supply of lumber for the prison and he wouldn't return until Saturday.

Maggie was glad he would be far away during Ben's escape — if she could pull it off today — which should prevent him from falling under suspicion as an accomplice. She had told Abby what to do and cautioned her against making any changes. She had a note ready for Ben, telling

74

him where the items he needed were located.

Maggie and Abby walked down Gila Street and veered toward Prison Hill. They pretended to stroll along, chatting and laughing and holding parasols over their heads to protect them from the sun's fierce rays. They halted at the base of the bluff and, as planned, Abby pointed up the dirt road as she talked. Maggie nodded, then they headed in that direction.

When they encountered the guard who was watching Ben and the convicts laboring near him, they halted and smiled.

"My best friend, Miss Margaret Anne Malone, is visiting us from St. Louis," Abby said to the man. "I told her she could get a lovely view of the entire area and a cooling breeze from up here. Is that all right with you, sir?" Abby asked, using her best southern charm and ladylike manner.

"Of course, Miss Mercer; and welcome to Yuma, Miss Malone. You can see for a long way off up here, but the wind is kicking up a big fuss today. Been blowing in stronger by the hour and tossing dirt in my eyes."

Maggie gazed across the landscape, smiling sweetly, and said, "It is a magnificent view, and so much cooler than down in the flatland. I — Oh, my!" she shrieked as she pretended to lose her footing during a strong gust of wind which billowed her full skirt and entangled her legs. She cunningly took advantage of that unforeseen incident by tumbling down the slope to land almost at her stepbrother's feet.

As Ben Carver rushed to assist her, Maggie pressed the note into his hand and whispered, "Go in the bushes somehow and read this."

The guard made his way down the slope, recovering her dropped parasol en route, and asked, "Are you hurt, Miss Malone?"

As Maggie brushed off her soiled and snagged dress, she smiled and said, "I don't think so, sir. That gust just blew me right off my feet and blinded me with sand. This man kindly halted my fall and assisted me." She looked at Ben and said, "Thank you for the rescue, kind sir."

Ben touched his fingers to his hat and said, "You're welcome, ma'am." He pulled the guard aside and asked in a low voice, "Can I go in the bushes over there? I got a grippy stomach and ladies are present, so I can't squat behind a big rock."

The distracted guard nodded before he grasped Maggie's elbow to steady her while they cautiously scaled the slope to where Abby was standing with a frightened expression on her face, having been joined by another guard.

"Are you injured, Maggie?"

"I'm fine, Abby, just a little dirty and scratched up, and my hair is a mess. Nothing is broken. This gentleman was most kind and helpful," she said of the guard as she smiled at him again.

"Thank you, sir, for assisting my friend. Her parents would be most unhappy with us if we allowed her to get hurt while visiting us."

"Your arm is bleeding, miss," the second guard

remarked. "I have a clean handkerchief if you don't mind me binding it so you won't get blood on that pretty dress."

"Please do so, sir, and I will be most grateful."

As the second guard tended her scrape and the first one watched him, Maggie furtively noticed that the other guards along the road also were watching their group instead of the laboring inmates. She lifted her head and took a faked breath to assess the situation; she sighted no guards standing on the wall on this side of the prison or any others leaning out tower openings. She knew they were out of visibility range of the main guard platform. The setup was perfect for Ben to sneak away, if he was brave enough to do so. She dared not glance in his direction to see if he was making an attempt at that moment.

As Abby chatted with the two guards while one tied a makeshift bandage around Maggie's left forearm, the bubbly blonde began, "I —"

"What was that?" Maggie asked as she looked around in panic following the ominous noise which sounded like cannon fire or . . .

Chapter Four

Both guards came to alert and glanced upward as another roaring peal of thunder rumbled overhead. As if from nowhere, wild winds swept across the setting, stirred up dust and sand, violently shook the leaves and limbs of bushes and trees, and yanked fiercely at wildflowers and grasses. The second guard's hat blew off and he raced off to retrieve it. A previously clear sky now darkened rapidly to a deep slate color as rain-ladened clouds suddenly stretched across it for countless miles. Anything loose was sent flying off into the distance; and anything held by another object was whipped about with awesome force. The muggy air caused faces to shine and garments to dampen. Lightning flashed, and more ear-splitting thunderclaps boomed. The breeze gusted stronger and cooler.

"Since you're closer to town than the prison, you best get home fast. That storm's gonna be a bad one and it's coming in at breakneck speed; that's the way they are out here, no warning. When one like this comes along, it sneaks up like a thief and catches us off guard."

Peals of thunder roared like cannon fire going off in rapid succession and echoed across the landscape. Lightning flickered like glowing fingers trying to claw open the heaven so the rain could begin, which it did before the startled people could react.

The second guard returned and shouted above the din, "It's going to be a long and maybe dangerous one; you ladies want me to see you home?"

"That won't be necessary, sir, but thank you. Let's go, Abby, or we'll be totally drenched soon," Maggie coaxed, taking her friend's wet hand and shouting farewells and another thank-you to the guards.

The two men waved and focused on rounding up the inmates to get them back inside the prison. As soon as the return signal was given, the striped-clad men scrambled up the slope with their tools and hurried up the dirt road where gushes of water were already running toward them.

Maggie glanced back to see the first guard quickly check the bushes where Ben had gone earlier, then rush to join the other guards and convicts. Did he assume Ben was bunched up with the fleeing group that was scurrying for cover and safety? Was that true, or was her step-brother using this surprise storm to get away? *You must be innocent, Ben, or Mother Nature wouldn't be helping us.*

From a concealed location in the nearby hills

and using fieldglasses to observe the action, a drenched Hawk lost sight of Ben in the ensuing torrential downpour. He knew he was too far away to trail Ben, who hadn't reappeared after heading into the dense bushes after speaking with a guard who was obviously distracted by the brown-haired beauty. Even if he could reach the scene fast, the rain would be destroying Ben's tracks as fast as he made them.

Hawk was certain Maggie's visit and tumble down the hill were tricks to make contact with Ben, and her clever attempt had succeeded. No doubt she had found a sly way to conceal items Ben would need. He was vexed with himself for allowing that slip to occur and warned himself to not underestimate her skills again. Apparently, when she almost landed at Ben's feet and while Ben was assisting her, she had passed along a message revealing the whereabouts of those items. By now, Ben probably had collected them and was on his way to a hideout.

Hawk realized that all he could do now was shadow Maggie when she left town to rendezvous with Ben, which would still enable him to locate and capture his three targets. He would entrap her, take her to a private spot, and extract Ben's location from those pretty lips. After Ben was in his tight grasp, he would force out the others' whereabouts from that sorry scum. How, he wondered, could a woman have such a convincing air of sweet innocence and ladylike refinement about her and ally herself to such vermin? She certainly had an enormous talent for duping people. *Well, Miss Malone, you don't have me fooled. You and Ben better kiss good-bye forever when you see each other again because I'm going to make your next separation a permanent one.*

As lightning flashed and thunder clapped, Hawk mounted his black mustang. Born and raised in the wilds, Diablo was surefooted, fast, spirited, and loyal to him. He would return the animal to the stable, tend him, then go to his hotel room to get out of his soaked clothes.

As he left his lofty position in the hills, Hawk's mind filled with contradictory thoughts and his body with conflicting emotions. He couldn't help but be amazed that she had pulled off such a seemingly impossible feat, and in only one week to the day after meeting with Newl in Wilcox! Of course, she had had unexpected assistance from a furious Mother Nature whose wrath increased by the minute. Yet, even without that help, he had a gut feeling she would have somehow succeeded anyway.

Hawk admitted he was impressed by her daring, intelligence, and courage. Although he was swayed by Maggie's talents and even enchanted by her beauty and fascinated by the mystery surrounding her, he was angered by her strong connection to at least one criminal on his list; maybe to others if she knew Barber and Jones.

Suddenly an unexpected idea struck him: what if Maggie was Ben's trusting sweetheart? What would Ben tell her if or when she discovered his guilt? If she was madly and blindly in love with Ben and Ben was deceiving her, she might refuse to accept the dark truth or Ben might continue to withhold it from her. Whatever their bond was, he needed to uncover it; and he needed to find an unsuspecting way to get close to her now that Ben was on the loose. If he lost track of Margaret Anne Malone, he would lose his path to swift revenge.

The force of the wild winds and downpour increased as the storm's fury mounted, as did the frequency of the lightning and thunder. With the gusts blowing so forcefully, the two women couldn't use their parasols. They walked as fast as they could toward the hotel, almost blinded by the thick sheet of water. Their movements were restricted by their saturated dresses which clung to their bodies and by softened ground which grabbed at their shoes. Both squealed as a bolt of lightning struck a tree and seared off one of its limbs, which immediately crashed to the ground.

"Let's run, Maggie, before lightning strikes us dead!" Abby screamed, and the friends bolted for cover as fast as their almost entangled legs would carry them, kicking up mud and soiling their clothes.

After she opened the door, Lucy gaped at the two young women, and pulled them into the sitting room. "My heavens, you're both soaked to the skin! We have to get you dried off and changed, but don't move from there or you'll ruin the rug." After she fetched thick cloths, she softly scolded, "Thank goodness your father isn't here or he would be angry. Those shoes and dresses look awful, so we'll need to clean them before he returns. Wherever have you two been? I've been worried witless. Why didn't you hurry home when the storm threatened or stay where you were until it stopped?"

"There was no warning, Mother, and we were out in the open. We hurried back as quickly as possible. You know we couldn't take shelter with strangers or in a horrid place like a saloon. I'm sorry about our clothing. We were strolling near the base of Prison Hill and started talking with two of the guards. None of us noticed the change in weather; it altered like magic, in the blink of an eye. Maggie took a spill and one of the guards was bandaging her arm when this calamity struck."

"Are you all right, my dear? Were you injured?"

Lucy turned her attention to Maggie. As Maggie dried her hair, she said, "Only my pride and dress, Mrs. Mercer. A gust of wind just swept me off my feet and threw me down an incline, but two of the guards assisted me. I shall have to purchase blue thread tomorrow to repair a rip in my skirt."

"First, we must take it to Mr. Kee's laundry to see if he can remove those stains. He's worked wonders for me on some soiled garments."

After they washed off mud and changed

clothes, they scrubbed their shoes and conditioned the abused leather. Then Lucy served them hot tea and warm muffins from downstairs and the women relaxed and chatted.

As the storm raged, Maggie waited in mounting suspense to learn if Ben had succeeded in escaping. If he had managed to elude the guards during the commotion, all he had to do was use the strange but propitious weather to get far down the Gila River and hide until he could catch the eastbound train at a distant station as her note with the items told him to do. She had been fortunate so far, and she hoped her good luck held out until this matter was resolved.

When Maggie heard a faint tapping at her door late that night, she assumed Abby had sneaked away from her sleeping mother to chat with her. She would have been asleep herself if the storm and her tension weren't keeping her awake and edgy. She unlocked the door and gaped at the person standing there, dripping wet and grinning. She seized Ben's arm and almost yanked him inside her room, unmindful of her state of dress. She relocked the door, turned, and whispered, "You should be long gone by now! It's up to you to get yourself to the pick-up point with the train. What are you doing here? How did you find me? This is crazy, Ben; you're endangering both of us."

He smiled and said, "I found the things right where your map said they would be. While you and that other girl distracted the guards, I slipped deeper into the bushes. After that storm struck, I got my fanny out of there fast. I figured I wouldn't be missed until lock-up time and by then, it would be too late, and the weather's too bad for them to search for me tonight. Besides, that rain washed away my trail, and I stuck my old shoes in the mud at the river to lead them in that direction. After everybody here was asleep, I sneaked in downstairs and used the registry book to locate your room."

"How did you know I was at this hotel?" She saw him grin again as he pushed soaked sandy hair from a darkly tanned nice-looking face. Eyes as green as grass sparkled with vitality.

"I didn't know, but it was the first one I checked. Everybody knows the Mercers are staying in a hotel, and this one's the best. I couldn't leave town before thanking you for getting me out of that hellhole. It surely does feel good not standing in the shadow of that hangman's noose. Papa and your letter said you're gonna try to exonerate me. What's your plan, my amazing stepsister?"

"We don't have time for a get-acquainted visit and I don't have time to explain the matter to you again: I thought I included everything in my note. I'll do my best to expose those two witnesses who lied and to apprehend the guilty men. You know them, right?" As Ben responded, she observed his expressions and manner and listened to his tone of voice to see if she could detect even a hint of deception. She didn't and was relieved.

"I've met Pete Barber and Slim Jones a couple of times; a man don't travel this territory much without running into them on occasion. The Law's certain they were involved in that Prescott bank job, so I hope you kill them for letting me be framed for their crime. Papa said he told you I was hunting with him when that bank was struck. All I know about that robbery and shooting is what I was told in jail and court and read in the newspaper. Papa also told me you're one of the best detectives in the country, but you be careful when you go up against Pete and Slim; they're mean and dangerous and unpredictable."

"If or when I locate them, I'll be careful," she promised.

"We're counting on you to help me, Maggie, or I'm a dead man. Papa says you're the only one who can do this for us, and Papa chooses only the best in everything, like when he picked your mama for his wife. She's a real nice lady. I know I've done some wild things in my life, but I swear I wasn't in Prescott that day."

Maggie found his manner genial and sincere, yet, she knew from experience that some criminals could be deceptively convincing. Either Ben was being open and honest, or he was one of the cleverest snakes she'd met. "You have to go, Ben. Every second you're here is wasted get-away time. If you and I are even glimpsed together, our efforts were for naught."

"If I get captured, Maggie, I swear I won't tell them anything about your help. By the way, it's good to finally meet you; I just wish it wasn't in this crazy situation. You best get me cleared fast because you're gonna need a big brother around to keep the boys from chasing you day and night. You're a whole lot prettier than the pictures I've seen of you."

"Thank you, Ben; now, get moving, pronto."

"Don't take any bad risks because of me, little sister, and I'll be seeing you again real soon. I'll be waiting in Sante Fe with Papa's friend while you prove I'm innocent."

"I only have one more thing to say, Ben: if you're lying to me and you're guilty, I'll work just as hard to see you back behind bars as I did to get you out. Understand?" She watched him squint his green eyes to look her over from un-bound hair to bare feet before he responded.

"I understand, but you don't have any call to worry about me. Thanks, Maggie. If you ever need anything from me, you'll get it; I swear."

She was surprised when he kissed her on the cheek before he smiled and crept to the door. "Wait," she whispered. She fetched a drying cloth, grinned, and said, "Dry up the floor on your way out or that wet trail to my door might look suspicious. And toss the used cloth into the outhouse so it won't be found by one of those Quechan trackers who'll be trying to earn fifty dollars by bringing you in. Good-bye, Ben, and good luck."

"You, too, little sister."

Maggie waited for fifteen minutes before she peeked outside her room to check the floor. Ben had done a perfect job of concealing the evidence of his nocturnal visit. She returned to bed, put aside the book she had been reading, and doused the oil lamp. She let her mind roam in contradictory directions.

Ben was exactly as her mother had described him: nice, polite, genial, likable. But for some reason, that reality unnerved her. She couldn't help but remember that her mother had deceived her for months about her father's death, told her what she wanted and needed to hear to remain in school during that final year. Was her mother deluded again about what was right and best for another person? Did Ben have her mother tricked? Was she, herself, fooled by a clever act?

The storm halted during the wee hours of the next morning, long before Tom Mercer returned from Los Angeles and after the *Arizona Sentinel* had been published and copies delivered to the hotel. A wide-eyed Lucy had just finished reading the lead story to Maggie and Abby when Tom entered the sitting room and set down his bag.

"You won't believe what's happened, dear," Lucy said. "A man escaped from the prison work detail during a storm yesterday. The weather was absolutely horrible. Fortunately we didn't suffer any flooding and the water appears to be drying up as fast as it came down. We were just reading about the shocking escape."

"What does the paper say?" Tom asked. "How did it happen?"

"When the storm broke, the convicts working outside the prison on the road were rushed back inside and sent to the bathing rooms to get cleaned up and dried off. Afterward, they were left in the main building to work on crafts. When suppertime came, the guards on duty assumed the man's seat was empty because he was either sick in bed or working in the mechanic's shop or doing a task for the superintendent. His absence wasn't noticed until it was lock-up time hours later. Mr. Vander Meeden sent out men to search for him where he was last seen but he couldn't be found and his tracks had been washed away. The paper says Quechan Indians were summoned this morning to look for him. So far, the trackers found his shoes stuck in mud at the riverbank, but there was no trail to follow. It's assumed he sneaked aboard a ferry or boat and got away."

"Not for long. Who is he? What was his crime?"

"Ben Carver from Tucson. He was convicted for robbing a bank in Prescott and shooting the teller. The article said they never caught his accomplices or recovered the money and that Mr. Carver pleaded innocence."

"You said he's a Carver from Tucson?"

"That's right, dear."

Tom looked at their guest and asked, "Your

stepfather is a Carver in Tucson; do you know who this man is?"

Be as honest as you can. "Yes, sir; he's my stepfather's son, but I've never been to Tucson and he never came to St. Louis with Mother and Mr. Carver. I didn't even know he was in prison until recently; I suppose Mother was too embarrassed to tell me earlier."

"Why didn't you ask to visit him while we were touring there?"

"He's a stranger to me, sir, a criminal, so I didn't think it would look appropriate to others for your guest to be visiting her . . . Well, we aren't actually related by blood. Do you think I should leave before anyone makes that discovery and thinks badly of me?"

"Of course not, Margaret Anne, and I'm terribly sorry this happened while you're visiting us. I'm certain no one here will discover your connection to him. Was her name mentioned in the article?" Tom asked his wife, "Was his father's?"

Lucy shook her head to both questions. "Of course, Mr. Dorrington probably didn't have much time to gather the facts before printing time. A reporter went to the prison this morning and talked with the guards and superintendent, but it says more facts will be released later. I'm so sorry about this . . . incident, Margaret Anne; I know it must distress you, dear."

"Yes and no, ma'am. He's a stranger to me, but he is the son of my mother's husband, so I suppose that makes him part of my family. I just

90

wouldn't want to cause any of you any embarrassment or trouble."

Lucy smiled and said, "You won't, my dear, so don't worry about us. Besides, it's a secret only we know, so it can't cause us a scandal."

"I suppose you're right, ma'am. Even if they print his father's name and my mother's name, no one in Yuma knows I'm her daughter. I agree it would be best for all of us if we don't tell anybody that secret." Maggie was glad the couple didn't suspect her of duplicity. "I don't think I should telegraph Mother and Mr. Carver about his escape because that would expose my connection to them, and you know how gossip can spread quickly, especially in a town this size. If the story is sent to Tucson and printed in their newspaper, I know they'll be embarrassed and worried about him being chased down and slain."

"I'm sure he'll be recaptured and be safely back in his cell within a day or two." Tom sat down on the settee beside his wife, facing Abby and Maggie in matching chairs. "I can't imagine why any prisoner would risk more trouble and have years added to his sentence when he's got it so good over there. The inmates are properly clothed and well fed with nourishing and ample food. They're given plenty of water and rest breaks during chores, and given every Sunday off. They have places to do their laundry, take baths, and entertain themselves. There's a machine shop to learn a trade, and those who are qualified teach others to read and write and do arithmetic. The tour money that's collected is for a library, but townfolk already donate books and magazines. The prison is in good condition and being improved and expanded at the present time. Some townfolk are jealous and resentful of the fact that prisoners get better food, clothing, and shelter than they do. We haven't had any bad trouble since I came to work here. Your stepbrother's going to be mighty sorry he made his situation worse on himself."

Maggie thought that despite what she had been told by Newl and Ben and what she had viewed during her tour, the prison did not sound as bad as those descriptions and how it had appeared to her biased mind. "Maybe he was scared of other prisoners, sir, or afraid he would hang for murder if the man he shot dies."

"I doubt he'd be hanged, Margaret Anne; he'd probably just be given life in prison, and still have a chance for parole one day."

"Maybe he panicked during the storm, saw a chance for freedom, and grabbed it before thinking clearly. Perhaps he'll turn himself in today."

"I bet you two probably saw him during your stroll yesterday," Lucy ventured, "but didn't realize it since you've never met him and don't know what he looks like."

"What stroll?" Tom sounded shocked. "You ladies didn't go to the prison alone, did you?"

"No, Father, we didn't climb Prison Hill. That wouldn't be proper. But we walked to the edge of the bluff and watched the men work for a while; then the storm drove us inside."

"Obviously Ben Carver is a dangerous and clever man to be able to get away from his work detail, and right under the guards' noses. It's too bad the convicts weren't chained together during their road labors. I'll go to the prison to see what I can learn about this matter. Please unpack my bag, dear wife, and I shall return for the evening meal with you ladies. As for you, Margaret Anne, please don't worry about this."

"Thank you for being so kind and understanding, sir. But if you change your mind and think it's best I leave early, I won't be offended."

"We wouldn't hear of you leaving early, isn't that right, Lucy?"

"Of course it is, my dear," she responded.

Not long after Tom left, Abby asked her mother if it was all right if Maggie and she went shopping for the thread Maggie needed. "We won't go far or be away for very long," she promised. "We can use the exercise and diversion. You can come with us."

"Thank you, dear, but I must unpack your father's things. It should be safe to stroll in town; I'm sure Sheriff Tyner is on alert for any possible trouble, though I imagine Mr. Carver is long gone from this area. You should both change clothes before you leave; you must look your best because I imagine the streets will be filled with people discussing the news. It's important that you dress and behave as ladies in case our secret leaks out. Besides, Matthew Lawrence could be in town today," Lucy hinted.

To please Lucy, Maggie and Abby changed into their best outfits. Maggie donned a white batiste polonaise that was trimmed with morning glory blue Valenciennes lace at the square neck, along the three-quarter-length sleeves, and around its bottom hem. Below, she wore a matching multiruffled walking skirt with a soft bustle created by the material's drapery rather than with a metal-framed undergarment. She secured a blue ribbon with pink-and-ivory cameo at her neck. She donned a hat whose brim slanted down toward her ears and upward in the back and front and was adorned lightly with morning glories and cloth strips at the base of its crown. She completed her attire with soft leather boots, a lace fan for cooling herself if needed, and a fancy parasol for shade.

Maggie felt as if she should be heading for church, an afternoon tea, or stroll in a large city rather than one in a small and dusty western town. But if this action made Lucy happy, she decided, it was worth the effort.

Maggie purchased the blue thread, looked around the large mercantile store for other needs, and bought a long and wide strip of white cotton cloth to replace what she'd thrown away during her menses.

As Maggie used her buttocks to push open the door to leave and turned aside quickly to make room for Abby to exit past her while she held it in place, her loaded arms crashed into a man about to enter the store. Startled, Maggie loosened her grip on the packages and they fell to the porch as she gasped in surprise. "I'm terribly sorry, sir; I didn't see you. Are you injured?"

"No, ma'am, and it was partly my fault; my thoughts were elsewhere and I wasn't paying attention to where I was going. Are you all right?"

"Except for embarrassment, I'm fine."

"Let me fetch those things for you," Hawk offered when she started to bend over to retrieve strewn objects. As he did so, she spoke to him again in that angelic voice which teased his senses and sent a rush of heat over his entire body.

"Thank you, sir; that's very kind of you, especially considering I almost smacked you in the face with a door."

Hawk glanced upward at her from his kneeling position and smiled. "Accidents do happen on occasion, and there's no harm done." He gathered the few spilled items and returned them to a sack. Mercy, she looked beautiful and smelled good! No matter what else she was, she was a real lady; or knew how to dress, speak, and behave like one. What a contradiction she was!

Accustomed to making fast and thorough observations and judgments, within moments many things about the handsome stranger registered in Maggie's mind. Obviously he had just ridden into town because he was wearing a below-the-knee linen coat and dark Stetson which were covered

95

with dust, as were his black boots and fringed chaps over Levi pants. The heel on his footwear and the high crown of his hat made him appear even taller than his over six feet. His shirt was dark blue, as was a bandanna around his neck. She couldn't see his weapons, but imagined he was well armed. His eyes were golden brown and his gaze was awesome. Ebony hair curled at the ends where it grazed broad shoulders, though a few strands caressed his forehead near his right temple. He had high cheekbones which created shallow hollows between them, and a strong almost squared jawline revealed a slight stubble that matched his hair. His lips were full; his teeth, white and straight; and his smile, irresistible and magnetic. He revealed good manners and respect for ladies. Unexpected emotions like swirling wild winds assailed her body, sending sparks of an instant and powerful attraction to him racing through it.

Maggie took her packages from him, smiled, and thanked him again for his assistance. She watched him touch his fingers to his hat brim, nod, and smile as he spoke in a stirring voice that made her feel almost limp.

"No trouble at all, ma'am," he said, and walked past her into the store where he would pretend to be looking around while he watched her departure from its front window. He concluded it wasn't wise to spend too much time with her during their initial contact or to show overt personal interest in her, not when she mistakenly assumed the incident was her fault and she was slightly beholden to him.

Maggie used her hip to let the door close quietly and slowly. She headed down the street with her friend, forcing herself not to glance back a single time. At a safe distance from others, she whispered, "That's what I call a real man, Abby. Have you ever seen him here before?"

"No, and I would remember a face like that one. He's almost as handsome as my Matthew. He got to you, didn't he?"

Maggie sent her an affirmative smile. "I wonder who he is and why he's in town. I wonder if he's married or engaged. Oh, well, it doesn't really matter who or what he is; I'll be gone soon."

"Oh, Maggie, must you leave so soon? Our visit has been too short."

"I must go, Abby, and you know where and why."

"Let me come with you. I can help you locate and capture those —"

"No, Abby, I can't let you endanger yourself again; I'm trained and experienced for such work, but you aren't. Besides, I need you to stay here and listen for news about Ben. You must read the paper, listen to everything your father and mother say, and collect the town gossip. I'll let you know where I am so you can send word by coded telegram if the worst happens. Agreed?"

"Agreed. And besides, I have a romance to handle."

"Yes, my friend, you do, and good luck with it."

After they returned to the hotel and gave Lucy the items she had ordered, they went to Maggie's room to chat while Maggie repaired the dress she had torn while making contact with Ben. As agreed, they did not discuss the successful escape or her stepbrother in case somebody decided to eavesdrop on them; instead they turned the conversation to Abby's romance.

"I don't know anything about ranching, so why would Matthew consider me for a rancher's wife?" Abby asked her friend. "Perhaps I'm only deluding myself about a future with him."

"I doubt it or he wouldn't be courting you. Besides, we're much alike, so you'll love ranching. It's a wonderful life, Abby, and I still miss ours. Matthew and his parents will teach you everything you need to know about it. Then, one day after they're gone, the ranch will belong to you and your husband."

"You should be my teacher so I won't appear dumb to them."

"I tell you what, for the remainder of my visit, every spare moment we have, I'll tell you everything I know about ranchers and ranching."

Abby hugged her and said, "You're the best friend I could ever have."

"You're the best friend *I* could ever have. Let's begin your first lesson right now," Maggie said, then started relating facts she had learned from her father and his ranch hands during a happy childhood in Fort Worth.

After attending church, eating Sunday dinner downstairs, and talking in their sitting room for a while, the Mercers excused themselves to visit with friends near the edge of town for the remainder of the afternoon.

Although Maggie knew that Abby's parents assumed she would stay with their daughter and suitor as a chaperone during their absence, she left the Mercer home only fifteen minutes after their departure. It was obvious to her that Abby and Matthew were deeply in love; and she liked Matthew, so she decided to give them a little privacy. "If you two don't mind, I'd like to take a short walk to get some exercise and fresh air after that big meal. I shan't be gone for more than thirty minutes, an hour at the most. I think you two are old and wise enough to do without a chaperone."

"That's true, Maggie," Abby said shyly, "but if Mother and Father see you out, they'll know you left us alone here."

"If Matthew promises to be a gentleman," Maggie said, "then I promise to stroll in the opposite direction from theirs."

"Hard as it will be with a beautiful and special lady beside me, I'll behave myself during your brief absence," Matthew teased with a broad grin.

"I'll take you at your word, Matthew, because a true gentleman would never deceive a lady."

Maggie exited the hotel and headed toward the Colorado River. She didn't get far before a horse's neighing caught her attention. She looked in the corral next door and saw a magnificent black animal standing at the fence, his head pointed in her direction. When he tossed it backward several times as if summoning her, she couldn't resist the pull, so she walked to him. "Hello, you handsome boy. Are you bored with nothing to do?" He seemed to accept her company and didn't give any signs of tension. His ears didn't stiffen and his gaze was calm and clear. "Would you rather be galloping across the countryside?" she asked as she stroked his neck several times.

"You must have a magical hand, ma'am, because Diablo doesn't allow anyone except me to touch him unless I'm around and give the okay."

Recognizing that stirring voice, Maggie half-turned as the handsome stranger joined her, and the horse instantly moved close to its master who touseled its forelock with apparent affection. Today, he was attired in a just-above-knee black frock coat, pale-blue shirt, dark-blue jeans, red bandanna, clean black boots, and dust-free black hat. He was wearing two pistols on a brown leather cartridge belt, yet there was nothing about his voice, expression, or manner to indicate he was a cold-blooded or cocky gunslinger as most were she'd seen during her travels.

"I can see you survived your collision with me yesterday. I realized afterward that I didn't introduce myself: I'm Hawk Reynolds."

Maggie extended her right hand to let him know it was all right to shake it, as a real gentleman knew it was improper to reach for a lady's hand before or unless she offered it to him, which he hadn't. As he did so with a gentle grasp, she responded, "My name is Miss Margaret Anne Malone. I'm visiting the Mercers; Mr. Mercer's daughter and I are old and close friends." If he had a reputation as a gunslinger, she hadn't heard of him; neither had she met him before Yuma, as he wasn't a man any woman would forget.

She blushed as she realized she had given more information than necessary to a stranger during a casual encounter, especially her marital status. "Do you live in or near Yuma, Mr. Reynolds?" she asked.

Hawk was surprised and oddly pleased by her openness and honesty, and he was warmed and baffled by the slight pink glow which came to her cheeks. "Nope, just passing through." As he propped one boot on the fence's lowest rail and his elbows on the top one, he added, "Actually, I came to Yuma to solicit business, but I haven't found anything useful here, so I'll be heading for Tucson on Tuesday to do the same thing."

"What type of business are you in?" she asked in rare boldness.

Hawk chuckled and said, "I have one of those kinds of jobs that a lot of people frown at; I hire out as a bounty hunter sometimes; a tracker, at others. Seems as if somebody's always losing

somebody or something they love and want returned. I do a lot of missing person jobs, and I
sometimes escort travelers through perilous or
unknown territory."

Maggie liked the fact they had something in
common. "That sounds like interesting work to
me, stimulating and exciting."

"It can be; mostly it's just a lot of time alone
on the trail in all kinds of weather, but the pay's
usually good and I get to be my own boss."
*You've made your clever points, so ride another trail
before she gets suspicious.* "I take it you know and
love horses from the way Diablo responds to you."

*Surely a man with his job couldn't be married or
stay in one place long enough to have a sweetheart.*
"I was born and reared on a ranch before my
father died and my mother sold it years ago. I
was a pretty good cowpoke as a young girl, and
I love horses."

Hawk smiled. "I've been a pretty good cowpoke in my day, too, but years ago. That surely
explains why he took to you so fast and easy."

"What kind is he? How long have you had him?"

"He's a mustang; I roped him, broke him, and
trained him myself. I couldn't have a better
mount or friend. Diablo and I have been together
for nine years, since I was eighteen."

"That means you're twenty-seven," she unin-
tentionally figured aloud.

"I will be in three months. Where do you live,
Miss Malone?"

Maggie went on alert, knowing it was unwise

to reveal too much about herself to anyone, so she half-lied, "I came here from Sante Fe."

"That's a nice town; I've been there a few times in the past. How long will you be visiting in Yuma, if that's not being too nosy?"

Impolite? You have wonderful manners, Hawk Reynolds. You seem genial, educated, and respectful. "I'll be leaving this week. Where was your home before you went on the road?"

Hawk knew he was being studied and appraised on the sly, which was exactly what he was doing with her. *Want to ask somebody to check up on me, do you?* "I'm from Wichita in Kansas, but I've been gone for a long time."

"Speaking of being gone for a long time, I have to get back to my friend. I told her I was only going to take a short walk to settle my dinner, but I didn't get past Diablo's summons. It's been pleasant talking with you, Mr. Reynolds. Good-bye."

"Been a pleasure talking with you, Miss Malone. Good-bye."

Maggie and Abby sat cross-legged as they faced each other on Maggie's bed, their skirts laying neatly across their laps to keep them from wrinkling. Matthew had left ten minutes ago, but the Mercers had not returned from their visit.

"Tell me everything," Maggie coaxed. "Did he kiss you? Did he ask you to marry him or hint in that direction?" She saw Abby's face and gaze glow with exhilaration and heard her voice fill

103

with joy when she responded.

"I shall love you forever for giving us our first minutes of privacy. Mother and Father would be vexed with us if they discovered that secret, but if they do, it will be well worth their anger. Oh, Maggie, he's absolutely wonderful, a dream come true. I felt weak and hot all over when he held me and kissed me. He said he loves me, and I told him the same thing. He said he's going to approach Father about asking for my hand in marriage if I agreed to his proposal."

"Which I'm certain you did, right?"

"Without a moment's delay," Abby admitted.

"When is he going to take that huge step?"

"In a month. We decided we should wait a while longer and see each other regularly for appearance's sake. Since we've only been courting for a short time, my parents and others might think we were being too hasty. It will be difficult to wait, especially since we won't get any more privacy after you leave. We decided, if my parents agree, we'll become betrothed next month and get married Christmas."

"What a marvelous holiday gift that will be for both of you. That means, by next Christmas, I should be an aunt," Maggie jested.

"If you get busy and find a good man like mine, you could be married by then yourself. Too bad you're leaving soon and won't get a chance to see that handsome stranger again."

"I've already seen him again; his name is Hawk Reynolds; he's from Wichita; and he has a job similiar to mine, except he's self-employed."

"When and how did you learn all of those facts?"

"During my stroll." Maggie related the unexpected episode to her friend. "I like him a lot, but this isn't the right time or place to begin a romance, and he might not be interested in one with me or any woman. He struck me as being a loner and wanderer, not the settling down type. Besides, it would be wrong to get involved with any man when the matter of Ben Carver is looming over my head. I must wait until that matter's resolved."

"By then, dear Maggie, he could be long gone and lost forever."

"If that's true, then we weren't destined for each other. But aren't we talking awfully serious about a man I just met? For all I know, he could be a villain who's only wearing a handsome and clever disguise."

"You can pretend to be joking, but I know you well, Maggie Malone: you want him badly, my friend. Why not give up your work, stay here, and go after him? I bet he would be responsive. You got Ben out of jail, so let some other detective try to exonerate him."

"I can't do that, Abby; I gave my word. I started this job, so I have to finish it; I have to either prove he's innocent or return him to prison if he isn't."

On Monday morning, Maggie sneaked down

the street while Lucy was bathing, Tom was at the prison, and Abby remained on look out at the hotel. She sent a cleverly worded telegram to her mother and Newl, a preplanned method of getting her out of town so she could begin her investigative work in Prescott. She sent it to the bartender who worked at the Paradise Club in Tucson so the Carver name wouldn't be on it and perhaps arouse suspicions about her. Afterward, she returned to her room and started packing for her departure tomorrow.

Maggie went to see Lucy after receiving a response to her wire. "A telegram was delivered to me just now," she explained. "Mother wants me to join her and my stepfather in Tucson as soon as possible. She said they need me to be with them at this difficult time. I'm sure they're worried about Newl's son's safety, since he's on the loose and subject to added charges and punishment when he's recaptured. I'm also worried, ma'am, about the local authorities discovering my identity and causing all of us trouble and embarrassment."

"Oh, my word, did Catherine expose your relationship to him?"

"No, ma'am; she worded the telegram carefully so as to not give away any clues about me, and she simply signed it, 'Mother.' I'm sure the men in the both offices didn't suspect a thing. If I know Mother, she was smart enough to let someone else send the telegram for her."

"That's good. But if there are repercussions, we'll handle it."

"Thank you, ma'am; you and Mr. Mercer have been so kind and wonderful to me concerning this nasty situation."

"Don't worry about it, dear, and tell Catherine we're thinking about her during this trying period."

"Thank you, ma'am, I'll tell her. I'm going to the depot to check the train's departure schedule and purchase a ticket. I'll see you at mealtime downstairs. May Abby walk there with me? We won't be gone very long."

"Of course, she can. You two should spend as much time as possible together until your departure. You're fortunate we have two passenger trains daily, so you shouldn't have trouble finding a seat on one in a day or two."

Yes, it is fortunate, except for what — no, whom — I'll be leaving behind forever. Maggie took a deep breath and concluded she and Hawk Reynolds weren't meant for each other, much as she wished it were otherwise.

On Tuesday at one o'clock, as the engineer blew the locomotive's whistle to signal its impending departure, Maggie took a quick and final look at Prison Hill, then smiled and waved goodbye to Abby and her parents. As the train headed down Madison Avenue at a cautious pace and she was wondering if Ben had made it to Sante Fe and was safe in hiding there, someone tapped her shoulder. After she half-turned, her gaze widened and her lips parted in astonishment. She glanced around to see if any other passenger was observing them, but no one was. She leaned toward him and whispered, "Whatever are you doing here?"

Chapter Five

"I'm sorry if I startled you, Miss Malone."

Maggie gathered her scattered wits and tried to appear poised, though she was thoroughly unsettled by contradictory emotions of joy and panic. "What are you doing here?"

Hawk perceived her mixed feelings about his unexpected appearance. He was pleased by that effect, as few things evoked slips quicker and easier than being caught by surprise. "I thought I told you I was leaving for Tucson today."

"You did, but I assumed you meant overland by horse."

"I decided taking the train would be faster and more comfortable for me and Diablo; there's no need to endure a long and dusty ride when this is faster and easier and don't cost much. That desert gets mighty hot and dry this time of year." Hawk grasped the back of the seat and spread his legs to brace himself as the train's speed increased. "Do you mind if I join you?"

"Yes, you may sit next to me; I don't mind, as long as you remain a gentleman."

"Thanks, Miss Malone, that's mighty kind of

you, and I will be."

After Hawk settled himself, his long legs a little cramped in those less than spacious confines, he told her, "I intended to take the early train, but I had a sudden change of plans. A man hired me to go to Prescott to check on his missing daughter."

Maggie went on full alert and three questions raced through her mind as the conductor reached them and checked their tickets. Was this meeting a coincidence? Or was a displeased God going to use Hawk to punish her for the illegal deed she had committed? Or was Fate throwing them together for generous reasons? Whichever was true, his appearance couldn't be worse timing. She told herself she had to come up with a credible explanation, and fast! When they were alone again, she voiced her question. "You're heading for Prescott, not Tucson?"

Hawk saw her blue gaze widen so he knew that revelation made her nervous and perhaps suspicious. He smiled and hurried on with his fabricated excuse, "That's right, Miss Malone. She took off with a fancy-dressed and smooth-talking gambler yesterday, and her parents didn't know about it until last night and they're worried about her. Her father heard about me from a friend, looked me up just after sunrise, and hired me to locate her. He asked me to see if I can convince her to return home; if not, to make sure she's safe and knows what she's doing. By the time I traced them to yesterday's train using fake names, I almost missed catching this one. I thought they might have taken that steamer that left Yuma yesterday because gamblers love to travel on them and ply their trade during the trip. I'm glad they didn't, because it would've taken them twenty or more days to reach Prescott using that means; that river's slow, winding, and treacherous; and she makes lots of stops. I surely didn't want to hang around for weeks awaiting their arrival."

The news that he was heading to the same destination told Maggie she would have to be careful not to arouse any suspicions; after all, he was a bounty hunter and she was going after men with big prices on their heads. Though her criminal act had not been detected at this point in time, she might soon be exposed and have a juicy reward put out on her, one he might be tempted to collect! Tension and suspense flooded her as she realized his presence could intrude on her carefully made plans. *Just stay calm and clear-headed, if that's possible around such an irresistible and potent force.* "I'm sure her family is terribly worried about her. How old is she?"

"Twenty-one, and has a slight wild streak according to her father."

Don't you dare let that sexy grin and handsome face distract you and cause a hazardous slip! "She must be impulsive to take off with a gambler — and without being married. I assume they didn't wed before they left town or her parents wouldn't be so worried about her?"

"Nope, I checked with every preacher there. But her note said they were eloping, so maybe they'll tie the knot in Prescott or in some town along the way."

"If they wed, surely you won't be able to persuade her to return home."

"The main thing her family is interested in is her safety and happiness. If she's made a terrible mistake, they want her to know she shouldn't be too embarrassed to return home. They don't want him using her and dumping her somewhere, and then having her being too ashamed to admit her error."

"I'm sure that happens plenty of times to unsuspecting and trusting young women when a 'smooth-talking' man sweeps them off their feet," she said. She knew for a fact that occurred, as she'd had a few jobs that involved tracking down such girls; she'd found several in dire straights and too humiliated to go home. It had required a lot of fast and clever talking to convince them otherwise.

Don't give her time to uncloud her wits; just keep her talking. "You heading back home to Sante Fe?"

Maggie wished she hadn't mentioned that town to him, not with Ben hiding out there. "No, I'm also en route to Prescott, for a job."

Hawk faked a look of surprise. From following her on the sly in Yuma, he knew about an exchange of telegrams and assumed it was with Newl Carver in Tucson. He also knew from eavesdropping at an open window at the S & P depot that she was heading for Prescott. If what Toby Muns had told him wasn't true, he couldn't surmise why Ben would return to the scene of his last crime just to rendezvous with her. Yet, he had no choice except to tag along until that reunion occurred. Besides, if Toby told the truth before his death and Ben — not Coot Sayers — had betrayed Barber and Jones, those two snakes should be searching for Ben as eagerly as he was, if they'd heard Ben was on the loose. "You mean we'll be traveling together for days and wind up in the same town again?" After she nodded, he smiled and said, "That sounds pleasant to me. What kind of work? You already have a job waiting or you're planning to look for one later?"

"In a way, neither and both. Actually, I'm from Virginia and did my last job in Sante Fe. Since I was so close to Arizona, I decided to visit my old and dear friend, Abigail Mercer, and to see if I could do another job in Yuma. I have a close friend in the newspaper business." *That much is true, so now come the lies.* "He hired me to write stories about the Wild West. I'm on a year's try-out basis. While I was visiting Abby, a man escaped from Yuma Prison. I did some checking and realized it would make an excellent story. Since his crime was carried out in Prescott, I'm heading there to talk to the witnesses, judge, lawyers, and maybe some of the jurors and townfolk. I suppose it sounds foolish to you for a woman to want to become a journalist."

So, you can think fast and clever; well, so can I. "Nope, in fact, it sounds exciting and challenging to me. Just be careful, because the Wild West can be dangerous and unpredictable, especially for a beautiful lady who's traveling alone."

Maggie felt a rush of heat sear over her body. "Thank you for the compliment, kind sir, and for not laughing at me. I suppose I, too, am guilty of having one of those wild streaks you mentioned earlier; but I'd rather think of it as an adventurous vein."

Hawk chuckled. "Well, you'll certainly have plenty of adventures and challenges out here if you go nosing around. And you'll want to be far away if those stories are printed locally; men like that escaped convict don't like people asking questions about them; they might come looking to see who you are and why you're intruding on their lives, maybe want to put a stop to your curiosity. What you need is somebody to protect you and help you gather information so you won't get yourself into trouble."

Maggie glanced at the weapon closest to her, a '76 Remington New Army single-action .44 caliber revolver. His dual holsters were secured to muscled thighs by leather thongs that dangled downward, once more hinting at a skilled gunslinger's preference. A Spencer rifle, a lever-action repeater, was wedged between his right leg and the armrest of his seat. "You appear to be well armed and ready for trouble. Perhaps I should hire you, Mr. Reynolds; you seem quite capable of defending anybody, and you're clever about extracting information. I don't normally talk with strangers, and certainly not to this revealing extent."

Hawk chuckled as he removed his Stetson and lay it on his lap. His fingers lightly gripped its dark brim when what they yearned to do was grasp the mysterious and enchanting beauty, pull her into his arms, and taste those tempting lips. He cautioned himself to ignore her many charms as he jested, "I must have a trustworthy air about me, Miss Malone, and I guess that's a good trait to have in my line of work. If that weren't at least partly true, I doubt the missing persons I track down would allow me to help them so I can collect my payments. Of course," he added with another chuckle and mischievous grin, "that trait could be hazardous when I'm on a bounty hunting trip if certain men looked upon it with suspicion."

"Oh, I'm sure that a man in your line of work adjusts his behavior to the needs at hand so he can succeed in his task."

"Well put, Miss Malone. Your offer sounds tempting, but I'm already working for somebody else. Of course, if that girl's not in trouble when I locate her and she doesn't need escorting back to Yuma, I'll be available. At least I can offer you my protection during our journey there, free of charge."

Maggie shifted her position, putting her left side closer to the window in order to break the wit-clouding contact of their arms and shoulders. She hadn't — not consciously — been serious about offering him a job, but perhaps he would be useful in several areas. As a bounty hunter and apparent gunslinger, Hawk would know how to locate and disable culprits such as Barber and Jones and prevent her from jeopardizing herself and her mission. Even so, she must keep the tempting male at arm's length until her dilemma was resolved, as an emotional involvement could be hazardous to both of them. "Why would you do that, Mr. Reynolds?" she asked ingenuously.

"In exchange for pleasant company and interesting conversation. I don't get much of those two while I'm on the road."

"A man in your line of work must have come across many infamous men and participated in blood-stirring events that would make terrific stories. Perhaps I should pick your brain about them between here and Prescott, if you're agreeable, for a fee of course."

"If you'll call me Hawk and, instead of payment, also tell me all about being a newspaper woman, you have a deal."

"If you'll call me Maggie, you have a deal," she countered, extending her hand for him to shake on it.

Hawk grasped it, delved her blue eyes for clues about the woman, and smiled. *Mercy, you're one bewitching and enigmatic creature! What is it about you that shouts you're nothing like Carver, even after what you've done for him? Why in blazes are you really going to Prescott? If you were heading there to reunite with Carver, you wouldn't be hiring me to tag along. You're up to something strange, woman, and I'm gonna learn what it is.*

Maggie responded to the infectious smile, aware he hadn't released her hand and she made no attempt to withdraw it for a few moments. His touch was gentle, yet it was strong and implied self-confidence. His hands were work-calloused, but not exceedingly rough. His golden brown gaze arousing. His scent, clean and masculine, inflamed her senses. She wanted to trail her fingers over his arresting features and drift them through his ebony hair. Afraid he would detect her trembling and sense her attraction to him, Maggie extracted her hand from his as she asked, "You really don't think I'm being foolish or reckless?"

"No, Maggie; you're following your heart and dreams."

"Those are strange and sensitive words for a tough man."

You got her roped, Hawk, so pull her in slow and easy. "Maybe that's because you remind me of my mother; she was a brave and strong woman who followed the callings of her heart and dreams; until she died she worked beside my father in just about everything he did. They were a good match."

Maggie yearned to learn more about him. "You said she's . . . deceased?" she asked. "I'm sure you and your father still miss her." She saw his

117

body stiffen and his expression alter before he stared at his hat, as if trying to master unleashed emotions. Her gaze followed his to where his fingers gripped the Stetson's brim tightly. His gaze had narrowed and chilled. "I'm sorry if I mentioned a painful topic, Hawk."

Hawk swallowed the bitterness almost choking him. Here he sat next to the very person who had a connection to his vicious enemies and he was craving her as a woman, chatting and laughing with her like a friend! He was allowing her to get to him, to soften him, and that must stop pronto! *Give her a little taste of the truth so when you wring her pretty neck, she'll understand why.* "Yep, she's dead, murdered last December. My father and younger brother, too. They were slain by a gang of outlaws during a bank robbery. Their killers were never captured and punished, so I guess that's why I hire out at times as a bounty hunter. Even if I don't come across them, which I hope I do one day, I get rid of other snakes who've harmed good people." *Bite the bullet and paint a good picture of yourself if you hope to ensnare her and use her.* "I enjoy helping nice folks in trouble or getting them to where they need to go safely. But I don't want to spend all of my time and energy going after lowlifes. I have to spend too much time around that sorry sort, and in the types of places they frequent. I even have to act like one of them on occasion to win their trust. I am well armed and skilled as you said, but I don't like to engage in any fight unless

I have no choice. Unnecessary killing has a way of hardening a man too much, so does endlessly searching for revenge; so I try to keep all that under tight control."

Maggie was surprised by the intensity of his emotions. He seemed like a good and decent man to her, but one who could turn mean if he wasn't careful to control his dark side. "So you don't have any family left now?"

"Yep, my grandparents on my father's side. I send them most of the money I earn on my jobs. Being a loner, I don't have need for much of it."

Maggie liked the love and respect she sensed for his grandparents, and the fact he helped support them. "You told the truth, Hawk Reynolds; you are a trustworthy man. I'm sure I would be safe in your protective care, so I hope your Prescott job is a quick one."

"You haven't even asked what I charge for my services," he jested, *which is far more than you could imagine or be willing to pay.*

"Whatever your price, I'm certain it's a fair one. Besides, I have an expense account, so I can afford to hire you."

"Considering the challenge you have in mind, it sounds like an exciting proposition. If you happened to lure some villain into the open with questions and stories, I could grab him and collect his reward. Getting paid double or more suits me just fine."

Walk this unfamiliar terrain with caution, Maggie girl. "I was told that four men helped that Yuma

119

escapee rob the Prescott Bank, and the authorities suspect it was a gang led by Pete Barber and Slim Jones. Have you ever heard of them?"

"Hasn't everybody in these parts? If they're involved, you're talking trouble, Maggie, big trouble."

"That means huge stories if we can ferret out the truth about them. An even bigger story if they come after us and you capture them. Just think what I'd get paid for an article with pictures about infamous outlaws."

"If you lived to write and publish it. Barber and Jones are known gunslingers who fight at the blink of an eye. But from what I know, none of the numerous allegations against them have been proven, so they come and go at will. I doubt you could find anybody who'd incriminate them. Word is, they don't leave witnesses behind; but even if they did show mercy, their victims would be too scared to talk."

"If that's true, wouldn't it indicate they weren't involved in the Prescott crime? By the same token, if Carver rides with them, he wasn't involved, which is what he claimed during his trial. If the authorities are mistaken about Barber and Jones, couldn't they be mistaken about Carver?" She watched Hawk shrug in response. "If Barber and Jones are involved in this matter, does that change your mind about hiring on to me?"

"Nope, I'm as good with my pistols as they are. Besides, I recently heard two of Barber's men were killed, so that about evens the odds if they challenged us. Still, you'll be taking a great risk going after them because you're talking about soulless men."

"Wouldn't it be your job to keep me alive and safe?"

"Yep, if I hired on to you. That remains to be seen, Maggie Malone."

"Yes, it does, doesn't it, Hawk Reynolds? I should warn you now, I can be awfully persuasive and determined when I want something badly."

I'm sure that's true. "And you want this story and those men badly?"

"I want the truth; you can have the villains and their rewards."

"Just the truth? That's all?"

"I swear it."

Blazes if she doesn't look and sound as if she's being honest! Does she think "the truth" will clear Ben Carver of that crime? Is that what you're after, Maggie, what Newl Carver meant by your "other task," exoneration or a pardon? You won't get either one, because the man you helped escape is as guilty as sin itself!

Even if Toby Muns lied about Carver's participation in Prescott and in his own tragic losses, Hawk reasoned, Carver was guilty of other crimes. There was no way Carver could ride with scum like Barber and Jones and keep his hands clean, and Carver had been seen with those two devils on more than one occasion and in several locations. It riled him that Sayers and Muns were dead and couldn't testify against the other three

121

villains, but they wouldn't have made credible witnesses anyway. Carver had to be one of the remaining three men he was after, so Carver was his path to finding the other two. Just as the woman beside him was his path to Carver.

As the locomotive's whistle blasted and the train lurched as it was braked and slowed for a water and passenger stop, both Maggie and Hawk glanced outside and neither made another comment about that topic.

During the next few hours as they crossed the cacti-studded Sonoran Desert, Maggie listened and took notes as Hawk related some of his past adventures, partly to learn all she could about the wicked men and about her companion and partly to give her necessary ruse credence. She was fascinated by the stimulating tales of perilous and cunning incidents. If he would come to work for her, she was certain they would enjoy each other's company. Yet, it would compel her to stay on guard to conceal her true motive and the crime she'd committed. Even so, if he helped her locate Barber and Jones and force the truth from them and kept her safe, she reasoned, wasn't that worth the risk? She surely stood a better chance of accomplishing her goals and staying unharmed with him.

At their six o'clock stop, Hawk purchased two cloth-wrapped suppers with cold fried chicken, still warm biscuits, and fresh California fruit, to be downed with water from canteens. He also watered, fed, and walked his horse for a short time, as was his practice during the longer stop.

While he did so, Maggie visited the depot outhouse and freshened up at a table with water and a basin.

After they were en route again and as they ate on the cloths spread over their laps and sipped from canteens, they conversed on several subjects, including books which both or either had read. For a while, they talked about the desert and its creatures and vegetation, the Indians who used to roam this area freely, and the settling of the territory by whites.

Hawk decided it was too soon to expose his part-Cheyenne heritage, as he didn't know how she'd react to his "half-breed" status. If she'd guessed his secret, she didn't let on that she knew or suspected it. Perhaps, he reasoned, if Maggie was from Virginia as she claimed, she wasn't that familiar with the troubles and animosities between the whites and Indians. But if she was from the South, how had she met Ben Carver? He noted how she ate daintily and used a lacy handkerchief to dab grease and food specks from her lips and fingers following each bite. She certainly gave every indication of being a real lady with education and superb social breeding. So, he mused, how had she gotten hooked up with a snake like Carver and why had she involved herself in a perilous crime to rescue him? And why had she told him in Yuma that she'd been reared on a ranch? He had to learn more about her, but without creating suspicion.

"I've been doing most of the talking," Hawk said, "so why don't you tell me about being a newspaper woman? I believe you called it a journalist?"

Maggie was forced to elaborate on her concocted tale, despite the fact the lies tasted bitter and came forth with reluctance. Thankfully she did have a friend in the newspaper business and had toured his publishing company, so she was familiar with its workings. She had even feigned being a journalist as a cover for one of her past investigations, so she was well prepared to carry off the necessary pretense. She found the perfect excuse to drop that subject when she noticed a coyote chasing a jackrabbit and pointed it out to Hawk. "Do you think we can save its life if we toss out the remains of our supper to distract its predator?" she jested.

"I see you're a tenderhearted female who doesn't like to see anything suffer and die needlessly." He saw her smile and nod. "If you're finished, I'll toss out these scraps, but we're too far ahead of him for that coyote to catch their scent and be lured off that rabbit's trail. But take my word for it, that rabbit won't be in the coyote's stomach tonight; Jack's too swift and sly, and he's skilled at escape on that terrain."

After Maggie dampened her handkerchief and washed her fingers and mouth, Hawk capped and put away the two canteens. He collected the unfinished food and tossed it out the opposite window so nothing would blow back in on her.

"You're a most thoughtful person, Hawk Reynolds. Thank you for the delicious meal, but I really should pay you for it from my expense account."

Hawk grinned. "Since I don't want to step on any of those independent toes, you can buy them the next time, at breakfast."

"It's a deal, partner." Maggie said. She already had been given a month off by her boss in St. Louis, but she would notify him later if she required more time to resolve her current task.

They were silent for a time as they relaxed and watched the landscape slip past at a steady pace of twelve miles per hour. The train made routine stops along the route whose scenery was familiar to both. The above eighty-degree temperature was pleasant due to a breeze created by the train's speed, open windows, and the lowering sun behind them. The ever-darkening blue expanse above them had only a tiny smattering of white clouds with rosy and gold reflections from the sunset.

As she gazed at the enormous saguaros with their uplifted arms and at other vegetation, most in spring bloom, Maggie sighed and murmured, "This is such a lovely and peaceful time of day. The desert is so beautiful this time of year that one can forget how hazardous it can be. I still remember the first time I saw it when my father took me with him to El Paso when I was a child. It was during late summer, and the weather was scorching hot. I recall my arms blistering right through my long sleeves, which Papa had insisted I wear for protection. I must have drank buckets of water, and I loved every time a large cloud shaded us if only for a few minutes; the brief drop in temperature amazed me, even at that young age. I loved ranching and I loved Fort Worth; I still miss them, but I miss my father most of all."

Maggie leaned her head against the train and continued to correct the contradiction she had made in her story to him. "I think I already told you I was born in Virginia, but Papa moved us to Texas after the war with the North because we lost our home and most of our family to the Yankees. We ranched until Papa died in '77; then Mother sold out and we moved away because the spread was too much for her to manage. At least, that's what she told me, but I think it was just too painful for her to remain there with Papa gone and with all of the memories there of him. She remarried a few years ago after I finished school; that's where I met Abby and we became best friends. I decided to get out on my own so the newlyweds could have privacy. I know what it's like to lose a parent, Hawk, so I empathize with your loss. You're fortunate you still have grandparents, and I'm fortunate I still have Mother."

Hawk heard emotional strain in her voice. He believed her moving and enlightening words, but he wondered why she was revealing such personal

126

things to him. "I like Texas, too. My grandparents live in San Antonio, and my parents ranched near there before they were slain." *That was a stupid slip! If she knows about Carver's crimes in that area, she'll become suspicious of you.* Yet, he noticed, that information didn't appear to have an adverse effect on her. He was relieved, but warned himself to stay alert to avoid another mistake.

"I guess that makes us both part Texans, right?"

"Yep. We're both from ranching backgrounds and we're both trackers of a sort by trade, and we both like challenges and enjoy adventures, so we have a few things in common. Our similarities are amazing for recent acquaintances, aren't they?"

Maggie agreed and added, "Nice, too."

"Do you get to see your mother and stepfather often?" Hawk asked.

"No, the distance between us is too great for frequent visits. But we correspond regularly and I'll be going there after my next job is finished." She turned her head, looked at him, and quipped, "That is, if my partner keeps me safe and sound in Prescott."

His response leapt from his lips and heart before he could stop it, "Don't worry, Maggie, I promise I won't let anything bad happen to you."

She tingled all over with desire and warmth at his words. "Thank you, Hawk; you're a good man, like my father was."

He saw a glimmering of unshed tears in her blue eyes and was touched by her lingering anguish, one he also had experienced and still endured. If she was for real, and he was getting that impression, she was too good for the sorry likes of Ben Carver. Mercy, he worried, how was he going to keep his promise to keep her safe and sound when she had broken the law and she was interfering with his quest for revenge? "I'm sure that's the highest compliment you could pay a man, so I'm mighty grateful, and I hope I live up to it," *but I won't.*

I'm certain you will, but I doubt I'll live up to your expectations of me as a lady and good person, a woman worthy of — Stop it, Maggie, you're dreaming now, and dreaming never got anybody anywhere. Heaven help you escape my wrath, Ben Carver, if you've deceived me, Mother, and your father because what I've done for you may cost me the perfect man!

As Maggie's expression altered from soft and sweet to dismay and then to anger, Hawk wondered what she was thinking. "Are you all right, Maggie? You look upset."

As she gazed at the full moon rising on the eastern horizon, she said, "I'll be fine in a few minutes, Hawk, I'm just a little unsettled by this talk about the past. It's astounding how certain events alter our lives so greatly, isn't it?"

"Yep, I understand," *more than you realize.*

As Maggie dozed with her left shoulder

128

propped against the train's side and her head leaning against a folded jacket she had kept out of her baggage to ward off the chill of the desert night, her neck eventually stiffened at the strain placed on it. Without her awareness, her body shifted to another position to her right.

Hawk smiled to himself as the slumbering beauty nestled her head against his shoulder and sighed dreamily in comfort. He glanced down and noted the way moonlight played over the other side of her body and across her lap. He allowed his gaze to trace the curve of her jaw, the line of her dainty nose, the fullness of her lips, the swell of her breasts as she breathed evenly. He inhaled the fragrant smells of her shiny hair and her subtle cologne and felt the warmth of her flesh through his shirt. Mercy, she was captivating!

Maggie, my reckless beauty, why did we have to meet under such difficult circumstances; and why do you tug so on my heart if you're a wicked person? You make it so hard for me not to respond to you, and impossible for me to mistrust you completely. Lord help us both if I'm letting you blind me to your evil streak. Either way, I have to snare you.

With caution so as to not awaken her, Hawk eased his left arm upward and around her back as he angled his body toward her. Almost immediately, she nestled closer to him on the padded bench they shared, snuggled her cheek to his chest, and slid her left arm across his waist. To hold her there safely, he cupped her shoulder with his hand. Later as he dozed, his cheek drifted to the top of her head.

An hour later, Maggie awakened when the train changed speeds and found herself cuddled in Hawk's embrace, warm and cozy and comfortable. She listened to the steady beating of his heart and the evenness of his breathing which implied he was asleep. She yearned to gaze at his handsome face; but she knew if she moved, it would no doubt awaken him and propriety would compel them to separate. She glanced toward the front of the car where the other passengers were snoozing, two of the men snoring softly. With most of the windows closed and the others only opened a few inches for fresh air, the noises of the wheels against the rails and those of the steam engine were muffled, and were familiar sounds by now. The sweet bouquet of night blooming flowers wafted in the air, mixing with the faint aroma of soap from Hawk's recently laundered shirt and jeans. There was a trace of mingled horse and leather scents where he had handled both the previous morning.

It felt wonderful — oddly natural — to be in his arms in the moonlight-dappled shadows. She liked the romantic feelings flowing over her. She was enkindled and fascinated by the man himself. Never before had she experienced this kind of intense pleasure and rampant desire. To kiss him had to be sheer bliss, to bond physically with him would be rapturous. She smiled to herself, boldly remained where she was, and longed for this to be only the beginning for them. If God and Fate were favorable to her, she would resolve her dilemma before the Law exposed her wicked deed and the man nearby lost all respect and budding affection for her. She closed her eyes and drifted back off to dreamland.

A light sleeper, Hawk knew Maggie had awakened for a while, but didn't move from his arms. He couldn't surmise if her reason was to prevent disturbing him or to seek a more comfortable position, or because she was as drawn to him as he was to her. He hoped being snuggled in a man's embrace, especially during the night, wasn't a familiar situation to her. He prayed to the white deity — God — and to the Cheyenne Great Spirit — Maheoo — that she didn't love and intend to marry Ben Carver. He also prayed that she had an unknown and well-intentioned objective for freeing Ben, just as he did. Whatever motive compelled her to aid that lowlife, he needed to discover what it was and decide how and when to deal with it. *I've always been a pretty good judge of character, Maggie Malone, and you don't strike me as being a woman who could love a sorry bastard like that. I have to earn your trust before you'll open up to me completely; and that's the only way I'll learn if you're worthy of my help in this mess you've created.*

Maggie awoke with sunlight streaming into the railroad car on the other side, as the tracks had veered northeastward during her slumber. She didn't know when she had reverted to her original position against the train's wall or how she had slept deeply enough for Hawk to make a pillow out of his folded duster and place it beside her head and to tuck her jacket around her for warmth. She turned her head and sighted him reading a newspaper. Heaven's above, he looked good enough to stare at for hours! "Good morning, partner; thanks for the pillow and cover. I see you're earning your salary already by taking care of me when I'm asleep."

Hawk chuckled as he lowered last Saturday's Yuma *Arizona Sentinel.* "You're lucky you can block out this Iron Horse's noises and get some shut-eye. We'll be coming to our next stop soon. How does stretching your legs and eating a hot breakfast sound to you?"

"Marvelous; I'm stiff and starved. What about you?"

"The same. Boy, that coffee's gonna taste good, and a walk is just what I need for getting rid of these kinks. I'm not used to being cooped up in a small space or being confined inside for so long."

"Ah, that restless spirit is itching to break free and that loner streak is begging for solitude, aren't they?" she jested.

"You got me pegged about right. What about you?"

"I'm not much of a loner, though I do enjoy my privacy. But I do get antsy when I'm forced to sit still for a long period. That bad trait got me and Abby into mischief and trouble several times in school."

"I seem to recall suffering from that same trait and having to stay after school to dust erasers for the teacher as punishment and discipline."

As he looked forward and spoke, Maggie sneaked a wilted mint leaf into her mouth to freshen her breath. "Did it work? Did you learn to behave in class?"

"Oh, I eventually learned how to control myself, or at least learned how not to get caught again."

"So, you developed a cunning streak to avoid trouble."

"Yep, 'cause it was doubled when I got home."

"Well, it appears as if your schoolmarm and parents did an excellent job of teaching you manners and self-discipline."

"Thanks, and so did yours. She's slowing down, so it won't be long now before we can stretch our legs and fill our stomachs."

Maggie noticed that he didn't say bellies as most cowboys would. Yes, he was intelligent, interesting, and utterly charming. If she wasn't mistaken, he was mutually attracted to her. But was she only a temporary and pleasant diversion?

After the train halted, they deboarded and used the facilities to wash up before she purchased them huge and hot catshead biscuits with a fried egg and slice of ham inside and steaming coffee. While the railroaders unloaded freight, they ate the food and sipped their drinks at a wooden table at the depot.

They finished just prior to the engineer blasting the whistle to tell everyone to reboard for impending departure. Hawk assisted her onto the train, and they were seated only a minute before movement began.

At last, the fifteen-hour journey on the Southern Pacific ended when they reached Maricopa at four o'clock that afternoon. Hawk told her the wells was a favorite and necessary stopping point for immigrants and other travelers to rest, take on water, and replenish supplies before heading across the harsh and lengthy desert. The Pima Indians who once lived there in great numbers, now dwindled by white man's conquest and disease, still grew and sold corn, wheat, barley, melons, and other vegetables; and they also collected wood for purchase by the railroad company to use as fuel.

Maggie noticed that the town was small, with spread-out structures in adobe and crude livestock fences of either rock or sticks. There was the railroad depot, stage depot, post office for inland service, telegraph company, businesses of various types and sizes to supply travelers and locals with their needs, one simple hotel, several restaurants, a few boarding houses, and the ever-present abundance of saloons.

It was obvious to her that it was populated by a variety of races which included Chinese, Mexicans, and Indians, along with those who called themselves Americans whether or not they were born in this country. It also was apparent that men vastly outnumbered women and children, and the location was infested with an offensive portion of unsavory males. It certainly wasn't the kind of place for a lady to be alone, and Maggie was glad to have the ebony-haired tracker and bounty hunter as her escort and guardian.

Maggie took a hasty sponge bath using a large basin in her hotel room because she didn't trust the public water closet down the hall to assure privacy, and she doubted it was clean enough to suit her. To allow her travel garments to air out, she donned a plain dress to prevent calling unwanted attention to herself. Since she couldn't wash her long hair, she brushed as much of the trail dust from it as possible and secured it with a ribbon at her nape. Afterward, she opened her door to go join Hawk to eat supper together but found him leaning against the wall nearby.

Hawk looked her over, grinned, and said, "Wise choices, Maggie, or I might have been fighting men away all evening."

She smiled in pleasure. "I take it you were on guard duty?"

"Yep, so I wouldn't be forced to whip anybody I caught spying on you, which was a big possibility considering the stares you got between the train depot and here. I guess you noticed ladies are far and few between in this area, and a refined

135

and beautiful one like you is even rarer to come by."

"Thank you for those compliments, kind sir, and for your generous protection. Do you think our possessions will be safe in our rooms?"

"Yep, because we'll only be downstairs for a short time, and I'll keep my eyes and wits alert. Nobody will take any risks with us that close by."

As she locked her door, Hawk asked, "How much more of that year's trial basis do you have left?" He saw her hands pause on the knob.

Maggie hated to lie to him, but she did, "A few months."

As they headed down the hallway, Hawk deduced she had deceived him with reluctance, and he was glad. "Since you're still roaming around the Wild West, I take it your boss is pleased with your work so far."

"I always do my best in whatever endeavor I begin. Don't you?"

"Yep, I give every job I take on all I have to offer."

I would love to earn all you have to offer a woman, but I doubt that will happen. "And you've never failed or been defeated, right?"

Hawk shrugged and grinned. "So far, so good, I'm pleased to say."

"And without boasting; I like that quality in a person," she told him as she took his elbow to descend the stairs, stimulated by their contact and easy rapport.

"Would it be forward or impolite of me to ask

how old you are?"

Maggie laughed and said, "Considering we're partners, not at all. I'm twenty-three until late June." She laughed again and whispered in a merry tone, "I suppose that makes me sound like a spinster."

Hawk liked the cunning way — and hopefully the reason why — she revealed that personal information. "That only means you haven't been married so far, but I bet you have a sweetheart eagerly waiting for your return home. Isn't that correct, Maggie, if it's all right to ask?" *Now, let's see if or how you lie your way out of that trap you set for yourself . . .*

Chapter Six

"No, I don't have a sweetheart pining for me. Do you?"

"Nope," he said at the base of the steps. "I haven't stayed put in one place long enough to find and court a woman. Considering that adventurous streak of yours, I guess it's the same for you." He watched her nod. "Let's sit at this first table, so I can keep an eye on the door and stairs. I don't want anybody sneaking past me and running off with our belongings."

"Are you sure Diablo is safe outside at the hitching post?" Maggie asked Hawk as he assisted her with her chair.

He leaned toward her and almost whispered, "Yep, he wouldn't let anybody get near him without kicking up a big fuss. He'd probably bite and stomp anybody fool enough to challenge him. I fed and watered him before I came upstairs to stand guard, so he's fine." He also had made a hasty trip to the telegraph office to ask a friend in Texas to check up on her for him, and he felt a mixture of eagerness and reluctance for that response.

Maggie watched Hawk take a seat opposite hers, facing the archway into the tiny hotel lobby. At least, she reasoned, he didn't seem to be afraid of or averse to the subject of marriage; that much was good news, though it probably wouldn't profit her any. With the small room crowded and noisy, she didn't continue their private talk. She smiled at the Chinese waiter who took their orders, then scurried away in rapid and short steps.

It wasn't long before the black-clad man returned with their plates of chili piled atop tortillas, baked beans, and rice speckled with spices and their drinks; and they began eating immediately.

She observed that Hawk sat with enough space between his firm body and the table and between his broad back and the chair to allow for swift action if necessary. To her disappointment, he didn't chat during supper, but she was certain he caught every word spoken near him and noted every motion others made. Though he looked relaxed, she was sure he was on full alert, ready to react to danger in the flicker of an eye, and no doubt with great skill and courage. In her opinion, his movements and expressions were the result of years of experience and practice. Long light blue sleeves rolled to his elbows revealed a smooth hardness in his forearms, the shirt's pale color a vivid contrast to his dark tan. From beneath lowered lashes, she saw the enticing span of hairless chest which showed above the few buttons he had left unfastened. He was so virile and appealing that he almost stole her breath and wits. Yet, there was so much more to that special man than his good looks, prowess, and charms. She felt so at ease around him, so drawn to him, as if she had known and waited for him all of her adult life. She found herself wanting to talk with him, hear his mellow voice and laughter, but thought it unwise to distract him from his self-appointed guard duty.

Hawk knew Maggie was scrutinizing him on the sly. He liked her interest in him, but found it most diverting when he should be keeping his attention on their surroundings. In his attempt to get close to Ben and his cohorts through her, he had allowed Miss Margaret Anne Malone to get under his thick skin, to imbed herself deep within his aching and lonely heart. Mercy, it was going to be painful to lose her atop of his parents and brother! And lose her he probably would for one reason or another.

He wished he hadn't linked up with her, just kept his distance and followed her to those bastards; then his mind wouldn't be in this turmoil. Now, with Ben in hiding, he had to carry out his rash deception in order to reach his family's killers and punish them. In doing so, he would betray and jeopardize her, and that reality cut at his heart like a sharp and lethal knife. *What am I going to do about you, Maggie, my love? With good luck, I'll soon discover just who and what you are, especially to Ben Carver. Maybe those facts will reveal your motives and goals for freeing him. And tell me if I'm misjudging you and being a blind and self-deluded fool.*

After finishing their food, Hawk said, "It would be nice to take a stroll, but this is a rough place after dark and we don't want any trouble. Besides, we should turn in soon to get a good night's sleep to be prepared for our overland ride tomorrow. We pull out early, and I'll warn you now, it won't be a short or pleasant trip."

It will be more than pleasant with you at my side, Maggie's mind countered, but she smiled and said, "Whatever you say is fine with me."

You don't know how wrong you are, woman, and I dread the day you make that discovery. He paid for their food, after joking about putting it on his "expense account", and escorted Maggie to her room. There, he said, "Good night. Just yell for help if you need it. I'm next door and a light sleeper, so I can be over fast. See you at seven for breakfast. We leave at eight."

"Thank you, Hawk, for everything. I feel totally safe knowing you're nearby and watching over me; your services will be worth any amount you charge me for them. Good night. See you in the morning."

"I appreciate your confidence and trust in me," *but it won't be long before you realize I don't deserve them, and I wish that weren't true.*

Maggie entered her rented room and followed Hawk's instructions to drop a chair under the door knob, then added two other precautions. She placed a revolver on the second pillow and,

141

after making sure the window was locked, spread sharp tacks along its sill in case an intruder tried to use that means of approaching her.

She went to bed and hoped her roaming thoughts would settle down so she could get to sleep, as a weary mind and body made perilous mistakes. After sleeping in Hawk's embrace last night, she felt alone and miserable, denied and yearning. *You said to "yell for help if" I needed it, but what I want and need is you, Hawk, here beside me and holding me, kissing me, telling me I'm doing the right thing. Now that I've found the perfect match in a man, I fear I'll lose you soon and I'll never be happy again without you sharing it.*

She wondered if her mother felt that same way about Newl Carver. For certain, Catherine Malone had loved Jed Malone without reservation, and his loss had been a tragic one. Perhaps loneliness and anguish had driven her mother into Newl's arms and life, but she hoped and prayed her mother loved him and he loved her and they were truly happy.

Thursday morning Maggie and Hawk boarded a coach belonging to the Arizona Stage Company to head for their next overnight destination.

Within the first hour, as he had warned, Maggie realized the ride was going to be a long, dirty, and bumpy one along a winding road between Maricopa and Phoenix. Although the distance wasn't great, the conditions en route and numerous stops resulted in a lengthy and arduous trip.

With a full load of passengers, she felt crowded in those confines, but it did allow for her to be pressed close to Hawk who rode between her and another man. She could imagine how the interior would smell if not for a breeze wafting through the windows and if the journey was a longer one without facilities to bathe and change clothes. She hoped rain didn't force them to lower the leather shades and cut off the refreshing air supply. She felt safe with Hawk nearby, a derringer in her pocket, and with the driver and a guard riding on the box seat and another guard positioned on the rooftop, though she marveled at how that second one managed to stay aboard at their swift and bouncing pace.

She overheard other passengers talking and laughing in soft voices as they whiled away the boring hours, but none attempted to converse with her or Hawk, not even the weasely-looking man beside him. While her companion watched the scenery from their backseat, she listened to the combination of noises: luggage thudding against the wood of the coach, the jangling of harnesses and snap of the jehu's whip, the flicking of the ribbons on horse flesh, the driver's shouts as he urged the animals to a swifter pace, and the rumbling of the wheels against rock-hard ground. Her eyes, throat, and nose burned and itched from dust and the minute debris which was thrown into the coach.

The Sonoran desert landscape was much the same as she had seen for days, but she still enjoyed looking at the amazing saguaros, some rising to heights of fifty feet and many with oddly positioned limbs. Most relay stations where they stopped were nothing more than rock or adobe structures with flat roofs and narrow windows. The stock-tender was fast and efficient as he switched the spent team of six horses with a fresh and eager one.

The established routine was carried out smoothly, stops made only briefly at those relay stations to change teams, and with a longer halt at one to eat a hurried and tasteless meal of beans, corn dodgers, and stewed antelope which had been cooked much too long.

Between stops, Maggie thought about Abby, wondered how her friend was doing, if any problems had arisen or if Ben had been recaptured, and how her romance with Matthew Lawrence was progressing. As soon as she reached Prescott, she must telegraph her best friend for the news, and she hoped it was all good.

After they reached the hotel, Hawk tended Diablo while Maggie was being shown to her room. Then he went upstairs to freshen up as she was doing. When he thought he'd allowed her enough time for that task, he knocked on her door to go eat supper. He grinned when he noted she had taken the same precautions in her appearance as in Maricopa. Yet, no matter how plain she tried to look to avoid excessive attention, it failed from his point of view, because she was always beautiful and tempting.

Since it was still light after they finished eating supper and Hawk said Phoenix was safe, they took a stroll.

Maggie was surprised to see that this town had lush green areas with wheat and barley crops, thanks to the cunning efforts, Hawk told her, of Jack Swilling and his Irrigation Canal Company which began in '67 and brought in water from the Salt and Gila rivers. She listened as he told her about the adventurous man who — after being an Indian fighter, Confederate officer, Union scout, and early settler of that area — had helped find gold in the Bradshaw Mountains, but had perished in the Yuma jail of a crime he hadn't committed. That revelation caused Maggie to think about Ben. If life had dealt such a dark and deadly fate to a well-liked, upstanding man, she reasoned, the same could be true for her stepbrother. If it was, she had to prove it; and if there was no error, she had to recapture him, no matter if she was incriminated in his escape.

Hawk pointed out many interesting sights, and she enjoyed the walk and their harmony, mainly because Hawk seemed relaxed and was conversing freely again after a bout of near silence on the stage. It was evident he knew a lot about this area; in fact, a great deal about the entire territory, so she presumed he must have traveled it many times, which was advantageous for her.

The stimulating outing ended too soon to suit

Maggie, but the sun had set long ago and the temperature had dropped. The air had grown chilly and she was without a wrap, which he pointed out before guiding them to the hotel beneath a rising full moon.

They paused for a while to visit with Diablo, who seemed to enjoy their company and attention. He even nuzzled his nose against Maggie's hand, then shifted closer to her to encourage more strokes.

As Hawk watched them, he concluded that Diablo knew she was sincere and was showing his approval of her. "He likes you and trusts you, he doesn't usually take to strangers."

"We aren't strangers anymore, are we, boy?" she said in a soft tone as she stroked his neck. "He's a fine animal, Hawk; you're lucky to have him."

"Yep, we make good partners. He's quick and smart, and he's gotten me out of trouble and danger plenty of times. I can always depend on him."

"I know what you mean; my father taught me that if you treat a horse right, he's a friend for life. Jed Malone was a good and wise man, and a perfect father. Good night, Diablo, see you tomorrow."

Hawk saw her eyes shine with tears, which she removed with a fingertip and without making an excuse for her show of emotion. He knew she still missed her father, just as he missed his family. When the motives for his deceitful and lethal

146

actions came to light, surely she would understand and not fault him for them. If she left him or was taken from him by the authorities, he would have to live with that bleak sacrifice. No matter how much he wanted her, justice must be done for him, his lost loved ones, the Law, and others who had suffered by their bloody hands; that he had sworn on his family's graves and on the badge he carried, a six-pointed silver star hidden in a leather pocket beneath his left holster.

At her door, Maggie wished Hawk would embrace and kiss her, but he didn't. He looked nervous, as if he wanted to kiss her but thought he shouldn't. He gazed deeply into her eyes while giving her those same defensive instructions from last night, then said a hasty good night and left.

Maggie leaned against the inside of her door, took a deep breath, and closed her eyes. Her heart pounded with love and her body flamed with desire. Had she really known him for only a few days, five glorious days? They were so compatible. They liked, respected, and enjoyed each other. They appeared to be a perfect match, and she hoped that was true.

On Friday morning at eight o'clock, an Arizona Stage Company driver snapped his whip and shouted, "All aboard! Awaaay!" and a team of six impatient horses lurched forward, jerking the coach in the throes of their frantic run. Once more, the familiar routine was established at departure to maintain a tri-weekly twenty-eight-hour schedule toward Prescott.

Maggie surmised that the bold red coach with bright yellow wheels could be seen approaching the relay stations and any road travelers from far away. It was larger and better built and more comfortable than the model used between Maricopa and Phoenix: It had big and narrow wheels which moved easier over hard ground, but the ride was still bruising and jarring because of their swift pace. She was glad she and Hawk, side by side, had the best seats available this time, behind the front boot and facing backward. She also was glad Hawk distracted her from worries about what awaited her at their destination by telling her things about Prescott so she'd know what to expect when they reached the territorial capital. His potent allure assailed her senses as they were jostled against each other from the rapid motion, despite the fact they had the entire padded bench to themselves, and provided another distraction. She assumed he was talking freely this morning because only two other people were making the trip, a man and a woman, who sat in the back. That left the bench between them on the nine-passenger coach empty, and plenty of distance between them not to be heard over the loud noises from outside.

Following many stops at relay stations and a scant and bland meal at midday, the Sonoran Desert was left behind as they entered the cooler

High Country with its drastic change in land-scape and topography. She saw awesome rock formations in brown and black, with spires that reminded her of various-sized chimneys. The red sandstone bluffs at some locations — many with multiple colored striated bands — were called "slick rock" because they appeared to be as smooth as glass. She saw precipitous cliffs, am-bling ridges, lush valleys, and flood-washed draws.

In the Black Canyon, the road stayed close to the mountain base and Aqua Fria River with its vivid blue water and swirling white edges as it splashed over or detoured around numerous rocks. Occasionally they passed other travelers, as the road also was used by freighters, lumber-men, trappers, military, and men going to ply their trades or seek their fortunes on the sur-rounding terrain. The steepest grade and sharpest curves were at Antelope Hill, where the driver used firm foot pressure on the brake lever to slow their pace on its intimidating descent. He an-nounced their presence at hairpin curves with a shrill blast of a tin horn. The jehu, she concluded, earned his pay with the skills shown as he handled three sets of ribbons in one hand and a whip in the other.

Late that afternoon, the sound of gunshots and their echoes filled the air, calling Maggie and Hawk to full alert, along with the others, as they were in ideal country for outlaw or renegade

149

Indian attacks. She looked out the left window, and Hawk did the same on the right side. Both sighted outlaws on horseback in their front and rear, gradually closing in on the coach. Within minutes, shots rang out from both of their sides from men sheltered in the rocks, warning fire of an imminent assault. Surrounded, and with the uphill terrain preventing a rapid flight from peril, the two guards returned the gunfire.

Though it was company policy to yield to robbers to protect its passengers' safety, Hawk knew that action wouldn't be taken until defeat was a proven certainty. Even so, whatever it required of him, he would not allow Maggie or the others to be injured, nor Diablo, who was trailing behind them with his reins secured to the coach.

As Hawk grabbed his rifle to aid the guards, he whispered to Maggie, "Best hope and pray it's not Barber and Jones because they don't leave witnesses behind to identify them; that's why it's impossible to prove their guilt; being sly and daring is why they're still running free." *I should know because I've been chasing them for months.*

She already had noted that Hawk was well equipped with a Spencer lever-action repeater rifle which held numerous cartridges in its butt. Though it came with ready-to-fill tubes for quick reloading insertion, she assumed those extra ones were with his belongings elsewhere. A Bowie knife with its long tempered-steel blade, serrated top edge, curved crossguard, and wooden grip was in a leather sheath on his belt — the first time she had seen that weapon on him. His two Remington .44 revolvers were in holsters on a wide cartridge/money belt. It seemed evident from the arms he wore that her companion had anticipated trouble and had prepared himself to thwart it.

Maggie wished she had the Winchester rifle and Colt Frontier pistol which were in her trunk. The only weapons she had with her were a Remington two-shot derringer in her skirt pocket and a seven-inch-long Spanish blade in a hand-tooled leather sheath under her top garment at her waist. Even though she had a drawstring pouch with extra cartridges in her handbag, the tiny pistol performed best at close range and had to be reloaded after firing it twice, which would be time consuming. She asked Hawk if she could borrow one of his revolvers to help defend the stage, though she knew that most men were reluctant to loan out their weapons.

Hawk looked over at her. "You know how to fire and reload one?"

"Yes, my father taught me; and I'm a good shot. It looks as if they need all the help they can get or we'll all be endangered."

Without delay, Hawk passed her one of his pistols. "Just pull out more cartridges when you need them. I count one in front, two in back, and at least one way over there with a rifle. How many do you have?"

She half-turned her head and said over her shoulder, "Two in the rocks, afoot but keeping up with our slow pace. Armed with pistols."

"Then let's show 'em we won't be an easy target."

Maggie and Hawk opened fire on the culprits, letting the guards know they had help from the interior, which might dissuade the bandits. Both heard a bump and yelp from the roof and realized a guard was down, either wounded or slain. The driver kept the stage moving slowly up the steep grade after the second guard took out the outlaw in the road beyond him.

Maggie concentrated on the men ensconced in the rocks, wounding one as he tried to change positions. Bullets zinged and thudded against the wooden coach and one whizzed past her shoulder and out the other window, barely missing Hawk's broad back. Angered and alarmed by his near hit, she emptied her revolver in the bandit's direction to force him to keep his head down; if he couldn't sight his target, he couldn't shoot at them.

Hawk's fire struck one of the villains behind them before he reached the coach to leap aboard it. Maggie saw his body jerk backward from the impact of the bullet before he fell from his horse. She slid onto the floor and removed cartridges from Hawk's belt loops and reloaded the borrowed weapon. As she did so, Hawk told her he got rid of another one, the sharpshooter in the distant rocks on his side. Once more she prevented the culprit behind a boulder from moving closer. To conserve their ammunition supply, she didn't fire in rapid succession; only whenever he showed his face or body. When he finally dashed for the next boulder, she succeeded in putting bullets in his right arm and thigh. She heard him shout to his friends that he was wounded.

Admitting defeat, the remaining rear outlaw and those only wounded scurried into concealment and allowed the stage to continue without further assault. The uninjured guard shouted, "Anybody hurt in there?"

As the other passengers returned to their seats and adjusted their clothes, Hawk leaned out the window and yelled, "We're all safe and sound!"

"Good, and thanks for the help. Jeb's wounded, but he'll live. We'll be pulling into Black Canyon City soon, so we'll take a breather there. Can't stop here; those snakes might come crawling back for another strike."

As the stage reached the base of the steep hill and its speed increased, Hawk settled back in his seat, and smiled at Maggie. Above the noises of rattling coach and pounding hooves, he said in a low tone, "You're one surprise after another, Miss Malone. That was fine shooting, and you stood your ground like a grizzly. You have a cool head, and lots of skills and courage. I'm pleased and impressed. I can see I don't have to wonder or worry about you being able to take care of yourself."

As she passed his weapon to him and smiled in return, she said, "Thank you for the compliments, kind sir; you did excellent work yourself.

I hope that opinion doesn't mean you'll renege on my job offer because I still need somebody to watch my back and keep me out of trouble and danger. I hate to think what may have happened to us if you and your guns hadn't been here today. I doubt that remaining guard could have held off six men and I was in no position to assist him without proper arms. Perhaps I should strap on my sixguns the next time I take a stage ride alone," she jested.

Hawk chuckled as he imagined her weighed down with many pounds of iron belted around that tiny waist and over a fancy dress. He envisioned her drawing them and shooting at those bandits. Even so, he had no doubt she and the guard could have driven off that gang. Yep, there was far more to Miss Margaret Anne Malone than he had seen or guessed, and he was looking forward to obtaining the whole picture. "I've never teamed up with a woman before, but it looks as if you'll make a good partner. Yesiree, this is going to be a mighty interesting experience and big challenge. I wonder what other surprises you have in store for me."

Maggie sent him a saucy grin and quipped in boldness that astonished her afterward, "Lots of them, Mr. Reynolds, just wait and see. I can promise your work with me won't be boring."

Hawk was amused and warmed by her words. "I have no doubt that's the truth, boss lady," he countered. He told himself it was a good thing they weren't alone because he'd probably make a romantic move toward her, so great was his desire. He loved the way her blue eyes sparkled and her cheeks glowed with vitality. He was almost certain she would be responsive to his overture, but he wasn't ready to discover where it would lead them, which could be down a perilous and painful road considering they were on opposite sides of the Law. He told himself he had to keep his hunger under control until he learned more about her.

They stopped at Black Canyon City to rest for thirty minutes and eat mesquite-cooked venison steaks with beans and biscuits, washed down with strong coffee, at a location operated by the station keeper and his wife, and their two vivacious teenage boys.

Maggie observed as Hawk chatted with the youths about the attempted holdup. Her companion was patient and obliging with their many questions, and even gave them ten cents each for serving the meals and clearing the table afterward for their mother while she washed dishes. Her feelings for him were growing stronger every day, and she knew that she was falling in love with him. She hoped it wasn't foolish and futile in her current predicament. She wanted to resolve her dilemma fast so she could concentrate on winning Hawk, if that was possible, and it seemed so with the way he responded to her. He brought out a hunger in her to settle down with him, to have his children, to give up her adventurous existence for a glorious life with him.

After they were en route again, Maggie and the other two passengers dozed off and on for most of the night, but Hawk only napped here and there during his self-appointed defensive vigil.

As he had done on the train, Hawk watched the moonlight coming through the window gleam on the sunny streaks in Maggie's brown hair, and kiss her flawless complexion. He wished she were sleeping in his arms again, but her head was propped against a jacket pillow placed between it and the coach. He had to content himself with only gazing at her and adoring her with his eyes.

As Maggie shifted positions and curled sideways on the bench, Hawk realized she was chilled. Without disturbing her, he lowered the leather shades and secured them to halt the night breeze, then tucked the shawl around her shoulders for warmth. If his gut instinct was right about her, Maggie was everything he wanted and needed in a woman; she would make a perfect wife for him and a good mother for their children. He also was certain that his grandparents would love Maggie and be delighted if he married soon and carried on the family name and ranching heritage, though his grandfather had given up that lifestyle years ago and become a merchant.

Hawk reminisced about his years on the Circle R Ranch near San Antonio, which he had inherited months ago. His parents' foreman and cowhands were running it for him until he decided to either settle down there or sell the three-hundred-acre spread. When he began his current task on January second, the day after burying his family on Reynolds land, love and marriage were the last things on his mind. Then Maggie Malone blew into his life like a wild desert wind. He couldn't explain why she had such a potent effect on him, but he couldn't deny it or ignore the possible grim repercussions.

It amazed him to realize he was lonely and ready to settle down. He was soul and body weary of being on the trail alone and in all kinds of weather, and of being around scum and in rowdy places so much of the time. He wanted to put down roots, have a family, and enjoy the important things in life. But not with just any woman; he wanted Margaret Anne Malone, or rather the woman he believed and hoped she was. Yet, she was in deep trouble and he wasn't sure if he could extricate her, though he would certainly try. On the other hand, even if she wasn't promised to Ben Carver or heading for prison, perhaps such a proper and refined lady wouldn't want to unite herself with a half-breed Cheyenne and trail-dusting loner, or perhaps after learning his other secrets . . .

The next morning, Hawk told Maggie about the gold and silver camps in all directions from them, camps with unusual and amusing names, such as Grief Hill, Yellowjacket Gulch, Lone-

157

some Pocket, Blind Indian Creek and Battle Flat.

She listened with interest as he related facts about the ancient Indian cliff dwellings and hilltop pueblos not far away. She learned about the Apaches, Navajo, and other tribes that had dominated this territory before the white man came. She heard about Fort Whipple which was on the doorstep of Prescott, placed there to protect the rich mining district and settlers.

The stage veered northwestward around Mount Union and entered Prescott Valley, south of the long and beautiful Chino Valley. The territorial capital was situated on Goose Flats on Granite Creek. It was bordered by mountains, forested wilderness, buttes, rolling hills, and abundant water. To the north, snow-capped peaks were visible. There were plenty of trees and bushes, but most — cedar, sagebrush, mesquite, pine, and thorn — stood alone in ballish forms and were scattered across grassland and knolls.

The many roads entering town and wide streets there — named for living or deceased figures of importance to the capital or encompassing territory — were all in good condition, Hawk told her, as a result of the soldiers' labors. Though there were some rancherias, pueblos, and adobe huts en route and near town, most homes and businesses were constructed of wood and had raised roofs. Hawk told her that Prescott wasn't as wild and perilous as places such as Tombstone and Nogales due to the presence of the military, a tough sheriff, and swift justice. It was apparent that Prescott was prospering and expanding because of its importance as the capital, its abundant timber, fertile soil, strong military defense, and vast mineral wealth.

They passed Courthouse Plaza between Montezuma and Cortez streets and halted at the depot. After deboarding, Hawk hired a wagon driver to take their possessions to a hotel on Gurley Street. Maggie rode with the man while Hawk walked there with Diablo, giving him a chance to visit with the mustang before he was corraled, fed, and watered.

While he did so, Maggie registered them and had their belongings placed in their rooms. She freshened up in a hurry and joined Hawk in the downstairs restaurant where she gave him his room key.

Between bites of succulent roast and spring vegetables, Maggie said, "I plan to take a bath and change clothes after that long and dusty trip. Then I'm going to the newspaper office to introduce myself and seek information. I need to see the articles published about the trial; and I need to get the names and addresses of those involved in it. Why don't you take care of your work while I do mine; then we'll meet back here for supper at seven? That way, I'll know if you're for hire before I'm ready to leave town."

Hawk swallowed his coffee and said, "Sounds fine to me, boss lady."

Maggie smiled and returned to her meal. *I also*

need to telegraph Abby and Mother on the sly. Hope-fully I'll have their responses by the time I return to the hotel. Please, God, let it all be good news.

Chapter Seven

Maggie stopped eating a moment and looked at Hawk. "I remember what you said about Pete Barber and Slim Jones when the stage was attacked and while we were on the train. You weren't exaggerating, were you?" She watched him shake his head. "Have you ever met them in your work or during your travels?"

Hawk lowered his fork. "Never met them, but I've seen them several times in other towns. Just about everybody out here has heard plenty about them, and none of it is good. They're mean, cold-blooded, and greedy. Few men, even famous gunslingers out to make a name for themselves, challenge either one to a showdown, no matter what they say or do to provoke one. Barber in particular likes to goad men into fights, and he's skilled with those pistols he wears. He enjoys killing, so that makes him dangerous and unpredictable; it's about the same with Jones. In my line of work, I have to keep up with such men's deeds and reputations and who they're riding with at present. If I didn't listen close to saloon talk and read newspapers, I could go up against a wanted man who has lots of friends nearby. When Barber and Jones started out years ago, word was that any victims of their foul deeds either refused to testify against them or came up dead before their trial began. The Law knows they're guilty of plenty of crimes, but they can't put them away without proof. Nowadays, it's said they don't leave any witnesses behind unless they get in a big hurry to escape, and those lucky folks hold their tongues."

Maggie continued her probe for more information. "I asked you before but you didn't answer: if they were involved in the bank robbery here with Ben Carver, why didn't they murder the witnesses as usual?" she questioned Hawk. "Or return later to kill them or bust him out of jail, because two of them didn't hold silent afterward."

Hawk knew the answers to those queries from Toby Muns, but he couldn't reveal his knowledge or how he had obtained it, so he said, "Those are good questions to ask the *Sentinel* editor or sheriff, or Barber and Jones when we catch up with them. I suppose it was one of those rare times when they got in a rush to leave."

"It doesn't take long to fire an already drawn weapon, especially since two of the witnesses saw Carver's face." *Careful, Maggie, or he'll wonder how, when, and where you gathered your facts. You can't reveal how you got hold of the trial notes and Prescott articles weeks ago, prior to Ben's escape!* "Exactly how do the authorities know they're

162

involved in a crime without evidence and if nobody will testify against them?"

"Answering the sheriff's questions in private is different from taking the witness stand in public. Besides, they didn't expose Barber and Jones."

"But they exposed their alleged partner and friend. I find that omission contradictory and suspicious. Perhaps it's a clue to a much bigger story than I imagined. What do you think?"

"Maybe there were reasons why they couldn't rescue him or slay those witnesses later. Since those witnesses didn't expose them and the other two gang members, maybe they just kept moving on and sacrificed Carver because he didn't mean anything to them or they were riled at him for being seen. To answer your other question: Barber has bright red hair and Jones has weird gray eyes; a bandanna and hat can't hide those features. They're smart in one area; they use stolen horses so their mounts and saddles can't be recognized."

"Why wouldn't Carver reveal the names of his accomplices? Surely turning in criminals like those two and recovering the money would have helped his case, maybe gotten him mercy or a pardon."

"Carver isn't a fool or he wouldn't be running with those two, so he'd never betray them. If he did, nobody could keep him alive afterward, even in jail, because Barber would pay some other inmate or bribe a guard to slay him. Terror tactics give Barber and Jones their power; folks know they'll carry out their threats."

Following those enlightening words, Maggie speculated, "I was told Carver had problems with other convicts and guards at the Yuma Prison and spent time in that awful Dark Cell I visited. I wonder if that incident was a paid warning to keep his mouth shut and that's what panicked him into escaping." She worried that she had stumbled onto a clue to Ben's guilt. When Hawk only shrugged, she went on. "Yet, knowing all you do about those horrible men, you aren't afraid of them, are you?"

"Fear is something a man has to keep under tight control, not allow it to rule his thoughts and actions. But having a healthy dose of caution and wisdom keeps him alive."

"So, you would agree to go after them with me?"

"Yep, because if I didn't, you'd probably go alone and get hurt."

"How else can I obtain the truth and my big story if I don't follow that lead?" she jested.

As they focused on their meals and their own thoughts, Hawk realized that instead of the truth about Maggie becoming clearer to him, it was getting cloudier! He called to mind the conversation overheard in Wilcox. In some instances, from her tone of voice and words used, it didn't sound as if she knew Ben at all; and in others, as if she did, as she'd called Newl and Ben by their first names. Since then, whenever she talked about him or spoke his name, nothing in her voice or expression or words implied she knew him or was pining away for him. In fact, instead of hurrying to a lovers' reunion, she had rushed to Prescott as if to study the crime's details for loopholes in Ben's favor. Was it possible she hadn't been told everything in advance, then gotten suspicious of Ben when certain facts were revealed to her after her bold feat?

Perhaps the Carvers had convinced her Ben was innocent of wrong-doing, and that false belief was why she had been willing to "rescue" him. Had she come to Prescott to search out the "truth" for herself?

Hawk realized it was possible — but not probable — that Toby Muns had lied to him about Ben's involvement in the bank robbery and in his family's murders. He had heard from other sources that Ben sometimes rode with Barber and Jones, but neither he nor another marshal had ever seen the three together, and there were no warrants out on Ben for other crimes.

Was it possible Muns lied about Ben to avenge some past wrong while riding together or to protect the identity of the real fifth culprit, especially if it was Barber's notorious brother? If Maggie knew Ben well enough to determine he was being honest with her, that would explain why she was helping him. It would also explain why his gut instinct and years of experience told him she didn't know Barber and Jones and, in fact, hadn't even heard of them until recently. He found that omission odd since they were Ben's alleged accomplices. Yep, Hawk concluded, this case and woman were becoming more complicated and confusing by the hour!

Maggie approached the structure that housed the *Arizona Sentinel*. It was built of wooden slats and painted white and had a large floored porch with "printing office" painted on the sides of its roof. A huge free-standing sign on tall poles reached the second-story level and read "Daily & Weekly."

She already had sent her two telegrams and requested replies be given by the recipients and delivered to her hotel and slipped under her door. She was certain she looked every inch the lady, clad in a day dress with set-in three-quarter-length sleeves, a high stand collar, a draped apron front, and knife-pleated skirt in a flattering blue-berry shade with ivory trim. She wore fine leather boots in black, a straw hat with an upturned brim with lace edging, and carried a parasol. She also held a leather-bound case with paper and pen for making notes. She took a deep breath and mentally prepared herself for the challenge ahead. She pasted a sunny smile on her face, readied a heavy southern drawl and feminine charms, opened the door, and entered the newspaper office.

Almost two hours later and with her head brim-ming with ideas and with bountiful notes re-corded, Maggie left the duped and smiling editor and headed to seek the two witnesses.

She walked to the edge of town and found the house the editor had described. It was a white two-story wood structure with a large front porch with rocking chairs and blooming bushes planted around its sides and up to the steps. The yard was fenced off with tall and sharp and sturdy white pickets, and behind the home was a small barn and corral. Everything was clean and in excellent condition.

She knocked on the door and a brunette responded, a rather plain woman in her forties clad in a simple green day dress. "Are you Mrs. Frank Moore, previously Miss Matilda Sims?"

"Yes. Who are you? What do you want? My husband isn't home yet."

"If it's possible, ma'am, I would like to come inside and speak with you about a certain matter. I'm a journalist for a newspaper back East and I was asked to come West to write stories about interesting events and people. I was recently in Yuma and happened upon what I think would be a good story for my editor. I suppose you've heard by now that Ben Carver escaped from the Territorial Prison and is still on the loose."

The woman paled and almost lost her voice as she struggled to speak.

"Ben Carver . . . escaped? No, my husband didn't tell me that bad news. How? When?"

"He escaped over a week ago, ma'am, on the twentieth. Sneaked away during a work detail outside the prison walls during a violent storm.

The authorities haven't been able to find him or any clues to his whereabouts so far. Since you were a victim during his crime and testified against him, I was hoping I could interview you. It would be an enormous help to me. To be honest, I'm working on a provisional basis; so if I don't obtain good stories, I won't be hired permanently by the newspaper. I would be ever so grateful if you could assist me."

"I don't know . . . I'm not sure Frank would want me discussing it."

Maggie observed the woman's anxiety as she softly reasoned, "Whyever not, ma'am, since you testified in court about the matter?"

"Yes, but Frank made me — I mean, he asked me to testify so that wicked man wouldn't go free. I didn't want to do it because I was scared he or his friends would harm us for exposing them."

Maggie caught what she hoped were two slips. She let the first partial sentence go unchallenged, but she pressed with a sweet smile, "Them? You mean you also recognized the other four men?"

"Not exactly. They were all masked. I did see one's red hair and the other's ghostly eyes. Only Ben Carver's mask slipped down, and we saw his face before he recovered it."

"You know this infamous Ben Carver well enough to recognize him?" Maggie pressed, noting Matilda's odd look during her last statement.

"Frank told me who he was. Frank knows him

and his father. I identified him in jail after he was captured."

"It's alleged that two of the other bandits are the notorious villains, Pete Barber and Slim Jones. It's a miracle they didn't murder all of you to prevent recognition."

"I don't think they saw Ben's mask slip, and they had to flee in a rush. Someone came to the door, saw what was happening, and shouted for help. The sheriff and some soldiers in town came running to rescue us. All of the robbers ran out the back door and rode away with the money."

Is it wishful thinking, Maggie, or does she sound as if she's speaking from rote instead of actual experience? "Barber and Jones never tried to approach you to threaten you about not testifying?"

"No. Why?"

"That's just strange, considering they normally do that kind of thing to avoid being captured and prosecuted. So, you were positive the man from the bank was Ben Carver?"

"Yes, and that's what I said on the witness stand."

"How did your husband —" Maggie saw Matilda's tension increase as the woman looked past her, and she heard the fence gate open and close.

"Here's my husband now. I think you should speak with him."

"Speak with me about what?" Frank asked as he joined them.

As his wife explained in a weak voice, Maggie felt as if the man were examining her thoroughly from hatted head to boot-clad feet, and in a manner she found offensive, but she smiled at him nonetheless.

"I'll handle this matter," he assured Matilda. "What is it you want from us, Miss. . . ."

"Miss Margaret Anne Malone, sir, from Virginia," she replied in the exaggerated southern accent she had been using since her arrival. She related what she had told his nervous wife earlier and asked, "Would you allow me to interview you for my story, sir? I would be most grateful."

"What have you learned so far?"

"Not enough for an interesting story, only what the Yuma prison superintendent told me after the escape and what the *Arizona Sentinel* editor and his articles added. I spent the last two hours with him, and he directed me to you and your wife. I don't want it to sound as if I'm reporting news, mostly old news at that; I want to concentrate on the people involved, how it affected them and their lives. Since you and your wife were major participants in that frightful event, a great portion of my story should feature you and your courage in court."

"Come inside and have a seat, Miss Malone; this could be quite an interesting experience. Mattie, please make us some coffee."

"Yes, dear, immediately."

The woman entered the house before Frank held the door open for Maggie, who praised herself for spotting one of his weak points: vanity. She sat down on a couch in an immaculate parlor

170

with nothing out of its proper place. She watched Frank settle himself on a matching one beyond the low table between them. He was well dressed in an expensive suit and leather boots, the image of a gentleman and prosperous businessman, but she didn't like him.

Maggie opened her case and prepared her paper and pen for taking notes. "Would you tell me what happened at the bank that day?" She saw how his bold gaze lowered to her pad and locked on it, not on her face, before he began his narrative.

"Mattie and I were there doing business, along with several others, when four bandits came in the back door and robbed us while a fifth man stayed with their horses. They took the bank's money, and the customers' valuables. A gray-eyed, skinny man collected the cash from the teller's drawer and another one cleaned out the vault while a red-haired, tall man held his guns on us. We had to stuff everything we had with us in a sack Ben Carver passed around. When a customer at the door window saw what was happening, he hightailed it down the street shouting for the sheriff. That redhead heard him and told the others it was time to make a run for it. The teller reached for a gun under the counter, so Ben shot him and escaped before help arrived. We never got any of our belongings or money back."

Maggie tapped her pen against her lips to distract him as she said, "That's almost what the editor told me earlier. Why was the bank vault open? Isn't that unusual?"

"The owner opened it to remove some papers he was holding for me. He was knocked unconscious by that redhead right after they sneaked into the bank, so he didn't see anything that happened afterward."

As Maggie continued her questioning, she noticed that Frank stared at the booted foot resting on his knee when responding.

"Why was the back door unlocked? That sounds strange."

"The owner said he must have forgotten to relock it after his arrival."

"Did the sheriff ever discover who the other four bandits were?"

"No, but he suspected the identity of two from our partial descriptions. Everybody knows how Pete Barber and Slim Jones look and know they ride together, and usually Toby Muns and Coot Sayers tag along. But none of us could swear it was any of them since we didn't see their faces."

"But you and your wife did see Ben Carver's."

"Yes, when his mask slipped down for a moment."

Maggie observed he still didn't look her in the eye when he talked, but his rude gaze traveled the rest of her body with frequency. "Did Carver or any of the others present realize you two had seen Carver's face?"

"I'm sure they didn't or we'd all be dead. The others had their attention elsewhere and Ben was looking down at the collection bag he was holding. Fortunately Mattie and I averted our gazes before he looked up again. Ah, here's our coffee. How do you take yours?"

"With two spoons of sugar, please. Thank you, Mrs. Moore," Maggie said as the cup was passed to her.

Matilda smiled and nodded, then prepared her husband's beverage.

"That will be all, my dear." Frank said, "You can return to your chores. I'll call you if I require anything else."

Maggie waited until the woman left the room, before turning her attention back to Frank. "It was fortunate for you and your wife that none of the culprits realized you had seen Carver's face," she said, "because I hear Barber and Jones are notorious for not leaving witnesses behind, or for returning later to get rid of them before trial. I'm sure that possibility must have worried you."

"Yes, but a man can't shirk his duty or live in fear. Besides, we didn't say they were involved, so they had no reason to come after us."

"But you exposed their friend and helped send him to prison. Are you worried about Carver coming here for revenge now that he's on the loose?"

"No, because his face is too well known for him to go unnoticed."

"But he could sneak in during the night, couldn't he?"

"I have a big and vicious dog I keep in the

yard at night. I'd keep it there during the daytime, too, but Mattie's afraid of him and he only obeys my commands. He's locked in the barn in daylight hours."

That revelation explained to Maggie why the picket fence was so tall and strong, to contain the "vicious" animal during the night. Yet, if Moore wasn't afraid, why did he need a guard dog? "I understand, because big and mean dogs frighten me, too." She changed the subject abruptly to ask Frank, "Exactly how do you know Ben Carver?" She saw him straighten his position, put aside his cup, and look her in the eye.

"Me and his father have had several . . . disagreements in the past over the location of the territorial capital. Since I'm in the lumber business and he's in the . . . entertainment business, that location is important to the prosperity and growth of a town. We butted heads over that rivalry. Newl wouldn't admit to the real reason why we got the capital: that Tucson leaned toward the Confederacy during the war with the North and was being punished by the government. Those Southern sympathizers actually held a convention in Tucson and declared Arizona a Confederate territory and elected a delegate to its Congress. As soon as the war ended, the fight was on for who would get the capital. Besides, we had Fort Whipple to protect the new government like it was protecting the mines and timber here, along with settlers and ranchers."

"But Tucson lured it away for ten years, from

'67 to '77, right?"

"Yes, but it's back here now, and this is where it will remain. I wasn't the only one spending his hard-earned money to recover it. Our Buckey O'Neill has fought Bob Leatherwood of Tucson as fiercely as I've battled with Newl. We garnered enough votes to get it back because every man in this area turned out at the polls. I made sure of that by putting my money where my mouth was."

"You purchased votes; is that what you mean?" She saw him glare.

"There's nothing illegal about compensating men for taking time off from work to come vote. Poor folk can't afford to lose a day's wages."

"Oh, I didn't mean it to sound as if I were implying otherwise, sir. Please forgive me if I failed to word my question properly. I'm still learning this reporting and interviewing business. It's just that I was so fascinated by the history you were relating that I didn't think before I spoke. I fully agree with your motive and applaud your generosity toward those less fortunate than you are," Maggie slyly masked her intentionally provoking statement.

"Don't worry about it, Miss Malone; I realize you're a greenhorn."

"Thank you for being patient and understanding with me, sir. Let me check my notes for a moment," she said, and feigned doing so. She looked up to find him gawking at her, but pretended not to notice as she needed more information from him. "I understand Mr. Newl Carver testified his son was on a hunting trip with him when the crime was committed and that Ben Carver swore he was innocent."

"That's true, but Newl and his son both lied on the witness stand, and the jury and judge didn't believe them. Ben couldn't be in two places at one time, and I saw him here that day. Newl's lucky they didn't toss him into jail for perjury."

Methinks that's sheer hatred in your voice and eyes; I wonder why. "It's propitious you and your wife recognized Carver or that crime would have gone unresolved and at least one villain unpunished. But I can understand why a father would lie to save his only son."

"I wouldn't know; I don't have any children, not yet anyway."

Maggie detected a suspicious bitterness in Frank's voice. She deduced that Ben's lawyer had overlooked two vital points during the trial to evoke a crucial "shadow of a doubt" with jurors. She broached the first one with Frank, "Is Ben Carver what you westerners call a legendary gunslinger?"

"No, why?"

"I just presumed he must be fast, skilled, and alert to have been the one who drew his weapon and shot the teller when there were two villains standing closer to him — and especially with the customer counter and protective bars separating them, plus Carver holding a collection bag with both hands. He must have drawn and fired as fast as lightning strikes." She saw him scowl for a minute before relaxing.

"After a warning shout from the leader, the other two ran for the back door and Ben drew his pistol. I suppose he saw the teller's movement and reacted to it. At that point, things happened fast and furious, so we all hit the floor to elude stray bullets."

"That was hasty and clever thinking on your part, sir, and probably saved your life," Maggie said. As Frank smiled in pleasure, she broached the second intriguing point. "That leader sounds like a careless man since he didn't assign a look-out — I guess that's what it's called — on the front door or keep a watch on it for intrusion himself. Perhaps such an oversight in the future will be his undoing; I hope so."

"Me, too, Miss Malone."

She asked a few more simple questions, then said, "I want to thank you and your wife for assisting me with this story. After it's published, I'll send you a copy of the newspaper, auto-graphed by me, of course. If you can't think of anything else to tell me, I'll be leaving now."

"Nothing more. I wish you luck with the article and your new job."

Maggie closed her case and stood as she said, "Thank you, sir; that's very kind and generous of you, as were your help and hospitality."

As they were heading for the door, she paused, turned, and said, "Oh, if I hear or read about

Ben Carver returning to Prescott, may I come back and interview you again?" *Get that lecherous glaze out of your eyes, you snake in the grass! For heaven's sake, your new wife is in the next room!*

"That will be fine with me, and I know I would find it just as enjoyable as your visit today, but I won't be seeing his face again. I'm sure the Law will have him back in custody and prison very soon."

"I hope so, sir, because criminals shouldn't be running around loose and committing more wicked deeds against innocent people. Good-bye."

Maggie stopped by to see the sheriff, who believed Ben was guilty. He was certain Newl had lied on the witness stand in a vain attempt to save his son from prison but that a merciful judge and court hadn't filed any perjury charges against the distraught father. When she asked the lawman why Ben wasn't hanged, she was told that wasn't the type of punishment for bank robbery.

Afterward, she met with the bank teller who had a permanent limp but was in no danger of dying from his past wound, as Newl had claimed in Wilcox sixteen days ago. The reedy-framed man told her he didn't see Ben's face or hear any names spoken that day. He also said he shouldn't have gone for a gun hidden under the counter, but he panicked because he feared the bandits would kill all of them before leaving and it was his duty to protect the bank's money and customers.

He said he didn't know why they weren't all killed, "because the robbers certainly had plenty of time to do us under and get away clean. I guess God protected us."

When she queried him about the same two overlooked points she had asked Frank about, she found his responses interesting.

As she departed, Maggie told herself that so far Ben's conviction still relied solely on the Moores' testimonies, claims she now found dubious, which led her closer to believing her stepbrother truly was innocent.

When she returned to her hotel room, weary and befuddled, Maggie found two telegrams — Abby's and her mother's — shoved under the door as she requested earlier. As prearranged for safety and secrecy, both replies were identical: *Everything fine here.*

She sighed in relief, though she yearned for more news, then headed for the wash basin to freshen up before meeting Hawk for supper downstairs later. She knew if she hurried, she would have just enough time to finger through the trial notes the *Sentinel* editor had made; that would explain her knowledge of the details to Hawk when she discussed them with him this evening to extract his professional opinions.

As they awaited their food, Maggie told him

about her talks that afternoon and her plans to visit the judge and prosecuting attorney tomorrow and some jury members to see if they voted their consciences or fears. "According to what I've learned so far, Ben Carver and his father vowed he was innocent," Maggie confided. "The Moores acted strange during my interviews with them, as if they were hiding something. I got the distinct impression that Frank Moore hates both of the Carver men, especially the father, and he appeared to take exceptional joy in putting the son behind bars. He's well liked and respected and trusted here, but he didn't give me that same opinion of him. In fact, I found him most unlikable."

While their food and drinks were being served, Hawk remained silent. Although he had shadowed her the entire time, he hadn't gotten close enough to her meetings to overhear any of them. He had seen her go to the telegraph office, but didn't know if she sent or received messages or both. But the coded telegram waiting for him, which he had collected and read after her return to the hotel, had been a pleasing one. He learned she had been forthright with him in most areas. She and the Mercers were from Virginia, and she had attended boarding school back East with Abigail. The Malones had moved to Fort Worth after the war between the States, where they ranched until Jed's death in '77. The widow had sold out and moved away, but he didn't know yet to what location; perhaps it was back to Virginia, but no newspaper there had a Margaret Anne Malone as an employee. Hopefully when he checked for another telegram in the next town they visited, he would receive more facts about her and her life since '77, especially clues about her relationship with Ben Carver.

Alone again, he ventured, "So, you think they lied about him?"

After sipping tea, Maggie said, "I don't know, but there seem to be a lot of convenient coincidences and mysteries."

"What do you mean?" Hawk asked as he speared a piece of roast.

"First, the bank vault was unlocked at Frank's request. Second, the back door wasn't bolted by the owner. How did the bandits know to check it and use it to slip in without notice from the street? Third, the one man in the gang whom Moore knew had his mask slip down just as the culprit was standing in front of him; yet, none of the outlaws or others present observed the Moores actually seeing his face. Fourth, the accused just happens to be the son of an enemy, a man who didn't have a credible alibi for his whereabouts that day. Fifth, why didn't the leader — if it was a clever man like Barber — post a lookout on the front door, or stand guard on it himself? Sixth, if as Moore said, 'Everybody knows how Pete Barber and Slim Jones look,' why didn't he recognize them? Even if you tied a bandanna over your mouth and nose, I would recognize you by your eyes and hair, especially if it was bold red hair or ghostly gray eyes. Why would Moore be brave and civic-minded enough to expose Carver, but hold silent about Barber and Jones, when he would be safer with them behind bars?"

Hawk stayed silent and nibbled at his food as she paused to wet her throat because he didn't want to derail her from her line of thought.

"The *Sentinel* editor gave me a copy of the trial testimony and notes he used to write his many articles; and I read them earlier and made some intriguing discoveries. Either Carver's lawyer was incompetent or careless or was bribed because he missed many of those points and others." She told him details about the teller's wounding, then reasoned, "Even the teller doesn't know who shot him; he said his head was lowered at that time. If Carver was holding a bag of valuables he was collecting, I doubt he could draw and fire that fast. Moore also said they all hit the floor after the leader shouted a warning, so how could he see who shot that man? And with obstacles between them, how did Carver shoot him in the thigh, not in his chest or head or an arm? The guilty verdict hinges on the Moores' testimonies, and I'm unconvinced they're credible."

Maggie sipped more tea and continued. "Then there's the angle of witnesses being left alive and later no retaliation toward them when the Law is almost certain two of the other villains were Barber and Jones. The trial took place on Moore's terrain, where his word would be accepted by jury members, the judge, and the town-folk. People here hated Newl Carver for his work opposing having the capital situated here. I got the distinct impression that Moore wasn't being totally honest with me, and I'm doubtful his wife even saw the culprit's face; I think she lied to please her husband. In case you don't know it, Hawk, they weren't even engaged at that time; they married right after the trial."

To Hawk's amazement, in a few short hours, she had obtained clues of which he wasn't even aware! "What do you mean by that insinuation?"

Maggie leaned toward him and almost whispered, "I charmed the newspaper editor into telling me about the great romance that resulted from the crime and trial. Frank and Matilda hadn't even been seeing each other until that time. Supposedly their being thrown into the jaws of peril together created a bond between them, so they up and wed as soon as she verified his testimony and Carver was convicted."

"You think Moore offered her marriage in exchange for lying?"

"Yes, but the editor believes Moore's claims about a sudden romance. I watched them together, and for newlyweds they didn't seem madly in love. I think their marriage is another one of those convenient coincidences. What if the robbery was an inside job and those bandits were hired by Moore and/or the owner? There was a lot of money, gold, silver, and other valuables in the safe on that particular day. I find it suspicious that it and the back door were left open at just the right time. Also, only Moore saw the gray eyes of one of the villains and he was inside the teller's cage, a good distance away and with obstacles between them. As for the redhead everyone saw, that could have been a coincidence, or a dye like henna could have produced it. Or Moore and the owner could have hired Barber and Jones to carry out their wicked plan, which would explain why they both let Carver take the blame and he perhaps wasn't even there that day. That also would explain why Moore refused to point a finger at those two miscreants."

"You sound as if you believe Ben Carver was railroaded into prison."

"If he was, wouldn't that be a fascinating story to expose?" She took a deep breath. "Maybe it's just my wild imagination or naturally suspicious mind at work, but the idea intrigues me. I did do one wicked thing to the Moores: I asked what they would do if Carver came here looking for revenge, and it seemed to panic both of them." She related that portion of her talk with Frank Moore, but omitted revealing his lecherous behavior so Hawk wouldn't think her conclusions were biased by it.

"So, you do believe Carver was framed?"

"To tell the truth, partner, I honestly don't know what to think. I need more facts and evidence to prove me right or wrong. Remember what you told me about Jack Swilling? If a man like that could be wrongly accused and incarcerated, why couldn't that be true of Ben Carver?"

Or you hope it is? "Well, you said you were looking for challenges and adventures, so it appears this mystery might provide both of them for you."

"That and a whole lot more." *I could stare at you all day and night.*

"Such as?" He saw her react as if she'd made a slip. Her cheeks rosed slightly and she averted her gaze from his.

"As I told you: this story could make my career."

Hawk struggled against the gnawings of jealousy that chewed at him because she seemed so determined to believe Ben was blameless and to clear him. He couldn't ignore the facts she'd uncovered or the suppositions she'd made. What if Toby Muns and the Moores had lied, and he helped Maggie prove it? What would happen to his budding relationship with her if Ben Carver was exonerated and became a rival for her affections? No matter how much he wanted Ben's competition removed and his family's killers punished, he couldn't let an innocent man pay for them. "You don't think Carver's escape proves his guilt?" he pressed.

"Perhaps it only means he's desperate and afraid. If he's innocent, how could he prove it from behind bars? Who's to say he didn't bust out to find and expose the real robbers or unmask lying witnesses? Why would he peacefully serve time for a crime he didn't commit? Why would he willingly stay penned up with evil and dangerous men and labor like a slave?"

"Are you planning to make a suffering and wronged hero out of Carver like in those dime novels?" Hawk teased.

"Only if he deserves it."

"And if he doesn't?" Hawk ventured, her gaze a captive of his.

"I'll let the Law deal with him. If I uncover something beneficial to his case, I'll turn it over to the proper authorities. But if we prove he's guilty and prove Barber and Jones were involved, we'll do the same thing, right, partner? First, we have to find and interrogate them."

Hawk knew where they were, thanks to his telegram and a newsworthy showdown between Barber and a reckless man near the Mexican border recently. "You're right, boss lady. Now, we'd better eat before our food is stone cold. We can talk more over coffee and pie."

On Sunday morning, Maggie asked Hawk to attend a local church service with her, and he seemed perfectly at ease sitting on the pew and being in God's house. When they stood to sing hymns from a shared book, their shoulders made contact. It felt wonderful to be at his side, sharing things. As she observed the smiling families around them, she longed for one of her own, for Hawk to be her husband, to have their children surrounding them. She couldn't help but say a selfish prayer for those golden fantasies to become realities, for Ben to be innocent and for her to be able to prove it, and for Hawk to understand and forgive her for deceiving him until that day.

Afterward, they ate lunch and went to see the judge and prosecuting attorney, to discover both were out of town; so they headed to visit with several of the jury members from a list provided by the newspaper editor.

As they strolled late that afternoon, Hawk was baffled by the way Maggie had conducted those meetings. She had talked in a heavy southern accent, used her best charms to captivate and relax those people into speaking freely, and sounded to him as if she were handling an investigation rather than doing story interviews. Just as amazing to him were some of the past jurors' responses.

"Now, do you see what I meant, Hawk?" she asked as if her mind traveled in that same direction. "Everyone we talked to said the Carver men were convincing in court and they would have believed them if not for the Moores contradicting their testimonies. They didn't think the open vault was strange or the unbolted back door, or that witnesses were left alive. Everyone here seems to be a loyal friend of Frank Moore's and to hold Newl Carver in contempt for his politics. It's as if their minds were made up Ben was guilty even before the trial began."

Hawk noticed she said "Ben" and not Carver as usual; and heard frustration edging her tone of voice. "Isn't it human nature to believe our friends over strangers?"

"Yes, but people have to draw the line somewhere between serving good and evil, just as the pastor said this morning. Even if one ignores his duty to the Law and his fellow man, when he places his hand on the Bible and makes an oath to God, he should refuse to allow friendship to color his decision. How can one vote *guilty* when he has a shadow of doubt, which they all do? Don't you agree?"

"Yep, the preacher's message was accurate; and what you just said is true." As they passed other strollers, Hawk went silent, but his mind asked her, *Where do you draw that crucial line between good and bad? Do you believe Ben is innocent? Do you believe his life was in jeopardy in prison? Is that why you helped him escape and why you're nosing around in his case? It surely isn't for a newspaper story. I agree Moore is withholding something, but I doubt he lied about seeing Ben in the bank. I wonder how you're going to feel when you discover Ben's evil to the core.*

During that quiet interlude, Maggie pondered a troubling mystery. After speaking with Newl and Frank, she was convinced there was a missing angle to their fierce rivalry which neither had disclosed to her. She had witnessed sheer hatred in both men's gazes and heard it in their voices. A gut feeling shouted there was more than opposing politics involved. She surmised that Newl had wanted Ben out of prison before more charges, real or fake, were leveled against him, possibly resulting in his execution. In any case, Newl had deceived her about the bank teller's condition, which forced her to be skeptical about some of his other claims. She needed to go to Tucson to speak with her stepfather, to clarify those hazy points. Besides, Newl was supposed to be trying to discover the whereabouts of Barber and Jones for her. She wondered if she should approach him with Hawk in tow, but quickly realized she had no choice. She needed him along for protection when and if she came upon the two cutthroats who held the key to Ben's exoneration or reincarceration.

When they were secluded again, Maggie looked at Hawk and asked, "What are your plans now? Have you resolved your business here so I can hire you?"

"I guess I forgot to tell you last night: one of the gamblers on Whiskey Row told me he saw my targets on the train, but they decided to head for Tombstone instead of Prescott. Since that's a good place to start our search for Barber and Jones, I can take care of both jobs at once."

"Can you spare time for a stop-off in Tucson? I'd like to question Mr. Carver about his son, and I need to retrieve my horse. I stabled her there because she wasn't taking to the train ride very well and she had a leg that needed rest and treatment from a stone bruise."

Mercy, woman, I wish you couldn't lie so easily and that observation pained his heart and tormented his mind, though he knew he did it himself when necessary. Maybe she had no choice under the circumstances. She couldn't tell a law-abiding bounty hunter what she had done in Yuma and what she was trying to do. And if she had any idea who and what he was, an ex-Texas Ranger and current U.S. marshal on a mixture of official and personal business and a family member of that gang's victims, she'd flee him in a flash quicker than lightning. Then he'd not only lose his chance to be near her for protection, he'd also lose his path to Barber and Jones through Ben. Besides, there was somebody he needed to see in Tucson, and he also needed to check on some facts in another enlightening telegram about her. "Suits me fine. I'm sure Diablo will enjoy having a traveling companion as much as I do." He paused suddenly, then said, "Wait here a minute. That elderly lady across the street looks like she needs help with her carriage."

Maggie watched him cross the wide street to assist the woman, and was warmed by his thoughtfulness. She saw them chatting and turned to look at things displayed in a store window, as she didn't want him to see her staring at him with what was sure to be a hungry gaze.

Soon, Maggie heard steps approaching, then a raspy voice to her rear. She turned to find a rough-looking man eyeing her up and down.

"Hello there, you purty thang. Why don't we sally on down to where you work and have us a good time? I just got off my digs, so my pockets are full of shiny nuggets. Whatcha say to earnin' some of 'em off of me?"

"I beg your pardon, sir, but you've made a mistake. I'm a lady."

"Shore you are, and I'm a gentleman, so let's go have us some fun. I'd be willin' to pay plenty to roll in the bed with you. I bet you'd be worth —"

"A sock in the nose if you don't stop insulting me and leave!"

"Now, don't go gittin' your bloomers bunched up. I got money."

"I do not work on Whiskey Row, if that's what you think."

"Oh, yore in privit bisness for yourself. That don't matter none."

Maggie glared at him and threatened in an icy tone, "If you don't cease this crude talk and leave, I'll shout for my husband. He's across —"

"No need to call me, my love, I'm right here. I think you best move along and stop offending my wife before I have to clean up the street with you," Hawk warned the grungy man.

"This here's yore woman, yore wife?"

"That's right, and I don't take kindly to men insulting her."

"I didn't mean no harm. I jest made a mistake. I thought she was —"

191

"You thought wrong, so hightail it before my anger boils over."

"I'll be goin'. No need to fuss or fight. Sorry, ma'am."

Maggie saw the rumpled prospector almost run down the street to avoid her "husband's" wrath. She lifted herself on her tiptoes and kissed Hawk's cheek. "Thank you for the rescue. I was just about to punch him in the nose and knee him . . . where it hurts. I only hesitated because I didn't want to cause a scene, with it being Sunday."

Hawk smiled, and wished he had dared turn his head and compel the kiss to land on his mouth instead of his cheek. "A guard has to earn his salary, right?" he jested as he tried to cool his burning loins.

"I hope so," she murmured, her blue eyes fastened on his.

"You're a beautiful woman, Maggie Malone, so I can see why he lost his wits over you." *Lordy, I surely have!*

"That's nice of you to say, but that kind of man can keep them where I'm concerned."

"He's not your type?" Hawk jested with a broad grin.

"Absolutely not." *But you are.* "Shall we return to the hotel?"

Hawk let her place her hand over his elbow and guided her that way. "So, what kind of man are you looking for?" he asked.

Maggie glanced at him, and murmured, "Why,

one like you, Mr. Reynolds: smart and brave and kind. Thoughtful and generous and handsome, too."

"Since I'm not one to argue with a lady, thanks for the compliments."

"You're welcome, and you've earned them. Here we are. Do you want to eat a light supper before we go to our rooms?"

"Suits me just fine." *So do you, woman, more than fine.*

After they ate in cautious silence, Hawk escorted Maggie to her door. "We best turn in because we've got that long and bumpy stage ride coming up soon."

"Good night, and thanks again for the rescue and help today. I hate to think of being here alone. I guess seeking adventure has its price."

"Yep, I suppose it does, like everything else."

For what seemed like a long time but was only a minute or so, they gazed into each other's eyes and tingled with suspense and desire, both wondering if they should reveal their feelings for each other.

Hawk knew she was excellent in her pretense; she had everybody convinced she was who and what she claimed to be, except for him. But if he didn't know the truth and wasn't emotionally involved with her, she would probably have him deluded, too. Yet, she appeared reluctant to dupe him, as if dishonesty was unnatural for her. If only he knew what her tie was to Ben and Newl and how she had been persuaded or coerced into committing a crime for Ben, he would have answers to questions about her and his impending course of action. If she loved Ben, why lean in his direction without a good reason? Maybe she was just trying to beguile him so he would help and protect her along her route . . . Or maybe she hadn't expected to fall for him during her ruse.

"You're a very special person, Hawk Reynolds, and I'm glad we met; even happier we're working together and have become good friends."

"The same's true for you, Maggie; you're a real lady and I enjoy being with you." *I'd like to say more, but this isn't the time or place to go getting romantic, and especially before we both discover where the other stands.* "I hear somebody coming, so I'll say good night. I'll see you at seven in the morning."

"I'll be ready. Good night."

Hawk walked to his room next door, his heart pounding with love for her, his mind plagued by doubts and fears, and his loins afire for her.

Maggie entered her room to prepare for bed and their journey in the morning. For a while in the corridor, she thought Hawk was either going to kiss her or tell her something important. Did he want to draw her closer or discourage an unwanted interest in him or just slow down what was happening between them? Surely she wasn't mistaken about his desire for her, but were his feelings nothing more than just physical? Did he

194

love her? Would he be interested in marrying and settling down with her? Should she make it clear she was available for his pursuit? If so, should she do it tomorrow or soon or wait until she completed her hazardous task?

She reasoned that it wasn't fair to entangle Hawk romantically while she was in trouble. But with his pull on her increasing daily, could she resist him until her self-made predicament was resolved?

Chapter Eight

At a relay station late that afternoon, Hawk rounded the corner of the stone structure to see what was taking Maggie so long to return from an outhouse which was situated a lengthy distance away and partially enclosed by boulders and a steep cliff. Using amazing speed and skill, he was astonished to see her hook one ankle around a dark clad man's who was behind her, loop an arm around his neck, and toss him to the ground to his back as if he were as light as a feather — or she was as strong as an ox. The man rolled over and bounded to his feet, stared at her for a moment, then started a new approach. The nimble Maggie grasped her full skirt with both hands, slightly raised it, and kicked one foot upward to land it across the man's jaw. As he staggered from the blow, Maggie withdrew a knife from under her top garment, glared at the scowling man, and said something to him before replacing the weapon. The way she wielded the blade told Hawk she knew how to use it and would if need be.

As the man's fingers inched toward his pistol,

Hawk's did the same. But Maggie was faster than either of them, withdrawing a small derringer from her pocket and leveling on her attacker, once more revealing she knew how to use it and would if challenged. Whatever she said caused the man to relent, stalk toward his horse, and gallop away. Hawk could hardly believe she had faced down a gunslinger alone and without appearing the least bit afraid. He recalled the shooting skills and courage she had displayed during the attempted coach robbery while en route to Prescott and how she had helped free Ben and the way she had carried out her ruses in Yuma and Prescott. There was much more to Miss Margaret Anne Malone than met the eye.

He watched the mysterious woman adjust her clothes and hair, then walk in his direction. After she sighted him at the corner, she sent him a playful smile and shrug.

"What was that about?" he asked. "Do you know him?"

"I've never seen him before today. He got fresh with me and wouldn't accept no for an answer, so I had to take him down a peg or two."

"I got worried when you were gone so long. I started to come and help you, but it didn't look as if you needed any."

"A friend of mine from Japan taught me those moves for self-defense, I caught him off guard with them." As she glanced toward the dust clouds the rider was leaving behind in his hasty retreat, she said, "I suppose he was too embarrassed a woman bested him to remain here. He shouldn't have put his hands on me; he had no respect for a lady and needed to be taught a lesson."

As they paused at a clean-up table, Hawk said, "Well, it certainly appears you gave him one. I can see you're well-armed beneath those lovely clothes."

Maggie grinned. "A woman traveling alone has to be able to protect herself since her bodyguard isn't always around to do so. Following the incidents on the stage and then with the prospector in Prescott, I thought it would be wiser to have weapons at hand rather than out of reach in my baggage."

"As I said in Prescott, you're too beautiful and tempting for your own good, boss lady. I'll have to keep a closer eye on you from here on because the next admirer or assailant might not be dissuaded so easily."

After washing her hands in the water basin, she said, "Thanks. Now, let's go eat; I'm starved, and we'll be pulling out soon."

The remainder of the two day-stage journey to Phoenix and Maricopa — including an overnight stay there — passed without problems and with little conversation, as did the seven-hour train ride in the Sonoran Desert as they railed toward their next destination on Wednesday, the second of May.

At last, the sprawling Santa Catalina Mountains northeast of town and the cacti and yucca-studded Tucson Mountains west of it loomed ahead. They traveled in the rugged and densely vegetated Santa Cruz Valley and near a tranquil river with the same name. The striking location was rimmed with multi-peaked ridges and surrounded by picturesque desert.

Maggie recalled from her mother's letters and her own observations while passing through weeks ago that Tucson was populated by a medley of people from many countries and walks of life. Most homes and businesses were flat roofed and built of sunbaked mud bricks which were held in place by straw-laced mortar, or were of adobe and mud with unplastered wattle work of ironwood branches lashed to cottonwood or saguaro slats and posts. Some homes and businesses were built of wood with raised shingled roofs and with wide porches to provide shade from the desert sun and protection from occasional but torrential and violent rainstorms. The ground and air were dry and dusty; and little non-native vegetation grew, just the usual variety of cacti, mesquites, and scrub brush. Dark stone from Sentinel Peak, meaning "Dark Mountain" for which Tucson was named, was used in abundance for foundations and walls. The town was considered modern and civilized, thanks to the S & P Railroad, gas streetlights, good law enforcement, varied types of businesses and professional services available, telegraph, and even a few of the "magic talking box" telephones which arrived in '81.

Maggie and Hawk deboarded at the depot at three o'clock to head for a nice hotel on Congress Street. After registering there and having their possessions delivered to their rooms, they walked to a livery nearby to purchase feed for Diablo and to have him stabled there overnight. While Hawk was tending his black mustang, Maggie spoke with the owner about leaving with her mount in the morning. After their business was settled and she was told the mare had been properly fed and exercised regularly, she visited with Blaze. The chestnut roan was as delighted to see her mistress following a long separation as Maggie was to see the almost prancing animal.

"That's my girl," Maggie cooed as she stroked the roan's neck and head. "I missed you something fierce, Blaze. I hope you were given good care. Soon we'll be riding together again, but this time we'll have company, you'll like them."

After speaking with the owner, Hawk approached and smiled as he witnessed the strong bond between woman and horse. "She's a beautiful mare, Maggie; and I can tell you two are close friends, like me and Diablo."

"She's the best horse I've ever owned, aren't you, girl? She's smart, sure-footed, and totally loyal."

Hawk watched Blaze nuzzle her nose in Maggie's upturned palm as she collected the treat her mistress gave to her. He saw Maggie kneel, lift the right foreleg, and examine it and the new shoe. She released it and rubbed the creature's leg, lightly fingering the entire area.

"She seems fine now, no tenderness or swelling; and the blacksmith did a fine shoeing job."

"He's changing Diablo's this afternoon. I don't want to head out across that desert with him in old ones. I'm having him stabled inside tonight; it'll be quieter and more restful in here than on that dusty and noisy street."

"My father taught me that if a man takes good care of his horse, his horse will take good care of him; I've always found that to be true. If we're lucky, Diablo and Blaze will become good friends, like we have."

"Since she's not in season, they'll do fine, because Diablo hasn't had a sweetheart in ages; I keep him moving around too much for romance."

Maggie laughed with him. "It sounds as if mount and master have the same dilemma," she jested.

"Yep," he agreed with a smile. "So, what are your plans for the rest of today?"

"As soon as I freshen up, I'm going to the Paradise Club to see if Mr. Carver will speak with me about his son. I was told he owns that establishment, and it isn't far down the street. If you don't mind, I think I should go alone. I think he would be more amenable to a lady by herself. He could tense up if I have a tall and tough-looking hombre beside me," she asserted with a playful grin and tone to make her excuse sound plausible.

"That's fine with me, boss lady, and it sounds sensible, as usual."

"Thanks for understanding. Afterward, I'm going to soak in a tub and wash my hair. It normally takes hours for this thick mane to dry, but as hot as it is here, if I sit near the window, it shouldn't remain wet for very long. If I'm wrong about that, I'll just eat in my room. If not, I'll meet you downstairs at seven for supper. Is that schedule all right?"

"Suits me fine. I'll probably stay here with Diablo for a while, then maybe wander around town."

"Just stay out of trouble so I won't have to bust you out of jail. You must leave with me tomorrow. I need you in Tombstone, partner."

Hawk saw her cheeks pinken slightly and she averted her blue eyes from his to her horse. She had chosen the wrong thing to joke about, though she was unaware of his knowledge about it. "After the skills and courage I've seen you use, woman," he jested, "I have no doubt you'd succeed. Then some other bounty hunter would be tracking us for rewards; so I promise to behave myself, hard as that might be. You do the same."

"As always, kind sir, I'll be on my best ladylike behavior. Good-bye."

"See you later, Maggie Malone, and be careful."

"I always am. You, too."

Instead of heading for her rented room to freshen up, Maggie walked to the Paradise Club.

She entered the open double doors and paused to allow her eyes to adjust from the bright sunlight to the dimmer setting and to give herself time to study the place. She was surprised by how respectable and elegant the business was, despite the fact her mother had told her it was one of the best on the frontier. It was busy inside, but quieter, she presumed, than it would be at night. She saw a variety of men talking and drinking and some gambling. Many were accompanied by pretty females who were attired in just-below-the-knee, décolleté red satin dresses trimmed with black lace and ribbons, and displaying "painted faces." She saw other *filles de joie* either heading upstairs or returning from those carnal duties, and a few standing on the upper landing and conversing. The piano bench was vacant, so no music was being played at that early hour. The same was true for the rear stage for entertainment later, singers and dancers according to her mother. The numerous tables and chairs for customers were stained in mahogany and were shiny from recent waxing, as were the floor and artistically carved railings, posts, and trimwork. The place was lighted at night by lovely suspended fixtures. There were several types of gaming tables such as faro and roulette. Red velvet swags were hung at the windows, held in place by gold cords with tassels. The bar was long and clean, also polished to a high sheen; behind it were bottles of wine and assorted whiskeys and various-size glasses and barrels of beer. It definitely was as nice as the place she had worked in Sante Fe recently.

She approached a bartender, who was now eyeing her with curiosity, and asked to speak with the owner. She was told Newl Carver was out of town for the day, to come back tomorrow. She thanked him and left.

As she returned to the hotel for a thorough bath and hair washing, Maggie hoped her step-father wasn't off somewhere meeting with his son. She penned a note to Hawk, telling him about Carver's absence and her decision to wait until another date to interview him and slipped it under his door.

Following supper, Hawk escorted Maggie to her room where she said she was going to bed soon to prepare for their trip tomorrow, which was partly true. She had told him Newl Carver was out of town, but omitted revealing he was due back tonight. She was eager to leave Tucson before somebody who had seen her in Yuma and perhaps Prescott saw her here and thought it was suspicious.

After she unlocked her door, Maggie turned and spoke with him for a few minutes. She feared and dreaded exposure, or incarceration, which might separate them for years, perhaps forever if Hawk couldn't forgive her for deceiving him. She hated being parted from him for even a few hours, but she had a crucial task to carry out tonight. Once more, her gaze melded with his, and they simply looked at each other in silence.

Maggie was surprised and pleased when Hawk grasped her hand, guided them into her room, closed the door, and pressed her body against the wall as his mouth met hers. The kiss was long, deep, and full of yearning. His lips were gentle yet commanding. Her senses spun slightly as he exchanged their positions and pressed his back to the wall and banded her body with his arms. As his mouth roamed her face, her arms looped around his neck and she leaned against his virile frame. He fused their lips once more as his fingers drifted up and down her back. She noticed when his breathing quickened, as did hers. She felt hot and tingly from head to feet as her passions were ignited to a fiery blaze of desire. She quivered when his mouth found her ear and whispered into it.

"Maggie, sweet and beautiful Maggie, I've craved to do this since we met, and I couldn't halt myself for a day longer. You've gotten to me as no other woman has." He pressed his lips to several spots on her temples, then cradled her head against his chest as he struggled to releash his freed emotions and to douse the fire searing his loins. That was difficult considering her re-action to his overture. She had yielded willingly and eagerly, a response he needed to discover before allowing himself to become hopelessly en-snared by her. "You're the most fascinating woman I've met. Mercy, you're tempting. I can hardly breathe or think straight while holding you and kissing you."

Maggie heard his heart pounding, its beat strong and swift. She snuggled into his embrace as she replied to his stirring words, "So are you, Hawk, far too tempting for our own good. I've wanted to kiss you since I first saw you. I was so surprised and happy to see you on the train that day I left Yuma. No man has ever made me feel the way you do. Just looking at you or hearing your voice brings me pleasure and joy. I'm so eager for us to get to know each other better, and we will while working together."

"I agree. I don't want to rush because these feelings are new to both of us. You're special, Maggie Malone, real special to me. Right now, I best get out of here so we can give some serious thought to what's happening between us, or I might lose my wits and offend you. You're a real lady and I respect you, so I wouldn't take advantage of an unexpected moment like this. I just wanted you to know how I feel about you, in case it changed your mind about traveling with me. And I had to know if you felt the same about me."

"I do, Hawk, and I want to be with you as much as possible." She looked at him and met his gaze. "Your mother reared a fine gentleman and a good man; she would be so proud of you tonight."

"Yep, she would, because walking out of this room will be one of the hardest things I've ever done. But you understand why I must go now?"

"Yes; we don't want to be impulsive, but we will be if you stay much longer."

His hands cupped her face as he gazed into her blue eyes and smiled. "Good night, Maggie. I'll see you in the morning. Call out if you need me."

Maggie grinned and teased as she stroked his jawline, "I think you should clarify that last sentence because I already need you."

Hawk chuckled, and tried to ignore the twitching in his loins. "Call out if you're in trouble. How's that?"

"Better and worse. Seven o'clock sharp, Mr. Reynolds. Good night."

"Good night, Maggie," he murmured in a husky tone, kissed the tip of her nose, and left fast before he changed his mind about departing.

She bolted the door and danced across the floor, whirling until she was dizzy, and fell on the bed. Her heart beat with elation. She was ecstatic, deliriously happy, supremely lucky. She was in love with Hawk Reynolds, and he so much as confessed he was in love with her, found her as irresistible as she found him. Surely a glorious future awaited them.

Then she bolted upright in bed in a panic. What she had done for Ben could spoil her happiness. She should never have broken the law for any reason, but it was too late to take back that deed.

Please, God, help me to do the right thing and fast; and please don't let anything turn Hawk against me. I love him and need him so much.

Dear, sweet Abby, please don't reveal to anybody you helped me, in case I'm exposed. Just marry Matthew and be happy. I can imagine how shocked and delighted you'll be to hear my news about Hawk. I must write you a letter tonight and mail it before I leave Tucson . . .

Long after dark, Maggie sneaked from the hotel to see her mother and Newl. She felt drained by the time she neared their house behind Newl's Paradise Club. She remained hidden for a while as she watched and listened to make certain the house wasn't being observed by lawmen or bounty hunters looking for Ben. The home was huge, two stories with a raised roof of shingles and with a porch that spanned the front and both sides, its decorative woodwork in the Victorian style. A combination barn/shed set behind it with an oblong corral to its side, probably for stabling Newl's horses and for storing his carriage and other gear and tools. The entire setting was fenced off with wood rails and posts, along which grew clusters of prickly cacti to perhaps discourage intruders, be they human or animal.

Maggie surmised from light filtering through curtains in various rooms that somebody was home. After she was assured it was safe, she made her way to the back door. As soon as she responded to her mother's query of who was there, Catherine opened the door. With haste, she darted inside, closed it, and bolted the lock.

"Maggie, dear, it's so good to see you," Catherine said as she hugged her daughter, then examined her with misty eyes. "Are you all right?"

"Yes, Mother, I'm fine. Is Newl here?"

"No, not yet. He went out of town this morning, but I expect him to return any time now. Come in and sit down; you look so nervous and pale."

"Make sure all of the drapes are drawn," Maggie said, "I don't want anybody peeking in and seeing us together."

"I've closed up for the night, so we have privacy. I'm glad you're here, but why did you come? I thought you wouldn't contact us until much later."

As Maggie followed her into an ornate parlor, she explained, "That was the original plan, but we need to have a serious talk."

Catherine sat on a floral patterned couch, her body angled toward Maggie. "About what, dear? Is anything wrong? Was Ben captured?"

Since time was limited, Maggie didn't comment on the lovely house or ask to see more of it. "As far as I know, Ben's still free and should be hiding in Sante Fe as we agreed. I have to ask, Mother, are you sure he's innocent? Are you sure he was hunting with Newl the day of the Prescott robbery?"

She saw her mother stare at her in astonishment. "What an odd and stunning question. Why do you doubt us now?"

"I'm sorry if it sounds that way and if I've hurt

you, but I've come across so much contradictory information that I'm puzzled and have to know the truth before I proceed any further on this matter. I've broken the law, Mother, and could get into deep trouble, so I need to be reassured I've done the right thing. Please be understanding."

Catherine nodded before responding to her daughter's concern. "That's what they told me. Even if I doubted Ben, which I don't, I believe Newl, he is a decent and honest man. On the day in question, Newl left to join Ben elsewhere and they returned home together afterward with a bag of quail. Ben was here with us when the Law came from Prescott and arrested him; he appeared totally shocked by the charges. To me, he sounded as if he were telling the truth. He seems to be a good and decent man like his father. Will it be helpful if I tell you what I know and think about him?"

After Maggie nodded, Catherine related, "Ben doesn't care for the type of business Newl's in. He reminds me of you in many ways; he loves challenges, adventures, and excitement. He likes to travel and hire on for temporary jobs, but he promised Newl he would settle down here one day and probably run a mercantile store or a gun shop; he's very knowledgeable about weapons and skilled with them. Every time he's been here, he struck me as a genial and easygoing young man who loves and respects his father and has a good sense of humor; he makes me laugh easily and often, and he helps out around the house with chores. He's kind and polite to me and to others. Some of the people he's helped tried to testify in Ben's favor at his trial, but the judge wouldn't allow it because he said it was irrelevant to the charges. I like him, Maggie, and he appears trustworthy. On occasion when he's between odd jobs, Newl gives or sends him money, and Ben insists his father keep a tally of the amount so he can repay him later. If he were robbing people and places, he wouldn't think of that. Ben just doesn't strike me as a criminal. And I don't think he would do anything to hurt and shame his father, or risk going to prison and lose the freedom he loves so dearly."

Although some of those descriptive points troubled Maggie, she smiled and said, "Thank you for being honest with me, Mother, and that gives me a better picture of my stepbrother. From what you've said and from things I learned, it certainly sounds as if they put the wrong man in prison."

"They did, Maggie, surely they did."

"I hope so, Mother, and I pray I can prove it soon. I'll tell you what happened in Yuma and Prescott, then I have some other questions."

Catherine was wide-eyed as Maggie related the events in both towns and the information she had uncovered to that point before asking, "Do you know why Frank Moore and Newl really are such fierce enemies? If there's another reason besides opposing politics, I have to know, because it could provide a reason for Frank framing

Ben. Without a stronger and more plausible catalyst, I'm stumped for a motive." Maggie saw a look of mingled indecision and dismay cross her mother's face, then watched Catherine glance at the door as if to make certain it was locked.

Catherine moved closer to her daughter and almost whispered, "What I'm about to tell you, dear, can't ever be repeated to anyone, including Newl himself, who confided this secret to me."

"I swear I won't reveal this secret, not even to help exonerate Ben."

"Before Newl married his first wife," Catherine disclosed, "she was Frank Moore's sweetheart. He left Tucson to head northward to seek his fortune; after he succeeded, he was supposed to send for her. Of course, there wasn't a town or fort there in the fifties, so it was impossible to get mail out of that area. Frank had told her it might take a long time, but she promised to wait for his return or summons. When the town and fort were established in '63, Frank gave up his work in the gold fields to go into the lumber business. He used his earnings to build a sawmill, buy freight wagons and teams, and build a home for them. Something happened to the two letters Frank wrote to her that year telling her what he was doing and that he was coming for her before Christmas. But after waiting such a long time and without any word from him, she presumed she had been jilted or Frank had died or been killed. To avoid being a spinster, she turned to Newl. When Frank came to Tucson that winter

212

and learned she'd married and had a son, he thought he'd been the one jilted, so he left without seeing her. I suppose it never occurred to him that he had been gone for years and she hadn't received his letters; maybe it was a wicked twist of fate that kept them apart. Or maybe Indians and outlaws attacked the carriers and made off with their satchels as often happened. The perils to mail delivery to and from the territorial capital was one of the arguments Newl used to get it moved to Tucson the following year."

Maggie nodded, but held silent for her mother to continue.

"When Ben was a teenager, Newl discovered his wife and Frank were meeting on the sly and she intended to leave him for Frank. In fact, she was carrying Frank's child." When Maggie inhaled sharply, Catherine said, "That's right, dear, she had betrayed her husband and marriage vows. During the preceding year, she had told Newl that her . . . wifely duties were painful. They hadn't shared a marriage bed for over seven months, so there was no doubt about whose baby she was carrying. She told Newl she had never loved him or been happy with him and wanted a divorce to marry Frank. Newl was devastated, so he told her to leave. She took off in such a hurry to get to Frank that she didn't even take her belongings with her, told him she would send for them later. She didn't get far out of town before she was thrown from her horse and killed.

Frank blamed Newl for her death and that of his unborn child, even accused Newl of killing them. Yet, no matter how he felt, Frank didn't report his foolish suspicions to the authorities because he didn't want to stain his reputation now that she was gone; you can imagine what a scandal it would have been if it became known he had impregnated and enticed away another man's wife. We think Frank was punishing Newl for those losses, and punishing Ben for not being his son. He knew Newl wouldn't expose the real reason in court why they hated each other because Ben doesn't know the truth about his mother and Newl couldn't bear to tarnish his son's memories of her. Since there were two witnesses against Ben and they didn't appear to have any connection, Newl felt that it wouldn't help Ben's case for him to try to discredit Frank by revealing their troubled pasts."

"At least I understand their hostilities now," Maggie said when her mother concluded. "It could be that Frank framed Ben for revenge, or he could be honestly mistaken, and it could be that Frank and the bank owner were in on that robbery." After reiterating her speculations about the bank door and vault, Maggie added, "But I can't imagine how I could prove that possibility; and without evidence, I can't even mention it to the Law. I'm heading for Tombstone in the morning to see if I can find a trail to Barber and Jones."

"I've heard they're mean and sly, Maggie, so

please be careful."

"I will, and I've hired a skilled gunslinger as my partner, so you won't have to worry about my safety. He doesn't know who I am or what I've done or plan to do." Maggie reminded her about the journalist cover story she was using and how it had worked on a past investigation. "He thinks he's helping me gather facts for my article and being my bodyguard and tracker. He's very nice, Mother, you'd like him and trust him, but I can't afford to introduce you to him and expose our relationship."

"But traveling alone with a man, a near stranger, isn't proper."

"Nor is busting somebody out of prison, Mother. I have to do what I think is best. Don't forget, I'm a trained and experienced professional. This isn't my first sojourn into peril. I'll be fine."

They heard footsteps on the porch, so Maggie hid in the first-floor bedroom while Catherine opened the door.

After she heard Newl's voice, she joined them and returned his smile. He beamed with joy as he embraced Maggie and kissed her cheek.

"You've made me the happiest man alive, my dear girl. It's good to see you, Maggie. You look wonderful as always, even in that unusual garb."

Maggie laughed as she glanced down at her black shirt and pants, and fingered the hair-concealing dark shawl draped around her neck. "This is my sneak-around outfit so I can blend in with the night. I already know Muns and Sayers are dead, but do you have any news on the whereabouts of Barber and Jones?"

"Your timing is perfect, Maggie. That detective I hired to trace them just told me yesterday by telegram they were in Nogales on Friday and heading for Tombstone. Since I knew you were coming this way, I told him to stay put so he wouldn't spook them. Using that cover you mentioned to me in Wilcox, not to mention your good looks and elegant manners, you shouldn't have any trouble getting them to talk freely. Cocky men love to boast and impress other people; they'll probably be tickled to death to have colorful stories written about them and their exploits. They'll never suspect your real identity and motive, and you'll be safe there. Tombstone is a wild town, but the Law's real strong there. So, tell me what you've been doing and how the work is going."

Maggie repeated what she'd already told her mother. She watched Newl's elation and excitement increase by the minute.

"You did it, my girl; you actually got Ben out of that awful place, and you're making enormous progress on his behalf. I'm so happy and so proud of you; I couldn't love you more if you were my own daughter. I knew you were sent from God to help us. I told you Frank lied about Ben. I wouldn't put it past the bastard — please excuse my foul language, but I wouldn't put it past that scoundrel to be responsible for the robbery. I tried to convince Frank he was wrong and not to seek revenge on me through my son. I told him he had no reason to bear a grudge against me for our past troubles, because I don't bear one against him; at least, I didn't until he framed Ben. I even tried to buy his silence, but he said he had plenty of money and didn't want any of mine. If he was in on that theft as you suspect, he told the truth for once; but I won't let him get away with harming my son for revenge or for filling his greedy pockets. I have every confidence you'll get Ben cleared of these fake charges. And it will be an added bonus if Frank's unmasked and punished for his foul deeds."

"An inside job is only a speculation at this point, Newl," she reminded him, "so don't get your hopes up in that direction." She looked Newl straight in the eye before asking, "Why did you tell me that bank teller might die and Ben might hang?" She noticed he didn't look uneasy or guilt-riddled.

"When my detective checked on him, his leg was badly infected and the doctor said he could lose it and his life if gangrene set in; fortunately for him and for us that didn't happen. But I fibbed a little by not telling you I'd just learned he was better, and I admit it. I'm sorry, Maggie, but I was desperate and scared. Besides, it is true that Ben was in danger of hanging if they pinned other crimes on him, and the Law's surely trying to do that, as you learned in Prescott. And his life was in danger there at the prison from other inmates, sadistic guards, or sickness from the foul conditions. You're our only hope, girl, so please don't lose faith in us now; I'm begging you."

"I won't, if from now on, you tell me anything and everything relevant to helping me clear Ben. And don't forget our deal: if I can't succeed in two months, Ben turns himself in while I continue to work on his case. I know you want him safe and free, but the longer he stays on the loose without vindication, the more crimes he may be accused of committing, which will worsen his chances for exoneration or a pardon. There's always a possibility that Barber and Jones won't confess their guilt or Ben's innocence, no matter how charming I am to them. There's also a possibility they'll claim Ben was with them; since he was accused, convicted, and imprisoned for that deed, they might allow him to remain a part of it for amusement."

"Do anything necessary to obtain the truth, Maggie, please. Find a way to force them to clear my son. I swear to you, Ben wasn't in Prescott that day and he hasn't committed any crimes. Ask your mother."

"Even if Newl didn't say Ben was hunting with him," Catherine said, "I don't see how he could have gotten from Prescott to here during the time span involved. Please do whatever you can to help him, but don't endanger yourself."

Newl drew Catherine closer to him on the couch and said in a tender voice, "Don't worry, my beloved wife, Maggie knows what she's doing or I wouldn't have asked her to take on this task."

"I know, dear, but she's a woman, a young woman, my only child."

"She's much more than a mere woman, my sweet. She's discovered and accomplished more in a short time than Ben's lawyer and my other detective combined did in months."

Maggie watched them as they talked and cuddled as Newl tried to appease his wife's fears. She was certain her mother loved Newl and trusted him. Newl was a tough and sometimes vain man, but he appeared to truly love his son and wife. He also seemed to be the good and decent man Catherine believed him to be, but she wondered if he would do or say "anything necessary" to protect them from harm.

"Did the authorities come to visit and question you after Ben's escape?" Maggie asked.

"Yes, within two days. They even watched the house for about a week, then gave up and left town. I made sure they were gone, because I also was having them watched. I haven't dared to contact him in Sante Fe, and Ben knows it would be foolish to come here or telegraph me. At least he's out of that hellhole and safe. He'll stay put like I told him."

"I hope so, sir, or he'll ruin everything we've worked on for weeks. If he allows himself to be sighted and recaptured, there's no way I could rescue him again; they would guard him day and night. He'd never be permitted to go out on work detail again, and he'd probably spend some time in that Dark Cell and in leg irons. I hope he's smart and obedient."

"Don't worry, Maggie, he knows what's at stake. He also knows he's not too big for me to tan his hide if he disobeys me."

"I want you to tell your detective to catch the train to Prescott and see what he can learn about Frank and that bank owner. I need to know about their finances and holdings prior to and following the robbery. If there were any big changes in them, it could provide clues or evidence against them."

"That's a smart idea, my girl, and I'll put him on it immediately."

"Well, for certain there's no way I can prove the Moores lied in court or persuade them to tell the truth. From what I could tell, Frank Moore detests you with an evil passion. I just don't understand how a difference in politics could cause such hatred."

Newl drew in a slow and deep breath of air and released it swiftly. "I guess I should tell you why he truly despises me and wants me harmed; after all you've done and are doing for us, I owe you the whole truth. This is humiliating for me, Maggie, so please bear with me while I explain."

She listened to him disclose what her mother had told her earlier, but pretended she was hearing it for the first time. She paid close attention to Newl's expression and tone, to find both convincingly sad and sincere.

Newl finished his revelation with, "I never told

Ben what his mother had planned to do to us. He loved her deeply and cherishes her memory, so I couldn't bear to hurt him by telling him she was wicked and selfish, and she had lived a cruel lie with us. A boy doesn't need to hear that his own mother was going to abandon him. It wasn't my fault she duped me and married me instead of waiting for Frank as she promised. And it wasn't my fault she and his unborn baby were killed. It was wrong of him to rekindle their romance and sneak around behind my back. The only reason nobody guessed the dirty truth was because she didn't have any belongings with her that day. After the accident when he came to confront me, I told him I could prove I was in town when she died, but he wouldn't believe me. If I had thought for one instant exposing the past would help clear Ben, I would have revealed everything on the witness stand. I swear to you, Maggie, I never harmed my wife on that or any day."

Afterward, she asked, "How much do you love your son?"

"What do you mean? I love him more than my own life, as I do your mother."

"Do you love him more than your reputation? Would you risk staining it to save his life? You have nothing to be ashamed of and you did nothing wrong years ago, Newl, so we might need to use that story as evidence in court. It provides a credible motive for Frank lying and seeking revenge; it might at least cast doubts on his testimony if we can obtain enough evidence to seek a new trial. Any resulting scandal should die down eventually and your son's injured feelings should heal; but even if they don't, Ben would be free and safe." Maggie observed Newl as he deliberated the pros and cons of that strategy. Her opinion that he was being straightforward with her endeared him to her, as did the difficult choice he made.

"If you're positive it would work in his favor, you can use it."

"That's very generous and wise, Newl. I promise it will remain a secret unless I'm convinced we need to use it in court. If you can't think of anything else to tell me, I should leave now."

"Must you go so soon?" Catherine's tone held disappointment. "We haven't talked about anything except this matter."

"I can't risk being seen returning to the hotel too late, Mother. And I need to get a good night's sleep for my departure tomorrow. Thanks for taking care of Blaze for me. I'm glad you had her taken to the stable under my name. We can't reveal our relationship or some sly detective or lawman might add up the clues and expose us. I'll send word whenever and wherever possible, but don't worry if you don't hear from me soon."

Catherine walked Maggie to the back door, hugged her and kissed her cheek several times. "I love you, Maggie, so please be careful."

"I love you, too, Mother, and I promise I will

be. Good-bye for now."

"Good-bye, my precious daughter. May God protect you."

"May He guide and protect all of us, Mother. Good-bye."

Maggie told herself that all she had to do now was sneak past Newl's establishment and get back to her hotel room without being seen or detained by anybody . . .

Inside the Paradise Club in the room of a pretty "soiled dove," Hawk was making some shocking discoveries of his own . . .

Chapter Nine

Hawk was relieved to learn that Maggie had told him the truth about Newl Carver being gone for the day, and he was glad the owner was absent when he paid Callie a visit tonight. It wouldn't do for Newl to notice that Maggie's helper was a "customer" of his on occasion, nor for Maggie to be given the false impression he was there buying sex. He had waited until Maggie retired to her room before heading to see the lovely blonde with hazel eyes who worked in the Paradise Club and often fed him information about desperadoes with rewards on their heads. He used the facts she supplied to aid his ruse as a bounty hunter and tracker, and to put outlaws behind bars. Long ago, he had convinced his superior to pay Callie a portion of those rewards for her valuable assistance in locating and capturing wanted men, money she was saving to begin a new life with in another town someday. Callie was a good woman who had fallen on hard times following her husband's death. She had taken the only job available, then had gotten trapped in that lifestyle by never making enough money to free herself . . . until Hawk came along.

Despite their long friendship and cooperation, Hawk had never told the "soiled dove" the truth about what he really was, an undercover U.S. marshal. Sometimes he felt bad about deceiving her, but secrecy was necessary to carrying out his assignments and protecting his life. Now that his task was personal, he was especially grateful to Callie: she had been the one to discover Newl's plan to hire somebody to break Ben out of prison and had alerted him.

"There aren't any rewards out on Barber and Jones, yet," Hawk reminded Callie, "but there will be if I can prove they were involved in the Prescott crime. I know the two of them, along with three others, one of them probably Ben, murdered and robbed my family in Texas last December. I've been tracking those sidewinders ever since, but they keep eluding me, except for Toby Muns and Coot Sayers, who're both dead. No matter what or how long it takes, Callie, I'm going to prove it and punish them."

"I'm real sorry about yore family's murders, Hawk," Callie told him. "I know Barber and Jones were supposed to be in on that robbery, but I ain't been able to learn where their seats are apolishing saloon chairs now. You know I hafta be careful who I ask about 'em and how I do it, or they could come looking for me to shut my mouth for keeps. But I learned a lot of other good stuff. I been spying on the old man and his wife since Ben was dragged away. Lordy, was that a happy day for me and the other girls. Until the Law rode up, he was spending half the day and night here, going from room to room to get a taste of all of us, like he was stocking up for lean times. And he shorely got 'em," she added. "I can't believe that bastard escaped. I hope you catch him fast, Hawk, so he won't go sneaking back here to pester us agin. Lordy, I hates 'im. He wants things from the girls no decent man oughta want or even think about. He acts all sweet and proper in public, but I knows 'im, and he ain't good atall."

"What have you learned from your spying, Callie?" Hawk returned the topic to his main interest. "It won't be much longer before my time's up in here with you and I have to leave."

The blonde trailed her fingers over Hawk's lower thigh as she hinted, "You sure you don't wants me to ease yore urges first?"

"Thanks, but this is business and we're rushed." He captured the fingers that almost had reached his groin and smiled. "I'm afraid I can't concentrate but on one thing at a time."

"I could have you con-cen-trating on just me for a while. I'm the best girl here. I really know how to treat a good man like you."

Hawk smiled again and explained in a gentle tone, "You know I can't do that with a friend, Callie, and we are friends. But thanks for caring."

"Oh, well, it was worth a try, you handsome devil. Lemme see . . . Oh, yeah, the old man has hired another detective to work on Ben's case, a woman. How about that? She's beautiful and must be plenty smart. I was sneaking around when the old man got a telegram from her a few weeks back. His wife got it and brought it over and I heard them talking about it. The old man said he was gonna hire her to bust Ben outta prison and to prove he's innocent. I don't know how he thinks she can do what's impossible."

"She did bust him out of prison, Callie, remember?"

"I mean, prove he's innocent, 'cause he ain't; he's as guilty as sin, and I surely know plenty about sin. Anyhow, the old man musta done some tall talking, 'cause Miss Margaret Anne Malone — ain't that a fancy name for a lady from St. Louis — made a bargain with him."

"Miss Malone is a detective from St. Louis?" Hawk could hardly believe what he was hearing.

"Yesiree, but when the Law learns what she's done, she's in big trouble; and the old man and her ma won't be able to helps her outta it."

Hawk's alert heightened. "What do you mean, 'her ma'?"

"This lady detective from St. Louis is Mrs. Catherine's daughter; she's Ben's sister of a sorts, I guess."

"Miss Malone is Ben's stepsister? Her mother is married to Newl?"

"Yesiree, about two years past, if I remember right as rain. The old man has both of them womenfolk blind as bats in sunlight; Ben wasn't with his pa that day; Ben don't hunt no more than I'm a boy. That bastard is wild as a buck, mean as a rattler, and greedy as a sneaky little packrat. Luck's with you tonight, Hawk, 'cause I saw her sneaking a visit with them earlier when I was catching a breath of air on the upstairs porch. If you follow her after she leaves town, she might lead you to Ben and his friends, 'cause she's supposed to try and clear him. Her capture — and Ben's naturally — could earn us big rewards, and you'd have a chance to get your revenge on that malicious gang."

Hawk was shocked at Callie's revelation. "How do you know Maggie Malone is Mrs. Carver's daughter?" he asked. "Are you sure you understood them correctly?"

"The old man hires me to clean their house when the woman who works for them has too much to do by herself, it's too big for his proper wife to tend alone. I saw her daughter's picture and heard her name. And I saw letters to her on the table, heading right for St. Louis. I can read; I ain't good at it, but I ain't dumb neither."

"Nope, you're very smart, Callie." *Smarter than you know.* "Is Maggie close to Ben?" Hawk asked.

"After the old man married Mrs. Catherine and brought her here from St. Louis, her daughter stayed behind for this is her first visit. Far as I know, she's never met Ben, and she would hate him if she did. I know I hate him and I hate his visits to me. So do the other girls. Catch him, Hawk, so he can't ever bother us agin. Please. He's bad to the core —" Callie paused as if suddenly remembering something. "I'll tell you what Mrs. Catherine did a few weeks past — she hid all of her daughter's pictures. I guess so the Law wouldn't see 'em and guess she was helping Ben. That Maggie's in for a big surprise and big trouble when she learns she's been fooled."

"You keep your eyes and ears open, Callie, but don't get caught snooping or eavesdropping, or you'll be in big trouble yourself."

"Don't go worrying about me, Hawk; I'm plenty careful. If you keep paying me good, this time next year, I'll have me enough money to leaves this job. I might even open one of them fancy dress shops or a nice restaurant somewhere far away."

"I have no doubt you'll do fine with whatever you choose to do, and I'll help all I can so you can afford to make the changes you deserve. Well, I best get going; we don't want to arouse anybody's suspicion. Thanks for the help; you always come through with something important for me. Just make notes up here," he advised, tapping her head, "and I'll check with you soon to see what else you've learned. Stay safe, Callie Mae."

"Ride careful, Hawk; these men are the worst of their kind."

He nodded, then left the Paradise Club and went to the hotel. He saw light coming from beneath Maggie's door, so he assumed she was back from her stealthy visit to the Carvers', and he was moving with enough caution not to be overheard returning from his own task.

After he was inside his room, his senses whirled with the mixture of what he had learned tonight and with what had taken place between him and Maggie earlier. He could almost taste the sweet flavor of her. She had felt wonderful in his arms; as if that was where she belonged — and that was definitely where he wanted her to be, forever. He needed her at his side day and night to make his life complete. Until he met Maggie, he had never been tempted to marry; now, he looked forward to that state with eagerness and joy. It was strange, he mused, that they had lived less than two hundred and thirty miles apart for years, both had lost a father, and both had lived on ranches.

Since Maggie didn't know Ben, she couldn't be in love with that snake, just drawn into his dilemma with colorful lies and family loyalty. But that didn't mean she lacked a sweetheart else-where, say in St. Louis. Yet, if that were true, she wouldn't be leaning romantically toward him, and she surely was. Well, at least he now had solved some of the mysteries about her.

Hawk was relieved he had an ace up his sleeve which might prevent her arrest when the truth was exposed, if he could persuade her to let him use it. If he could capture Slim, Pete, and Ben and prove their guilt and recover the stolen money as he'd vowed when his superior agreed to the unusual strategy, she might avoid any charges against her and be safe. To ensure that possibility, he must keep her trusting him and close to him. He couldn't tell her the truth at that point since she might think he was only using her for ulterior motives. She might take off on her own out of a feeling of betrayal or to prevent him from capturing Ben in her misguided belief her stepbrother was innocent. He had to wait until she saw the bitter truth for herself, then confess everything to her and hope for the best.

As he peeled off his shirt, Hawk remembered the telegram he had stuffed into its pocket earlier. He retrieved and opened the envelope and studied the message. Fortunately for him, Maggie was using her real name during this investigation. He was impressed to read that she was one of, if not the best, female detectives anywhere, and was employed by the prestigious Carlton Agency in St. Louis.

He told himself he should be ecstatically happy with the progress he was making on his assignment and especially about finding the perfect woman for himself. Yet, his mind and heart were troubled. He was worried about being able to save Maggie from a grim fate following her exposure and tormented about what that loss would do to him. He was concerned about not winning her after she learned the truth about him. He was tense about the perils looming ahead for them as they confronted their evil foes. He was pained about how the truth about Ben and her futile deed would affect her.

He was also worried about a secret he held

that could repel her — his Indian blood. He recalled what his parents had told him and he had witnessed while growing up about what they had endured when they met and married, a white man to a Cheyenne maiden. The fears and animosity many people held toward any Indian had made it difficult for their relationship to be accepted. His parents and even his grandparents had confronted resulting hostilities, prejudices, and rejections. It had gotten better over the years as his beautiful mother, with her ebony hair and fawn-colored skin, learned to dress, speak, and behave as a "proper white woman." She was often mistaken for a lady of Spanish descent, with the abundance of Mexicans in Texas. As so many of the tribes were conquered and confined to reservations, anti-Indian feeling had diminished a little years ago.

Now, Apaches under Geronimo were raiding and skirmishing again. That great Chiricahua leader could not accept the loss of his freedom and homeland to invaders. Part of the whites and Army officers considered him vile, while others understood his feelings and befriended him to a certain degree. With Geronimo and his band on the move again in Arizona, New Mexico, and Mexico, it refreshed many people's distrust and enmity for all Indians.

Hawk's gut instinct told him Maggie Malone wasn't like that; but at this crucial and unpredictable point in time, he couldn't risk discovering if he was wrong. With that "flaw" added atop his deception, he fretted, were her understanding, forgiveness, and acceptance too much to hope for? Was he dreaming of and seeking the impossible? God and Maheoo have mercy on him if he was being blind and foolish.

He removed the remainder of his clothing and lay down, needing to sleep before their journey to Tombstone tomorrow morning. As a shocking idea came to mind, he bolted upright on the bed. After deliberating it, he grinned, nodded his head, and reclined once more . . .

Following their midday meal and while sipping tea, Maggie wondered where Hawk had gone after excusing himself from the table. They had reached Benson earlier on the Southern & Pacific Railroad and would catch the Southeastern train to Fairbank in less than two hours, then ride their horses the remaining three miles into Tombstone to arrive there before dusk.

As she waited, Maggie's thoughts were in a turmoil. She wanted and needed to believe in Ben, but something within her prevented her from doing so. Maybe, she reasoned, it was a combination of intuition and years of experience that birthed distrust. Her mother had told her that Ben was highly skilled with weapons, had faced down a gunslinger, and wouldn't "harm innocent people." Yet those facts could explain how Ben might have shot the teller and why the man hadn't been slain. Considering Ben's impulsive and daring visit to her hotel room after his escape, maybe he had a hazardous wild streak. And maybe a cocky one made him think he couldn't get caught and wasn't taking any risk of going to prison. Now that she knew the truth about the trouble between Frank and Newl, she was tempted to believe that Frank hadn't tried to frame Ben with false testimony and had instead acted out of sheer and sadistic joy at having an opportunity to punish Newl through his son. Yet there were several dubious points concerning that Prescott crime that baffled her . . .

Please, God, guide me toward the right path.

When Hawk returned, Maggie noticed his broad grin. "What's going on? I can tell something is from that animated look."

Hawk took a seat next to hers and leaned in her direction to whisper, "Hear me out. We're heading after one of the slyest ruffians alive in Pete Barber; and Slim Jones isn't a fool, either. If Barber does any checking on us, we can't allow him to find any holes in our story or he'll try to take us down. If we're going to claim to be a just-married couple who's visiting Tombstone to see if that's where we want to settle, we might need proof."

"I don't understand. What kind of proof?"

I'm going to rope you in, woman, and never release you. "A marriage certificate. I talked with a local preacher and he's waiting to perform the ceremony." He saw her blue eyes widen in astonishment. "Don't worry about getting stuck with me forever," he said with a chuckle, "I have good friends in a judge and a lawyer, so they can remedy the situation later."

"You mean, actually get married?" She watched him nod. "Then have our union dissolved after we finish our work?"

Hawk chuckled. "Unless we decide we make a great team and want to stay partners. I promise you I'll behave as the perfect gentleman my parents tried to rear, and I'll bed down on the floor in our room; we'll have to share one to be convincing. Think about it for a minute before you answer, but that piece of paper could save our lives, and get you that big story."

Marry you and perhaps get the chance to convince you to remain wed if you like the arrangement . . . If I'm exposed by the Law, I can protect you by swearing you didn't know the truth about me and I can vow I tricked you into a wedding with sweet lies and captivating charms . . .

"Well, the preacher's waiting. You want to do it or have me go tell him we changed our minds?"

"Actually, Hawk, it sounds like the perfect precaution."

"Then let's get moving, boss lady, so we won't miss our train." *The faster I get you out of Ben's romantic reach, the better I'll feel. And, God willing, I'll find a way to persuade you to stay married to me. It might also be just the thing I need to keep you out of prison.*

Maggie could hardly believe she was standing in a Benson, Arizona, church about to pledge herself to Hawk Reynolds, all the while hoping their commitment would last "forever."

"Are you of legal age to enter into a holy union without parental consent, Miss Malone?" the pastor asked.

"Yes, sir," Maggie responded in a distinct and polite tone, "I'll be twenty-four next month. My father is deceased; and my mother is rewed and living far away, so she can't be with us today."

"Do you enter into this holy union of your own free will and without legal ties to another man elsewhere?"

"Yes, sir. I want to marry Hawk, here and now."

The genial man smiled at them and said, "Then let's go on with tying this knot snug and proper so you young folks can be on your way as man and wife. My own dear wife and her sister will be your witnesses if you have no objection or others to stand with you."

Maggie returned his genuine smile. "None, sir, and we're grateful to them for their kindness."

Hawk's heart leapt with elation at hearing Maggie's replies and at her confident tone of voice and sincere expression. He listened as the pastor read appropriate scriptures from a well-worn Bible and made stirring remarks after each one.

As the pastor explained the meaning of those passages, Hawk wished his parents and younger brother were alive and present, and wished his grandparents were sitting on a nearby pew to share this special moment.

The reverend shifted his gaze back and forth between them as he read the last verse of a passage, then said, "Now, face each other, join hands, and look into each other's eyes to speak your vows."

Maggie and Hawk followed his instructions; they turned toward each other, clasped hands, and their gazes locked.

Maggie was aware that Hawk's attire — frock coat, pale-blue shirt, dark pants, and recently polished boots — implied he had dressed for and planned this event before they left Tucson this morning, and it wasn't a spur of the moment idea. He looked so handsome and virile and his gaze was so tender and tranquil that he almost stole her breath and clouded her wits. The contact with his hands sent quivers racing over her susceptible body.

"Do you, Hawk Reynolds, take this woman whose hands you hold to be your lawfully wedded wife? Do you promise to love, honor, and cherish her in sickness and in health, in good times and in bad, in riches and in poverty, until death do you part?"

"I do," he responded, and meant it with all of his heart and soul. Afterward, Hawk observed Maggie as she gave her response. She was wearing a medium-blue day dress whose color enhanced that of her eyes and flattered her skin tone, silky flesh his fingers and lips yearned to caress. Before reaching the church, she had loosened her hair from its ribbon confinement to allow the long brown strands to flow down her back in a mass of curls and waves. His breath caught in his throat and his pulse raced with elation as he told himself she would soon belong to him, and forever.

"Do you, Margaret Anne Malone, take this man whose hands you hold to be your lawfully wedded husband? Do you promise to love, honor, obey, and cherish him in sickness and in health, in good times and in bad, in riches and in poverty, until death do you part?"

Maggie knew she was about to seal her marital future and to take that step in willing eagerness, though she had met him only a few weeks ago and still had much to learn about him. "I do." *With all my heart and soul.*

Maggie and Hawk were so caught up in the heady episode that both forgot for a time that it was supposed to be only make-believe. Their hearts throbbed with love and happiness; their minds spun and their spirits soared from excitement and anticipation. Their bodies flamed with desire and reminded them of what normally transpired the night following a wedding ceremony . . .

"The ring," the minister prompted Hawk, who freed his hands to remove one from his coat pocket and place on the older man's palm.

"A circle without an end, as true love and marriage should be. It is a symbol of your sacred vows to each other before God. May your love and commitment remain as precious and shiny as the gold within it. Place the ring on Maggie's finger and say after me: With this ring, I thee wed until death."

Hawk guided the band onto the correct finger, lifted his gaze to hers, and said, "With this ring, I thee wed Maggie Malone until death."

"Hold your groom's hands and say: I accept this ring and thee I wed until death."

Maggie grasped his hands, gazed into his eyes, and repeated those sweet, meaningful, and honest words.

Hawk had told the minister that he didn't want just a hasty and formal exchange of legal words, and the pastor was doing a superb job of making the ceremony special and romantic, which he hoped would have a favorable effect on the woman he loved.

"By the authority given to me by God above and by this Territory, I pronounce you husband and wife. As Matthew, chapter six commands, 'Wherefore they are no more twain, but one flesh. What therefore God hath joined together, let no man put asunder. Let us pray."

The pastor placed their right hands on his Bible and covered them with his wrinkled one as he blessed their marriage. Afterward, he added, "May your union be long and happy. God bless you both. Congratulations, Mr. and Mrs. Hawk Reynolds. Son, you may now kiss your bride."

Hawk and Maggie shared a tender and tentative kiss, all the while craving a longer and more private passionate one.

The two older women also congratulated the couple and kissed their cheeks before Hawk smiled and said, "We hate to rush, sir, but we have a train to catch. I'm much obliged for your help today."

"So am I, sir," Maggie added, "and it was a lovely ceremony. Thank you."

On Thursday afternoon, the fifth of May 1883, Maggie and Hawk boarded the Southeastern Railroad train to head for Tombstone as a legally married couple, both wondering what that unusual night would hold for them . . .

Chapter Ten

As the train left the depot to head southward to their next destination, Maggie gazed out the left window at the lofty Dragoon Mountains which rose from the desert terrain. Her life had changed drastically in a short time span; she had become a criminal and a wife, and a woman in love with the man nearby. She was tempted to confess the entire truth to Hawk, but decided it was too soon. After all, their marriage was only a pretense at that point. She wanted to do everything she could to keep him, and nothing to repel him. She wanted him to get to know her better and move closer to her before she revealed something that could prevent a glorious future together.

She glanced at the gold band on her finger, with pleasure. Their marriage certificate was tucked into his coat pocket, and she wondered if there was more to their union than a cover for safety. *Mrs. Hawk Reynolds . . . Margaret Anne Malone Reynolds . . . Maggie Reynolds . . .* How wonderful those names sounded, and she longed to keep them forever.

She couldn't resist telling her handsome

groom, "The ring is lovely, Hawk, and it was clever of you purchase it. How did you know what size to buy, because it fits perfectly?"

"Remember when I asked to see the one you usually wear this morning?" When she nodded, he explained, "I slid it on my little finger, memorized where it stopped, then tried on rings in Benson until I found one that fit the same in that spot."

She looked at the ring she had moved to her right hand and said, "This amethyst was a gift from my parents on our last Christmas together. It's very special to me."

"That's how I feel about my Bowie knife; it was a gift from my father, and it's saved my life a couple of times."

"It's nice to have special things with us when we're away from home, and meaningful keepsakes of those we love." To keep him talking so she could listen to his voice, she asked, "The pastor did a fine job with the ceremony, don't you think?"

"Yep, he surely did."

"Even though it was make-believe, were you nervous?"

Hawk chuckled. "Yep, a little. What about you?"

"A little," she echoed with a matching grin. "It's amazing what people will do to achieve their goals, isn't it?" she jested.

"Yep; if one's worthy of going after, we should give it our best."

"We think a lot alike; that pleases me."

"Maybe that's because we *are* a lot alike in many ways. You have plenty of good qualities, Maggie Malone, and you're a beautiful woman."

"Thanks, but it's Maggie Reynolds now," she said and laughed.

"That'll take a little getting used to, won't it?"

"Yep," she replied with one of his favorite words, then laughed again.

"What's amazing to me is how easy and comfortable it is being with you, since I haven't spent much time around women unrelated to me."

"I find that hard to believe, Mr. Reynolds; you're far too handsome and charming for women to ignore. Are you only trying to make sure you don't create a jealous demanding wife to irritate you?" she jested.

Hawk chuckled. "Somehow I can't see you in that role."

"As a wife?"

"Nope, as jealous and demanding if you don't get your way."

"Oh, you'd be surprised at how mischievous I can be at times. When Abby and I were away at school, we did all sorts of wicked things."

"Abby is Miss Mercer from Yuma?"

"Yes, she's my best friend. We became roommates and fast friends the minute we met. She's going to be shocked when I write and tell her about this," Maggie hinted as she tapped the gold band on her finger.

"You tell her everything?"

"I have few secrets from her. She's being courted by a local rancher's son and they expect to marry around Christmas time. She'll make Matthew Lawrence a perfect wife, and I'm so happy for them. If we're still partners in December, you can attend their wedding with me."

"Sounds interesting to me, boss lady, so I accept."

They exchanged smiles before they lapsed into silence as each tried to read between the lines of that conversation to assess the other's feelings and intentions.

They passed St. David, a Mormon community which was settled in '77 on fertile farmland in the lovely San Pedro Valley and river between the Dragoon and Whetstone ranges.

"Those mountains over there is where the notorious Cochise and his Apaches had a stronghold," Hawk related. "He chose well; you can see for miles from those peaks, and some of those meandering and tight canyons are like mazes for enemies. He used to give wagon trains and the cavalry hard times; he and his band would attack without warning and vanish into those hills and rocks before a rescue came. You can bet your boots nobody wanted to ride in after him, and was a fool if he did so. The Apaches know every crook and cranny of this territory, and they know how to live off of its harsh terrain and travel it with speed and ease, so soldiers are at a big disadvantage when they go up against them. I heard Geronimo and Chato are kicking up their heels again, but the Army is striving to keep them pinned in the Sierra Madre Mountains in Mexico. I guess I can't blame them for wanting to stay free and trying to hold on to their homeland; they're a proud and defiant people. Of course, that will be difficult with men like Mickey Free riding with the Army. He was captured as a child and reared by a band of Apaches; now he's one of General Crook's best scouts against them. Years ago, I met a *Hechicero* — that's an Apache medicine man. He was one of the wisest, gentlest, and kindest men I've known, and he taught me a lot about his people."

"It's tragic what's happened to the Indians all across the West, Hawk," Maggie said with a sigh, "but peace is difficult between two such different cultures, especially with the Indians being so hostile toward whites. I mean, innocent whites. I can understand them battling soldiers and wicked men, but not settlers or people simply passing across land they claim is theirs, land they stole from others years or even generations ago. Since I don't know any Indians personally, I'm not a good judge of their character and motives."

"I've met and known plenty. Just like whites, there're good and bad among them."

"That sounds logical."

So, how would you feel if you knew your "husband" was half Indian?

They made a brief stop at Contention City, a

town that served as a stamping mill for silver and gold, and was named after one of the richest mines in the area. It already had a colorful history of mining disputes and robberies involving famous and infamous gunfighters.

To pass time, Hawk told Maggie about one stage robbery where $26,000 in bullion was saved by a Wells Fargo agent. The attempted theft in '81 was rumored to be plotted by Doc Holliday who had been arrested, released on bond paid by Wyatt Earp, and had his case dismissed for lack of sufficient evidence.

Recognizing two of those names from newspaper articles and rumors, she queried, "Have you ever met the Earp brothers and Doc Holliday?"

"Yep," Hawk disclosed, "while they were big in Tombstone." Hawk related the colorful tale about the gunfight on Fremont Street near the O.K. Corral between them and the Clanton gang two years ago. "To a lot of folks, it's still unclear who was in the right and who was in the wrong. Those two sides had been at each other's throats for a long time, so trouble was bound to erupt. There was a big funeral for the Clantons afterward. The streets were packed with people; and those boys were laid out in black caskets with silver trim and little windows over their faces. They were hauled to Boot Hill in a fancy hearse and with a brass band playing music; I read Ritter and Ream Undertakers paid eight thousand dollars for that hearse. Wyatt and Doc were jailed for a while; Morgan and Virgil were laid up with wounds. After a thirty-day trial, Wyatt and Doc were acquitted. The judge ruled they were only doing their duties as peace-officers, trying to disarm and arrest troublemakers who resisted and attacked them. Out here, it's common on every day for at least one man to lay down forever with his boots."

It was evident to Maggie that this portion of the territory was hard land which bred hard men, many with a total disregard for human life. Their sacrifices and demands were countless. The perils confronting them almost daily were numerous. Greed was frequently a driving force among dreamy-eyed men who came there to seek or to steal fortunes. The strong and sly often preyed on the weak in body or will. Lives were taken without emotion, and sometimes without exposure and punishment. She had seen and read about men who could "throw lead quick and straight." She was certain her husband fell into that last category.

"They hope to extend the tracks to Bisbee within the next few years," Hawk said. "Hauling copper, silver, gold, and zinc ores to Fairbank is long and hard work. Bisbee's situated in two canyons in the Mule Mountains south of Tombstone. They have so many breweries, one area is named Brewery Gulch; that section is wild and rough. I hope we don't have to go there, because it's no place for a lady like you."

"From the way it sounds, I hope so, too. But it would be our bad luck that's where Barber and

Jones will lead us."

As they neared Fairbank, Maggie learned it was a vital location for mail, freight, and ore shipments. A supply point for other towns, ranches, settlements and mining camps, Fairbank was a busy and important place. Hawk told her how the surrounding area was favored by outlaws for robbing trains on deserted spans of track and stages along secluded stretches of dirt road, with ample concealment nearby for surprise attacks and ridges to gallop over for rapid and easy escapes: the kind of terrain villains such as Barber and Jones liked and frequented with daring raids.

At the depot, they claimed their horses and possessions. After Blaze and Diablo were saddled and loaded, the couple mounted and got under way.

En route to town three miles east of the river, Hawk told her how legendary prospector Ed Schieffelin was warned that all he would find in this "Apache-infested" area was his own tombstone; after he discovered silver and great wealth, he aptly and humorously named the settlement for that warning.

"It sounds as if you know everything and have been everywhere out here, Hawk, so I'm fortunate to have you as a partner."

"The same can be said about you, boss lady. Now, hopefully, we'll find what we're looking for ahead of us." Hawk doubted that she realized his words had dual meanings. He wondered how he would sleep in the same room with her without making romantic overtures, as his desire for her was enormous and increasing by the hour.

As Maggie's dreamy thoughts traveled that same path, she sighted Tombstone, perched on a high desert plateau between distant mountain ranges. The large town was sprawled over a lengthy distance, with mines studding the near harsh landscape in several directions.

"So this is the infamous Tombstone," she murmured.

"Yep. She has over one hundred and ten saloons open around the clock to empty reckless prospectors' pockets of weeks or months of work. While you settle in at the hotel, I'll take a quick look around to see if I spot our targets. You can visit the newspaper office in the morning while I scout the rest if I don't find them tonight."

"Don't forget why you came here."

"What do you mean?"

Maggie laughed and prompted, "The missing Yuma girl and her gambler sweetheart, your original job."

Except for family and a few close friends, he had never been one for small talk, but Maggie had a way of relaxing him and drawing him out. He enjoyed their conversations, and enjoyed making her smile and laugh. Hawk chuckled and said, "I had forgotten about them for a minute. I guess you and our adventure distracted me. Thanks for the reminder."

"Since you added me to that short list, I'll take it as a compliment," she said with a saucy smile.

"It was meant as one, Mrs. Reynolds. I hope you don't mind if I practice using that name for times I must introduce you."

"Of course not; do it as often as possible to avoid a future slip."

They walked their horses into the windswept town. On the first of numerous saloons, Maggie saw *Whiskey, 12¢ a shot* painted on its window. They continued down Fremont Street as Hawk pointed out sites involved in the already famous Earp/Clanton showdown: Fly's Photography Gallery, the Harwood house, Papago Cash Store, and entrance to the O.K. Corral. She saw Bauer's Union Market, pool halls, shops, homes, and businesses in a mixture of sizes and heights and constructed of adobe bricks or wood. In fact, she noticed that despite the lack of trees in that area, more places were built of wood than of adobe. With a population of over ten thousand plus visitors, the streets were crowded with people. The air was dry and dusty; the sky, clear and blue. Horses' reins were secured to countless hitching posts, and wagons sat here and there either being loaded or unloaded of various goods. She saw miners and prospectors who had come to town to purchase supplies and sometimes to drink, play cards, or seek out carnal delights. Despite the approaching dusk, carpenters still labored on new structures, the pounding of their hammers and slicings of their saws giving the raucous music stiff competition for volume.

Hawk guided them down Fifth Street so he

could point out the *Epitaph*'s office she would visit tomorrow.

On Allen Street, Maggie didn't have to be told what some locations were: cribs and bordellos where prostitutes were licensed at seven dollars a month to ply their trade. She watched a group of cowboys enter the infamous Bird Cage as they elbowed each other and joked in anticipation of watching the bare-breasted Fatima belly dance before assauging their carnal needs with a "soiled dove" behind one of twelve curtained-off balcony boxes referred to as "cages". Every few buildings was another dancehall, saloon, gambling hall, or a combination of those.

But, Maggie observed, there were plenty of "respectable" businesses and shops, even several ice cream parlors. There were churches, a school, two firehouses, Victorian courthouse, city hall, hotels, boardinghouses, and theaters. It was evident that Tombstone was a booming town.

Hawk told her that one street over on Toughnut was one of Ed Schieffelin's mines, the Goodenough which ran beneath the town itself.

Maggie glanced in that direction. "One would think that tunneling under a well-established town would be hazardous. Don't they worry about hungry cave-ins that might gobble up businesses or homes?"

"Nope, because there's too much silver down there and being dug out for folks to think clearly about such possibilities."

"If it ever rained here enough to flood those

tunnels and weaken them, I'm sure that would cause a panic and fast property sales."

"Maybe, but some folks go blind where greed is concerned."

"Ah, yes, that dark side of human nature. I suppose we all have at least a tiny one, don't you think?"

As Hawk fastened his gaze on hers, he grinned and said, "I can't imagine a fine lady like you having one. Do you?"

"Oh, I admit I've done things I shouldn't have. Haven't you?"

"I suppose so. Here we are, Mrs. Reynolds. Does this suit you?"

Maggie eyed the lovely Victorian-style hotel and said, "Excellent choice, my dear husband."

"Only the best for you, my refined wife."

"Don't forget I'm covering our expenses. I'll slip you the money so you can pay the clerk and retain that masculine pride."

"Well, you don't have to worry about that where I'm concerned," he told her as he assisted her from her saddle. "I'll get you to our room, then I'll tend our horses. Diablo, keep an eye on Blaze for Maggie."

She watched the black mustang's head move up and down as if he understood his master's command. She followed Hawk into the lobby where he set down their bags to register. She had left her trunk in Tucson where the Paradise Club bartender would have it taken to her mother's house for safekeeping. She had packed what she

252

thought she would need for the impending portion of her journey inside her saddlebags and two brocade satchels with corded handles for looping over her horn. If Hawk had noticed the missing item, he hadn't mentioned it. If he did, she would tell a partial truth by saying it was too bulky for horseback travel.

Inside their room, Hawk placed the bags on the bed for unpacking. "You rest and tend your chores while I look around," he told Maggie. "I'll return for supper in about an hour."

"That suits me fine. See you later."

Hawk left to head to the Silver Dollar Saloon where Ella Mae, another paid informer, worked; he needed to find out if she had seen his two targets in town.

Maggie removed her garments and shook them to remove as many wrinkles as possible. Some she hung on a peg and others she put in drawers of a dresser. She tucked her pistol and holster beneath one stack, as hers and Hawk's rifles were propped against the wall in a corner. She laid his saddlebags atop the dresser after deciding he would rather unpack them, resisting the urge to peek inside to check out his possessions.

After that task was finished, she used a ceramic basin and water from a matching pitcher to freshen up. After brushing her hair, she sat on a comfortable chair to relax while awaiting Hawk's return. Her gaze settled on the double bed nearby. Her dreamy mind imagined them lying there together, hugging, kissing, and making love. She had been kissed before, but never as Hawk had done to her in Tucson. She tingled just recalling that romantic episode.

Her gaze shifted to the gold band she was wearing. She grasped it between her right thumb and forefinger and stroked it. Married . . . The wife of a man who stirred her heart and soul and inflamed her body . . .

Well, Abby, I wonder what you'd say and think if you knew about this shocking behavior. Was I impulsive? Am I deluding myself about keeping him? Whatever shall I do when he discovers the dark truth about me? Will he try to help me extricate myself from trouble, or will he reject me? Would he — a law-abiding man and bounty hunter — be so hurt and angry he would turn me in to the authorities?

Whatever possessed me to break the law? What if I can't prove Ben's innocence? What if he's guilty and refuses to surrender to the authorities as he and Newl promised? Could I look the other way and ignore my conscience in order to keep Hawk, or will I be compelled to right that foolish wrong? Even if I keep that prison break secret, Hawk will soon discover I lied about being a journalist and he'll learn I am Ben's stepsister. He'll add up the clues correctly and surmise what I've done. And what then?

"Are you sure you're all right down there?" Maggie asked Hawk after he climbed inside the bedroll he had spread out minutes earlier. He had given her enough time to change clothes and get under the covers before he entered the room

254

to settle down for their first night together.

"Don't worry about me, Maggie. This floor isn't any harder than most ground I sleep on when I camp out on the trail."

Maggie propped up on her elbow and looked at him, though he was barely visible in the light of a half moon filtering through the window. "To be fair, partner, we should take turns using the bed."

Hawk squinted his eyes to peer into the shadows to obtain only a glimpse of her. "No need. I'm used to such conditions, but you aren't, so you wouldn't get any rest. Honestly, I'm fine," *except for this ravenous hunger for you.*

"What did you learn this evening? Anything useful?"

He surmised she was seeking a distraction from the unfamiliar and arousing circumstances, so he complied by saying, "Yep, they're both here. Any time somebody of their reputation comes to a town, news spreads as fast as a wildfire because folks suspect trouble isn't riding far behind them. I didn't see them, but I'll locate them tomorrow. If I can catch them apart, maybe I can fool Slim Jones into careless talk. He isn't as smart as Pete Barber, but he's a wary sidewinder, so I'll have to be cunning."

"You will be careful?"

"Always. You should be safe taking care of your task at the *Epitaph*. This town has plenty of badges strolling the streets, and you've proven you can defend yourself in a bind. Besides, all you'd have to do is scream and help would be there in a hurry. Just stay off of side streets and in the open."

"I'll follow your good advice. Did you locate that missing girl and the gambler?"

"Nope, but I'll settle that matter tomorrow." *I have to deal with it one way or another, or it'll keep coming up between us. I have to decide if I'm going to lie again or tell you it was only a ruse to be with you — but withhold the reason I needed to be at your side.*

Maggie thought Hawk's tone sounded a little odd during his last sentence. Maybe he was worried he would find the girl in dire straits and have to leave his "wife" alone in order to honor his prior commitment to her parents by escorting the impetuous female back to Yuma. Or perhaps he was unsettled by the unusual situation. After all, they were partly undressed and sharing a cozy bedroom. Too, they were married, if in name only, and were highly attracted to each other. Since it was normal for men to have sexual urges, surely his were aroused. Perhaps, he, too, was uncertain as to how he should behave under those provocative circumstances.

"Good night, Hawk," she said to still her speculations. "We'll continue our conversation in the morning."

"Good night, Maggie, sleep well." *Me, too, if I can.*

Maggie could hardly believe Hawk had risen,

256

dressed, put away his bedroll, and departed without awakening her, since she normally was a light sleeper. She attributed part of her restless night to ceaseless music and rowdy merriment, but most of it was due to agonizing thoughts about her awful dilemma coupled with severe hunger pangs for Hawk. She'd forced herself to breathe evenly and lie still to prevent disturbing his slumber until she finally fell asleep near dawn from sheer exhaustion.

What if, her weary mind shouted, Hawk decided he made a terrible mistake in coming to work for her and especially for marrying her so he sneaked off the first moment he could? No, her heart argued, he would never do anything like that. *Get your lazy fanny out of bed and get dressed! You have work to do if you want to extricate yourself.*

The surprise she received moments later was the last thing she had expected to happen on that or any day . . .

Chapter Eleven

As Maggie's bare feet touched the thick rug and she stood beside the rumpled bed, she halted her movements and came to alert as the door was unlocked and pushed open. She watched Hawk bend over and retrieve something before entering the room and closing the door with his right boot.

"What's that?" she asked as she nodded toward the tray in a grinning Hawk's hands. Although her body was partially visible through the material that traveled from throat to ankle and elbows, she made no attempt to grab a matching robe to cover a white cotton gown trimmed with embroidered sprays of blue and pink flowers and green stems and leaves.

Hawk forced himself not to stare at the vision of beauty before him, though it was difficult to master that temptation. Being this close to her without touching her was harder than he had imagined it would be, but he must not press her to yield to him after promising to behave as a gentleman. He wanted and needed more than physical release; he yearned for a future with her, a home, a family, and her love. He wanted to do nice things for Maggie, show he cared deeply about her. He had to prove she was special in order to win her and keep her.

"Your breakfast, boss lady: bacon fried crispy, eggs scrambled well, biscuits with little butter and no jelly, and coffee with two sugars," he replied as he placed the tray on a round table with a chair beside it. "I hoped you were awake by now. I figured after not eating much at supper and enduring a restless night, you'd be hungry and moving slow this morning."

"Thanks," *and do you notice everything I say and do?* She was pleased and flattered he remembered her food preferences. To avoid seeming a tease, she donned her robe and buttoned it before she went to the washstand. As she washed and dried her face and hands, she said, "Please forgive my appearance, but I was just dragging myself from the bed."

"You look lovely, Maggie; you always do," he told her as she brushed her hair while eyeing him in a mirror hanging over the stand.

"Thanks, but you're biased since you're my husband and partner," she replied in a jesting tone, which she had to fake to mask how he was affecting her with his engulfing golden brown gaze and husky voice. She watched him grin and nod agreement.

"As you learned last night, Tombstone's noisy around the clock, but quietest right before and a few hours after sunrise. This way, you can eat before you dress for your visit to the *Epitaph.*

Anything else you need?"

Probably what I can't have: release from my self-made reckless plight, freedom from prison, and you as my husband forever. I want and need your love, respect, and acceptance; but I've probably spoiled any chance of earning or keeping them. "Thank you, Hawk; you're very kind and thoughtful. But your job doesn't extend to acting as my servant."

Although her last sentence was said in a playful tone, Hawk had seen a sad look dull her eyes only moments before it and wondered what she'd been thinking. "I kinda like making the boss lady beholden to me. I never can tell when I might need rescuing from trouble and she's mighty skilled with those hands and feet and with weapons."

"So," she quipped in return, "you had an ulterior motive, did you? Just teasing. So, where's your food?" she asked after lifting a thick cloth to find only one filled plate.

"I ate long ago; I'm used to rising early. I've already checked on Diablo and Blaze down at Mr. Tuttle's corral; it's on Fremont between Second and Third streets, in case you need her for a swift getaway."

"An escape from what?" she asked as she sat down and sipped coffee. *Not from you, never from you, my love.*

"Barber and Jones if you rile them too much and too fast. We have to move slow and easy with them, agreed?"

"Agreed. I'll let you take the lead where they're concerned."

"Good. You eat while your food's hot. I'll get busy elsewhere while you dress and nose around at the newspaper. I'll meet you back here at noon."

Maggie suppressed a frown of disappointment after she left the *Tombstone Epitaph* office on Fifth Street because the editor hadn't allowed himself to be charmed into making any useful disclosures. Perhaps, she reasoned, since the two men she asked about were in town, he was afraid to discuss them with a stranger. Perhaps the *Epitaph* editor feared similar retribution from Barber and Jones if they felt challenged by his loose tongue.

To get a closer look at the town, Maggie turned left onto Fremont Street and pretended to be taking a stroll and doing window shopping. She passed the O.K. Corral entrance beside Papago Cash Store and Bauer Union Market and paused on the boarded walkway before Fly's Photograph Gallery. To its rear, she had noticed the man's photography studio. Since villains and gunslingers were known for their love of having their pictures taken, perhaps she could glean helpful clues from the owner or from his display of works.

Maggie entered the gallery and sighted two men near its rear. One, a short and lean fellow in a suit, spoke to a well-dressed gentleman with him before heading in her direction while the other man left by the back door.

"May I help you, ma'am?"

"Yes, I want to see samples of Mr. Fly's work and, if I like them, I want to speak to him about taking a photograph of me and my husband while we're in town for a visit."

"I'm Mr. Fly, and I'm certain you'll be pleased with my work. My assistant is out sick today, so his absence is keeping me busy and traipsing between my two businesses. Are you in a hurry?"

"No, sir," she responded in an exaggerated southern drawl. She was glad she had kept one fashionable day dress and leather shoes with her, though she'd left all of her hats, two parasols, and crinolines in Tucson.

"Excellent. If you'll look around for a while and give me time to finish in the studio with my other customer, I can show you my work, discuss my price, and make the appointment. I shall return in about twenty minutes, thirty at the most. Is that agreeable?"

As he was speaking, Maggie heard the bell over the front door jingle behind her. The photographer smiled at her after she nodded, then went to speak with the other person whose name brought her to alert and caught her immediate interest. She heard Mr. Fly give the stranger the same spiel as she had received, and the newcomer also agreed to wait.

Well, Maggie, you prayed for help and an opportunity was just laid in your lap, so take advantage of it. When you made your promise to Hawk earlier, you didn't foresee this fortuitous event, so he'll have to understand and accept your apology for disobeying him. You're a professional, so put on your best front and charm this snake in the grass into complying with your needs.

After Fly left by the back door to work in his studio, Maggie turned to the redheaded customer and asked, "Did I hear you say your name is Pete Barber?" She watched his narrowed dark gaze walk over her with cocky boldness. There was a coldness in his brown eyes that almost made her flinch, but she controlled that reaction and kept her expression pleasant. He was a good eight inches taller than her five-feet-six-inch height, so she had to look up at him. His body appeared to be muscular and strong and his posture and movements implied he was ever ready to confront dangers! A lack of smile lines near the eyes and mouth told her he probably found them often and dealt with them rapidly and lethally. The man didn't respond until after he completed his slow and thorough scrutiny of her.

"Yep. Who's asking and why?"

She saw him glance in all directions, as if suspecting a trap by a rival, the fingers of his right hand grazing the butt of his pistol and his body rigid with alert. *Relax and dupe him fast, Maggie girl.* "Oh, my goodness! It's so exciting and such a great honor to meet a real western legend that I can hardly think straight or speak correctly. Since my arrival in the Wild West months ago, I've heard and read so much about you, Mr. Barber. My name is Margaret Anne Reynolds and I'm a newspaper journalist from Virginia."

Maggie hoped Hawk was right about not being well known as a bounty hunter, as too many people knew his name for them to go by Maggie and Hawk Malone; the name Reynolds shouldn't seize Barber's attention, and it didn't appear to. "I was sent out West to gather detailed information and write fascinating stories about famous men and their exploits. Everywhere I've traveled so far in Arizona and New Mexico, I've heard your name mentioned as one of the fastest and smartest gunslingers. Yet I find it amazing that no one has written dime novels or in-depth stories about you. I would be honored and thrilled if you would agree to be interviewed by me for that purpose. And if you'll allow Mr. Fly to take a photograph of us together to print with the article, I would be the envy of every journalist. Would you be agreeable to that, sir?"

"You wanna write a story about me for your newspaper?"

"That's correct, if you don't mind, of course. You see, I never like to write stories about unwilling subjects or to do them from gossip I've heard. If the person involved doesn't participate, the story is boring and is usually inaccurate or biased in one direction or another."

"I've already had lots of stuff printed about me, so I'm plenty famous."

"But it was all written as news, sir, not as your life story. I want to write about who you are as a person; what you've done; how you feel before, during, and after a showdown with a challenger;

how you stay out of trouble with the authorities; where you've been and who you've met. You have a huge reputation, Mr. Barber; I want to know how you got it and keep it."

Barber's tone was flat and cold as he explained, "I got it by being good with my guns and being faster than anybody who's been fool enough to draw against me. I don't take to nobody calling me out or talking against me. I ain't never shot no man who didn't need killing for one reason or another. If I hafta empty my holster, he's gonna be sleeping under dirt before the sun goes down. If a man needs killing, it don't trouble me none to oblige him. I'd say I probably put thirty or more to sleep permanently. There ain't no man out here I can't outdraw."

"How do you earn a living, Mr. Barber?"

"I do odd jobs here and there. I don't like to tie myself down to one place for long. I like to stay on the move."

"Do those 'odd jobs' involve the use of your weapons?"

"Whada you mean?"

Maggie noted that the man's expression, gaze, and tone stayed the same, as if he held tight control over his reactions to avoid exposing his feelings or next move. "Like riding guard for stages, silver shipments, or freighters. Or acting as a troubleshooter for people with problems, such as with outlaws or rustlers. Scouting or fighting for the Army. Bounty hunting."

"I ain't never turned no man in to the Law;

them bounty hunters are the worst of their kind. I kill one every chance I get if he crosses me."

"Have you ever broken the law and not gotten caught?"

"That's a mighty nosy and dangerous question to be asking."

Despite his choice of words, Maggie noted there was still no change of expression or voice. "I wouldn't print anything you told me in private and didn't want the public to know. But being clever enough to outsmart the authorities makes for interesting reading and colorful exploits."

"Let's just say I'm a clever man, but that's not for writing in your newspaper. Who else you done stories about?"

Thank you for asking that evocative question. After naming two famous lawmen and one notorious outlaw, Maggie alleged, "I came to Tombstone to do preliminary research on Wyatt Earp, Doc Holliday, and the Clantons. I'm sure you've heard about their showdown here in '81. I wanted to read the local newspaper's articles, interview witnesses to that event, and buy photographs of the deceased and their grand funeral from Mr. Fly before I try to locate Mr. Earp and Holliday for interviews." Barber interrupted her before she could reach her needed destination, but she relaxed when his snide remarks put her back on the right trail.

"Ain't nothing special about Earp and Holliday. One's a coward and the other's a weakling. After his brothers were shot up, Earp turned tail

266

and ran for cover, and Doc weren't far behind him, coughing all the way."

"After what I was told by the *Epitaph* editor earlier, you could be right. Actually, I wanted to do a different story next, but I ran into a box canyon as you westerners call it. I was in Yuma recently when a convict escaped from the Territorial Prison, an incredible feat according to the superintendent. I was told he robbed a bank in Prescott and shot the teller, but he claimed he was innocent at his trial. I went to Prescott to study the matter to see if it would make a good story, but nobody there wanted to discuss the episode. Tell me, have you ever met Ben Carver? Is he a famous gunslinger or outlaw? Would he be a worthy story?" Maggie realized she had elicited a reaction from him; she didn't think it was possible, but his expression hardened and his gaze chilled even more. The voice which replied to her queries was edged with ice, his words, clipped and forced out between near clenched teeth.

"Yep, I heard of 'im, met 'im, too. If'n I get 'im in my gunsights, he's a dead man. I could take him down with my eyes closed."

"I take it there's bad blood between you two, a past quarrel?"

"The bastard tol' the Law me and Slim was with him on that robbery."

"The one in Prescott?"

"Yep, and he's a damned liar. Me and Slim weren't nowhere near Prescott in March. He's damned lucky the Law didn't believe him and come after us. If they hadda, I'd busted 'im outta jail and shot the bastard."

"That's strange, Mr. Barber, because I didn't read anything about you and your friend in the Prescott newspaper articles and no one there mentioned your names to me as alleged accomplices."

"Like I tol' you, nobody talks against Pete Barber and lives to brag on it. He better hope the Law throws his ass back in prison afore I come across him or he's full of my lead. I gotta go; hanging around don't sit well with me. If'n I was you, I'd forgit about Ben Carver; he's trouble."

"You mean he's dangerous? If I do a story about him, he might come after me while he's on the loose; is that what you mean?"

"Nope, the dead kind of trouble, one way or another."

"Thank you for the warning, sir, and I'll surely drop that story. If you change your mind about letting me interview you, I'm staying at the Carson Hotel."

"Forgit about me, too; I don't like people reading about me."

"As you wish, Mr. Barber, but I'm glad I got a chance to meet you and speak with you." She watched his frigid gaze travel her entire length before he left the gallery and headed down the street. Maggie took a deep breath and prayed she hadn't gone too far with the villainous creature.

When Fly returned, she told him the other customer had left. She repeated her fabricated story to the photographer, in case Barber returned later to question the man about her. Fly appeared delighted that she wanted to purchase some of his pictures to accompany her story on the Earps and other famous outlaws. Without delay, he retrieved a batch and let her select the ones she wanted and gave her a fair price. After paying him, Maggie discussed the previously mentioned photograph of her and her husband, and an appointment was made for the following afternoon for a sitting and for an interview about the showdown years ago involving his business.

Maggie strolled down the street, clutching the pictures in one hand to make them visible to any spying eyes. She entered a mercantile store a block away and pretended to shop while keeping near the front window. Just as she suspected, Pete Barber returned to the gallery, no doubt to check out her claim for being there earlier. She smiled and complimented herself for taking the necessary precautions to dupe him.

She walked to the telegraph office and sent three messages. One went to Yuma to let Abby know she was safe and in Tombstone; she sent it from *"Maggie Reynolds"* at the Carson Hotel. She assumed Abby would think she was using a cover name, but Abby needed to know where to reach her in case an emergency resulted from their misdeed.

The second telegram went to Newl, via his

loyal bartender, telling Newl to "check property safety. Found news items. Threat to property. Hold fast to original terms." She knew her stepfather would use her code list to discover her meanings: contact had been made with her targets, they were a threat to Ben and to warn him without exposing his location, and for Ben to stay rooted where he was and ready to surrender if need be.

The third went to her boss and friend in St. Louis to tell him due to "family problems. Need another month here. Will send return date later." She had asked for a month off to spend time with her mother, but hadn't known she would be working for Newl. Her time had elapsed, but she couldn't leave now. She had promised Newl and Ben two months at the most, and she would hold them to their bargain with her. She also wanted to remain with Hawk and to work things out with him the moment that opportunity arose.

She returned to the hotel minutes before noon and sat down in its restaurant area to await her beloved's arrival, sipping coffee as she did so.

Forty-five minutes later, Maggie assumed something important had delayed Hawk, so she ordered her meal and ate without him. Afterward, she went to their room and gave her dilemma careful study. Her eyes soon became heavy and she drifted off to sleep.

She awoke at four o'clock, took a bath down

the hall, and donned a casual skirt and blouse. She pulled a novel from her drawer and read for a while, her concentration strained by her husband's continued absence.

At seven o'clock, Hawk still hadn't returned, and Maggie was worried about him. What if something terrible had happened to him in this rough town? What if he'd had an accident and the local doctor and sheriff didn't know who he was and to contact her? What if Pete Barber and Slim Jones had connected them, and had ambushed him as a warning to her to stay out of their business? Should she go to the sheriff and report him missing? Should she search for him?

Stop fretting, Maggie; he's a grown man, and he can take care of himself. Maybe he found that missing girl and he's with her, getting her settled somewhere until he can send or take her home.

At seven-thirty, Maggie closed the drapes and lit a lamp beside the bed. The sun had set and it was almost dark outside beneath a waning moon that would be invisible in a few days.

She came to alert when she heard somebody at the door. She lifted her pistol and aimed it in that direction as it opened. After Hawk entered and closed and locked the door, she put aside her weapon and hurried to him. She hugged him as she asked, "What have you been doing all day? I've been so worried about you."

Hawk's arms banded her body and held her

close with her cheek nestled against his chest. He was elated when she remained there with her arms looped around his waist. "I'm sorry I frightened you, Maggie, but there was no way to send you a message." He was touched by her show of concern and affection, and aroused by their contact. It quietened the fury raging through him at being so close to his family's killers and having to restrain himself from a hasty revenge. "I've been shadowing Barber and Jones since I left you this morning. After they separated, I followed Jones to a meeting with two other men who are camped about five miles outside of town, which I found mighty suspicious. It looked as if he was hiring them, so they must be planning a job nearby or picking up men to ride elsewhere to pull one."

Maggie leaned her head back and looked up at him. "If that's true, maybe we can catch them red-handed; that would give us the evidence the Law needs for finally convicting and punishing them. It would also provide a justifiable reason for arresting them so they can be interrogated about the Prescott robbery and a connection to Ben Carver."

He noticed her choice of words and knew why she selected them: she was a detective, licensed by the authorities to solve crimes and capture criminals. He also had seen the weapon in her hand upon his entry, the pistol she had put aside in haste to almost run into his arms. "I hope so."

"How did you trail him on such barren terrain

without being seen?"

"I have my tricks, and I'll teach them to you sometime. Mostly I used the hills for concealment and kept up with him by his dust trail. Remember I told you about the Apache medicine man who taught me a lot of things; one of them was how to stay and move unseen on this terrain."

Maggie laid her face against his chest once more, relieved he was safe. "So you think they're planning a robbery?"

"Yep. It's my guess they'll do it close to Tombstone because those men had four extra horses with them, probably stolen from some rancher. I think I told you how Barber and Jones use others to mask their identities; for certain that big pinto of his would be remembered. I also saw Jones pull black hoods from his saddlebag and show the others, so I figure Barber doesn't want his red hair seen again since it's a dead giveaway. Right now, they're both settled in for a card game in a saloon on Allen Street. The way they're drinking, whatever they're planning won't take place tonight." *If they do leave soon, Ella Mae will alert me pronto.* "I don't know what Barber's been up to in town alone. After he went into Fly's gallery this morning, I stayed on Jones's tail."

"I know he was there; so was I. It was after my visit to the *Epitaph,* where I learned nothing of use to us. I went to Fly's to see if he had any photographs of interest, perhaps a group picture of Barber with his old gang; or maybe one of Ben Carver taken on the same day. I need to know if they were friends and riding together. I pretended to be checking out the quality of his work and setting up an appointment for a photograph of the newlyweds. We're scheduled for a sitting tomorrow. If you don't mind," she added. "I thought it would aid our cover and give me an excuse to go there."

"I'm glad I hooked up with you, boss lady; you're a clever and brave woman. A pretty one, too." *A photograph of us would be mighty nice for hanging in our home later.*

She smiled and said, "Thanks, so are you, partner."

To conceal her potent effect on him, he asked, "So what happened?"

Maggie deduced that reality from his adoring gaze and how he refused to release her from his stimulating embrace. Since she wasn't certain if she should bring their matching feelings into the open just yet, she stalled having to deal with them by telling him how Barber had come into Fly's gallery to have his picture taken at the very same time she was there.

"So you got a good look at him?"

"Yes, and more. We talked for a while. Please don't be angry with me, but the opportunity was tossed in my lap and I took advantage of it."

That news made him uneasy, but Hawk chuckled and teased, "I can't imagine Maggie Malone doing otherwise. What did you think of him?"

Hawk's hands drifted to the sides of her waist as hers moved up his chest and toyed with the collar of his dark shirt. Taking a cowardly path, her gaze settled on his bandanna to prevent fusing it with his where he could read her heightened emotions. "Cold-blooded, arrogant, nerves of iron, on constant alert, and tries to intimidate others."

"You've got him pegged right. Did he make eyes at you?"

Maggie laughed and replied, "Not in the least, though he did seem to be inspecting me to be certain I wasn't a threat to him."

Hawk noted how she kept her gaze averted from his and hoped he guessed the reason why with accuracy. "Good; that means I won't have to call him out for going after my wife. So, what did you two talk about?"

As she related the conversation, Maggie lifted her eyes and watched Hawk's expression alter from pleasant interest to worry and surprise.

Hawk's fingers moved to her shoulders, and his thumbs under her chin kept her from lowering her head, which kept their gazes fused. "He's dangerous and unpredictable, woman, why did you risk angering him?"

"I had no choice, Hawk. As I said, the opportunity presented itself and I had to take advantage of it. How else could I check out his reaction to hearing Ben's name — and he did react. But as a man who had been duped and betrayed, not one who had been implicated by an acquaintance. As I told you, I used a heavy southern drawl and acted every bit the part of a southern belle who was thrilled to meet a legendary gunslinger. I'm sure I fooled him."

"If that's true, why did he return later to question Fly about you?"

"He could have been returning for his photograph, but I'm sure he asked about me. That's only natural for a man in his position. I'm also sure he was tempted by my idea; he just didn't want to agree too quickly. You've met enough men like him to know how vain they are. I told you I covered myself by talking to Fly about Wyatt Earp and others and by purchasing those pictures of the Clanton funeral. After telling Barber I intended to write about them, he should be duped by my precautions. Besides, I didn't mention Ben Carver before Barber gave me that opening." Maggie felt almost weak from the nearness of him so she couldn't help herself from saying, "I had to act fast so I can get this intrusive matter settled as soon as possible."

"Intrusive". . . . . *On what? Draw it out of her before you go loco.* "You anxious to get back on your own again and be rid of me?" he jested to evoke an explanation; whatever it might be, he had to know and know now.

"Of course not. I enjoy being with you and I care deeply about you."

"I feel the same about you, Maggie. I don't want you getting hurt."

"I won't, because I have a talented husband to protect me."

"So you're not trying to hurry just to be rid of me and that condition."

"No, Hawk. In fact, I like our . . . arrangement. I like you, too."

He cupped her face between his hands. "I more than like you, Maggie Reynolds; you're so tempting, it's hard to be around you without taking you in my arms and kissing you every chance I get."

Maggie realized a moment of truth had presented itself and she willingly faced it headlong. "What's stopping you from doing so, Hawk?"

Chapter Twelve

Hawk gazed deeply into her rich blue eyes before he responded in a voice made husky with emotion, "I don't want you getting hurt by me."

"The only way you could harm me is if you don't feel the way I do. I want to be closer to you, Hawk. I've never felt this way about a man before, but I know what we share is strong and special."

He wanted to bind her to him in more than name only. Once he proved his love, she should come to trust him enough to tell him everything so they could work on her problem together and he could protect her from all harm. Even so, he must not trick her into surrendering to him and their mutual passion. "That's true. I just don't want to lead you down the wrong trail and encourage you to do something that'll make you feel sorry later. But I do want you and need you, Maggie Reynolds."

"We are married, Hawk, and I am a grown woman with a clear head, at least as clear as it can be around you," she divulged with a smile.

"You cloud my wits, too, Maggie. I was taken

by you the first moment I saw you. I had to stay close to you to learn why you affected me like this, so I only pretended to have a job in Prescott. I was outside the depot when you bought your ticket for there. After you left, I went in and did the same. I even boarded at the last minute to keep from spooking you and having you get off to avoid me. Forgive me for deceiving you, Maggie, but I had to get to know you; I had to be with you. After you told me what you were going to do, I had to stay with you to keep you out of trouble. I never imagined things would progress so fast between us. For a loner like me, this predicament is new and a little scary. I've never been tempted before to change my plans just to hang around a woman. That strikes me as being a little loco, but I figured our paths might not cross again if I let you get away before I made sense of this situation. There was something about you that told me to take a closer look, and I've learned to follow my gut instincts or pay a price for not doing so."

Maggie savored his touch on her cheek and heady confession. "I'm glad you were bold and persistent. I hated to leave Yuma because you were there, but I knew you would be gone soon, so it was foolish to change my schedule. Besides, even though you seized my interest immediately, we were strangers back then, and a woman can't go running after somebody she just met."

"I don't want to put you in an uneasy position, Maggie, so I've tried to keep my distance and behave myself as I promised when we partnered up, but you surely don't make it easy. So far, that precaution isn't working for me; I just keep needing you more and more every day. I'm not used to dealing with a woman on this kind of terrain, so I guess it's natural to be a mite wary and nervous."

She recalled that he had lost his family only months ago, so he must still be suffering. As a loner, he probably didn't know exactly what to say or do in a romantic situation. Perhaps he felt insecure about his background as a trail man. She had to prove to him he was special, was a perfect match for her in all ways, and before he learned the dark truth about her and put distance between them forever. "I don't mean to make it hard on you, Hawk, and you have kept your word of honor. Actually, I think there's too much space between us."

As if fearing he would push prematurely, Hawk misunderstood, took a deep breath, and stepped to the dresser. As he removed his hat and holster and put them atop it, he said in a somber tone, "I'm sorry if I offended you, Maggie; that wasn't my intention. I suppose there is a wide space between a refined lady like you and a rough man like me."

Maggie waved her hand between them and clarified, "I was referring to this kind of space between us, Hawk. I meant to encourage you, not reject you. I must know the truth, am I a risk worth taking so we can figure out exactly what kind of force is drawing us toward each other? Neither of us is the kind of person who relinquishes freedom in rash haste; after all, we have retained ours this long, so there must be something different about our relationship that should be investigated."

Hawk told himself he shouldn't have approached her in this manner before certain matters were brought into the open and settled between them, but he couldn't find the strength or will to back down now. Besides, everything she just said made perfect sense to him. "Yes, Maggie, you are a reasonable risk. Am I?"

"Yes, Hawk, you are."

He admired her honesty and courage and was enslaved by his love and desire for her. She had come into his life at a time when his heart was frozen by hatred and a desire only for revenge; she had melted that terrain and brought him back to life. Mercy, he wished his other confessions would be as quickly understood and accepted as his revealed deceit, but he somehow knew it wouldn't be the same. But before he risked losing her, he must risk loving her and binding himself totally to her with the hope that bond would be too strong for anything or anyone to break.

"Even if you had rejected me, Maggie, I wouldn't desert you and our work together. I'll be at your side until you tell me to leave."

"That won't happen, Hawk," *because I've fallen in love with you.*

His pounding heart leapt with joy, and the

flames within his loins kindled to a greater height. For a moment, he did nothing more than hold her tight against him. "I have real strong feelings for you, Maggie, but you can slow or halt this ride if it starts to scare you," he murmured before his mouth covered hers with a tender kiss. When she looped her arms around his neck and responded, his embrace tightened and a moan of intense need escaped his throat.

Shared passion caused Maggie to quiver and ignite with pleasure and anticipation. She felt strange and wonderful all over. Her pulse raced wildly through her body, taking hot blood to every inch of it. Her dreamy thoughts danced like blades of grass in a wild wind. She hoped she would know what to do at the right time, and that such things would take care of themselves as nature intended. Once he realized how much she loved him, that should prevent him from turning against her later, at least from hating her. If she made their bond tight, surely he would forgive her recklessness in Yuma and remain at her side.

Hawk was almost staggered by the spellbinding way she clung to him, kissed him, and pressed against him. He wasn't a greenhorn where sex was concerned, but he was a stranger to romantic lovemaking. Even so, he instinctively knew she was an innocent, and he must move slow and gentle with her, though she was making self-control difficult with her ardent responses. He trailed kisses over her face where her skin was as soft as silk. His mouth journeyed down her throat as she leaned her head back to give him plenty of roaming room, and his actions evoked muffled groans from deep within her. He was elated that he could arouse such desire for him. He nestled his face against her brown hair and relished the feel of it against his cheek. He drifted his hands up and down her back and felt her curls tease over his fingers during each trip upward. He kissed her forehead and the tip of her nose. As his lips brushed over hers, he vowed, "Nothing in my life has ever felt as good as you do in my arms, Maggie. I've craved you every day and night for weeks. If I didn't know better, I'd swear I was only dreaming."

Amidst their mingled breaths, she said, "So would I, Hawk, but we're wide awake. That day at the corral in Yuma, I felt as if I'd known you" — *and waited for you* — "forever. I somehow knew my life would never be the same."

He looked at her radiant face. "If you never believe anything I ever say again, believe how much I want you and need to learn where this twisting path will take us." With those heart-stirring words, he lifted her and carried her to the bed, where he lowered her beside it. Maggie unbuttoned his shirt and peeled it off his broad shoulders, dropping it to the floor, unwilling to leave him even long enough to toss it over a chair or hang it on a peg. She untied his bandanna and let it fall to the rug. She waited in rising suspense as he removed her blouse and cast it aside, then undid the ribbon and unfastened the tiny buttons of her undergarment. After his mouth covered hers again, she felt his fingers slip the straps of her chemise off her shoulders. She held her arms down so he could free them of that white garment, which was left to dangle over the waistband of her skirt.

For a short time, they simply looked at each other, as if each was making sure the other had no reservation about what was going to happen next. Her palms were flattened against his bronzed chest while his hands cupped her face and his thumbs stroked the velvety skin near her parted lips. Maggie sent her fingers to toy with hair as dark as midnight which curled under at his nape, and he slid his into her long tresses and drew her head toward his. Their mouths united in a budding kiss that flowered as passion spread it throughout their bodies.

Maggie slipped her hands beneath his arms to rove his broad back and felt the strength that dwelled there. His shoulders and arms were taut and well muscled from ample use and her wandering fingers encountered defined ridges and planes amid the tanned flesh.

Time seemed to stand still and any reality beyond that room seemed to vanish as they explored their feelings and stimulated each other to a lofty degree. Their kisses became hungry and greedy, as did their hands.

As if receiving a mental message from her, Hawk unbuttoned her skirt and it slid to the floor, as did her chemise in its wake. He felt her move as she lifted one foot at a time to discard the pool of material around them. As he doused the lamplight to prevent alarming her with the sight of his jutting manhood when he undressed, Maggie tossed aside the covers, removed her bloomers, and climbed onto the bed. With haste, he shucked his boots, socks, pants, and lower undergarment. He eased down beside her and pulled her into his arms on their sides.

They shared a pillow as they kissed and caressed each other, eager to be as one. Her nipples hardened even more as Hawk's fingers tantalized them to firmer points after rolling her to her back.

Maggie was awed by how stimulating and profound it felt to have him touching her breasts. She had imagined it would be nice, but nothing as sensuously evocative as it was. Her astonishment and pleasure multiplied when his questing mouth closed over one rosy brown bud. His tongue lavished hot moisture and generous attention there. The sensations he created were deliriously arousing. She closed her eyes to absorb them, though the room was too dark to see him or any object there.

Hawk's right hand ventured over her bare figure as far as it could reach without dislodging his mouth from its splendid task. She had a firm and agile body, and every inch was an enchanting enticement. Her unflawed flesh was neither pale nor dark, but somewhere in between. She was almost too beautiful and angelic to touch, but too irresistible not to do so. His hand drifted over her rib cage and stomach, caressing its way to the fuzzy triangle between her thighs. He remembered being told that rubbing the small nub there evoked delight and ravenous hunger, so he massaged it with light and slow strokes at first, then with firmer and faster ones as her hips began to squirm and soft moans escaped her mouth.

Maggie's fingers played in her lover's ebony hair as he feasted at her breasts and drove her wild with his hands. A curious tension gnawed at her, though she tried to relax as she anticipated what was to come.

Hawk's lips traveled up Maggie's chest and neck at a snail's pace and at last fused with hers as he moved atop her. He hoped she was as eager to continue their bold journey as she appeared to be; he certainly was. He had never had to use this kind of restraint before or delay his release so long.

He entered her with as much gentleness as he could muster, then halted while she accustomed herself to his presence. She stiffened slightly and inhaled sharply before she relaxed again, her fingers pressing hard against his shoulder blades. When she arched toward him, he thrust himself deeper within her, kissing and caressing her all the while. He hoped he hadn't hurt her, as he had been told it could be painful for a woman her first time, or if a man was rough and too swift, whether it was a woman's first time or hundredth. He knew she had never lain with a man before, and he was overwhelmed that she had chosen him to be the receiver of her precious gift of chastity. After her ankles overlapped his calves and she seemed to open herself more to him, he penetrated her more deeply and began to move within her sweet heat.

One sharp pain and ensuing mild discomfort passed quickly for the highly aroused Maggie. Each time he moved within her, it was sheer ecstasy. It was beautiful and special and natural to have their bodies joined as one. To her, it was a total sharing of themselves, a consummation of their wedding vows, an exquisite foreshadowing of a golden future together.

Together, they climbed upward, seeking a goal that they could only imagine at that point. They urged their spirits skyward and grew dizzy at the awesome heights of their soaring passion. Maggie reached her precipice and toppled over it only minutes before an enraptured Hawk did the same, and they met in a tranquil valley afterward to cuddle as their bodies cooled and their pounding hearts slowed.

The minute Hawk's near breathlessness ended, he asked, "Are you all right, Maggie? Did I hurt you?"

A sated Maggie replied in honesty, "It was a little uncomfortable at one point; but on the whole, it was wonderful. You were very gentle and considerate. Thank you, Hawk."

"I'm the one who should be thanking you,

Maggie." *You're mine now, woman, and I'll fight anybody and anything to keep you at my side.* "Maybe this means I won't need to be calling on my judge and lawyer friends later to untie us," he murmured before thinking, which was unusual for him; so he chuckled as if jesting because he didn't want her to think he was trying to entrap her.

Maggie nestled into his embrace and rested her head on his shoulder. She liked the way his fingers trailed over her arm and shoulder, and the husky tone of his voice. Although they hadn't confessed love for each other, she was certain that's what they both felt; it definitely was what she felt. "I suppose this episode ropes us together good and tight, Mr. Reynolds; at least for as long as it works out between us." *There, that should relieve any pressure you might be feeling about being trapped in a hasty marriage.*

It'll work out somehow; you'll see. "Yep, I guess it does."

"We did say, if we liked our marital arrangement, we'd keep it. So far, I find it most pleasing and acceptable. We make a good team."

"I like it, too, boss lady; that's something I didn't expect to be saying and thinking when I took off after you in Yuma to see why I couldn't get you off my mind day or night. You're a sneaky critter, Maggie Malone."

After she laughed with him, she said, "Since we were thrown together unexpectedly and married by necessity, let's wait and see if we can discover why before we cut that knot. We don't want to toss away something which might be beneficial to us both."

"Yep, you're right; smart, too." Hawk realized she was relaxing more and more as he stroked her hair and bare flesh. He was surprised she didn't get out of bed and put on a nightgown, but was glad she didn't. He savored the feel of her bare body against his, the way her arm rested over his chest and a knee over his thighs, the way her soft nether curls tickled his leg, the way she cuddled up to him, and her occasional dreamy sigh. He knew they had been talking in jesting tones to conceal their real feelings from each other, as if they both were wary of each other and their sudden emotions because of their secrets.

As Maggie drifted off to sleep while locked in his embrace, Hawk's concentration drifted in another direction. He couldn't forget that two of his family's killers were within his reach; two were already dead, and the last one could be found through the woman in his arms. He had been tempted to call out Slim Jones this afternoon while the odds were even, then go after Pete Barber with the same intention. All he had thought about for months was finding them and punishing them. But Maggie had come along and changed his original plans and his feelings. There was more at stake now; he needed those culprits alive to help extricate her from her reckless deed. In order to protect her life and to save her from incarceration, he had to be satisfied with exposing their crimes in Prescott and Texas, arresting them, and seeing them either hang for multiple murders or rot in prison in order to get his justice and revenge.

Besides, as a U.S. marshal, he was sworn to uphold the Law, so he couldn't just kill somebody in cold blood and for personal reasons, even under the pretense of a justifiable showdown; that would make him no better than his wicked targets. Yet he sometimes had to battle violence with violence when a criminal tried to elude justice and punishment or threatened him or a victim. Since he had pinned on a badge years ago — first a Texas Ranger's for five years, then a U.S. marshal's for the last two — he'd bent some laws and stretched a few others while performing his duties, but he'd never broken one, at least with knowing willfullness.

His badge and authority were recognized everywhere as the highest rank of law enforcement, but that had never made him feel or behave arrogant around town sheriffs or local marshals, especially since he rarely exposed his status and worked undercover. He took his job seriously, and his jurisdiction included anywhere his missions took him. He even had the power to appoint his own deputy; to date, he hadn't felt a need for a partner since he preferred working alone and being responsible solely for his actions and safety. His duties included bringing to justice murderers, robbers, arsonists, rapists, railroad obstructors, whiskey sellers to Indians, mail thieves, Army deserters, swindlers, adulterers. He was a threat and scourge to anybody who broke federal laws.

Hawk listened to Maggie's even breathing for a while as his mind told him she should be under arrest at that very minute for aiding the escape of an imprisoned convict. His heart told him he would have to resign before he could be the one to carry out that deed. Yet if her action was exposed and a warrant was put out on her, he would have no choice except to honor it in order to prevent other lawmen and/or bounty hunters from snatching her.

Besides marrying her in Benson yesterday, he already had taken another bold step before he left Tucson to protect her from repercussions from her misdeed in Yuma; he could get into big trouble if his deceit was discovered, probably cost him his badge. All he required now was the arrival of a certain item to prove his good intentions before he revealed the truth to her and pleaded for her cooperation.

Hawk wondered what kind of assignments Maggie had carried out and where, and if she had ever been forced to kill a target in self-defense. He listened to her peaceful breathing and told himself she couldn't have a bad bone within her lovely and shapely body. She was much too gentle-spirited to kill anyone, so her assignments couldn't have been extremely dangerous ones.

Yet, during his sly observations and their travels together, he had seen her exhibit enormous courage, intelligence, and prowess. In that same vein, she couldn't have become one of the Carlton Agency's best detectives if she never had confronted and resolved major problems and the kinds of perils that went along with them. That fact, along with her relationship to Ben, would work in their favor if she let them.

But that involved her going up against vicious men. Could she stand up to cruel men like Pete Barber and Slim Jones if those bastards came after her to silence her? For certain, he would gun down those snakes without a second thought if they harmed a single inch of the woman he loved.

As dreamy thoughts of life together on his ranch filled his mind, Hawk drifted off into a light sleep, unsuspecting of a crushing blow that loomed ahead for them . . .

Chapter Thirteen

Maggie sat up in bed and held the sheet to her neck as Hawk entered the room with several items in his hands.

"Good, you're awake. I've already had my bath and shaved. I tried to be careful with that delicate skin of yours last night; I hope my stubble didn't rub your face raw." He watched her lift one hand and stroke her flesh before she smiled and shook her head. "I ordered you a bath; a Chinese worker is preparing it now in the water closet down the hall. I'll just put away my things and clear out so you can get up and get ready for breakfast." As he headed for the dresser to do so, he said, "Since we missed supper last night, I'm sure you're as hungry as I am."

Maggie nodded as her stomach growled in response. "I'm astonished I slept so soundly in that condition and with so much noise outside. I guess I was exhausted from the night before. I promise to hurry."

"I'll wait for you downstairs; I'll be having coffee." He grinned and chuckled. "I need a strong cup to clear my head of what's dazing it before me. I'm out of here, woman, because you're much too tempting like that."

"You seem to show me more and more consideration and kindnesses every day, partner; thanks. Did you sleep well?"

"Like a newborn baby, just as you did."

"Do I snore or toss or do anything else disturbing?"

"Nothing more than cuddle up to me," he said with another grin.

"I'll try to remember to stay on my side from here on," she quipped.

"I hope not; I like having you near me, asleep or awake."

My, aren't we bold and romantic this morning. "I feel the same way."

"You look mighty fetching with your hair all mussed like that."

"You look mighty fetching any way I see you." *No good morning kiss?* She watched Hawk boldly gaze at her for a minute, then grin and nod his head as if answering a mental question. "Is anything wrong?" she asked.

"Nope, things couldn't be much better. See you downstairs."

She observed his departure, his walk almost a swagger and his final glance as he closed the door most enticing. She would have adored waking up in his arms and making love again; and from his banter, that idea had crossed his mind, too. She was glad no strain existed between them this glorious new day following their intimacy.

Heaven above, I love you, Hawk Reynolds, and I must have you forever. If not, surely I'll perish.

At breakfast, Maggie ventured to Hawk in a whisper, "Why would Barber be angry at Ben Carver for betraying him when I didn't find any mention of incrimination in the trial notes or even any hints about it from the people I interviewed in Yuma and Prescott? As I told you yesterday, that was the impression he gave me, which I find odd."

Hawk recalled Toby Muns telling him Barber suspected Coot Sayers of stealing the holdup money they had secreted near a rocky draw on Mount Union on March first before they went their separate ways to avoid being seen riding together. But when they met as planned at that site on March fourteenth to split up the money, Barber had slain Sayers during a challenge over its return after he found it missing, despite Sayers' claim of innocence. Sayers had told Barber either somebody — perhaps a prospector — had happened upon its location or Carver had taken it. Since Ben had been captured in Tucson on the fifth and was in prison by the eighteenth, Barber didn't believe either Ben or a stranger had committed the foul deed. Barber also said Ben was too smart and too afraid of him to pull a crazy stunt like that, and had lacked the time and opportunity.

It was too bad, Hawk mused, that he hadn't thoroughly searched Muns after finding and arresting that varmint; if he had done so, Muns wouldn't have pulled that pistol hidden in his boot and forced him to shoot in self-defense, slaying his only witness against the others. From all he knew, but couldn't reveal at that point, Hawk speculated, "Maybe Carver made off with the robbery money and that riled Barber against him."

"How is that possible? Why would Barber let Ben keep it for him?"

"Carver could have doubled back after they hid it somewhere and took it with him or concealed it in another place. He could have stopped en route and telegraphed his father to meet him somewhere to set up his alibi. You can almost bet that hunting idea was Ben Carver's."

Maggie realized she must question Newl about that possibility, and do so immediately; it was looking more and more as if her stepbrother was guilty. If that was true, she was in deep trouble as his escape accomplice! "You could be right." *But I hope not.*

She reminded Hawk about their photography sitting at two o'clock. "After we finish, I think I'll go shopping for a hat and perhaps a new dress. I left my trunk with most of my possessions stored in Tucson because it was too bulky for horseback travel, and I want to look good for our picture. While I do that errand, why don't you nose around to see what Barber and Jones are up to today?"

Hawk surmised what she planned to do and

was glad. If Newl related the truth, and if it was what he suspected, that would draw Maggie closer to him and further away from Ben. It also would give him the perfect chance to use that valuable ace up his sleeve . . .

As soon as Hawk vanished down the street and around the corner, Maggie went to the telegraph office and sent a message to Newl via their regular method. She told him she was awaiting a rapid response. She told the office clerk she would return for a reply in an hour or so, so to hold it until she retrieved it in person.

Afterward, she went to a dress shop nearby and delighted in finding the perfect outfit for their impending photograph session.

It didn't take Hawk long to locate his two targets, who were engaged in a poker game in a saloon. Since they appeared to be settled in for a while, he walked to H.H. Tuttle's Tombstone Corral, saddled Diablo, and rode to Fairbank in hopes the small package he was awaiting had arrived . . .

Maggie stood in the front of the telegraph office and read Newl's reply. She was relieved he was honest with her, though his message dismayed her. Hawk's speculation had been accurate: the hunting trip was Ben's idea, and he had sent his request while en route toward Tucson from Benson, which would appear to make it impossible he had been in Prescott two and a half days earlier. She studied the map of Arizona on the wall and figured the timing required to cover that distance. If, after the early Thursday morning holdup, Ben rode like a wild wind almost around the clock, only halting for naps and quick snacks, and with two horses along as the gang was rumored to use, providing him with a fresh mount for frequent changes, he could have made it to Maricopa Wells to take a train to reach Benson by noon on Saturday. The two Carver men could have met near the Rincon Mountains that evening as they swore in court, camped overnight, hunted Sunday, camped again, then returned to Tucson on Monday in time for Ben's capture that afternoon.

Knowing or suspecting his face had been seen by someone who would recognize him, Ben would have been desperate to set up what he thought would be an unquestionable alibi; he would have sacrificed sleep and rest and even food and would have pushed his horses to their limits to acquire one. He probably never imagined his prestigious father's word wouldn't be accepted or that the authorities wouldn't be fooled by his sly precautions. The court had assumed Newl was lying about the hunting trip to protect his only son, but no doubt her stepfather had told the truth on the witness stand and truly believed Ben's vows of innocence.

Newl also disclosed that his detective had learned that neither Frank's nor the bank owner's monetary status or property had altered since that robbery, so she was inclined to think her original speculations were wrong.

Though the message was coded, Maggie shredded the paper, stuffed it into her skirt pocket, and headed for the hotel with her packages. In her distracted state, she encountered Pete Barber, who halted her to speak.

"I been thinking about what you asked me yesterday and I reckon I can tell you a little about me for a story. Where can we sit and jaw?"

Maggie's wits weren't so dazed by the offer that she didn't remember to use her exaggerated southern drawl and southern belle charms. "I'm sorry, Mr. Barber, but I can't interview you today; I have an appointment with Mr. Fly at two o'clock to have my photograph taken and to interview him about the gunfight between the Earps and the Clanton Gang. I just barely have time to eat dinner and get ready for my sitting. However, I have plenty of time after church tomorrow afternoon and evening. Would that be convenient with you? I truly hope so, because your life would make a fascinating story to write, and I'm sure everyone would love to read it." She forced herself to keep a pleasant expression around the offensive man, and cautioned herself to be alert and careful with him. Like yesterday, Pete Barber had himself under total control and was unreadable.

"If'n I'm still in town tomorrow, where'll I find you about three?"

Don't you dare panic and change your mind and appear too eager! "At the Carlton Hotel," she reminded him, though she doubted he ever forgot anything or anybody. "I'll wait for you in the lobby. They have a private sitting room to one side of it, so I'm certain I can arrange for us to use it for a few hours. I'll also arrange for refreshments served."

"I'll be seeing you about then, if'n I'm still around."

"I hope you can stay and tell me your story, but I'll understand if you have to leave. And yes, I shall be glad to pay you a fee for your time and cooperation." *Careful, Maggie, don't give him the impression you're wealthy, or he might try to rob you.* "However, it can't be much because my expense budget is small until I earn a larger one by submitting several great stories."

"Ain't no payment needed."

"That's very kind of you, sir."

"I'll be leaving, but we'll be seeing each other again."

Maggie watched him depart with a cocky strut, his spurs jingling in his wake and his boots thudding on the boardwalk almost as heavily as her heart pounded within her chest. She couldn't deduce if his last words were meant to be intimidating or threatening. She glanced around to see if Hawk was in the vicinity, since he was supposed to be shadowing Barber, but she didn't see him, and thought that was odd. She decided he must be trailing Slim Jones as he had the last time when the two men were separated.

After Maggie joined Hawk in the lobby following their meal and her retirement to their room
to change clothes, she saw his golden brown gaze
leisurely travel over her from the silk flower-and-
ribbon-trimmed straw hat to feminine leather
slippers.

"You look beautiful, Maggie, prettiest I've ever
seen you." *Blazes, I'm a lucky man!* "Is that the
dress and hat you bought this morning?"

Maggie glanced down at a lovely polonaise
with a softly draped bustle bottom and a square
neckline which were both edged with ivory lace.
The gored underskirt in ivory batiste featured
numerous ruffles from waist to hem. "Yes, it is,
straight from back East. They're perfect, aren't
they?"

He knew she wasn't fishing for a compliment,
just assurance he liked what she had chosen.
"Yep, they are. That color reminds me of Texas
bluebells. It matches those beautiful eyes."

"Thanks. You look handsome yourself," she
told him with a smile as she eyed his black frock
coat, black pants, black boots, stark white shirt,
and silver bolo on a braided black cord. With his
ebony hair, dark eyes, and bronzed flesh, the
black-and-white contrast with them was splendid, enormously masculine and inflaming to her
senses.

"Thanks. I had everything except the shirt and
tie. I bought them this morning and had my coat

pressed at that Chinese laundry on Toughnut Street. Mr. Fong even polished my boots for me and cleaned my hat."

So, that's where you've been hiding today; perhaps preparing yourself to impress me. And you certainly have, as always, even when you don't try at all. Since his hair was neatly combed for their photograph, he told her — even newly trimmed she noticed — he didn't don his Stetson, just held its brim between the fingers of his right hand. He cocked his left elbow toward her and asked if she was ready to leave.

"Yes, and we make a fine-looking couple, I must say."

"So do I."

In Camillus Fly's studio behind his Fremont Street gallery, Maggie stood next to a seated Hawk's right shoulder for the first photograph, her left side slightly behind him, and with her left hand lying atop the area between his shoulder and neck and the other resting lightly at the crook of his arm.

Several times Camillus peered through his camera on a stand which was situated a few feet away, then returned to them to make minor adjustments with clothing, head and body positions, or hand placements. It was evident the slender and genial man wanted everything to look perfect, which pleased both Maggie and Hawk.

As they held that initial pose for a few minutes while Camillus vanished beneath a black cloth and made the photograph, each was highly cognizant of stimulating contact with the other's body. With every breath taken, each inhaled the other's arousing smell. Each heard and felt the other's controlled breathing, and tasted the sweet flavor of elation coursing through their veins.

For the second pose, Camillus had them stand before a large painting that featured a lovely outdoor scene which looked real, one of many clever "backgrounds" he had in his studio, each arranged area providing different moods and settings. Maggie was in the front, her body concealing less than half of Hawk's left side, with his right fingers curled around the crook of her right elbow and with his left ones almost teasing around the curve of her waist, barely visible. In her left hand, resting casually near the edge of her polonaise parting, she held a lacy fan which Camillus supplied. Their heads faced forward, but were tipped slightly toward the other's.

Once more, Camillus made his adjustments until he smiled and said everything was "perfect, just perfect."

As they remained motionless, those previous heady perceptions assailed their senses again. Each hoped that the heat they radiated and tingles they experienced weren't noticeable to the other two people present. Neither realized Camillus saw the adoring expressions on their faces and assumed they were deeply in love, as newlyweds should be, and hoped he captured that shared aura.

Before they separated to assume their last pose, Maggie felt Hawk's fingers give her waist and arm light squeezes. She glanced over her shoulder at him and smiled, and he sent her a near beaming one in return. Each concluded that the other also was enjoying this adventure.

As they sat side by side on a short settee before another artistic painting simulating a lovely parlor, they exchanged grins as Camillus fussed with her folds and ruffles to get them just right. Each tried to seek distraction from further arousal by thinking about other things.

For Maggie, it was making plans to send her new outfit to her mother via the mail for safekeeping with her other possessions, and attempting to visualize the three photographs and decide where to hang or set them.

For Hawk, with that certain item in his possession now, it was trying to decide when and how to reveal the truth about himself to his wife . . .

At last the man said he was finished, and the pictures would be ready for pickup on Monday. To get their minds and moods focused elsewhere, Maggie pretended to do her feigned interview with Camillus. As she took notes, Hawk assisted her ruse by asking clever questions and making comments.

While Maggie changed clothes in their hotel room, Hawk lingered in hiding near Fly's gallery to see if Pete Barber paid the photographer a visit following their lengthy sitting to question the man about them. Just as he suspected, within minutes after their departure, the redhead appeared down the street, walked to the gallery door, glanced in three directions, then entered the structure. Within fifteen minutes, not long enough to have a photograph taken to provide his motive, Barber left the building.

Despite his curiosity, Hawk didn't return to question Camillus; that could make the slender man more nervous than he probably was. He returned to the hotel and told Maggie what happened.

"Do you think he's suspicious of us?" she asked. "Was it a mistake for me to have mentioned Ben Carver to him the other day?"

"I'm sure he was curious about you and your words, but our cover story should have him duped. Don't worry, men like Barber are suspicious of everybody and everything; that's how they stay alive and out of the Law's reach. I'm sure he's fooled by the precautions we've taken, so he won't be coming after us before we're ready to deal with him."

"I hope not, because he's dangerous, probably the most dangerous man I've come across in my work and travels. I don't want him becoming a threat to you because of me."

"Don't worry about me, Maggie; I can take care of myself. I've been doing so for a long time. I just don't want you catching his eye and —"

Hawk halted his sentence, and both looked toward the door.

"Ella Mae, what are you doing here?" Hawk asked after opening the door to find his Tombstone informer standing there and looking nervous. "Come inside; hurry." After peering down the hall in both directions and sighting no one, he closed and locked the door. He turned and asked, "Did anybody see you?"

"No, I came around the rear and in the back door. I used the back servants' stairs to sneak to your room; you told me the number the other night. I need to talk to you, alone, Hawk."

He glanced at a watchful Maggie, then faced Ella Mae. "It's all right; this is Maggie Malone, my partner on this hunt. You can talk freely in front of her. Maggie, this is Ella Mae, a friend of mine who works in the Oriental Saloon, one of the fanciest and most profitable businesses in town. I pay her to gather information for me on the sly."

Maggie smiled at the young woman she was scrutinizing with a masked expression and said, "It's a pleasure to meet you, Ella Mae."

"Likewise, ma'am."

The flame-haired, hazel-eyed visitor looked to Maggie to be in her early twenties, and was pretty. Her complexion was pale, with a smattering of freckles across the bridge of her dainty nose and rosy cheeks. Ella Mae was a little shorter than she was and had a more ample bosom. Her brownish green gaze stayed locked on Hawk's handsome face, and she stood as close to him as possible. Attired in a simple skirt and blouse, the female could have passed most places unnoticed except for those fiery red tresses which cascaded down her back and her voluptuous figure. Despite Ella Mae's occupation and obvious infatuation with Hawk, Maggie didn't sense any hint of past intimacy between the two.

"You ast me to keep an eye and ear open for anything Pete Barber and Slim Jones does, so I listened to a talk they was having with one of the new girls at our place; she's been here about a month or a little more. Her name's Conchita Vasquez, but she goes by Chita; she's Mexican, dark hair and eyes, a real looker the men say. She's popular with customers 'cause she knows all the tricks for pleasing a man. You know a customer can hire his favorite girl for the whole evening or for all night for a nice price; that's what Pete's planning to do, and pay her a hundred dollars in secret for helping him fool everybody."

Maggie noticed the redhead never even glanced at her or spoke to her, as if she weren't there. She wondered if a cunning Ella Mae was making intentional insinuations about a sexual relationship between herself and the man nearby.

"Pete told Chita to pretend to serve drinks and snacks and provide company for him and his friends on Monday night in one of the private card rooms. He told her they would sneak out about nine and return about ten or eleven but for her to keep the door locked and pretend they was there the whole time. Nobody in his right senses would try to get inside that room, not even our bossman. They're planning to rob the nine-thirty train to Fairbank. It's a special run that's supposed to be a secret 'cause it's bringing in a big payroll for the mines. Somehow Pete learned about it and he's gonna steal it before it reaches town. Maybe Chita told him; she coulda got wind of it from one of her customers 'cause we get plenty of railroad men along with miners and cowpokes. She coulda sent for him or she coulda told him after he come to town this week. It's amazing what some men will say when they're . . . busy with us girls and ain't thinking clear. They tell us things they won't tell their wives and sweethearts."

Hawk became uneasy as Ella Mae rambled on about such a crude topic in front of Maggie. At the first available moment, he sought to get the talk back on the right track. "So, Pete's using Chita to set up a clever alibi for that crime. With her bringing drinks and food in and carrying out empty glasses and dishes, everybody there will believe those snakes are playing cards and liquoring up all night while they're actually off robbing the train. You did good, Ella Mae, very good; if I can catch them red-handed, they'll pay off nicely with big rewards. For certain, the mining companies will pay big to have their payrolls recovered."

"Tell me, Ella Mae," Maggie asked, "how did

you get close enough to overhear that talk without being seen? Barber is a very cautious man; not many people catch him off guard. You must be very smart and brave," she added when the female turned to face her, unsmiling and gaze squinted as if vexed at what she considered an intrusion. However, her own smile, feigned look of flattering amazement, and final complimentary words caused the woman's gaze to soften.

"I was standing on the upstairs porch getting some air when Pete walked up to Chita. She was on the porch downstairs, under me. I heard him ask to go to her room to talk. I could tell they knew each other, so I figured he might reveal something Hawk needed. Like I just said, men tell us girls all sorts of things. I wasn't working, so I raced to her room — we all have our own rooms to use there — and hid under her bed. I curled up in a ball, stayed real quiet and still, and just listened. He weren't there long, 'cause it was just for talking. After they was gone, I sneaked to my room. I waited for a while to make sure nobody was watching me, then come here."

"Did he say anything to Chita about strangers being in town?" Maggie asked. "Did he mention either my name or Hawk's?"

"Nope, he just talked about the robbery and what Chita's to do."

"As Hawk said, Ella Mae, you did an excellent job. You're very brave and smart, and we're grateful to you."

"You be extra careful from here on, Ella Mae,"

he added, "so they won't get suspicious. It's best not to get near any of them again, so don't try to get any more information; it's too dangerous and risky for both of us."

Ella Mae nodded. "You can use my room to spy on the window below it to see when they leave, then follow 'em. You know which one it is. Course you'll have to rent me for the evening so you can stay in there for however long it takes."

"Thanks, but I'll do my spying from outside so I'll be ready to trail them. You get back to the Oriental before you're missed, and don't take any more chances," he stressed.

"Whatever you say, Hawk. You know I always follow your orders."

"As soon as I collect payment, I'll reward you good, Ella Mae."

"Thanks. I'll be seeing you later. Pleased to meet you, ma'am."

"It was nice to meet you, Ella Mae, and thank you for the help."

"I was lucky; this plan just fell into my lap by accident. I been helping Hawk catch bad men for a long time. We're good friends."

"Yep, we are, Ella Mae, and I'm much obliged for everything."

After Ella Mae left, Maggie remarked in a mischievous tone, "She's sweet on you, partner, and was disappointed you had company."

"Despite how she earns her living and how she misbehaved today, Maggie, Ella Mae's a good woman. But there's never been anything romantic between us."

"Is that supposed to appease my jealousy?" she jested.

"Do you feel any?" he retorted with a grin and approached her.

Maggie stroked his jawline in boldness as she murmured, "Perhaps. After all, you are my husband, which you didn't mention to her."

Hawk captured the hand on his cheek and kissed it. "I didn't want to distract her from what she came to tell me. I knew it was something important for her to risk getting caught. If this plan works, we could have Barber and Jones in deep trouble and custody very soon."

"Custody" . . . *That's an odd word for a bounty hunter to use.* "What happens after we entrap them and have them tossed into jail?"

"If we can convince them to talk, maybe we can learn where Ben Carver is hiding out and recapture him."

Maggie was surprised by that statement because she had never said anything about pursuing and ensnaring Ben. "For his reward and my story?"

Hawk placed his hands atop her shoulders, gazed into her blue eyes, and said, "Nope, arrest him to get you out of trouble with the Law."

Something in his grave tone, choice of words, and somber expression caused Maggie to panic. Her gaze widened of its own volition, and she gaped at him in astonishment and trepidation.

Her heart rate increased to a rapid pace, its responding pulse pounding — almost ringing — in her ears. Chills raced over her body, and she trembled in dread. She felt the light pressure of his fingers on her shoulders, as if he was holding her rooted to that spot. She clasped her icy fingers together before her waist and asked in a ragged tone, "What do you mean?"

Hawk slid his hands to her nape, his fingers buried in her thick hair and his thumbs beneath her jawline, to prevent her from lowering her head and severing their needed eye contact. "I think it's about time we were totally honest with each other. I know who you are, Maggie Malone, and I know what you did at the Yuma Territorial Prison."

Chapter Fourteen

Does he know, she wondered, *or is he only guessing and trying to evoke a confession? If I make one, what will he say and do about it?* "What do you think I did?" she asked as she observed him closely for clues.

Go slow and easy with the hard parts, then explain yourself to her. "I know for a fact you helped Ben Carver escape."

Maggie noted his tender gaze and tone, and was confused by them. "What brought you to that conclusion? How did I accomplish such a feat?"

"I was watching you from the hillside that morning with fieldglasses before the storm struck. You tumbled down that incline on purpose, passed a message to him, and distracted the guards and other prisoners while he sneaked away, using things you'd hidden for him nearby." He saw her stare at him in renewed astonishment and apprehension, her expression and reaction exposing her guilt. Her lips remained parted after a sharp intake of air. Her face paled, and her cheeks rosed. "Then you went to Prescott under the fake ruse of being a newspaperwoman to find evidence to get him exonerated. You're wasting your time and energy, Maggie; Ben's guilty of that and other crimes."

He sounded convinced of those last words, and as if he knew everything about her misdeed, so she asked, "Such as?"

Hawk was a little surprised she didn't query his motive for spying on her, and was pleased when she didn't tell him his assertions were wrong, as if she wanted to bring the truth into the open and see where it led them. "Such as helping Barber, Jones, Sayers, and Muns rob and murder my family in Texas a few days after Christmas." When she looked stunned by that claim, he said, "That's right, Maggie; Barber's gang is responsible, and Ben was riding with them that day. After I buried my father, mother, and brother on the first of January, I took off after them to punish them. I caught up with Muns on March nineteenth, and he filled my ears with facts before he pulled a concealed pistol and forced me to shoot him in self-defense."

"You killed Toby Muns?"

"He gave me no choice. I wounded him several times just trying to halt and disable him, but he kept staggering toward me and firing, so I put a bullet in his heart."

"Did you catch up with Coot Sayers and slay him, too?"

"Nope, Barber did him under on the fourteenth," he divulged, then related the details of that showdown as told to him by Muns.

"What makes you think Muns was telling the truth? He wasn't a trustworthy person. Why would he confess such hazardous things to you?"

"I didn't beat it out of him, if that's what you mean. He parted ways with Barber and Jones after Sayers' killing and was trying to steer clear of them. He was afraid they would think he took the money and murder him. It's my guess Ben took it and that's why Barber's so riled at him. Since he couldn't bust Ben out of jail during his trial with so many alert guards around him, I guess Barber decided all he could do was wait until Ben was released then hunt him down and riddle him with bullets."

"But you said Muns said Barber didn't believe Ben had the money."

"I suppose he changed his mind. It's my guess that's the real reason Ben and Newl Carver sicked you on them, to get rid of their threat to him. You can bet Ben has the money stashed away. If he hasn't already recovered it from hiding, he will as soon as it's safe."

"How long have you been spying on me?" Maggie's heart lurched and her spirits sank as she listened to his response, which implied he had been duping her and using her all along.

"Since you met with Newl Carver in Wilcox and hired on for the job of rescuing Ben. You see, Maggie, when I happened on that meeting between you three, I was heading for Tucson to take that position myself so I could hook up with Ben. You beat me to it, so I just hung back for a while until I got a chance to join up with you. I'd been chasing Barber and Jones for months and figured Ben could lead me to them if I got him out of prison. Even if I couldn't earn his trust and ride with him, I knew I could shadow him until they rendezvoused and I'd have all three within my reach. At that point, I didn't know Barber had turned on Ben — maybe sent him a warning in prison — and Ben would be trying to hide from him. Frankly, I was amazed and impressed when you pulled off his escape, and without incriminating or endangering yourself and others. I wasn't even sure I could do it, and was certain a woman alone couldn't do so. After Ben was free and I lost sight of him in that storm, I intended to trail you until you joined him somewhere, but you surprised and confused me by heading to Prescott instead."

Is that all you wanted and needed from me, a guide to them and Ben? Why not shadow me? Why become my partner? Why go so far as to marry me? Delay those questions until later. "As infamous as Barber and Jones are, why were you having such a difficult time locating them?"

"They've been laying low since my family's murders. The only job I know they've pulled since leaving Texas is that Prescott holdup."

"You're saying you just happened to be in Wilcox when we were meeting there?" After he nodded, she frowned and said, "As you recall from our talk in Prescott, I'm suspicious of co-incidences."

316

"I know, but it's the truth. I think it was fate or God throwing us together. A friend in Tucson alerted me to Newl's plan to hire a rescuer, so I was heading to see him when I sighted you three in Wilcox. The bad thing was, I overheard only the last part of your talk with Newl." He related what he had discovered that night, how he had done so, and what he speculated from their words and tones. "It's time to swallow the bitter truth, Maggie, stop being used, and extricate yourself from this predicament."

"So, our encounters in Yuma at the store and corral were tricks?"

"Only at the store because I wanted to get a closer look at you. I have to say, Maggie Malone, you took me by surprise. I couldn't get you pegged because too many pieces to your puzzle were missing, but I came to realize I wasn't judging you accurately or fairly."

"What made you change your mind?" she asked in a sarcastic tone.

"Learning you're Ben's stepsister; your faith in his vows of innocence; and your attempts to clear him. I don't think you believe in him anymore."

She realized he hadn't been bluffing or probing for facts, because he knew everything! "How did you make those discoveries?"

"I learned part of those things from getting to know you. As for your family ties, a friend like Ella Mae who works in the Paradise Club told me who and what you are; she learned those facts by accident and by intention from your mother and your stepfather."

Do you have a soiled dove in every town working to gather facts for you? Is your only payment to them in cash, a reward split? She felt as if her heart, her very soul, was riddled by verbal bullets. What, she mused in anguish, could he possible say or do to heal those cruel wounds? Would she and her life be scarred by them forever? Did he intend to betray her — Ben's stepsister — to the authorities? "So, you knew all along, watched everything I did, and hooked up with me only so I could lead you to Barber, Jones, and Ben so you can kill them?" Maggie asked the other tormenting mental questions and added, "That's all I meant to you, a path to revenge?"

"No. Well, yes, in the beginning. Then, somehow and somewhere along the trail, you stole my heart, woman. You have to believe me and trust me, Maggie, so I can help get you out of this mess. If not, you'll go to prison. I don't want that to happen."

Are you implying you love me and want me, despite what I've done? You finally have Barber and Jones within reach, so what more do you need from me? Ah, yes, a guide to Ben's location. "I should trust you when you've been duping me all along?"

"You've been doing the same thing to me, but *I* trust *you*. If I had been in your position, I would have done the same thing for one of my family if I believed he was framed and in danger. Now that you know it was a mistake, let me help you correct it and save you."

You look and sound honest and sincere; but are you? "Just how do you think a bounty hunter can help clear me?"

Hawk smiled and caressed her cheek, and was glad she didn't recoil from his touch when he murmured, "I'm your husband, Maggie Reynolds."

"In name and pretense only."

Hawk cupped her face between his hands. "Oh, no, woman, you're wrong there; our marriage has been consummated, as they call it, so it's legal and binding. You're also the wife of a United States marshal."

Maggie gaped at him. Had she heard him right? "A what?"

"I'm a U.S. marshal, have been for two years. Before that, I was a Texas Ranger for five years. I was appointed by President Arthur following a request from the governor of Texas. I have jurisdiction anywhere."

Of course he was serious, she told herself, which made perfect sense to past clues; or rather, slips he had made. "Why would a U.S. marshal marry a known criminal he was only duping and using?"

"For two reasons: I love you, woman, and want to protect you."

"You have a strange way of proving such feelings."

"So do you, Maggie. Isn't that right?"

"Even if it were true, you used me for ulterior

and selfish reasons."

"Guilty as charged, but I'm asking for forgiveness and understanding. I'm asking for your cooperation in capturing those villains."

"Cooperation with arresting them or slaying them?"

"Arresting, Maggie; that's the only way to clear and protect you. Sure I want them dead; they murdered my family in cold blood. But I wear a badge and that means something important to me. If all I wanted was revenge, I could have challenged and gunned them down by now. I know how to clear you, Maggie, but you have to agree to my plan. Will you?"

Was there a silver lining to the dark cloud looming over her? Was there a chance for them to have a bright future together? At what cost? "What plan? You of all people know I'm guilty, and you're a lawman who's sworn to do his duty at any price."

Hawk got an expected reaction from her when he asked, "How would you like to become my deputy? I have the power to appoint one or more as needed." He watched her stare at him in surprise and doubt. "We could say you've been working with me all along to locate and capture them. You being a skilled detective and, in a way, kin to Ben makes you the perfect choice for an undercover job."

"But I'm a woman. I've never heard of a female marshal before."

"I haven't been told I can't select a female to

deputize. You're more than qualified for the position, Maggie. You're perfect for it, and perfect for this particular job. Just accept my offer for the time being, until this case is resolved and you're in the clear."

"Planning and aiding a prison break is a crime, Hawk. Even if you look the other way, I'm still in trouble when it's exposed. If Ben's guilty, and he probably is, don't you realize he's going to shout about my misdeed the moment he's captured by us if I team up with you?"

"It doesn't matter if you agree to join up with me. You see, my impulsive and beautiful wife, after I learned about Newl's plan to hire somebody to rescue Ben, I came up with an idea for capturing hard-to-expose criminals like Barber and Jones and recovering stolen money or goods. My superior got that suggestion approved by the President himself. My strategy was to break a gang member out of prison and let him lead me to the others and the money. As my deputy and with Ben trusting you, we can say I let you carry out the first step of my plan. Then we pretended to try to prove his innocence to remove any lingering doubts he had about us so he'd guide us to his cohorts and the money. After we discovered they'd had a falling out, we used our guise as journalists to help lead us to Barber and Jones."

"You have permission to break the law?"

"Let's just say bend or stretch it a little to obtain justice."

"You want me to help you arrest Ben and send him back to prison?"

"That's right, but after we finish here with Barber and Jones. Their little plan for Monday night will be their last crime. Once they're in custody, we can use Ben to prove their involvement in my family's murder."

"But I can't lead you to Ben; I don't know where he is. He —"

"Maggie, love, I can't save you if you don't trust me and help me."

"Let me finish. He's somewhere in or near Sante Fe with one of Newl's trusted friends. I wasn't told the person's name or location. They promised if I couldn't find evidence to get Ben cleared within two months, Ben would surrender and wouldn't incriminate me. I was convinced he was innocent, even suspected maybe he was framed. I wouldn't have helped him escape except I was told his life was in immediate danger. I was told if I left him in Yuma while I investigated his case, he wouldn't be alive by the time I could get him exonerated. He's supposed to be in safe hiding until either I clear him or he surrenders on June twentieth."

"He won't ever surrender, Maggie, and you can't clear him."

"I realized that this morning after Newl telegraphed a response to my query about that hunting trip; you were right: it was Ben's idea. No matter what you feel about Ben, Newl honestly believes him and told the truth in court. It's going to break his heart. He's going to hate me for being responsible. He'll probably try to turn Mother against me, and she'll get caught between us."

"That's a risk you'll have to take, Maggie. Newl and your mother will have to accept the bitter truth about Ben and understand you had no choice in this matter."

"If I work with you, Hawk, they won't know the truth; they'll think I was against Ben from the beginning and lied to them just to capture the others and recover the stolen money. Even if I tell Newl the truth about our ruse, he might be so angry at us for sending his son back to prison or to the gallows that he'd expose your plan to save me. What if we incriminate Newl for hiring somebody to engineer the prison break and he gets into trouble? They might even send *him* to jail. What would happen to my mother?"

"My superior already knows about Newl's plan, and I'm sure any court would understand his paternal action. He'll probably just be scolded again like he was in Prescott. As for your mother, she's a smart and brave woman like her daughter, so she can take care of herself if the worst happens. In my opinion, she'll be glad nothing bad happened to you."

"You're right, of course. The main thing is, I can't get you into trouble to protect myself; it could cost you your badge and reputation."

Hawk pulled her into his embrace and cuddled her against him. "So what? I have a three-hundred-acre ranch in San Antonio. I can live and work on that. Besides, I have to make a home for my new wife. We can't be dragging our children down dusty or muddy trails chasing outlaws, so we'll both have to retire from our jobs after we close this case."

Hawk leaned back so he could look into her eyes as he said, "That is, woman, if you love me as much as I love you and want to stay married to me, have a family, and become ranchers. Do you, Maggie? Will you?"

That time when her heart rate increased, it was from elation and relief. She smiled and said, "Yes, Hawk, I do want to be your wife. I love you and I want to have a home together, and live as ranchers in Texas. Are you sure?"

"Never been more certain of anything in my life, Maggie love. Look now, I have a present for you," he said with a broad grin and released her. He withdrew his marshal's badge from a secret leather pocket on the underside of his left holster and showed it to her. As she held and eyed the silver star, he withdrew a deputy badge from a small package in his drawer. "This arrived this morning. I rode over to Fairbank to pick it up while you were shopping. After I pin it on and you take an oath, we'll be official partners."

"I would rather take something off than put something on," she told him, grasping the front of her blouse and shaking it for clarity. Now that they had revealed their mutual love and their marriage was for real, she yearned for the physical closeness that would unite their bodies.

Hawk grinned and nodded. "I like your idea best, Mrs. Reynolds, so this business can wait a while."

Hawk's passion increased in intensity and heat. She believed him and trusted him, understood his motivations and forgave his secrecy. She loved and desired him, only him, and had committed herself to sharing his life. She was his wife in more than name only. He almost could taste the delicious future that awaited them as soon as his mission was finalized.

As Hawk looked into her radiant face, he traced the delicate features and said, "I love you, Maggie, more than I could have imagined was possible."

"I love you, my arresting husband; I think that feeling started the moment we met. It was like being only half a person in many ways and finding my matching part. It was as if I knew immediately we were destined for each other. I meant every word I said during our marriage ceremony."

"So did I," he concurred before his lips claimed hers in a tender kiss.

After they walked to the bed, Maggie wondered if her brimming heart could burst with happiness or if she could melt from the sweltering flames blazing within her body. Her breasts felt heavy with desire and she moaned in delight when he removed her blouse and chemise to fondle them. A fierce craving for him attacked the center of her being and she yielded to its sweet and powerful summons.

They kissed several times as Maggie unbuttoned his shirt. They parted for her to shuck her remaining garments and shoes, and toss aside the covers while he undressed. They lay on the bed and cuddled as they sought each other's kisses. Their hands roamed and their fingers gave and took pleasure.

Hawk drifted his lips across her face, down her neck, and to the satiny skin of her breasts. Her nipples were taut and seemed to beg for his loving attention. He teethed, licked, and tantalized those points until he had her breathless and squirming in rapture. He adored the velvety texture of her bare skin and its intoxicating contact with his own flesh. She had taught him how unique and potent and consuming sex could be when it took place between true lovers who were bound to each other.

Maggie quivered in anticipation of what loomed before her as his hand blazed a searing path down her abdomen, across the space between her hipbones, and went lower where it teased and tantalized her to the brink of ecstasy. She felt special, treasured, loved deeply. When she became so aroused from his strokes and suckles, she thought she might cry out from sheer ecstasy. Her fingers sated their yearning to touch and stimulate him by journeying over his stalwart frame as far as she could reach. Just when she wondered if she'd perish from hunger if he didn't kiss her soon, Hawk's mouth returned to hers and he moved atop her responsive body.

He looked into her softened gaze as he thrust his pleading erection deep within her feminine core. Her long brown hair spread around her head on the pillow and he buried his fingers within those lustrous locks. He lowered his mouth to her throat where it felt blood pounding there with exhilaration. With leisure, generosity, and gentleness, he advanced and retreated numerous times at a steady and teasing pace. He heard her sigh dreamily, felt her cling to him, and savored her mouth meshing to his.

Maggie clasped his handsome face between her hands and tried to convey all of her emotions in a deep and loving kiss. She felt every inch of his magnificent shaft as he penetrated and withdrew over and over until she was engulfed by need. She wanted him urgently. She liked when he increased the speed, depth, and power of his thrusts. From their past encounter, she knew where this trip would take her, and there was no discomfort this time. She was ready to reach her destination and could not hold back from racing toward it with haste.

As soon as Maggie surrendered to the blissful sensations and writhed in the throes of her release, Hawk cast aside his weakened control and sought his own fulfillment.

They continued to kiss, stroke, and embrace until they'd savored every measure of the glorious experience. Then they nestled together as they relaxed and rested.

As current events returned to her mind, Maggie propped up beside Hawk and looked down at his peaceful face. "How do you plan to explain Ben's escape before we became partners? Won't that contradict our story?"

Hawk grinned as he placed a lock of hair over her shoulder and teased his fingers across her exposed collarbone and down her upper arm. "I took that precaution while we were in Prescott. I had a gut feeling about you and us even then, so I acted on it. I telegraphed my superior and told him I had somebody working with me who had assisted with Ben's escape and was traveling with me to carry out my assignment. After I learned more about you in Tucson, I sent him another telegram and said I wanted to appoint my partner as my deputy so you'd have the authority to help me make the arrests. That's when I requested a badge for you and asked for it to be sent to me at Fairbank."

Maggie laughed and jested, "So, I have a very sneaky husband."

He chuckled and quipped, "Nope, just a cunning and cautious one."

As Maggie nibbled on his strong chin in a playful manner, she said, "Now I'm working for you and you're the leader of our team. I guess you didn't like having a boss lady after all, right?"

"Oh, you can boss me around any time, my tempting wife."

"As long as my orders are agreeable, right?" she retorted.

"So far, you haven't given me one that isn't."

In a serious vein, Maggie said, "I'm sorry about what happened to your parents and brother, Hawk, and I'm sorry my family is involved in those tragic losses. I'm positive my mother will adore you as much as I do. Well, almost as much. But I can't surmise how Newl is going to feel about either of us later. We might not be welcome in their home."

"That reaction is to be expected in the beginning, Maggie, so don't let it hurt you or make you hesitate about doing what's right. In time, things should be settled between us; I hope that's true because I know how much you love your mother. One thing you've taught me is that hatred, anger, and a hunger for revenge can be tamed by love. In time, maybe Newl will accept that reality and forgive us for upholding the Law."

"That's one of the nicest things you could say to me, Hawk; thanks. I pray that Newl will be understanding, because those feelings can be so self-destructive and damaging to relationships with loved ones. You made the right decision to let the Law mete out justice for you and your family. You're a good and honorable man, so I think you would have come to regret killing them, despite what they did."

Maggie halted herself from stroking his chest as if trying to soothe the anguish he still endured within his heart. "How did you discover Barber's gang was responsible for their deaths?"

"My parents and brother had just returned from the bank in town, carrying a satchel of money Pa had collected to pay for a herd he was buying that week, when those varmints rode up to steal it. I figured one of them must have been in the bank, maybe checking it out for a robbery, when Pa made his withdrawal, so they considered him an easier and safer target."

Hawk's voice hoarsened with a mixture of sadness and anger as he said, "Whoever saw that pickup must have gathered the others and followed them home. They shot them down near the barn, right beside the carriage, took the satchel, and left in a hurry before any ranch hands could come running to help. Pedro Gonzales, a Mexican boy who does chores around the place, he was in the loft checking out a bird nest when the incident took place. From where he hid behind bales of hay, he saw and heard everything, including their first names. When he told me it was a tall redhead called Pete, a spooky-eyed skinny man called Slim, and two others called Coot and Toby, I knew who was responsible. Besides, they'd been seen in town that morning. I learned that when I returned to bury my family and investigate their murders. Blazes, Maggie, if I had stayed longer, maybe I could have saved them. But it's too late to think in that direction."

Maggie's heart ached over his sufferings and misplaced guilt. Yet, she thought it best to keep silent. Grief was something a person had to deal with in their own way and time.

"Pedro said a fifth man was with them, tall, sandy-haired, nice-looking. Nobody spoke his name during the attack. After I caught up with Muns, he told me it was Ben Carver, and that Carver was in prison. With Ben locked away until I dealt with him later, I concentrated on finding the others. As I told you, they laid low for a long time. Every clue I got to them only lead me into box canyons. Then, I received word from Callie — the girl who works in the Paradise Club — that Newl was looking for a hired gun to bust Ben out of prison. That's when I came up with my cunning idea and got my superior to agree to using it because the authorities want Barber and Jones real bad, and want that stolen money returned to Prescott. You see, part of that theft was the payroll for Fort Whipple soldiers, government money. Since federal laws had been broken, that gave me power to act."

"So, you have a witness against them this time; that's good news."

"I don't want to involve a boy in a trial. That could put him in danger. You see, Maggie love, Barber has a brother who's as mean or meaner and faster than Barber. His name is Berk and he's as dangerous as a villain comes." Hawk decided not to tell Maggie that Berk also fit Pedro's description of the fifth man because he didn't want her doubting Ben's guilt at this point in time, and he'd been told Berk was seen in New Mexico on that awful day.

331

"So you're afraid that this Berk would harm Pedro?"

"Yep, either before or during or even after Barber's trial. I don't want anybody to know about Pedro's existence, other than my superior and you. Pete and Berk are sorry excuses for men, but they are brothers. Whether they love each other or not, those kind of men go after revenge."

"You're right. I'm sure you felt frustrated knowing you might be unable to prove their guilt since you couldn't use Pedro against them."

"For a while, about as frustrated as I was about a mysterious woman who blew into my life and gnawed at my innards without mercy or relief."

Maggie smiled, allowing him to get off of the painful subject. "But you're appeased and calmed now, right?"

He caressed her cheek and smiled. "For a little while. You have this way of making me hungry and thirsty over and over again, no matter how good my last taste of you was."

"Speaking of taste, if we don't hurry, we'll miss supper again."

"I can take a hint, woman. Let's get dressed and go eat."

As they snuggled in bed later, Hawk asked Maggie about herself and her work. She talked about her childhood, schooling back East with Abby, life and work with her mother in St. Louis, Catherine's romance with and marriage to Newl, her job in a lawyer's office for two years, and about joining the Carlton Detective Agency years ago. She related tales about her various assignments: She told him about investigating a detective agency in Denver which was in reality a cover for the clandestine business of forcing gamblers to make payoffs rather than risk being searched for hidden cards or shot down from concealment. She told him about a ruse in Amarillo where diamonds were sprinkled on rocky sections to lure ignorant men into purchasing certain properties, only to discover no other stones could be found later and those picked up earlier were of low quality. She told him about burnings and so-called accidents at a newspaper office in Kansas City where a formidable cattle baron was being written about unfavorably and was trying to scare off the editor and reporter. She related other stories at his encouragement, then said, "You see, my value was in being a stranger to those areas, being a woman who wouldn't fall under suspicion by the culprits, and the ability to play a southern belle to great heights. That Kansas City case was where I got my newspaper experience I've been using during our work together."

"I married a very smart and brave woman. My family would have loved you, Maggie, and you would have loved them. I know my grandparents will feel that way. I'm eager for you to meet them. Grandpa owns a mercantile store in San Antonio. He retired from ranching years ago; as you know, that's hard work in all kinds of weather. He and Grandma are wonderful people; they started the ranch my parents had. It's a large and beautiful spread, three hundred prime acres and plenty of water. They raised high quality cattle and horses. Stone, my brother who was killed, took to ranching like a duck to water. As for me, I liked moving around and seeing places and being a lawman. It got lonely and the weather could be miserable at times, but it suited me too much to let the sacrifices and hardships get me down. Their foreman and hands are running the place for me until I return or sell out. Now that I have a wife and want a family of my own, the Circle R Ranch is where we'll live. Unless you want to settle somewhere else."

"Absolutely not. Living on your ranch sounds like a dream come true, Hawk: a home we and our children will love."

They lay on their sides and talked in whispers for a while before they went to sleep.

On Sunday morning, Hawk and Maggie attended a local church on the edge of town before they had lunch. They skipped dessert to savor one at an ice cream parlor on Fourth Street. While strolling back to their hotel, they paused here and there to window shop.

At Summerfield Bros., Maggie glanced at samples of new clothing in brocades, silks, and satins in many shades which were hanging inside the multipaned windows. On the *Tombstone Epitaph*'s window, there was a message for anybody who didn't read the local newspaper: it announced a meeting of the Rescue Hook & Ladder Company at Judge Wallace's court room at seven o'clock on Monday night.

After reaching the hotel shortly before two o'clock, Hawk changed garments and left her in their room while he went to check on their targets.

Since her tentative meeting with Pete Barber wasn't until three, Maggie did the same before she walked to the telegraph office, open even on Sundays, to send her boss all the news. She told him she would be sending in her resignation soon because she had gotten married, and would be settling down soon on her new husband's San Antonio ranch. She told him she would visit him when she came to St. Louis to pack and move her belongings.

She also sent Abby a telegram to tell her everything was fine and that she would write her a long letter soon which would include "wonderful news."

That errand required longer than she had imagined, so she hurried to the hotel to learn that Pete Barber had not arrived for his appointment with her. She told the desk clerk she would be in her room if the man came later, which he didn't.

When Hawk returned at four-thirty and she told him Pete hadn't showed up, he shrugged and said, "I didn't expect him to. After talking with Fly yesterday, he's probably satisfied we're no threat to him. We'll prove him wrong very soon, won't we, my love?"

"Yes, we will." After Maggie told Hawk about her two telegrams, she was mystified by his reaction. He smiled as she related her news to Abby but it faded fast and he actually stared at her when she revealed the message to her boss. An odd expression crossed his face before he could prevent it, though he quickly concealed it. Yet even his tone of voice sounded a little unusual when he spoke . . .

"I wish you hadn't done that before asking me, Maggie."

"Why?"

"We're working on the sly and can't afford any slips and exposure."

"Don't worry; I used our secret code as usual, so the key operators won't know what I said to him. I just didn't want to surprise him with a sudden resignation; I wanted him to be prepared in advance. I always work on the sly and report to him, so that won't be a problem for us. Besides, I needed to let him know why I extended my leave of absence. It wouldn't do for an emergency to arise and for him to try to contact me at Mother's in Tucson since we don't want my name connected to Newl's yet."

"I'm sure you'll be a big loss to him and his agency, and I guess a warning is understandable and he's trustworthy." Anxious to change the subject, he suggested, "I tell you what, why don't we take a ride before supper? We and our horses can use the exercise."

As Maggie changed into a split-tail riding skirt and boots, she stole a furtive glance at Hawk and wondered why he was frowning and what he was thinking about with such intensity. Although he had given her a plausible explanation, she didn't think he had exposed his real reason for being dismayed by her action. Or perhaps she was reading him wrong and her imagination was running wild.

They rode across the high desert terrain at a leisurely pace, enjoying their outing as much as Diablo and Blaze. The chestnut roan and black mustang delighted in having their owners atop them and seemed to revel in freedom from the corral. The day was still too hot for galloping or racing, though all four were tempted to do so. They weaved through red-blossomed ocotilla, flowering cacti, budding yucca and sotol, and scrubs of various types and sizes on the near-treeless landscape. They saw mines in several directions and talked about the wealth of that region. They sighted the reservoir atop Comstock Hill. They ascended a low ridge and gazed down at sprawling Tombstone whose streets were busy with people, horses, and wagons.

They talked a little, but mostly just took in the sites and each other's pleasant company in tranquil silence. Since there had been no rain in a long time, even the air smelled dusty and dry; but ever so often at certain locations or when a breeze wafted by, they caught the mingled scents of flowers and food cooking in homes and businesses nearby.

As the sun sank lower on the western horizon, Hawk said, "We'd better head back to town before dark. We'll need to tend our horses before we corral them and freshen up for supper."

Maggie concurred and guided Blaze toward their destination.

After supper, Maggie — who had forced this afternoon's mystery out of her head — and Hawk kissed and caressed and whispered endearments as they made love before she fell asleep.

Before Hawk did the same, he told himself his initial apprehension over Maggie's revelations to her boss was unnecessary. There was no way the man could or would jeopardize their assignment and lives, so he needn't worry about their exposure and survival.

Monday night, Hawk and Maggie prepared themselves and their horses before they went to spy on their targets at the saloon. Their mounts were saddled and waiting for them at a hitching post. Both were clad in a dark shirt and jeans, and Maggie's long hair was stuffed beneath her hat. Their weapons had been cleaned, checked, and loaded that afternoon. Each wore a knife in a belt sheath; hers was a long and slender Spanish blade, and his was a large Bowie. All precautions had been taken and their plans made in detail. Ella Mae had told them this afternoon that everything was going as scheduled, with Conchita and a private card room hired for the entire night by Pete Barber.

Concealed within sight of the window of that chosen room, Hawk looked at Maggie in the dim light of a fast-waning moon, and whispered, "This is it, woman, so be careful. I love you."

Maggie squeezed his hand and murmured in his ear, "I'll follow orders, sir, and I love you, too." She was anxious to get this episode started and finished so they could wind up the case soon and head for home. Home . . . what a beautiful word, her mind echoed. *Please, God, guide and protect us tonight during this perilous ride.*

Chapter Fifteen

At nine o'clock, Maggie and Hawk watched Barber and his men sneak out the window and make their stealthy way to where they had either stolen or borrowed horses waiting. The gang mounted and rode in a direction that would take them north of Fairbank to the Southeastern Railroad tracks. With caution, the couple mounted and followed at a safe distance, a waning moon refusing to illuminate any dust they might kick up en route and their horses' hooves covered with thick cloth to prevent any telltale noises. Riding gloves covered their own hands. With little light available and with such a space between them, they felt it was unnecessary to soot their faces to prevent reflective shines.

The landscape altered to a more protective one as they left the high desert plateau. They rode over knolls or around rolling hills. Tall agave, ballish sage, spreading mesquites, cottonwood, and other trees appeared; and increased in numbers and sizes as they entered the San Pedro Valley where lush and tall grass grew in abundance.

At last the four outlaws reached a site east of the San Pedro River which Pete had selected for his daring crime. After secreting themselves in nearby trees in the fertile valley, the couple observed as the gang donned black hoods and waited until a locomotive pulling a wood car and an express car appeared, moving slow at that winding location and time of night to avoid striking animals which might wander onto the rails.

Maggie and Hawk saw Pete gallop alongside the engine, leap aboard it, and draw a pistol with one hand as he held on to a bar with the other. With her rifle and his revolvers at the ready to defend any victims — though they surmised Pete didn't intend to shoot them or hoods wouldn't be worn for disguises — the train came to a stop and the others joined their leader. Above the hissing of steam, they overheard Pete's shouts as the engineer and fireman were ordered from the locomotive. After Pete threatened to blow up the express car with dynamite if the two guards inside didn't open the door and turn over the money, the wide wooden gate was slid aside and two weaponless men came into view with hands lifted upward. They, too, were ordered to "hop down and kiss the ground."

Within minutes, the safe was blasted open, the money sacks removed and loaded on the horses, and the deed completed. As hoped, Maggie and Hawk heard Pete warn the men to stay there for at least an hour until they got the train under way again; he said he would be watching them from a concealed location, until and if they moved an inch, he would blast them to pieces and dynamite the entire train.

Then Pete changed his mind; he had the men bound with their hands behind their backs, shoved to sitting positions, and secured two by two with ropes encircling them so they couldn't walk or run for help in Fairbank a few miles down the tracks.

As all that took place, Maggie whispered, "How did Pete know the train's schedule and how many guards would be aboard? And why did they give up so quickly and easily? They had cover and the gang was in the open, so that gave the guards an advantage. They aren't brave or dependable."

Without taking his gaze from the scene and while staying prepared to shoot Pete and Slim, who still had weapons in their hands, Hawk whispered in return, "We'll check out that strange angle later." Even after Pete and Slim holstered their pistols, Hawk relaxed only slightly. He knew Pete was dangerous and unpredictable, but he was confident he could use both of his hands and revolvers skillfully enough if necessary.

The alert couple observed in suspense as the gang mounted and left, both sighing in relief that the victims were alive and unharmed. Each had feared the vicious Pete might turn and shoot the disabled men just for fun.

Hawk told Maggie in a rush, "You wait about ten minutes, cover your face with a bandanna, and go untie the engineer so he can free the others and get that train moving before the morning one comes along and crashes into it. Make sure you don't talk and reveal you're a woman. They won't know what's going on, but they'll be glad to be freed. Then head back to the hotel and wait for me there. I'll follow Pete and his boys to see where they hide the money. For certain they won't go spending it around town and arousing suspicions; they'll wait for things to settle down before retrieving and dividing it. Be careful, Maggie, and don't get seen by anybody."

It was a long time after she reached their room that Hawk joined her. "Where have you been?" she asked anxiously. "What took so long? Did they change the plan?"

"Nope, they wanted to get back in a hurry to establish their alibi. It's clever of Pete to use other horses and gear so his won't be dusty and damp if they're checked out later. They discarded the saddles and released the horses before they reached town and walked the rest of the way. They sneaked back in the window; then Pete and Chita left the room hugging and laughing. I guess they were heading upstairs, probably making sure everybody in the saloon saw him there. I doubled back, hauled the money to another spot, and hid it, then brushed away mine and Diablo's tracks. Course, Pete shouldn't go checking on it for a while, not before we get to the sheriff in the morning and arrest them in their beds. I also rode over to Fairbank to relate our suspicions to the sheriff there; I told him he should hold and question both guards as soon as the train arrives. I also told him to do it quietly so he won't alert our targets we're on to them before we take action in the morning."

Maggie smiled and said, "He won't have to arrest both of them. The guilty man already confessed to the others. When I walked up with a mask on and drew my knife, they were scared witless. One of the guards started begging me not to kill him and swearing he wouldn't tell anybody anything about the robbery, that he'd followed the boss's orders and opened the car without resistance. It seems he convinced the other guard they were going to be blown up in the blast if they didn't surrender and they put up a fight. The other three began cursing and threatening him with jail. After I cut the engineer loose and returned to hiding, he freed two of the others, but they kept that guard bound to turn over to the authorities in Fairbank. As lily-livered as he is, it shouldn't take much to scare him into shedding light on how Pete learned about the delivery and got him involved."

"You're right, woman, and that won't sit well with ole Pete. Looks as if I'm finally going to see justice done toward those sorry bastards. Excuse the crude talk, woman, I forgot myself there for a moment."

"You're forgiven, but why are we waiting until

morning to talk to the sheriff and go after them? What if they panic and escape?"

"I doubt Pete Barber's ever panicked for even an instant in his entire life; he's too cocky and arrogant to think anybody or anything could harm him. It's late, so the sheriff's asleep. Besides, as I said earlier, those culprits aren't going anywhere until the excitement dies down and they recover the money. Pete will probably consider it an amusing challenge to bluff his way out of this situation if the Law even glances in his direction. He thinks his cunning alibi is unbreakable. Too, by taking them in the morning after they've had a long and busy night celebrating, they'll be asleep and groggy, so there's less chance of a shootout and people getting hurt."

Maggie unfastened the large buckle of Hawk's gunbelt, removed it, and laid it aside. "As always, my beloved husband, you're smart and right."

"I'm glad you think so. I know I was smart to lasso you."

Maggie was aroused by the way his eyes were devouring her face and gown-clad body. "And I was smart to let you rope me tight."

Although he ached to take her in his arms, Hawk said, "We'd best get to bed, you tempting woman; we have an early and busy day coming. I need to be up and seeing the sheriff at dawn."

Maggie deliberately danced past him to the bed and smiled as she murmured in a seductive tone, "I was hoping we'd have a busy night over here before the excitement starts tomorrow."

Hawk grinned and chuckled. "You were, were you?"

"Yep, boss man, I was." She sent him a mischievously playful look of disappointment as she purred, "But I guess I can wait until later to —"

Hawk grasped her arm to halt her from walking away. "Oh, no, woman, you can't start something like this without finishing it. Shuck those clothes, my arresting wife, and climb into bed. I'll join you faster than snow can melt under a blazing sun."

After they were undressed and cuddled, Hawk drifted his fingers over her sleek arm as he gazed down at her in the glow of a lowered lamp whose flickering light seemed to play across her flesh as merrily and freely as he did. "You're so beautiful and enchanting, my heart's pounding inside my chest like a Cheyenne war drum. I think I could just stare at you for hours; heck, for weeks or months without end."

Maggie smiled as she stroked his jawline and teased her fingertip along the cleft in his strong chin, then over his full lips. "It's you who's utterly irresistible, Hawk. Every time you look at me or smile at me or I hear your voice or inhale your scent, I want you," she murmured with another radiant smile.

"Then we're well matched, woman." He trailed kisses from over the joint of one bare shoulder, across her collarbone, and up the silky column of her throat before kissing her. His thumb stroked one cheek as his mouth deftly plundered hers for hidden treasures. Consumed by suspense and anticipation, his hands roved her naked body with delight.

Ensnared by the magic and pleasure of her husband's actions, Maggie clung to him and allowed her exploring fingers to chart his torso and face. She relished the taste and feel of his unleashed responses to her stimulations. He was the most exciting and alluring man she had ever met. Since their initial union, she couldn't get enough of him, in and out of bed.

Hawk separated their mouths so his could journey down her neck to take turns swirling his tongue around her taut nipples, teething them with gentleness, then kneading them with eager fingers. Soon, his questing hand sought out the moist heat between her thighs. She gasped as he began to pleasure her with his touch. Moaning softly, she surrendered to his masterful caress until she cried out in sweet release.

Maggie was astonished by climaxing from his kisses and caresses. Yet within minutes of receiving that unexpected gift, there didn't seem to be an inch of her that didn't beg for more. She wanted and needed her husband, her lover, her friend, her partner, to the fullest with all of her heart, soul, and being. She was surprised that he could ignite her passions to such a high degree so fast after sating her so wonderfully.

Hawk had reached a near feverish level himself. Unable to wait any longer to become one with his beloved, he took a position over her and buried his pleading erection deeply and snugly within her moist recess.

Maggie's hands journeyed over his virile frame. Her fingers clutched his buttocks and felt the muscles there contract and relax as he entered and withdrew from her feminine core. She lapped her legs over his. Her cravings mounted as they loved each other without hesitation or restraints.

"Mercy, woman, you're driving me loco. I can hardly control myself."

"Then don't, my beloved. Ride away with me, Hawk, now."

As she arched toward him, hugged him tightly, gasped for air, and kissed him, he knew she was claiming her prize, and he did the same. In a glorious burst of supreme ecstasy, he once more branded her as his wife.

Total tranquility settled over and within them as they relaxed in each other's arms.

"I love you, Maggie Reynolds; mercy, how I love you, woman."

"I love you, Hawk. We're going to be so happy together as soon as we complete our assignment. I can hardly wait to see our home."

"It won't be much longer now," he said and kissed her temple before he doused the lamplight and filled the room with darkness.

They cuddled and shared light caresses until they fell asleep.

Tuesday morning at dawn, Hawk ate a quick meal before he awakened the sheriff, revealed his identity, and related his story, including where the money was hidden. When asked why he didn't prevent the crime in advance or foil it while in progress and summon him for help last night, Hawk answered, "A man can't be arrested and tried for a deed he hasn't done yet. No court would convict him on mere allegations."

"If you'd come to me when you learned about his plans, we could have set a trap for him and caught him red-handed," the sheriff reasoned.

"I couldn't risk Barber smelling a trap or somebody overhearing us planning one and warning him. If shooting had started at the tracks or on the trail afterward, some of those railroad men or your deputies could have caught a bullet, and Barber might have escaped in the commotion. I also needed him to carry out that robbery so I could unmask everybody involved in it; that's how I discovered the identity of the guard who helped him. As for why I waited until now, I knew they weren't going anywhere soon. I figured it would be safer for everybody around him if we captured them early this morning while they're sleeping; we certainly couldn't have challenged them in a busy saloon. Barber's been known to take down three men in one gunfight, and a desperate man is unpredictable and dangerous."

"You're right, Marshal Reynolds, so let's get to it."

Within thirty minutes, several deputies had been summoned. With stealth, the group of lawmen sneaked to their assigned locations. The deputies found and arrested the two cohorts without any trouble, as both had been dead drunk.

The sheriff and another deputy found Slim Jones in the same condition when they busted in on him and disabled him; but Hawk found Pete's room next door empty, his bed still neatly made.

The vexed U.S. marshal almost stalked back to Slim's room and demanded, "Where's Barber? Talk before I lose my temper." The bony outlaw with a sharp and thin face, dirty hands and ragged nails, unwashed and mussed hair glared at him with fierce hatred in those pale gray eyes.

"I ain't tellin' you nuthin'. You cain't prove we robbed no train. We was playin' cards and drinkin' all night. Ask anybody at the saloon."

"We know all about your faked alibi, Slim, so it won't hold water with us or the court. You and your friends are heading for prison pronto."

"We ain't goin' nowheres. You ain't got nuthin' against us. I know you're just bluffin', and it don't scare me none. Ain't no court fool 'nough to accuse Pete, and ain't no bars strong 'nough to hold 'im."

"He must have spent the night with Conchita," Hawk speculated and saw Slim's look of surprise and fear, probably assuming Pete was still asleep and vulnerable. "I'll go after him while you take care of this varmint."

"If'n you goes after Pete Barber, you bastard, they'll be coverin' you with dirt afore noon. He's the fastest and best gun around."

Following Slim's taunt, Hawk used a slug across his jaw to silence his ensuing shouts to create a commotion to alert his friend to peril. He looked at the sheriff and deputy and said, "Barber's mine, so I'm going after him."

To Hawk's dismay, he found Conchita on a rumpled bed, but alone. From the pattern of her breathing and the way her cheek puffed out from a smile, he knew the dark-haired Mexican woman who was lying on her stomach and facing the wall with her eyes closed was awake. She must have heard the hinges squeak, though he'd tried to open the door quietly, Hawk reasoned. He walked to the side of the bed and nudged her bare shoulder.

"Come back to bed, you fiery *hombre*. It is too early to rise. *Dese prisa,* and I will make you squeal and squirm with *delicioso deleite.*"

So, you're in a "hurry" to give that snake "delicious delight," are you? "Where's Pete Barber?" he asked, and watched her flip to her back and gape at him, her dark gaze taking in the revolver still in his hand.

"*Que demonios!* Who are you? What do you want?"

"I'm Hawk Reynolds. Answer the question. Pronto!" When she remained silent, he hinted, "I'm not in a good mood this morning, Chita, so don't provoke me to anger. Where is he?"

"How should I know? He left earlier. Why do you want him, *perro?*"

351

Hawk wasn't even slightly aroused by the earthy female who sat up, allowing the wrinkled sheet to fall to her lap exposing her naked body. As she fluffed her ebony mane, she made no attempt to cover her ample breasts or the dark furry patch which was in partial view. He was amused and repulsed by her bold and seductive ploy to distract him. In case she made a slip in her language, he pretended not to understand her insult, though he was fluent in Spanish, as well as Cheyenne, and knew a smidge of Apache. Besides, a "dog" wasn't the worst thing he'd been called during his work. "For that train robbery he pulled last night, with your help."

"I was here working all evening, *lastimoso gato.*"

Hawk still didn't react to her calling him a "pitiful tomcat" but confronted her with her complicity as he said, "You were pretending to serve drinks to an empty room downstairs while Pete and his gang robbed the payroll train. You're just as guilty, and you're going to prison for a long time. If I were you, Chita, I'd go for mercy by helping us catch Pete."

"I do not know what you're talking about and I can not help you catch him because I do not know where he is."

Although she tried to look and sound calm and ignorant, Hawk perceived her rising anxiety and took advantage of it. "Then you're in big trouble, Conchita. We know for a fact you helped set up his fake alibi last night, and you're close . . . friends, shall we call it? What happens to a pretty

352

woman behind bars ain't nice. At the Territorial Prison in Yuma, men and women are incarcerated together. Some of those guards and male convicts are known to get itches in their pants they like to scratch when nobody's around to stop them. Be smart for once and talk to me. You're already under arrest, so stop acting dumb before I toss you in jail to look for him. If I have to find him on my own, I won't be merciful toward you. I'll throw you in a cell with Slim and those other two cohorts, and let them think you did a lot of blabbing before you arrived. I wonder how ole loyal Slim will react to a traitor within his reach when the sheriff steps out of his office for a few hours."

A wide-eyed and pale-faced Chita asked, "What are you?"

"A U.S. marshal, so I have the authority to help you all I can," he said, not revealing that was little to nothing for cooperation. He told himself he shouldn't feel guilty about misleading her because she was a criminal who could help him capture a worse one. "Well, time's a wasting. What's it to be, woman: a cell alone or one with your friends?" He saw Conchita glare at him as she considered his intimidating words.

"All I know is he left about fifteen or twenty minutes ago to head for Fairbank. *Vete al infierno, sucio cerdo.*"

This "dirty pig" isn't going "to hell," ardiente puta. "Has he gone to meet with that guard from the train?" When she hesitated to incriminate herself further, he frowned and warned, "I can't ask for mercy for you if you don't tell the truth, woman. Hurry, my patience is wearing thin."

"*Esta bien, feroz lobo!* He went to silence him."

"*Fierce wolf,*" *now that's better, so is "all right."*

The sheriff arrived at that moment to see what was taking Hawk so long and to check if he needed help. Hawk related what he'd learned to the man and said, "As soon as Barber realizes that guard has been exposed and arrested and he discovers the money is gone, he'll guess the truth and hightail it. I'm going after him as soon as I run tell my wife and grab some supplies and a canteen."

"Don't you want us to ride with you? Pete Barber's as mean and sly as they come."

"No, thanks, I can travel faster alone, and it's easier for one man to trail him unseen to an ambush point than for a posse to sneak up."

After the sheriff nodded agreement, Hawk glanced at Conchita and said, *"Gracias, tonto bruja."* He watched her gaze enlarge as he thanked her and called her a foolish and reckless witch, letting her know he had grasped her many insults and curses.

"You speak Spanish?"

"*Si. Adios,* Chita."

"You can't go after Pete Barber alone, Hawk," Maggie pleaded with her husband when he'd related the plan to her. "He's dangerous and cunning. He'll suspect a pursuit and try to ambush you. I stayed behind this morning, but I'm going with you this time to back you up."

As Hawk grabbed his rifle and gear, he urged, "No, Maggie love, please stay here. I can ride faster if it's just me and Diablo, and Pete already has a head start on us. We know this terrain and we're used to challenging its harsh conditions and the desert heat; you and Blaze aren't. I'll be careful; I promise. Don't forget I'm an experienced marshal; I'm used to pursuing outlaws like Pete Barber, but you aren't. I'll return for you as soon as I catch up with him and capture him."

"But, Hawk, you might need my help. If he's such a vicious killer, surely two armed officers are better than one."

"I won't be able to keep on alert if I'm worrying about Barber shooting you out of the saddle. I've always worked alone and never been harmed, so I'll be fine. When I return, we'll go after Ben together; I promise. Please agree, woman, time's short and I have to get on his trail fast."

"All right, Hawk, I'll do as you say this time. But if you aren't back or I haven't heard from you within a week, I'm coming after you two. And if he harms you, I won't rest until I track him down and punish him."

Hawk smiled, gave her a rapid kiss, and said, "I love you, Maggie Reynolds, and I'll be seeing you again soon. Stay on guard just in case Barber doubles back for revenge or to rescue Slim."

"I'll stay alert and be careful. Good-bye, my

beloved husband."

From the hotel window, Maggie watched Hawk load his gear, mount his eager horse, and gallop down the street. She observed him until he was out of sight and his dust cloud had settled. She didn't know why, but her last words to him had caused her heart to lurch in a premonition of trepidation and goosebumps to rise on her flesh, though the day was warm already. She prayed for God to protect her husband and his cherished mustang, and for Pete Barber to be brought to swift justice.

At midmorning Maggie visited with the sheriff in his office, identifying herself as an agent of the Carlton Detective Agency in St. Louis and Hawk Reynolds's wife. She noticed Slim Jones, Conchita, and the other two hirelings glaring at her as she spoke with the Tombstone lawman about the current episode and the past one in Prescott she was investigating. She was surprised and puzzled as to why Hawk hadn't mentioned that was what brought them to Tombstone in search of Pete and Slim . . . She speculated to the sheriff that, during the sunrise commotion and his hasty departure, Hawk probably had lacked the time to explain the matter fully.

She discovered that the guard from the train had been brought to town earlier to be held with the other villains until they were either tried in court there or taken elsewhere for their trials. The guard had related that Pete had learned about the payroll shipment from a drunken miner recently, then approached him about aiding his plans. He said he had cooperated for two reasons: money and fear of Pete Barber, fear of retaliation for exposing his intention or refusing to assist it. Conchita had told the sheriff that Pete approached her to help establish his alibi after finding her in town following his arrival; Chita claimed she helped him for the same reasons the guard had, but neither the sheriff nor Maggie believed her.

She was allowed to stand near the cell to question Slim about the robbery in Prescott on March first, his past involvements with Ben Carver, and the lethal incident near San Antonio on December twenty-ninth. Maggie was annoyed but not astounded by Slim's belligerent refusal to relate any facts or even — in his great ire — to drop a single clue about any of those matters.

"That trash in the next cell is lyin' about us; we ain't done nuthin' wrong. Who's gonna believe a cheap whore and a law-breakin' guard and saddletramps like them two? They're probably coverin' up for the gang who done it, or bein' paid to lie about us."

Maggie reminded the ghostly-eyed man whose skinny body was taut with the same rage that flamed in his gaze, "My husband and I followed you and the others from the saloon after you climbed out the window and sneaked away, and we were concealed nearby when you robbed the train. The money's already been recovered from where you hid it and it'll be returned to the mining company today. We aren't afraid to testify against you in court, and we will. You'll either hang for murder or go to prison for a long time for your many crimes. You might get a year or so taken off your sentence if you help us resolve those cases in Prescott and San Antonio."

"We ain't been to Prescott or Texas in over a year, and you can't prove we have. We're bein' framed for revenge, or you done accused the wrong men. You might as well buy yourself a black dress, 'cause your husband ain't comin' back. Ain't no man smart enough or good enough with his guns to capture Pete Barber. I'll be outta jail afore you knows it, and you'll be sorry you ever went up against me and Pete."

"No, Mr. Jones, you'll be the one who's sorry you got caught for your crimes and will be suffering greatly very soon. So will Ben Carver after we arrest him and return him to Yuma Prison. Tell me, is Pete riled at Ben because he doubled back and stole that money hidden outside of Prescott before he was captured and sent to prison?"

Before he could stop himself, Maggie saw a look of astonishment cross Slim's face, just as she watched him mask his reaction in haste. "You two have realized by now Ben stole the money, not Coot Sayers or Toby Muns, right? I suppose you've also heard that Muns is dead, and you already know Pete murdered Sayers because you were there with him. I'm amazed you and Pete

358

didn't go searching for Ben after he escaped from prison last month. By now, he's probably retrieved the loot and he's off somewhere spending it and celebrating, maybe even boasting about duping you two."

"You ain't gonna trick me into sayin' nuthin' crazy, you bitch."

Maggie observed Slim's glare of fierce hatred before he stalked to his bunk, threw himself down on it, and faced the stone wall. "If that's how you want it, Mr. Jones, so be it, but silence won't help you any. Nor can Pete Barber because he'll be joining you in there very soon. Pete might be skilled with his pistols and wits, but he's no match for my husband's talents." After those taunts failed to provoke Slim into making reckless shouts at her, she talked with the sheriff again before leaving the jail.

For the rest of that long and frightful day, Maggie ate two meals alone as she waited in their room for Hawk's return or good news from him. She fretted over his safety and kept a watchful eye and ear out for any treachery from Pete Barber. None came, and she deduced that Pete would surmise his cohorts were under heavy guard at the jail, which they were, so any attempt to free them would be reckless and lethal.

With a lightweight and short-barreled Colt .45 revolver at the ready at all times, Maggie gazed at the three photographs again Camillus Fly had delivered to her near dusk. Once more, her heart filled with love and joy; her mind soared with plans and with pride; and her body flamed with desire for Hawk, but ached with loneliness and concern for him. She felt it wasn't vain to think they made a lovely couple; they looked happy and compatible in the three poses. She had purchased all of them immediately upon viewing them, which had delighted Mr. Fly.

She could hardly wait to frame and position them in their new home. She decided to package the three photographs, along with her new outfit and any other unneeded items, and mail them to the ranch where they would be safe until she and Hawk arrived there, hopefully within the next month. Since they would be in a rush to leave for Sante Fe as soon as he returned with Pete, she would send the pictures on their way tomorrow and surprise him with them later.

After placing them on the table, she wrote Abby a long letter relating the news about her sudden marriage and recent adventures. *I can imagine your expression and reaction to this amazing turn in events, my dear friend. I only wish I could be there to tell you in person, but I can't.*

Maggie knew that the *Tombstone Epitaph* editor, as was common practice, would send out word about the colorful episode last night to other territorial newspapers, perhaps even include copies of his article about it which would appear in tomorrow's local paper. Yet, he had promised not to print that those notorious villains had been exposed and captured by U.S. marshal Hawk Reynolds and his detective wife. He had promised to keep that fact secret following requests from Hawk via the sheriff so that others involved in those crimes wouldn't be alerted to their identities and impending pursuit.

She wondered how Ben and Newl would feel and what the Carver men would think after learning that Pete and Slim no longer posed a threat. She wished there were some way she could reach Ben and capture him before he made that discovery, but time and distance prevented it. She would have to trick Newl into revealing Ben's location to her; surely she would face his wrath for doing so, but that couldn't be helped. She was certain now that Ben was guilty not only of the Prescott bank robbery and other crimes but also of complicity in the murder of Hawk's family members, and must pay for those deeds.

At least Hawk didn't hate and mistrust her because of her stepbrother. No matter the personal cost to her and her family, she must help him arrest Newl's son so he could be punished. She hoped and prayed Ben wouldn't bolt to unknown places before they reached him; he couldn't be allowed to get away with such crimes, and possibly commit new ones.

At ten o'clock, a weary and anxious Maggie went to bed to spend a restless night, waking up many times to worry about Hawk and their final task with its possible repercussions on her relationship with her mother and Newl before dozing off again, totally unprepared for the two shocks she would receive on Wednesday . . .

Chapter Sixteen

After breakfast, Maggie went to a mercantile store where she bought wrapping materials and was given assistance by the owner's genial wife with packing the photographs and her unneeded possessions. As they worked, the older woman remarked that the pictures and the dress she had chosen were lovely and romantic, and that the couple's expressions revealed their deep love for each other, to which Maggie agreed with a beaming smile. She walked to the post office and mailed the package to the ranch in San Antonio, in care of her husband. She also sent a letter to Abby before she went to the telegraph office to send a cleverly worded message to Newl.

After she heard several knocks on her door, as a safety precaution in case Pete Barber had doubled back to seek revenge on her, Maggie asked without unbolting it, "Who's there?"

"It's Matthew Lawrence, Maggie. Abby sent me with a message."

She unlocked the door and stared at the man who was standing there with an expectant expression on his face. "Why did she send you here?" she asked anxiously. "Is something wrong in Yuma?"

"No, everything's fine there; so is Abby. She's just worried about you."

"Why?" Maggie asked, then added, "Come inside," in the event her love-blinded friend had confided their secret in her sweetheart. "Have a seat," she offered, pointing to the short settee. "Now, why are you here?"

"Mr. Mercer received news that somebody has been checking on you back East at the boarding school."

Maggie tensed in apprehension, but masked that reaction. "Checking on me? Whatever for? Who?"

"He doesn't know, but a man went to the school and asked questions about you. The headmistress thought it was strange, so she sent word to Mr. Mercer. I suppose because he mentioned Abby several times since you two roomed together and were best friends. Mr. Mercer was going to let it pass as a mystery until he received another message that a man — perhaps the same one — was checking on you and the Mercers in Virginia."

Maggie's anxiety increased as she wondered if her misdeed had been exposed, or if she and the Mercers had fallen under suspicion because the relationship between her and Ben had been discovered and because she was visiting the prison Commissioner's family when he escaped. She

364

prayed they wouldn't be incriminated and jeopardized or face a nasty scandal. "Someone was investigating the Mercers, too?"

"Mr. Mercer's ex-business partner was at a newspaper office when the man came in to ask if you were employed there or maybe at another Virginia newspaper. The editor told him he'd never heard of you, or met you at any of the other offices he had visited. His ex-partner notified him because his name was mentioned again in connection to yours."

"What kind of questions was this man asking?"

"Where you live. If you moved back to Virginia after your father's death in Texas. What you're doing now. How he could locate you. Since nobody had those answers, he asked where the Mercers live in case they knew where and how to reach you through Abby. He seemed the most interested in where you work and your current address."

Who could be trying to find me and why? How does he know about my past? Did this news frighten Abby into breaking her promise of silence? "Is that all you came to tell me, about those two suspicious incidents?"

"Yes. Mr. Mercer told Abby to write and inform you, but Abby asked me to deliver the message and as fast as possible, and on the sly."

Maggie wondered if he thought Abby's actions were odd. "I guess she thought it was important I know immediately," she hinted.

"Yes, because of your work. Don't be upset

with her or worry about me revealing your identity, but she told me you're a detective and you're working secretly on an important case; so she figured it could be somebody involved in it checking on you. She figured somebody in Prescott traced you back to Yuma and them to get that starting point. If you've got a person worried to this point, Maggie, he could be dangerous, so if anybody strange comes around questioning you, you should contact the sheriff for protection."

She recalled she had used the journalist cover on one other case, but nobody involved in it had been told where she was born or where she had gone to school. In fact, the only person she had related those facts to was Hawk; but if he had asked an agent to investigate her, he would have revealed that action to her by now. "I will, Matthew, and thank you for coming to see me so promptly. You're marrying a smart woman, Abby's speculations match mine. But until somebody contacts me for information, I'm totally puzzled by this matter. Are you planning on staying here overnight?"

"No, I'm catching the return train to Yuma. I only have another hour before it pulls out, so if you'll excuse my rush, I'll be heading back to the depot at Fairbank. I hired a wagon driver to haul me over and return me; he's waiting outside for me."

"Tell Abby my current case is going fine and I'm perfectly safe. In fact, I just mailed her a long letter this morning telling her I'll be finishing and leaving in a day or two. I'll send her news of my new location soon."

"She'll be glad to hear you're safe; she was plenty worried. I guess your kind of work can be dangerous at times."

"Only on rare occasion; and I know how to defend myself and how to seek help when I can't. Thank you again, Matthew. By the way, how is your romance with my best friend progressing?"

"Perfect, just like Abby. Her parents know we're courting seriously now and they seem to approve of me and our match."

"The Mercers are wonderful people. You're lucky to be marrying into that family, and Abby's lucky she found you."

"Thanks, I'll be sure to tell her you said so in case it escaped her keen mind," he jested with a lopsided grin. "Well, I'd better hightail it for the depot. I don't want to miss the train. You take care of yourself, Maggie; so long for now. I'll be seeing you this winter at our wedding."

"I'll be there, Matthew; I wouldn't miss it for anything. I know you and Abby will be very happy together." She decided not to delay him by relating the good news about her own marriage; Abby could tell him later.

"I fully agree. I can hardly wait to get back to her."

"Good-bye, Matthew. Hug and kiss Abby for me."

"I will."

Maggie closed the door and leaned against it. Who was checking on her and why? Since the queries involved her current cover story, it had to be someone in Prescott because the timing was wrong for it to be somebody in Tombstone or from her past job. So, she pondered, whom had she intrigued so deeply in the territorial capital and why? Who had sicked a detective on her? Could it be Frank Moore and/or the bank owner? If Ben was guilty and they'd told the truth about him and the robbery, why would he or they be worried about her nosing around there? It was a very strange occurrence indeed.

She almost jumped at the pounding noise behind her as another knock came to her door. She unlocked and opened it, thinking Matthew had forgotten to say or give her something.

"Two telegrams, Mrs. Reynolds. One was sent to Margaret Malone, but you told our office that's your maiden name. Right?"

"That's correct, and thank you for delivering them. Wait a moment," she said and fetched a token to give him for his trouble.

Maggie hurried to the settee to sit down and read the telegrams. She hoped one was from Hawk saying he had captured Barber and was en route back to her. She quickly learned that neither message was from him, but both — in a way — involved her husband.

The first one, addressed to her maiden name because she hadn't exposed her marriage to Hawk, was from Newl in response to hers that morning. In their prearranged code, she had told him it was urgent she head to Sante Fe and speak with Ben about important discoveries in his case. It revealed Ben's location, so she sighed a breath of relief. Now, as soon as Hawk returned, they could head out fast to recapture Ben. She had told Newl about Slim's arrest for a local crime, but said to alert Ben to stay put because Pete was still on the loose and a threat to his survival.

The second telegram was from her boss in St. Louis and in code. As she deciphered it, her heart began to drum in trepidation and confusion:

Be alert for deceit and danger. Had a friend check on your new rank. Invalid. No marshal named Hawk Reynolds on record. Had him checked in Texas. Bounty hunter. In pursuit of family's killers. Repeat. Not a marshal. Put distance between you fast. Will continue to investigate mystery.

Maggie shook her head forcefully as if in a desperate attempt to clear it of doubts. She told herself that her boss and his sources had to be mistaken. Perhaps, she reasoned in near panic, Hawk's name wasn't recorded because he worked undercover. Yet, her defiant mind recalled, Howard Carlton had contacts everywhere who had clever ways of finding out anything and everything, even closely guarded secrets in government files. Several other facts leapt into her troubled mind to further distress it: Hawk hadn't told the local sheriff about the Prescott robbery, which was what had propelled them to pursue Barber and Jones. In addition, he had told her not to reveal she was a deputy marshal, to say only that she was a detective and his wife. He had known in Yuma that she had aided Ben's escape and had learned en route to Prescott about the boarding school, her journalist claim, and about being from Virginia — exactly the areas somebody had checked on in an attempt to verify her profession and address.

As pain knifed her heart and conscience, Maggie scolded herself for what she was thinking when surely Hawk could explain those curious points and coincidences. She was plagued by anguish and was speculating wildly about the man she loved and trusted, her husband. Or was he? If he wasn't a marshal who worked undercover, Hawk Reynolds might not be his real name. If that was true, her marriage wasn't legal under a false one!

No, Maggie, even Howard verified that's his real name. But if he isn't a marshal, you're wed to a bounty hunter and a liar and a cunning trickster. And if he isn't a marshal, he can't prevent your arrest by working with him on his alleged case. But as a bounty hunter, he can capture you for a reward, and as revenge for helping Ben escape, for being the stepsister of one of his family's killers. Would the authorities agree to a wild idea about busting a convict out of prison to let him lead you to his cohorts and stolen goods? That strategy doesn't sound likely. What if, after learning you were a detective, Hawk came up with a ruse he was sure you'd fall for: a marshal making you his deputy? Maybe he's blinded by hatred and a hunger for revenge and he's only using you to get it.

Perhaps, she fretted in torment, this traitorous dilemma was the reason for that premonitory feeling during their last talk before Hawk left!

Get a good hold on yourself, Maggie. Stop letting your imagination run wild and your emotions go crazy. Think calmly and rationally.

Despite that stern order, her ravaged mind asked how he had duped her so quickly and easily and completely about who he was and what he wanted from her. An answer came too fast to suit her: he had told her what she needed to hear in order to be ensnared; he had used her love for him to entrap her to obtain her assistance. He had convinced her Ben was guilty of both crimes and others, but was he? Had her speculations about a frame been accurate? Was the fact that Ben had suggested the hunting trip a clue to his guilt, or had Hawk only used that angle to inspire doubts within her? Had she tried to turn all she'd learned against Ben because Hawk had sworn Ben was partly to blame for his family's killings and she'd felt remorse for freeing him and she'd believed her husband's allegations? Had Hawk only needed her to help him get to Pete and Slim? Maybe he had no intention of returning to her later; maybe that was why he hadn't wanted her to accompany him during his pursuit of Pete; maybe he would just keep riding after Pete was either captured or slain. Maybe he knew Ben wasn't involved in his family's murders and had no interest in Ben, except for his reward.

Have I allowed you to dupe and mislead me? Should I wait for you here so you can explain, or should I continue my crucial mission alone? Can I trust you to speak the truth? And to not slay Ben when we reach him, if Muns really told you Ben's your fifth target?

Yet, it didn't elude Maggie's astute mind that Hawk had arrested Slim and had gone after Pete to do the same, not challenged either to a lethal showdown for revenge. Even so, Muns and Sayers were dead. And Slim and Pete hadn't yet made it to the gallows or prison alive . . .

Maggie went to see the sheriff and told him she was leaving town shortly to carry out her next assignment and she could be reached through her St. Louis agency when and if she was needed to testify at the villains' trials. She also told him she wasn't married to Hawk Reynolds, saying that claim was just a ruse to provide a safe cover for their joint investigation, which was over now that Barber and Jones — his targets — had been exposed.

On an inexplicable whim, she asked if he knew or had seen Berk Barber, Pete's notorious brother.

"Yep, I've seen him a few times when he rode into town either alone or with Pete and Slim." The sheriff confirmed Berk's notorious reputation.

"Could you give me a description of him in case I come across him?" Maggie asked. "If he somehow learns I was in on his brother's fate and he's the vengeful type, I'll need to avoid him."

"I can do better than words, Miss Malone. There was a reward poster put out on him about year back for cattle rustling. It was called off when Berk came up with an abili for that night, but I kept it for some reason. I got it in my desk. Yep. Here it is."

As Maggie stared at the worn paper, her emotions sank lower as she was given the last piece of evidence she needed to expose Hawk's pretense. The man drawn there strongly favored Ben Carver, down to the same height, hair and eye colors, age, the two men even rode the same type of horse. Hawk had to be aware of the similarities. There could be only one reason why Hawk had kept that crucial secret. . . .

She deduced that the fifth man Hawk was seeking for revenge — and possibly the fifth bandit in Prescott — was Berk Barber, not Ben Carver. And she wasn't about to lead a greedy and devious bounty hunter to her stepbrother!

A heart-sore and angry Maggie faked a smile, thanked the sheriff as she returned the old poster, and left his office.

Afterward, she telegraphed Howard to ask if he could gather more facts about Hawk and find out who was checking on her and why. She revealed she was leaving Tombstone alone to

question Ben Carver, her stepbrother, and out-
lined the facts about Ben's prison break and that
she was helping him prove his innocence, leaving
out the pertinent detail that she had effected his
escape. She told her boss and friend she would
contact him soon with her new location.

She went to the mercantile store again and
purchased trail supplies, relieved the owner's wife
wasn't there, as the woman might perceive her
change in mood and wonder about it. Had it
been only a few hours ago, she fretted, that she
had been happy and eagerly awaiting Hawk's
return? How quickly and painfully one's life
could be altered forever! She pushed aside her
distracting anguish, as she had work to do.

At the hotel, she bought food for her impending journey, filled her canteen, and packed her
belongings in a hurry. As she did so, she noticed
that Hawk had taken all of his possessions with
him, as if he didn't intend to return. But in case
he did, she wanted to be gone, vanished like a
mist following sunrise. She addressed an envelope to him at his ranch, inserted the wedding
ring and deputy badge — both fakes, to her mind
— and left the oppressive room where she believed for a while she had found true love.

At the registration desk, she handed the envelope to the clerk and told him, "If Mr. Reynolds
returns within the next few days, please give this
to him; if not, please mail it to him for me." She
paid her bill and gave him enough money to
cover the postage if necessary.

At the hitching post, Maggie loaded her gear on her saddle, having claimed Blaze at the stable before returning to the hotel. Since the last train at Fairbank had left for the day, she mounted to ride overland to Benson where she'd take the next eastbound one to New Mexico. Afterward, she would ride Blaze to Sante Fe for a rendezvous with Ben Carver and somehow extract the truth from him, whatever it might be.

Maggie covered the distance between Tombstone and Benson in two hours, riding at a pace that wouldn't overexert Blaze beneath the ninety-degree sun. It was a smooth journey in the San Pedro Valley along a well-worn road near a river by that same name. The sky was clear and blue, so she didn't have to worry about rain or a storm slowing her down. Yet she traveled with a heavy burden on her shoulders as she headed to see Ben, and another one gnawing at her heart as she abandoned a traitorous lover.

Fortunately, she arrived in town not long before the afternoon train's departure. She spoke with one of the railroad workers to learn that not only would other horses be transported in an open railed car for fresh air but also a man would be inside to keep them calm and tended along the route.

"I'm so sorry, but we have to move fast," she told the chestnut roan as she stroked the animal's forehead and neck before Blaze was led up a plank and into the car where her reins were secured to an iron ring. Maggie noted the water buckets, feed sacks, and fresh straw, which she was told would be changed frequently for cleanliness.

After her saddle was stored nearby, she took her seat in one of the many cars where other passengers were chatting and waiting. She sighed a breath of relief when the engineer blasted the whistle and the train left the depot on schedule without Hawk making a sudden appearance.

With many freight and mail stops to be made between Benson and her first destination of Las Cruces, the trip would take thirteen hours, with an expected arrival there at six o'clock in the morning.

Maggie settled back and watched the rocky outcroppings of the Little Dragoon mountains slip behind her. In an attempt to keep her mind off her troubles to her rear and the challenges before her, she glanced here and there at the rugged terrain where numerous scrubs, mesquites, agave, cacti, and other trees and plants grew. Grasses waved in a constant breeze which also cooled the car's interior, but her spirits stayed low.

As she ate a light meal of ham biscuits, fruit, and coffee, she was reminded of the time she had done the same with him while en route to Prescott. His arousing smile and laugh, those arresting golden brown eyes, the touch of his hands on her, and the tender way he made love to her kept assailing her senses and memory.

After the barely touched food was put away, Maggie realized her right thumb and forefinger were rubbing the empty spot on her left hand where the gold circle had been, left behind at the hotel for Hawk. She wondered what he would think when it was given to him, if he returned to Tombstone. She asked herself if she had acted too swiftly and impulsively. Should she have given him the benefit of doubt and waited for him to return and explain those heartrending mysteries? As a detective, she was influenced by evidence, and certain facts answered no. Yet how could he fake the sincerity of his words, the tender way his hands played sweet music over her body? Wouldn't her astute senses perceive emotional deception? Not if she was totally enchanted by him, she reasoned, which she had been.

Soon, foothills and snaking ravines appeared; vegetation lessened for a while except for sage and cacti; rocks were countless, as were doves; coyotes foraged and antelope grazed.

After passing the Chiricahua Mountains and crossing the San Simon Valley and River, they entered New Mexico where the topography altered to mostly flatland with mountains to their left and right miles away. Grass, tall sotol in bloom, and yellow wildflowers flourished in abundance on otherwise uncluttered land. It was what easterners called "the great open spaces."

As a new moon obscured the Chihuahuan

Desert landscape, Maggie ignored the lowered light of a hanging lantern near the car's front, closed her eyes, and tried to sleep; but only succeeded in sporadic dozing.

After sunrise, Maggie noticed that the train was heading directly for rugged brown mountains which were kissed with morning haze. Seemingly thousands of white yuccas and red ocotillos were scattered across the ever-greening landscape. A strong wind kept the plants and bushes in rapid motion, as if it were running wild and free. She sighted trees, large ones, and knew an ample water source loomed ahead.

Soon, the train left the elevated section and slowed as it descended into the Mesilla Valley and entered Las Cruces on the Rio Grande River.

As she deboarded, Maggie gazed at the towering and rugged Organ Mountains with their sharp spires in a cinnamon shade, visible despite the bluish white haze drifting over them. She heard bells ringing in what she was told was the St. Genevieve Church. She saw irrigated fields in clearings of mesquite and tornillo trees where corn, pumpkins, chiles, beans, and other crops were grown in the fertile location edging the great river.

She entered the depot and purchased a ticket for the next leg of her journey, the end of the line at Socorro. While she waited for departure, she purchased breakfast at a nearby cafe where ristras of *chile* peppers hung here and there, partly for drying and partly for decoration. Afterward, she walked Blaze for exercise, then let the roan drink and graze.

By eight o'clock, she was en route on a north-bound train, unaware that trouble was lurking ahead before the day ended . . .

A tired Hawk dismounted at the Tombstone sheriff's office, eager to be rid of his prisoner and to see his beloved wife. As he tethered Diablo's reins to the hitching post, he glanced down the street at the hotel and wondered if Maggie had sighted him and her heart was pounding with elation as was his. He had missed her something fierce and could hardly wait to embrace and kiss her. He wanted to spend the entire day and night showing and telling her how much he loved her before they took off to capture Ben. He wanted to complete their work so they could go home and begin a wonderful life together. He hauled a sullen, hostile, and bound Pete Barber from his own saddle and shoved him onto the boardwalk.

When the local lawman opened the door, his gaze widened in amazement. "I'll be darned, Reynolds; you caught the bastard."

"Yep, but he didn't make it easy for me. I've hardly been out of my saddle more than a few hours since I took off after him. I guess he got tired and butt-sore, too, because I found him grabbing a nap in some rocks over in the Santa Ritas. I'm hoping you've got a sturdy cell wait-ing for him."

"Yep, right beside his scraggly bunch. I'll send word to the judge we got 'em all so he can get ready to try and sentence the lot of them."

As Pete was being locked up, Hawk said, "As soon as you're finished with them here for that train robbery, I want them railed over to San Antonio to stand trial for murdering my family last December. I have to admit, it was tough bringing them in alive after what they did to my parents and brother. I was sorely tempted to force them into a showdown to punish the sorry varmints. But as a U.S. marshal, I'm sworn to uphold the law and seek justice, not revenge. I had to work to restrain myself, especially with Pete there. This is one time — no, two — he won't elude justice and punishment. If I have any say-so in the matter, they'll all swing from ropes."

"I agree," the sheriff said. "Then they won't be able to harm anybody else . . . so it doesn't slip my mind, let me tell you now that before she left town, Miss Malone said we're to notify her through her agency in St. Louis if she's needed to testify at the trial here."

Hawk stared at him for a moment in bewilderment and dread, then asked, "What do you mean? You saying she's gone?"

"Yep, yesterday sometime. Said she had to get on with her work elsewhere since yours together was finished."

Hawk's alarm and confusion increased. "Is that all she said to you?"

The sheriff chuckled. "She told me about your

380

marriage ruse; that was mighty clever of you two to pose as a couple to throw off suspicion. She did seem mighty interested in Berk Barber."

"What do you mean?" Hawk asked the same question again.

"She wanted to know his description in case she ran across him. She didn't want to tangle with him after helping to snag his brother. Lucky for her, I had one of Berk's old posters I showed her. You remember when they were floating around for a while on that rustling charge?"

Hawk's heart lurched in his chest as he surmised her reaction. She must have asked about Berk, viewed the poster, then added up two and two and gotten the wrong answer. But why would one omission on his part set her off so strongly against him? Why would she say they weren't legally married and take off like a wild wind? "I remember them, but I doubt she'll be crossing paths with him. Where was she heading?"

"Don't know; she didn't say, and I didn't ask. I guess she figured your pursuit would take a while and she had important things to do."

Hawk didn't want to arouse the man's curiosity about a personal problem between them, so he nodded and smiled. For certain, he had to locate her fast and learn what had happened to upset her. "I have one more task to carry out," he told the sheriff, "so stall their trials if you need us to come back and testify. I'll leave a note where I can be reached." He rapidly wrote down his superior's name and handed it to the sheriff. "I'll be riding out quick as I can. Guard them boys good; I don't want to go chasing after them again."

"They'll be safe here; I got plenty of extra guards on duty."

At the telegraph office and after he sent a report to his superior on his progress, Hawk showed his marshal's badge and asked the key operator about any telegrams Maggie had sent or received during his absence.

"You know the rules and law, sir," the man replied. "We can't reveal the contents of telegrams to and from other people, not without permission from the head office and a court order. You'll have to ask your wife about them. I will tell you this much: she received two telegrams on Wednesday — one from St. Louis and one from Tucson — and she sent one to Tucson early yesterday morning and one to St. Louis around midday."

Even at Hawk's urgings, the slender man firmly refused to divulge those messages, which he was certain hadn't made sense to the man, as they were probably in some type of code. At least he now knew she had been in touch with Newl Carver and Howard Carlton. If she had told her boss they weren't married — as with the sheriff — and she was leaving Tombstone alone, he doubted that Carlton would divulge any information about her plans to a stranger, that is, if she had reported them to her boss. It would be futile to contact the man. But there was another person he could go see for clues . . .

He hurried to the hotel to see if Maggie had left him a message, and was relieved when the desk clerk handed him an envelope. His joy vanished after he opened it to find her wedding ring and deputy's badge. He took the inclusion of those two items and the exclusion of a note as bad signs, and his apprehension and worry mounted by the minute.

The desk clerk volunteered that Maggie had left by horseback and too late to catch the last train to Benson from Fairbank. He also told Hawk that a young man had visited her earlier that morning.

Hawk was relieved when the description didn't match Ben Carver's, nor Berk Barber's. So who, he pondered, came to see her? What was said to spook her into secretive flight? What was in those messages sent to and from Newl and her boss? Where had she gone and why? Why hadn't she waited for him or left him a letter of explanation? Why had she returned the ring and badge? Trepidation consumed him as he thought of her being on the road alone.

He rushed to a mercantile store to purchase trail supplies. The owner's wife recognized him and told of Maggie's two visits yesterday. He wondered why she'd sent her clothes and the "absolutely exquisite and so romantic" photographs to the ranch if she wasn't planning on going there later. Something didn't add up, he told himself, unless she made a misleading and distressing discovery after mailing the items.

Then a horrible thought flooded his mind. What if she had been abducted as a hostage to be exchanged for Pete Barber? What if whomever kidnapped her forced her to make it appear as if she left willingly, and she believed he would take her strange behavior as clues to her jeopardy? No, he reasoned, she had been alone during her preparations to flee him. If she'd only gotten news about Ben which demanded immediate action, she wouldn't have handled matters with him as she had. It was clear she was eluding him for some unknown and serious reason . . .

After making as swift a ride as possible along a well-used road, Hawk dismounted before a large brown house in Tucson. He guided Diablo to a water trough behind it where the animal could rest, drink, and eat feed, which he poured from a sack into a metal container laying nearby. He approached the front. In less than a minute, a lovely woman responded to his knock and looked at him with an expectant blue gaze that reminded him of his wife's, though Maggie didn't resemble her mother.

"Yes, may I help you, sir?" Catherine inquired, having heard the stranger's arrival and observed his actions from several windows.

Go slow and easy. "Is your husband home, Mrs. Carver?"

"Didn't they tell you at the club he's out of

town today on business?"

Hawk held his hat between his thumb and fingers. "I didn't ask for him there, ma'am; this is a private matter; it's about your daughter."

Catherine's face paled and she trembled. Her voice quavered as she asked, "Is Maggie injured? Please tell me she isn't . . ." She could not bring herself to utter the word, dead.

Hawk quickly shook his head. "No, ma'am, she isn't hurt." He watched the lovely woman close her eyes and take a deep breath of relief before she looked at him again. "But I have to find and help her fast before she does get hurt or gets into worse trouble than she's already in." *You have to mislead her or she won't tell you anything.*

An anxious Catherine eyed the handsome man who was clad in black garments and wearing holsters secured to his thighs. "I don't understand, sir. Who are you? What do you want from me? Where is Maggie?"

"That's what I came to ask you, ma'am. After an exchange of telegrams between her and your husband yesterday, she took off alone while I was out chasing and capturing Pete Barber."

"You didn't tell me who you are, sir, and what you want with her."

"I'm United States Marshal Hawk Reynolds, ma'am, and we've been working together on Ben Carver's case since her arrival in Arizona." He saw the woman's look of shock at those revelations. "As hard as it will be for you and his father to accept the bitter truth, Ben Carver is guilty of that robbery in Prescott and guilty of committing other crimes elsewhere. I don't know why Maggie took off alone while I was chasing Barber, but she could be in danger if she confronts Ben by herself or runs across Barber's brother who's as mean as they come. You see, ma'am, I appointed Maggie as my deputy to give her the authority to help me make those arrests and to protect her during our work together."

"You're telling me that my daughter is a deputy marshal now and she's working with you on resolving that matter?"

"Yes, ma'am. I know everything, Mrs. Carver, about your husband persuading her to aid Ben's escape from prison and to try to prove he was innocent. I'm afraid all we've done is prove he's guilty. I'm sure she's gone to confront and arrest him, so please tell me where I can find them." He saw her expression alter to one of suspicion and alarm.

"Are you trying to trick me into telling you we're involved in crimes?"

"No, ma'am, I only want to get to Maggie to help her. You see, Mrs. Carver, I love your daughter and she loves me. In fact, we're husband and wife; we got married in Benson recently." At Catherine's look of astonishment, then disbelief, Hawk withdrew the marriage certificate and showed it to her, along with his badge. "She didn't reveal this news in a telegram because she was afraid it would panic your husband into coaxing Ben into hiding from us, and she also wanted to tell you the good news in person. I wish you and I weren't meeting under these grim circumstances, but that can't be avoided. I wish we didn't have to be the ones to arrest your stepson, but we have to do our duties. I don't know what provoked her to take off alone, unless she was afraid Ben wouldn't stay put much longer and she couldn't risk leaving me a message somebody might read. She's a skilled detective, ma'am, and is good at self-defense, but I doubt she's ever gone up against violent men like these before. You have to help me find her and keep her out of trouble by returning Ben to prison."

"Ben would never harm Maggie."

"Trust me, Mrs. Carver, he's dangerous and desperate. He doesn't know Maggie, so she means nothing to him, especially if she's out to send him back to prison, where he knows he belongs. Besides Ben's threat to her, she's on the trail alone where she could meet up with Barber's brother or other dangers. If you love her as much as I do, help me save her."

"What will happen to Maggie after you find her? You're a marshal and you know what she did. Will she be arrested and sent to prison?"

"No, ma'am. You see, I had permission from the authorities to bust Ben out of prison so he'd lead me to the others and the stolen money. Maggie took care of that first part for me; at least that's what I've already reported to my superior. The government thinks she's been partnered with me the entire time, so I'm the one who can protect her, with your help. There is one problem for you: after Mr. Carver returns home, you can't tell him I was here or you revealed Ben's location to me. If you do, he'll warn Ben to flee before I can reach him. If Maggie's already with him, there's no guessing what a furious Ben might do to her for revenge."

Catherine's heart pounded in dread. "Of course I love my daughter; she's my only child. But you're asking me to deceive my husband."

"Only for a few days, ma'am, then —"

Frantic, Catherine interrupted, "Newl would never forgive me for betraying him and for endangering his son."

"You have to make a choice, ma'am: you have to sacrifice a guilty Ben or an innocent Maggie. I know you and your husband helped Ben because you believed in him, but he doesn't deserve your loyalty, especially not at Maggie's expense. If we all work together and hold silent, nobody has to learn about Mr. Carver asking Maggie to break the law."

"Does that mean you won't tell the authorities about him convincing Maggie to rescue Ben?"

"That's right, so he won't be in trouble if he doesn't talk. To protect you, Maggie, and himself, surely he'll agree. He'll have to accept the fact his son is guilty and he can't help Ben elude justice. I know this decision is difficult, ma'am, but time is precious; she's already a day ahead of me."

Catherine turned her back to Hawk as she deliberated her dilemma. She must protect her daughter and husband — and the child within her body, a fact she had just learned today and hadn't yet shared with Newl. Her new son-in-law was right: Ben had deceived them and didn't deserve their loyalty, and certainly not at such a great price. Surely their baby's impending birth would soften the crushing blow to Newl when he lost Ben.

Catherine faced Hawk, grimaced in resignation, and said, "I'll tell you what you need to know." Afterward, she gave him a smile and added, "Tell Maggie how happy I am about her marriage. You seem to truly love and care about her. I'm glad she's going to quit that dangerous job and settle down. It's wonderful to meet you, Hawk, despite it being under these trying conditions."

"It's an honor and a pleasure to meet you, ma'am; you're as smart and special as she said you are. I promise I'll take good care of Maggie. I have a large ranch near San Antonio; that's where we'll be living as soon as we get this trouble settled. She told me about the ranch she lived on near Fort Worth with you and Mr. Malone, so she's excited about ours. I have to get moving, so we'll tell you more later."

"Good-bye, Hawk, and be careful. Hug and kiss Maggie for me."

"I will, the instant I see her. Good-bye, ma'am."

After mounting Diablo to head for the train depot to attempt to catch up with his wife, Hawk told himself he had been right not to divulge certain facts to Maggie's mother which might have evoked mistrust and silence: the return of the wedding ring and badge, and Ben's involvement in his family's murders. All he could think about now was getting to Maggie fast.

At dusk, Catherine was sitting in a rocker on the porch, daydreaming about the baby she was carrying and about her daughter's surprise marriage. She could hardly wait for their impending reunion so they could share their good news and she could get better acquainted with her son-in-law. It would be wonderful to have a second child and a first grandchild in the same year. She warmed with affection as she recalled the sound of Hawk's voice and look in his eyes when he spoke of Maggie, exposing great love for her. She was praying that Newl would be understanding and forgiving toward all of them when alarming news arrived. Within ten minutes, a doctor was being summoned for an emergency . . .

Chapter Seventeen

As Maggie — her shoulders covered by a railroad blanket to ward off the nippy mountain air — strolled beside the meandering rails with Blaze's reins in her grasp to give the animal exercise, she wondered if this impulsive trip was doomed. Only twenty minutes out of Las Cruces, a rider had chased them down and compelled them to reverse their direction to return for important freight which hadn't been loaded. That delay had added two hours to the scheduled journey, a slow route because it traversed mountains, hills, and the Jornada Del Muerto, a long stretch of desolate wilderness. Then, before they reached the halfway point at Engle, a water and shipping point and a base for miner's supplies and entertainments, they had encountered fallen rock and uprooted trees blocking the tracks.

With the terrain too dangerous at that hour to walk in search of help, they had sat there until they were missed in Engle and someone had been sent to check on them. That rider had gone back for assistance and tools before the lengthy clearing process began.

Maggie heard the thudding of axes and gnawing of saws against fallen trunks and limbs, the rumbling of rocks as they were rolled away, and swishings of branches as they were dragged aside. A lack of moonlight forced the workers to depend on lanterns and fires in order to perform their labors, which slowed the procedure even more. Often, they would halt to rest and drink water or warm their chilly hands near a blazing campfire.

Both as a money-making venture and kind service, the owner of a restaurant at Engle that stayed open all night hired down-on-their-luck prospectors to help him bring food and drinks to stranded passengers in exchange for a free meal. After the small group arrived on horses and mules, Maggie — who had stayed close to the train in the shrouding darkness — returned Blaze to the stock transportation car and went to purchase a late supper.

At two o'clock on Friday, May eleventh, Maggie checked into the Windsor Hotel in Socorro. She was fatigued from insufficient sleep, wanted a hot bath and delicious meal; she'd realized it was too late to head out for Albuquerque on horseback that afternoon. She was amazed and pleased to find such a large and charming place to stay. The oblong-shaped structure was three stories high with many chimneys rising above its flat-topped roof, and the exterior trimwork was artistically carved. The interior had a mixture of carpeted floors, polished hardwoods, and area rugs. The walls were a skillful blend of wainscotting, painted surfaces, and exquisitely designed paper patterns. The furnishings were of fine woods, with chairs and sofas covered in striking fabrics and colors. As she glanced around, she could hardly believe she was in the middle of nowhere, situated far from other large towns and almost nestled between mountain ranges.

Maggie saddled Blaze and took the roan for a ride before stabling her. They walked on a road west of town which traveled to the Billings Smelter and stamping mill for silver and gold mining companies, its towering round chimney sending forth thick and dark smoke toward a serene blue sky. A constant flow of wagons going to or from the enormous structure while hauling ore to be processed or while making deliveries to town for shipment on the Sante Fe Railroad provided ample safety in numbers.

Maggie — clad in a simple but flattering day dress — made sure she didn't ride too far before turning Blaze back toward Socorro. The surrounding area was picturesque with its mountains, hills, abundance of cottonwoods and pines and other types of timber, and the meandering Rio Grande River. On elevated sections, she saw ranches, vineyards, orchards, and farms where wheat, corn, and fruits appeared to be the major crops. As with other locations of that kind, miners, cowboys, drifters, swindlers, and other advantage-takers frequented the town where they traded, gambled, drank, played cards and other games, and visited "soiled doves."

Maggie made sure Blaze was tended at a nice stable, and would be ready for her to leave for Albuquerque at sunrise.

"It ain't safe for a lady to be riding that road alone, ma'am," the worried owner said. "We get all sorts of ruffains in this territory."

Maggie explained she had no choice as she alleged she was heading there to do journalist work and it was the only way to reach the town.

The man motioned to a group of horses in his corral and said, "They belong to a unit of soldiers who'll be riding that way at dawn, heading for Sante Fe. See that captain sitting in a rocker on the billiard hall porch?"

Maggie looked at the man in an Army uniform and nodded.

"If I was you, ma'am, I'd go ask if I could ride along with them; I'm sure he'll oblige. They came from Fort Craig, about thirty-four miles south of town on the tableland right of the river; you passed her on the way here. This area's been cleared of hostile bands, but we get renegades riding through ever so often, and get our share of outlaws; so soldiers still have to protect the north/south route along the river. You go ask him, ma'am."

"I will, sir, and thank you for the information and help. I'll see you at sunrise. Please take good care of Blaze for me." Maggie watched the man send her a genial smile as he nodded his head.

"Don't you go worrying about that roan, ma'am; she's safe with me. I ain't lost a horse yet. I give 'em clean stables at night, a clean corral by day, the best feed and hay around, and plenty of clean water. You won't be sorry you left her in my care."

Before she headed to the Windsor Hotel, Maggie crossed the wide dirt street and approached the officer. As she introduced herself, he stood and removed his hat and nodded at her, which implied to her he was a gentleman with manners and respect. She related her fabricated ruse and what the stable owner had told her and asked the captain if she could accompany the troop to the next town.

"We'd be honored to escort you to Albuquerque, Miss Malone. We strike out at dawn like he said, so meet us at the corral, ready to ride."

"Thank you, sir, that's very kind of you."

"If my wife or sister was stranded in the wilderness, I'd hope some man would offer them protection and assistance."

Maggie felt guilty about having alleged her travel companion was laid up in Las Cruces with a broken leg and she had a scheduled appointment to keep, but felt she had no choice except to mislead the officer. "If he were a gentleman like you, sir, I'm certain he would. I'll see you at sunrise at the corral. Thank you, and I'm deeply grateful you'll help me out of this bind."

Maggie was relieved when the captain and his

men bid her farewell on Sunday and rode onward for Sante Fe, as it prevented the kind officer from discovering her deception. As she placed her belongings on her bed, she smiled as she recalled his compliments about her not slowing them down. She had enjoyed conversing with him about his family and the territory during their long journey and as they camped last night. She was pleased that none of the men had spoken or behaved improperly toward her. The trip had passed without incident and placed her closer to her target: Ben Carver near Sante Fe, where she'd head tomorrow.

She ate a midday meal, took a bath, and washed her hair. She sat in a chair by an open window in her hotel room to help her long and thick locks to dry faster in the mid-eighty degree air and gentle breeze. Before reading a dime novel, she gazed at the contrasting landscape and local sites.

From a genial couple who had insisted she join them at their table for Sunday dinner, Maggie had learned that Albuquerque was situated on a flood plain created by the Rio Grande River and was bordered by the granite-covered and forested Sandia Mountains on the east and mesas on the west. Fields irrigated over sixty years ago were abundant and fertile. The town was mainly populated by a mixture of Anglos, Hispanics, and Indians. Its growth and prosperity had increased after the coming of the railroad in '80. The San Felipe de Neri Church anchored the center of

"Old Town" in its plaza. "New Town" was located a short distance away, with a mule-drawn streetcar traversing the center of Railroad Avenue. Legendary gunslingers and outlaws had visited there; colorful tales included one about Billy the Kid. When crime rose and justice was too slow to suit some citizens, vigilantes had dealt out their own punishments in the form of midnight lynchings.

When she had remarked on how clean the town was, she discovered that past ordinances still influenced people's behavior. Her dinner companions quoted her one as an example: "All houseowners or heads of families within the city limits . . . shall have especial care that their servants do not cast dirty water, sweepings, ashes or kitchen residue in front of the plaza, roads, streets, or alley-ways." How marvelous it would be, she had thought, if all towns enforced such ordinances.

As Maggie fluffed her hair to help it dry, she recalled how Hawk's fingers had played in her long light brown tresses. She missed him something fierce, loved him deeply, and ached over the breach he had created between them. She yearned to be held in his embrace and to taste his sweet lips on her. As she reminisced on their weeks together, she couldn't imagine how she had misjudged him so badly. Had he remained consumed and controlled by hatred and a hunger for revenge? Or had those natural feelings changed after meeting her? She wondered if the worst mistake of her life was in leaving him behind without asking for an explanation or by falling in love with and marrying him. How could she ever forget him and what they had shared? How long would this feeling of anguish and misery last? What if she was the one who was wrong?

Will you try to find me, my enchanting husband? If so, for what reason: love or to continue your quest for Ben? Whatever your explanation, will I be able to trust you again? If Ben is innocent, please don't come after me and him and force me to take action to halt you from harming him.

The dilemmas involving Hawk and Ben plagued her mind all afternoon. She needed the truth in both situations. She decided that if Hawk didn't come after her, she would locate and go to see him as soon as she resolved the predicament concerning her stepbrother. The only way she could get on with her life and healing was by facing the truth, whatever it was.

To distract herself, she thought about Abby and her mother; she longed to see and talk with both of them. Somehow she must prevent either of them from being implicated and jeopardized by her deed in Yuma, as well as the Mercers. Ben Carver was influencing every facet of her life and problems, she concluded, and he must be dealt with fast.

Hawk traveled as rapidly as possible to catch up with Maggie. A lengthy telegram he had received in the last town clarified the situation for him and revealed what must have provoked his wife's flight. He wished he hadn't involved other agents in his assignment, but he had needed the information about her they provided. He surmised that Maggie knew somebody had been checking on her at the boarding school, in Virginia, and in Texas; and she had suspected it was him. Fortunately, his superior and other agents assumed he had requested those studies to make sure she was trustworthy since she was a crucial part of his current mission.

Yet, it was the other two parts of the message that distressed him. Maggie must have tried to have him investigated, and had been told via her boss he wasn't a U.S. marshal. Despite the fact the Carlton Agency was a reputable company, the sources Howard had approached for answers had duped him out of the necessity to keep Hawk Reynolds's cover shielded. It was evident that Maggie believed he was only a bounty hunter and tracker, and a man out for revenge at any cost or sacrifice. She could even doubt that their marriage was for real, just as she doubted being made his deputy.

Even if that damaging "evidence" wasn't enough to emotionally hang him in her eyes, he worried, Berk Barber had ambushed Newl Carver days ago, most likely to extract Ben's location from him. Following his own visit to Maggie's mother, he had asked for a nearby agent to be assigned to observe Carver to make sure Newl didn't warn Ben of a marshal's impending arrival. That agent had reported that he didn't know if Berk had extracted the truth because Newl hadn't regained consciousness from his wounds since being found Thursday afternoon beside a trail near Tucson. Now, Newl was being treated at home where he'd been taken after he was recognized, and Hawk could imagine Catherine's anguish.

He was thankful they had been given an enlightening clue. Berk had hired an old prospector — who, for meals and board, did odd chores around town and at the Paradise Club — to watch Newl and to report to him in his camp outside of town if Newl made any trips, which he had done last Thursday morning. Berk had sworn that Newl wouldn't be harmed; the breaking of that promise had provoked the old man to tell the sheriff who was responsible. As soon as the agent learned who the shooter was and reported his name, the motive was clear. Hawk was all too cognizant that Berk, if he rode hard and fast, would reach the secluded cabin before or simultaneously with Maggie . . .

He didn't know how he could survive losing the last person he loved to another vicious Barber. If Berk or Ben harmed a single hair on his wife's cherished head, Hawk vowed, he wouldn't rest until he hunted the culprit down and killed him with his bare hands!

Maggie deboarded the train on a spur from the Lamy junction which was eighteen miles south of Sante Fe. She claimed Blaze and went to a cafe nearby to eat before riding into the wilderness to seek Ben. She didn't go into the plaza in order to avoid being sighted by the captain or one of his men, as soldiers from old Fort Marcy were now quartered there.

It was relatively quiet at that time of day. Most of the residents — especially the Hispanics and longtime peaceful Indians — followed the routine and custom of afternoon siestas or less demanding tasks inside the cooler confines of their homes and shops, a fact she had been told at the cafe as its owner and servers prepared for the respite.

After she skirted the occupied section, expansive vistas opened up to her line of vision. The highest elevations of the Sangre de Cristo Mountains were still capped by snow, offering a vivid contrast against the dark blue overhead and lush green below their white peaks and descending crevices. Knowing it would be cooler as she climbed into the foothills, she had a wool jacket across her lap, ready to don when necessary. She passed a large and lovely hacienda where a prosperous *charro* and his wrangling *vaqueros* relaxed beneath shade trees, talking and smoking and gaming.

While staying alert and having her weapons at the ready, Maggie rode into the forested hills north of Glorietta Mesa. As soon as it appeared to be safe, she took cover and changed clothes in a rush. To disguise her sex, she tucked her hair beneath a dark Stetson and donned Levi's, a dark cotton shirt, brown leather vest, and boots. Then she continued her journey.

Every time she heard a suspicious noise, Maggie concealed herself until either the rider or wagon passed her location on the dirt road. She had gotten fairly accurate at judging distances, so she knew when to start looking for the landmarks to indicate she was to veer into the woods. She smiled in relief as she sighted the huge and odd-shaped hardwood amongst pines, the pointed peak of a mountain kissing its right shoulder.

Since the sky had clouded after she left Sante Fe and obscured the sun's position as a directional reference, she used a compass to guide her southeastward. She crossed a stream with a large boulder on the left bank. She followed the remainder of Newl's instructions and saw the cabin, a tobiano paint — a white one with brown splashes — tethered to a scrub at its corner. She assumed Ben was staying prepared to flee in a hurry, because the animal was saddled and loaded. She frowned as she recalled being told Ben's paint had been left in Tucson after his arrest, because that meant either Ben had sneaked to see his father ensuing his escape or Newl had sneaked to see his son; that defiance of her warnings irritated her.

She dismounted, removed her hat, and shook her hair free. She knocked on the door and called out, "It's Maggie!"

"It's unlocked; come on in." She heard Ben's

response after a short delay, recognizing his voice from their short meeting in Yuma.

Maggie pushed open the door and entered the cabin. She froze as she simultaneously saw Ben bound to a chair to her right and heard an icy voice from behind her say, "Turn around real slow, woman, and hand over that pistol." Though he was trying to mask it, she read anxiety in Ben's green eyes and tight expression. She heard the squeaky door close and the bolt slide into place as she turned to stare into the hardened expression of Berk Barber. The first thought to race through her mind was that the notorious ruffian looked more like Ben's brother than Pete's. She saw his narrowed gaze give her a quick scrutiny, then lock on her hopefully controlled one. Her heart thudded in her chest and apprehension flooded her mind and body, reactions she struggled to master and conceal.

Maggie decided to bluff him by asking in a southern accent, "Who are you? Why is Ben tied up and why are you pointing a weapon at me?"

"Well, little sister, seems you came at a lucky time for me."

Maggie realized from his taunting remark that Berk knew who she was, or who he thought she was. She remembered — too late — that Ben's paint was an ovaro — brown with white splashes. How strange, her mind scoffed, that these two men who resembled each other so strongly had chosen the same breed of horse, their only difference being in opposite markings. "I don't un-

derstand," she murmured, trying to sound un-
enlightened and feminine, though her garb and
weapons probably belied her attempt.

"Old Ben there understands me just fine, don't
ya, Ben?"

"Leave my sister out of this, Berk; she's doesn't
know anything. She's a real lady from the South."
Ben looked at Maggie and said, "I'm sorry about
this trouble; I tried to tell Pa not to send you
with money for supplies. I can't believe you even
found this place way up here."

Maggie picked up on what she presumed was
Ben's hint and went along with it. "He drew a
map for me and I have a compass. He said you
needed money for food and no one would suspect
a woman of bringing it. What's going on, Ben?
Who is this horrible man? Why are you bound?"

"The pistol, little lady, pronto."

Maggie heard Berk prompt her as he nudged
her shoulder with the barrel of his. She frowned
as her fingertips gripped the butt, withdrew the
lightweight Colt, and held it out, dangling downward, to the infamous man. She faked disgust as
she said to Ben, "I don't know why your father
insisted I wear that silly and dangerous weapon;
I told him I didn't know how to load or fire one.
He said having it would scare off assailants.
That's what he also said about this ridiculous
outfit. I told him that no one with any intelligence
would think I was a man, but he insisted, so I
obeyed him. I can hardly wait to be in a dress
again." She passed a haughty gaze over Berk and

404

added, "It appears that Mr. Carver was wrong on both counts, since I now find myself at the mercy of a beastly scoundrel. I must insist you put away that gun, sir; it frightens me. As you can see, I'm no threat to you."

"Place your pretty butt in the chair by Ben."

At that icy order, Maggie straightened her shoulders and glared at him. "How dare you mention a private part of me in such a despicable manner!" she scolded. "That is no way to speak to a lady, nor is this any way to treat one! You, sir, lack manners and respect for the fairer sex and should be horsewhipped!"

"Sit down and shut your pretty trap afore I get real mad."

Although Maggie sent him another feigned haughty and shocked look as he glared in return and gritted his teeth, she took a seat, muttering, "You don't have to be so rude and surly, sir, or so —"

"I said, shut up, woman!"

"Leave her be, Berk; she's one of them southern belle types; she don't understand western ways and talk."

"She understands English, don't she? It's shut up or be gagged."

Maggie crossed her arms over her abdomen, exhaled in disgust, and donned a petulant expression to continue biding her time while awaiting a defensive opportunity. As she did so, she furtively observed the two men as they had a revealing and dismaying talk.

"Now, Ben, where's that money you stole from my brother? Pete's hoppin' mad and wants it back pronto. He knows it was you, not Coot, who took it. Where'd you hide it? He tol' me if I found your sorry arse and got the money back, he'd split it three ways. Course I mite keep half of it for my trouble. Tell me where it is or I'm gonna plug the little lady. Fact is, I might just plug her two ways with both of my pistols."

Maggie cringed as a lascivious expression danced over the villain's face. She didn't have to be told what he meant by the added threat as he stroked a rising bulge in his pants. She knew she would fight him tooth and nail and to the death if he tried to rape her. Her gaze jerked in Ben's direction as he shouted at the grinning man and strained against his bonds, his chair legs scraping against the floor.

"You touch her and I'll kill you with my bare hands, you bastard!"

"How you gonna do that with them all tied up? Now quit squirming and don't cuss at me again or you'll rile me up real bad. You don't wanna do that 'cause it makes my trigger finger get real itchy."

"Let her go, Berk, and I'll tell you where I hid the money."

Maggie stared at Ben as his guilt was divulged. Was he bluffing, she mused in disappointment, or telling the truth to save their lives? It was Berk who extracted more facts for her, but after she asked for her own benefit, "How could you do something so horrible, Ben? You told us you were innocent, that you had been framed or mistakenly accused. We believed in you, but you lied to us. My heavens, you're a real criminal." She didn't know if his contrite look and tone were faked or genuine. He had duped her in Yuma and was probably doing the same now. Hawk had been right about her stepbrother's wickedness all along. Did that mean Ben was also guilty of the Reynolds' cold-blooded slayings . . .

"I'm sorry, Maggie, but I got in over my head. I —"

"Hush up, you two! You can talk later. That ain't what I asked. How did you pull off that double-cross afore you was captured?"

Maggie pushed aside her tormenting thoughts about her husband to listen to Ben's response.

"I wasn't going to double-cross Pete and Slim. After we separated outside of Prescott, I got to thinking about the hungry way Coot eyed those sacks of loot, so I went back and hid them in another place. I was captured and sent to that hellhole in Yuma before I could join up with them and split it. If you promise to keep Maggie safe, I'll go fetch it for you. It'll take me about a week of fast riding, but I'll keep my word to you."

"Don't you dare leave me here alone with this . . . this scoundrel!" *I know what you're trying to pull, you deceitful coward! Save your sorry hide by sacrificing me to this ravenous wolf.*

"If Berk gives his word not to harm you, Maggie, he won't. The sooner I get myself out of trouble with Pete and Slim, the better. Hellfire, Berk, Pete should know me better than to think I would back-stab him! We've ridden together plenty, so he should know by now I can be trusted."

"Pete don't trust nobody but me and Slim. Where is it, Ben?"

Maggie observed the bound man beside her as he silently reasoned on the hazardous situation. She surmised he had disclosed certain facts in an attempt to sway Berk's opinion of him. He probably didn't care about what she would think and do if or when they got out of this predicament. If he knew her at all, he would realize she was as big of a threat to his survival as Berk was! His lies had entangled her in a terrible mess and had evoked awful decisions on her part, including the betrayal of her husband. Would Hawk ever forgive her for doubting and abandoning him? Would Newl ever accept the bitter truth about his son? Would Newl's anger and disbelief provoke problems between him and her mother? Ben had deceived and used all of them to obtain his freedom. Yet, there was one point she couldn't understand: why had Ben remained at the cabin when he could have recovered the stolen money and been far away by now? Had he believed she could find a clever way to clear him and get rid of his threats? She focused on Ben when he finally spoke.

"As soon as I tell you, you'll shoot us both and

go after it. I'll give up my cut if that's what Pete says, but I'll be the one to recover the money and turn it over to him. We'll all go after it. Or turn her loose and we'll go."

Maggie wondered if Newl had gotten the message to Ben about Pete's capture, as Hawk surely had the culprit in custody by now. It was fortunate for them that Berk hadn't heard about what happened in Tombstone last week and was ignorant of his brother's fate. She concluded that Ben was stalling for time or seeking an opening for escape. Even if someone was scheduled to arrive with supplies or to check on him, that person couldn't get near this place to get the drop on a skilled gunslinger like Berk.

"You're real protective of that sister of yours, ain't you?"

"I'll do whatever it takes to keep her safe and alive. You can have my share if you'll release her."

"So she can run straight to your friends for help? Nothin' doin'."

"I don't have any friends skilled or fool enough to go up against you, Pete, and Slim; and I surely wouldn't challenge any or all of you myself."

"Maybe we'll just leave her tied up here for somebody to find."

"She'd starve before she's found. Turn her loose or I'm not talking."

"Oh, I think I can convince you to run your mouth like the piles."

"Let her go, Berk, and I'll give you my share

of the money from the last three jobs we pulled; it's over sixty thousand dollars, some in gold."

"You givin' me the feelin' she means more than a sister to you. Don't tell me you done gone and got sweet on her. They got a name for that."

"Maggie's my stepsister; we're no blood kin. My pa married her ma a few years back. We weren't raised around each other; we didn't even meet but once, so don't go thinking and talking dirty around her."

"Yep, you done gone sweet on her. What would you do with a sassy lady like her? Hitch up to her so you can poke her all you want?"

"Shut up, you foul-tongued bastard!"

Maggie witnessed the keen way Berk was studying her and the way he was taunting Ben. What she couldn't surmise was how much of what her stepbrother said was accurate and sincere; he certainly looked infuriated by Berk's words and actions. Was Ben trying to save her, or was he only trying to instigate a cunning escape?

"Cut me loose, Berk; my hands are numb and my arms hurt. I'll sit right here where you can watch me with a pistol in your grip."

To Maggie's surprise, Berk complied with Ben's request. She had her Spanish blade nestled in her right boot, if she could only get to it . . . "Sir, may I fetch a cup of water?" Maggie requested softly. "My throat is cotton dry after that long ride."

"Nope, you keep your sweet arse stuck to that wood."

"Mine's dry, too, after all this talking. Let me get us some water."

"Do it, but if you try any tricks, I'll shoot her faster than you can blink, and I'll make you beg to die before I plug you."

"I won't twitch a muscle without your say-so, Berk, so relax."

Maggie watched Ben approach a wooden table and fill two metal cups with clear liquid from a canteen. After he asked Berk if he wanted any water or whiskey, the gunslinger shook his head, his gaze fastened on Ben.

"It's gonna be this way, Ben —"

A man's voice shouting, "Hello in the cabin! Permission to ride into camp!" sliced into Berk's words and brought him to alert.

As Berk glanced toward the door as if to make certain it was bolted, Maggie had time to mask her astonishment at hearing Hawk's voice. How had he found them, and so fast? Had he been spying on her and shadowing her, she fretted, the entire time since she left Tombstone? After all, he had accomplished that feat without her knowledge from Wilcox to Yuma weeks ago. Instantly she quelled those new doubts and scolded herself. No doubt he had reached town shortly after her departure and tracked her.

As she had, Maggie reasoned in haste, Hawk probably assumed the paint belonged to Ben, and of course he recognized Blaze, so he would deduce only they were present. She had to do something to prevent Berk from gunning down her husband before he could reach the cabin, but what?

Chapter Eighteen

Berk ordered fast and in a low voice, "Git over here, woman! Ben, you keep still and quiet or I'll kill her quicker than a sidewinder strikes."

"My boots are nailed to the floor, Berk, so control that trigger finger. I wouldn't do anything to endanger my sister or me."

Maggie joined Berk at the entrance and received additional orders before his last threat chilled her very soul.

"Git rid of him fast or he's dead afore his boots touch the ground."

Maggie's heart thudded in panic as she prayed Hawk wouldn't say or do anything to expose their relationship. She slid aside a bolt, opened the door about a foot and a half, and positioned herself in that limited space as a second call was heard and her husband dismounted at the edge of the clearing.

"Hello in the cabin! Can I ride into camp?"

She felt the barrel of Berk's revolver pressed into her back in warning as he leaned against the wall by the jamb, out of Hawk's line of vision. A wild wind whipped hair into her face and eyes, and she lifted a hand to move it away. "What do you want, stranger?" she yelled out, hoping he'd grasp her alerting clues by what she called him and the use of her exaggerated southern accent. With her free hand, she sent him another one by holding two fingers straight and wriggling them rapidly while the others and her thumb were balled toward her palm. She knew that signal was shielded from Berk's view by her body between them. She saw Hawk's gaze lower from her face for a moment, then his head gave a slight nod of what she presumed was understanding. She was relieved when he made no attempt to walk toward her and the cabin. His stance beside Diablo appeared deceptively relaxed, but she knew now he was wary. He removed his Stetson as he chatted in a genial tone, then held it before the left side of his waist; she guessed so his other hand could shift closer to his pistol in case he needed to withdraw it in a hurry for self-defense.

"There's a storm brewing, ma'am, and I was seeking shelter before it strikes. Looks to be a long and bad one. Got any hot coffee in there? I'd be much obliged to have a cup and a roof over my head before the rain starts."

As the wind gusted more forcefully, Maggie had to hold her hand over the hair at her right ear to keep it from blowing into her eyes. Her left hand imprisoned the edge of the door to keep it placed there as ordered. "I'm sorry, sir, but my son has the chicken pox and he's highly contagious, burning with fever, so you can't come inside. There's another cabin a few miles south-east of here. It's best if you take shelter there."

"Maybe I can make it before a downpour, which is sure to come within an hour or so. Thank you, ma'am, and I hope your son gets better soon."

"You're very kind, sir, and I wish you good luck." Maggie's body jerked as loud thunder pealed and dazzling lightning flashed overhead, confirming Hawk's assessment of the menacing weather. The sky was ominously dark as the storm closed in on them.

"So long, ma'am. Thanks again."

"You're welcome, sir, and you best move fast; it's looking dangerous here." She watched Hawk mount Diablo and rest his left hand on his hip-bone near his weapon. Blaze neighed as if to say hello to the familiar man and his horse, and she mentally urged her roan not to expose their acquaintance. Thunder roared and lightning flashed again, that time closer and longer and brighter. To keep Berk from getting tense and opening fire on Hawk, she whispered, "He's preparing to leave. He's putting on a rain slicker. I'll watch him and tell you when he's gone."

"That was quick thinkin', woman; you're real smart, ain't you?"

"I tried to come up with a logical excuse to keep him away so you wouldn't, I believe the word you like to use is, 'plug' him. There's no reason for an innocent passerby to be shot." She saw lust in Berk's eyes as he looked at her. The thought of this foul-smelling creature touching her made her queasy but she tried to appear calm. It seemed best not to offend or vex him, unless he made it necessary. "That stranger was right; it's going to storm fiercely very soon. The sky is getting blacker by the minute and the air is heavy with moisture." She was tense, but the weapon in her boot reassured her somewhat — if she could get to it and when Berk was off guard. The fact her husband was nearby gave her the greatest amount of courage. She had no doubt, no matter his motive for joining up with her, that Hawk Reynolds would give his best efforts to protect a woman in peril. "Is this area dangerous during bad weather?" she asked as more thunder and brilliant flickers came.

"Don't know. Why, pretty lady, you afraid of storms?"

"Let's just say, I don't like violence of any kind. Is there a shed or lean-to out back where we can shelter our horses?"

"Nope, they're just fine out there."

"What if we bring them inside? I don't want anything happening to that horse; she's special and she doesn't belong to me."

"Nope, they'll stink up the place and crowd us. Horses and cows stay out in pastures all the time durin' storms. She's safer in the open than tied under a tree; lightnin' loves to chew on them durin' storms."

A worried Maggie peered around the jamb as Blaze neighed again and pawed the ground with a foreleg. "It's all right, girl, settle down."

"I think that roan of yours is just in season. She wants to get at that big black mustang real bad. She don't seem to take to my paint, though."

Maggie saw Hawk vanish into the forest. She was relieved he was safe, and knew he was planning her rescue by now. "I wouldn't know about such vulgar things. But I can understand her repulsion if that animal is anything like his master."

She jumped as Berk's forefinger tapped her cheek and she half-turned to glance over her shoulder at him. She eyed his cocky grin, then gazed outside once more as he teased her. She allowed that sudden movement to widen the doorway opening and didn't force Berk to put distance between them; in fact, the stinking villain leaned closer. She endured his action with the hope Hawk had concealed himself and used his field glasses to check out the cabin. With luck, he would sight and recognize Pete's brother.

"You got a sassy tongue in you, woman, and you're real uppity."

"What do you expect, sir, when you speak so crudely to me? I fear you've given me no reason to think you possess even one gentleman's bone in your body."

"A loose tongue can be real dangerous in these parts. You best learn when and how to rein it in. Course I bet a pretty looker like you gets away

417

with foolishness most of the time. Don't she, Ben?"

When no response came, Maggie — as did Berk — turned to look toward the spot where Ben had been standing. As did Berk, she glanced right and left for concealing obstacles and found none, then closed the door to peer behind it to discover her stepbrother was gone! Her mind spun in alarm and her heart lurched in dread of Berk's instant revenge. *Calm yourself and use your wits, Maggie!* She stated the obvious with exaggerated amazement, "Where is he? There isn't another door. The windows are shut. There's nowhere to hide in here. He couldn't just vanish. I don't understand."

She watched Berk bolt the door, narrow his gaze, and step toward her. By intention, she widened her gaze and retreated. "Don't blame me, Berk; I didn't help him escape. That sorry stepbrother of mine will be in big terrible trouble when I tell his father he abandoned me."

"You distracted me while he sneaked away, didn't you?"

"Of course not! I did exactly as you ordered. Besides, whenever did we have a chance to plot any mischief? You've watched me like a hawk from the time I arrived. I've never been to this cabin before, so I didn't know it had a secret escape route. How did he sneak out so fast and quiet? He can't get far on foot."

"He's probably got a saddled and loaded horse hidden close by."

"Didn't you check out the surroundings before you captured him?" she asked, and saw Berk frown when she pointed out his oversight.

"Not everywhere. I got the drop on him while he was outside drainin' his lizard. Sit down and shut up while I look around."

Maggie did as she was told to stall for time so Berk could calm down and so she could seek an opportunity to get to her knife. She watched him look inside a cabinet filled with various items, then slam its doors. He examined the back and side walls, and obviously found nothing suspicious among their boards. He studied the floor, she surmised, for a trapdoor. He checked the rear and side windows and fingered sealing pegs which were still in place. He halted near a five-by-three-feet wooden rack with several shelves which held supplies. He grabbed one edge and pulled it away from the wall, exposing a small door that opened outward. Berk pushed the silently moving shelf unit back into place and eyed its other side.

"He kept them hinges greased so they wouldn't make noise. He had fresh-cut bushes hidin' it from the outside so nobody'd notice a trapdoor and to keep dried ones from makin' noise when he opened it. He cares more about that money and his hide than he does about you, little sister."

Maggie's gaze met Berk's. "He's my stepbrother and we hardly know each other; this is only the second time we've met. If he were my bloodbrother, he would never leave me in jeopardy for any reason. In my opinion, Ben Carver is a sorry excuse for a man and I was foolish to let his father talk me into coming here to help him. Mr. Carver is going to be heartbroken when he learns his son is a guilty man. Ben is a very good pretender because he convinced Mr. Carver he was innocent. He's probably heading straight for that money. If I knew where it was, Berk, I would tell you so you could catch him and refuse to share it with him. Your brother was right; Ben can't be trusted. I hope you horsewhip him when you find him."

"I'll do better than that, little lady; I'll give him the same thing I gave his old man last week. That's how I found this cabin and that weasel."

"What do you mean?" Maggie asked in dread, staring at him. Her alarm increased when Berk grinned sadistically and lifted one eyebrow.

"I gave him three of my bullets in exchange for a few words."

"You . . . shot Mr. Carver?" Maggie felt cold and weak as Berk gave her a nonchalant nod in response. "Did you . . . kill him?"

"Ain't no man still walkin' around with my slugs in him."

"My mother . . . Did you harm my mother? Is she. . . ."

"Never saw her. I got Carver on a trail outside town. He was alone."

Maggie closed her eyes and exhaled in relief. Yet anguish filled her. "I have to go see my mother. She must be suffering terrible grief. How could you gun down an innocent person? What kind of man are you?"

"You ain't goin' nowheres till I have that money."

Maggie noticed that he ignored her last two queries. "But I don't know where Ben hid it; I don't know where he's going."

"That's too bad for you, little lady, 'cause I'm gonna find them."

As Berk lifted a rope from the table, Maggie asked, "What are you going to do with me? It's obvious Ben won't talk or share it to save me."

"I'm gonna go look for the weasel. I'll drag him back here and make him talk. I'll skin his sorry hide inch by inch till he squeals, then plug him."

As Berk secured her to the chair, to dupe him, she reasoned, "You can't leave me bound here. Let me go with you. Ben could ambush you and keep riding. You could have an accident or be gone too long. Who will give me water and food, protect me if some villain arrives. And who will untie me later?"

"That don't concern me. I cain't let you slow me down. If I catch him fast, I'll be back to handle you."

Maggie knew it would look suspicious if she willingly accepted such a fate. "You're mean and heartless, Berk; I won't be safe here alone."

"That's too bad; you shouldn't be tied to that sorry bastard."

"That isn't my fault. Please don't leave me

bound and helpless."

"You're a mighty temptin' woman, but I done promised Pete to help him. Maybe you'll be nicer to me if I come back."

Maggie scoffed haughtily, "I could be dead by that time."

"I doubt it; you're too spirited to die quick and easy. I'll be seein' you again, mark my words; and we'll have us some fun next time."

As Berk left the cabin and mounted, Maggie wondered what Hawk was thinking when he sighted Pete's brother, as surely he was observing the location from the woods. Yet, if he was watching the front near the trail he had taken, he couldn't know Ben had fled from the other side of the cabin and would assume her step-brother was with her. All she could do was wait until Berk was long gone and tracking Ben before she yelled for help.

Then a horrible thought invaded her mind. What if Hawk had seen Ben escaping from the cabin or sneaking through the woods as he concealed Diablo before returning to spy, and deduced she had tricked him with her signals to give her stepbrother time to escape? What if Hawk was now trailing Ben to capture him or to let Ben guide him to the stolen money? What if Berk located both and ambushed them? She couldn't bear for Hawk to die.

Despite her peril, Hawk was her major concern. There was no doubt in her mind that Ben was guilty. He hadn't blinked an eye at jeopardizing her safety and survival, but how would he feel about costing his father his life? Her mother must be tormented by grief and worried sick about her daughter, if Newl's body had been found and if the authorities knew or suspected who was to blame. If only —

Maggie's worries were severed by sounds of distant gunfire. Who, she wondered, was the shooter and the target: Ben, Berk, or Hawk? She waited in rising distress to learn those answers, as struggling against the ropes accomplished nothing. Soon, the cabin door was shoved partially open, but she couldn't see around it to learn who was there. Her heart pounded in trepidation.

"Blaze!" she shrieked as her roan clomped into the cabin, and the horse's head jerked in her direction. "How did you open — Hawk!" She saw him step from behind the door and rush toward her.

"Are you all right, Maggie love?" he asked, cupping her face to study her quickly for injuries before he kissed her soundly as she gaped at him.

After their lips parted, he held his cheek against her temple for a moment as he exhaled in relief. Without another delay, he withdrew his Bowie knife and cut her bonds. The instant she almost leapt into his embrace, his arms banded her body and snuggled her close to his. "You scared years off my life, woman. You shouldn't have taken off like that alone. I've been half loco trying to reach you before Berk did."

Maggie leaned back and asked, "How did you know he was coming?"

"We'll talk about that in a minute. Are you all right?"

"Fine, now that you're here and you're safe. After I heard those gunshots, I was afraid you'd run into Berk or Ben out there."

"Neither. The shots came from the woods. I knew it wasn't a hunter 'cause it was pistol fire. I was worried sick when I saw Berk mounting alone. Then he walked his horse around the cabin while looking at the ground. After he left, I sneaked over and did the same thing. I found a trapdoor and boot tracks, so I figured Ben had somehow gotten away while we were talking and Berk was guarding you. That's what happened, right?"

"You're very astute, partner. Ben stole the hidden money and Pete asked Berk to recover it. He's mad as a hornet about Ben getting away while he was distracted. If that's who fired those shots, one or both might be returning soon. How did you find me?"

"We'll talk about that later. Right now, let's get out of here and conceal ourselves before we have company." Hawk grasped Blaze's reins and Maggie's hand to guide them out of danger.

"Wait, my pistol!" Maggie told him and fetched it from a peg near the door where Berk had suspended it by the trigger guard. She holstered the weapon, grabbed her hat, and joined Hawk in the entrance.

He led both into the forest where Diablo awaited them, and seemingly greeted them with affection. "You stay here while I take a peek around. Keep that pistol ready for use until I return. Then we'll talk and make plans." A few feet away, Hawk turned, smiled, and said, "I love you, Maggie Reynolds, and I'm glad you're safe. I'll be back soon."

"If not, I'll come looking for you because I love you, too."

She warmed when Hawk sent her a happy grin before he hurried to the cabin and vanished around the corner. She watched as he followed the boot and hoof prints he'd found into the forest and left her line of vision. She stayed on rigid alert and suddenly realized the storm hadn't struck yet and appeared to be moving westward at a swift pace. That was good, she decided, as it would prevent washing away trails needed for tracking Ben and Berk. She didn't want either man to escape capture and punishment.

Punishment . . . Berk's would be for murdering her stepfather. As soon as possible, she needed to send a telegram to her mother to let her know she was safe; and she needed to reach her mother's side for comfort. How sad and tragic to lose two husbands. At least Hawk was safe, and he appeared to be elated to see her. Soon, she would know the truth.

Twenty minutes later, Hawk returned alone and winded from his rush. He grasped his canteen and drank long gulps of water to wet his dry throat. He held it out to Maggie, but she shook her head. "Give me a minute to catch my breath and I'll tell you everything."

As he saw her gaze around in apprehension, Hawk said, "They're gone, love, so you can relax until we hit the trail. I found the spot where Ben had a horse hidden in the trees near a stream. I followed two sets of tracks for a short distance, but they kept going so I turned back. They're traveling fast from the depths of those prints. I didn't see blood anywhere, so I assume neither one is wounded."

"Did it look as if Berk caught up to Ben at the stream?"

"Nope, not from the positions of the tracks, and their pace. I'd say Berk fired at Ben to slow him down or stop him, but missed every time. Looks as if Ben's trying to put distance between them in a hurry. We'd best get moving before they get too far ahead of us. At least they're heading away from that storm's path, but dusk will be falling soon. You want to ride into Sante Fe and wait for me there? You've been through an ordeal here."

"No, I want to go with you, unless you object."

"That's fine, just stay alert and be careful, whatever happens. Good thing is, Berk and Ben won't know we're on their tails. We'll catch up to them and arrest them." He waited to see if she argued against Ben's guilt, since he wasn't certain if she'd come to aid Ben or to question and arrest him.

"My stepfather is dead, Hawk. Berk said he ambushed and murdered him last week. He said he didn't harm my mother, and I pray that's true."

Hawk pulled her into his arms to console her as he replied, "It is, love; she wasn't with Carver Thursday when it happened. But he isn't dead; leastwise he wasn't last I heard. He's hurt bad and was unconscious for days, but he's home and has a doctor and your mother tending him."

Maggie focused a teary gaze on him. "How do you know that?"

"I went to see your mother Thursday before I hightailed it after you and before news arrived about your stepfather's shooting. She told me where the cabin was located. The only reason I got here so soon after you did was because that trouble on the railroad slowed you down; they told me about it at the Las Cruces station, so I knew I wasn't far behind you. And I rode like a wild wind the rest of the way to hopefully beat Berk here. I retrieved a telegram from my superior before Diablo and I caught the train out of Albuquerque, it was faster travel on this mountainous terrain. Don't worry; I'm sure your stepfather is going to be just fine."

"If you left Tucson before Newl was found and he was unconscious for days, how did you know Berk shot him and was en route here?"

Hawk explained what he'd been told about the incident via a previous telegram he'd received earlier during his journey. "That agent's guarding Carver to make sure he didn't find a way to warn Ben I was coming."

"You met my mother, and she told you where to find us? Why?"

"I went to see her because I had to find you and fast. You left me a mighty skinny path to follow, even though I traced your final movements in Tombstone for clues. She's a good woman, Maggie, and beautiful like her daughter. I told her about our marriage and how much I love you. I also told her you're my deputy and we're working together on this case because Ben's guilty but that we kept those two facts a secret to prevent panicking Newl and Ben. I told her, while I was pursuing Pete Barber, you took off alone to reach Ben before the news broke about Pete and Slim, and he fled to escape justice. I convinced her you were in great danger and needed rescuing."

"Mother actually accepted such a shocking tale from a stranger? She actually believed you and told you where to come?"

"You trusted me at one time, Maggie love, but some crazy facts led you to think you were wrong about me. You weren't. When you had me investigated, you were told I'm not a marshal; that isn't true; it was said to protect my cover. I promise you I'm who and what I say I am, and I swear you're a legally authorized deputy marshal. I should have told you that Berk and Ben look alike; but back then, I was afraid it would sway your judgment. Later, I forgot to correct that mistake. In all honesty, I don't know which of them was the fifth man at the ranch, but I believe it was Ben because I was told Berk Barber was elsewhere that day. I wish we could talk longer and we will settle everything soon, but now we need to get going."

"You're right, Hawk, but can you answer two quick questions?"

When Hawk nodded, Maggie asked him, "Why didn't you tell the sheriff about Pete and Slim's connection to that Prescott robbery and reveal that was why we were pursuing them?"

"I didn't want the Prescott paper to pick up the story prematurely; the same's true of why I wanted your deputy rank to stay concealed. If those facts were reported and either Newl or Ben read them, they could have panicked and sent Ben into deeper hiding. I should have explained my motives to you, but things happened so fast in Tombstone that I forgot."

"Were you the one who had me investigated back East and in Texas?"

"Yep, but I convinced my superior and those agents I was only checking out your story to make sure you were trustworthy because of our work together. I took that step before I discovered who and what you are: Ben's stepsister and a Carlton detective. Everything else I told you is true, Maggie; I did have permission to pull a prison break for Ben. Since I told my superior you helped me, you won't be arrested for that deed. One last matter: we *are* legally married for as long as you want us to be."

"I'm sorry I doubted you even for a second and took off that way. I suppose I was afraid to believe my good fortune was for real. I didn't ask Howard to check on you; that was his idea. I was stunned by his message to me on Wednesday morning, especially following a surprise visit from Matthew Lawrence minutes earlier. Abby sent her fiancé to see me secretly after her father was alerted that somebody had been checking on us at the boarding school and in Virginia. She wanted to warn me to be on alert for trouble."

"Do you trust me and love me enough to put this on again, forever?"

Maggie gazed at the gold ring he pulled from his pocket and held up between his thumb and forefinger. She smiled and extended her left hand for him to replace it as she replied, "More than enough, with all of my heart and soul." Then he withdrew and pinned the six-pointed silver badge to her vest. She went into his welcoming embrace and shared a soul-stirring kiss that sealed their bond.

"Well, Deputy Reynolds, my beautiful wife, ready to ride?"

"Absolutely, my beloved and handsome husband."

Using great caution and all their skills, Hawk and Maggie tracked Berk and Ben for two hours and forty-five minutes. When the last rays of a sunset vanished and a waxing crescent moon denied sufficient light for further travel, they stopped for the night. They had covered twenty-five miles since leaving the cabin, traversing a dry plain with occasional ridges and picturesque mesas, and crossing railroad tracks which ran between the Lamy junction and Albuquerque.

As they dismounted, Hawk said, "They'll have to halt, too, my love; so we'll camp here and pick up their trail again in the morning. Let's tend the horses, eat, and get some needed rest; we may have a long and hard ride ahead tomorrow. From the condition of their tracks, they're using the same pace we are, but it's too dangerous to travel in such darkness. I figure they're an hour or less ahead of us."

"Do we risk a fire for cooking and warming our bones?" she asked as she unsaddled Blaze while he did the same with Diablo.

"The smoke wouldn't show in the darkness, but if they aren't far ahead and camp on higher elevation than us, they might either smell it or see its glow. I could hang a blanket to shield the fire's light from their direction, but the wind keeps shifting, so that wouldn't prevent them from catching a whiff of its odor. Sorry, love, but it's cold beans, jerky, and water."

"And biscuits. I purchased a few when I ate in Sante Fe earlier. My stars, was that only a few hours ago? So much has happened today that it seems ages ago."

"Now that I can see your beautiful face, touch your soft skin, and hear your sweet voice and laughter, woman, so does the fear I was riding with this morning. I've never been that scared in my life, Maggie, scared I wouldn't reach you in time to. . . ."

Touched by the emotion that choked his voice, she pressed her fingers to his lips and pointed out, "But you did, my love." She leaned against his virile body and murmured, "Speaking of fire, my brave husband, since we can't have one to keep us warm, I'll depend on you to ward off the night chill."

Hawk's arms encircled her body and held her close. "All I can do is share my bedroll and arms, woman, because I'll have to stay on alert for trouble. Just remember, you owe me later."

Maggie quivered in anticipation as she jested, "Owe you for what?"

"All of those lonely nights I spent without you nearby."

She nestled her face against his hard chest. "It won't happen again; I promise, and I'll gladly pay my debt whenever you're ready to collect it."

"As soon as possible, woman, but it can't be tonight. In fact, I won't ever get around to collecting it if I don't release you and clear my head. Berk and Ben aren't the only threats to us in this area. There are wild animals and renegades and other dangers in these parts."

"Then, you see to the horses while I . . . rustle up some grub," she quipped as he kissed her forehead. "I'll keep quiet so you can concentrate on your guard duty. Just for tonight, I'll even sleep in my own bedroll so you can keep a clear head and relaxed body."

"Ouch," he teased, "that'll hurt but I'll tend that wound later."

They broke camp a little after sunrise the following morning, relieved the ominous storm that had threatened the Sante Fe area yesterday had struck the landscape many miles east of their location.

They traveled past the Sandia Mountains, skirted Albuquerque below its southern flood plain boundary, crossed the Rio Grande River, and journeyed over terrain similar to what they'd covered yesterday.

As Hawk stayed on constant alert with one hand gripping his reins and the other grazing the butt of his left pistol, Maggie rode a short distance behind him and did nothing to distract him. Yet, his broad back and agile physique were enormous distractions for her as she trailed him, forcing her to struggle to concentrate on their work and surroundings.

At three o'clock, they reached a tragic sight and reined in their horses. Two scruffy prospectors halted them and gazed at Hawk's badge, then at Maggie's, as the couple dismounted.

"Afore you go to thinkin' wrong, Marshal, my partner and me didn't do this bad thing. We came upon him tied to that tree over there. We cut him loose and was gonna give him a decent burial with our picks and shovels. From the way he's cut up, we figured it was Injuns. We heard there's renegades ridin' these parts, prob'ly from over San Carlos way. Maybe some of Geeroneemo's bunch; heard he's kickin' up his heels again."

As Maggie stayed with their horses and averted her gaze from the sad scene, Hawk hunkered down and studied the bloody body. "Nope, this isn't the work of Apaches." He stood and said, "I'd be obliged if you boys would carry his body into Albuquerque and turn it over to the undertaker there. Tell him to place it in a nice casket so it can be sent home for burial in Tucson. He's from a good family over there. You should notify the sheriff before the casket's sealed so he can identify him. His name is Ben Carver, and there's a big reward out for his recapture, dead or alive. Since you boys found him, I guess you can lay claim to it."

"You don't want no share of the reward, Marshal?"

"I'm afraid lawmen don't qualify for them, but thanks for the offer."

"We ain't never seen no female deputy afore, ma'am."

Hawk chuckled and said, "As far as I know, boys, she's the only one that's been hired. And by me; she's also my wife and a good partner."

"You're a lucky man, Marshal."

"So are we, Clem. How much is Carver worth?"

"Last I heard, two thousand dollars, unless it's been raised."

"Yep, this is our lucky strike, Amos; we got us a new grubstake. Let's git him loaded and hauled into town. I guess who done shot him took his horse and gear, or he spooked and run off durin' the ruckus."

Hawk nodded as if he concurred, but surmised Berk took the paint to have a second mount so he could travel faster. "Just tell the sheriff you talked with U.S. Marshal Hawk Reynolds. His father's name is Newl Carver. Everybody in Tucson knows him and he's got plenty of money, so he'll pay whatever charge there is for the casket and railroad delivery." Since he didn't have any implements with which to write the information — or even a scrap of paper — he repeated those names so the prospectors would remember them. "I appreciate your help in this sorry matter, boys, and we gotta get riding. So long."

"Good-bye, Marshal, and thanks. Good-bye to you, ma'am."

Maggie forced out a smile and nodded before she mounted Blaze and followed Hawk until he stopped out of their sight. His voice was tender. He said, "I'm sorry about you having to see that, love."

"So am I. Newl is going to be heartbroken when he learns his son is not only guilty of that crime but also dead, and in a horrible manner. Do you think Berk is responsible?"

"Yep. Only a skilled gunfighter could wing a

man in both hands like that. Those cuts were made after he was bound. Berk must have tortured the truth out of him, because he's still riding toward Prescott. The only reason he didn't turn around to go back for you is because he knows where the money is hidden and he figures you've been found by now."

"By whom? That cabin was secluded."

"By that friend of Newl's who been hiding and supplying Ben."

"I suppose you're right. What do we do now? How can we arrest Berk for murder when Ben was wanted dead or alive?"

"We can get him on kidnapping and threatening a federal officer: you. We can also get him as an accomplice to that stolen money he's going after. But my motive is mostly personal, Maggie: I have to catch up to him to see if it was him or Ben at my family's ranch that day. Now that Ben is dead, only Berk knows the truth."

"Then let's get moving while we can still catch up to him," Maggie suggested before they headed out to ride their last wild wind together.

At five o'clock, Hawk and Maggie reined in once more as three men appeared before them as if by magic, and two others fell in to their rear.

No one had to tell her they were Apaches; their native garments and markings exposed their identities. With rising alarm, she watched Hawk exchange signals with them before he spoke with them in their language, one she didn't know.

Hawk pointed to himself and revealed his name and Cheyenne blood, *"Biishe. Heevaha-tane."* He motioned to Maggie and said she was his wife, *"Ghaasdza."* He then related his friendship to other Apaches and training by a legendary medicine man years ago in Arizona.

Maggie observed the interchange with great interest and was surprised when her husband withdrew a knife from his saddlebag and gave it to the foremost brave, perhaps as a bribe for sparing their lives. Yet, somehow she had a strong feeling the Indians were not a threat to them.

"Ixehe, ch'uune'," the Apache thanked Hawk and called him a friend.

Hawk spoke with the group for a while, telling them he was seeking a white man who helped murder his family and who rode a white horse with brown splashes and had another with opposite markings with him.

The Apache band leader revealed they had seen such a man, but he was riding hard and was far ahead of them. After he offered to help track the killer, Hawk reminded him of his training by an old Apache friend. The brave nodded and bid him good hunting and farewell.

Maggie was amazed at how fast the five men vanished into the surroundings. "Who were they? What did they want?"

"Apache from the San Carlos Reservation, just seeking a place to be free and to hunt. I've known many Apache in my day, Maggie, some were friends, good friends, one helped trained me in desert ways. I should have told you by now that I carry Indian blood in me: my mother was Cheyenne." He went on to quickly tell how his parents had met, married, and dealt with prejudice. "Does it bother you I'm what's called a half-breed?"

"No, Hawk, it doesn't, not at all. I love you, the man you are."

"That's a relief, and my last secret."

"One you never needed to worry about or keep from me."

"We'll talk more about it later; I'll tell you all about me and my parents and Mother's people, but right now, let's get moving again. They saw Berk pass earlier, but didn't approach him. Said he's riding fast."

They made camp around eight o'clock that night, ten miles west of Los Lunas in sheep country, though Hawk selected a secluded location. That time, he scouted the area for threats before they ate and slept, both aware they were still on Berk's trail and closing in on him steadily.

On Wednesday afternoon, they overtook Berk as he halted to rest on the bank of the Rio Salado which meandered in a valley between the desolate Ladron and forest-covered Gallinas mountains.

Hawk had noted from Berk's tracks that one of the horses had picked up a stone and was limping, and Berk had slowed his pace. From higher elevation, he studied the area ahead with his fieldglasses and sighted his target lazing on lush grass beside the river near a copse of trees.

"We'll dismount here and move in by foot," he told Maggie. "I have to know the truth. You keep a rifle aimed on him while I walk into his camp and have a chat with him. Maybe I can bluff information from him. I'll put your pistol in my belt behind my waist, because he's sure to demand I drop mine."

Maggie knew how important the truth was to Hawk and for the right man to be punished for those crimes, and it was the same for her. Yet she had heard how dangerous Berk Barber was. She couldn't forget what a man on the Sante Fe train had told her; it was said by many that Berk was the best gunslinger alive. Was Hawk, she fretted, fast and skilled enough to win a showdown with such an expert?

Chapter Nineteen

Maggie was worried about Hawk's illogical plan. In a gentle tone, she pointed out, "Won't it look suspicious to him if you walk up on foot? He might think you have friends or a posse hidden nearby."

"You're right, and I just realized that flaw myself."

After Hawk related a different strategy, she asked several questions to make sure she understood it fully, as she wanted no mistakes to imperil him. Blaze was concealed before she rode doubleback with Hawk for a certain distance. When he put her down, she secreted herself among trees and rocks and positioned herself where she had total balance. She leveled her rifle at Berk's chest, confident the site on the Winchester was accurate. She prayed her aim was true if her help was required to save her husband's life. Her suspense mounted as he appeared to ride casually along the riverbank, his badge in a shirt pocket to prevent spooking his reclining target. Once more she prayed; that time for Berk to stay calm and not start shooting wildly.

She watched Berk leap from the ground and draw his right pistol the instant he saw Hawk's leisurely approach. Her finger quivered on her trigger and her apprehension increased. *Steady your hands and clear your wits; this could be the most important shot of your entire life.*

Hawk sat nonchalantly in his saddle as he confronted the man, Berk's weapon pointing at him. He smiled, nodded, and used an embellished Texas twang to disguise his voice on the chance Barber might recognize it from their encounter days ago, "Howdy, Barber. Hope you don't mind me joining you for a spell." He saw Berk's steely gaze rake over him, assessing him for any threat. Maggie had told him that Berk had only glanced out the cabin door; so the varmint shouldn't know he was the man who had spoken with her; too, he was wearing different garments and wasn't the only man with a black horse.

"You know me, stranger?"

Hawk chuckled, and kept his hands resting on his saddle horn to keep Berk at ease. "Everybody recognizes you, don't they?"

"Who are you? Why are you trailin' me?"

"Two reasons. First, I was hoping to get my hands on that money. I saw Ben's body back there, so I'm guessing he told you where to find it." Hawk noted that Berk's only reaction to that news was a blink of his eyes, which told him Berk had himself under rigid control.

"Yep, he squealed like a stuck pig, but I ain't tellin' you where it is. Git rid of them pistols, real slow and easy, and git off of that horse."

Hawk obeyed those surly commands, dropping his two revolvers to the grass after he dismounted. He had practiced retrieving and firing a gun hidden behind him, so he knew he could do it if necessary. He also had practiced hitting the ground quick, seizing a discarded weapon, and firing it. What he didn't know was if he could carry out either trick swifter than Berk could react and shoot. "Well," Hawk questioned, "where did that sorry snake hide the money after he tried to cheat the others out of their shares?"

"Who are you? And why are you interested in that loot?"

"Name's Hawk Reynolds. I been chasing Ben ever since I spotted him after he escaped from Yuma Prison hoping he'd lead me to it. Before I could get to him and make him talk, I got laid up with a broken leg after my horse was spooked by a rattler and tossed me off his back. By the time I found that cabin where he's been hiding out, he was gone. I been trailing you two ever since I found your tracks in the woods. Course I didn't know he'd hooked up with you until I spied you from a hill over there. While we were riding together in March, Toby Muns was the one who told me how Ben double-crossed the others and had it stashed someplace near Prescott."

"You've gone to a lotta trouble for no good reason; I ain't tellin' you nothin'. And you ain't ridin' outta here."

"If you're going to kill me, why not tell me where the money is?"

"Naw, ain't good luck to go ajawin' afore you plug a man."

"Don't you want to know what my second reason was? Remember, I said I had two for riding into your camp today?"

"Don't make no never mind to me if it be one or ten reasons. I —"

Hawk interrupted Berk to distract him, "That's just about what Toby said before I plugged him. I would have gotten Coot, too, but your brother gunned him down before I found him. As for Pete and Slim, they won't be needing any money where they're heading soon, to the gallows. I got them stashed in the Tombstone jail."

"Ain't nobody can get a drop on Pete; he's near as fast and good as me; and there ain't no way he's gonna swing from a rope."

"That's about what he spit forth after I captured him and turned him over to the Tombstone sheriff. He robbed the Fairbank train last Monday, but I got the money back and lassoed those snakes. The railroad and authorities were mighty generous to me."

"You're a stinkin' bounty hunter, ain't cha?"

"I've been called worse, but that isn't why I was after Pete's gang. It was personal, for revenge. I planned to hunt down and kill all of you, but I'll settle for watching three hangings. You're my last target, Berk, so I'm lucky you were the man I've been trailing for days."

"What in hell's name you jawin' about? I ain't never met you afore."

"You and your brother's gang murdered my family in Texas late last December. Remember an Indian woman, a rancher with sandy hair, and a dark-haired man around nineteen who favors me, down San Antonio way."

"Yeah, I remember; that squaw was a real looker. I was tempted to have a taste of her afore we shot 'em, but Pete was in a big hurry that day. Somebody shoulda taught your little brother how to use that pistol he was wearin', 'cause he didn't even clear leather afore he hit the ground with a hole in him. Best I recall, we collected us a fat pouch full of money. Seems they just left the bank in town. That who you talkin' about, Reynolds?"

"You like to brag about who you've killed in cold blood, don't you?"

"Yep, and I never forgit a single event. I could tell you ever' person I shot and where I done it and what I took from 'em. You was a fool to ride into my camp and challenge me. You're a dead man, just like your folks. Maybe you'd like to have this back afore you die."

Hawk watched Berk grin sadistically as he withdrew something from his pocket and tossed it to him. His hand darted forth and caught it in midair. He looked at what he was holding: his mother's locket; it contained his and Stone's picture as children on one side and his parents' on the other. His body stiffened and fury consumed him as Berk taunted him.

"Toss it back; you ain't gonna be needin' it where you're headin'. It's a real pretty trinket; that's why I kept it."

"You sorry bastard," Hawk muttered in a tone of icy hatred. "If you're half the shooter you claim to be, why not give me a fair fight?"

"Nope. That's why I tossed you that necklace. You're quick thinkin' and actin', never looked at it afore you caught it. I know a good gunslinger when I see one. Ain't no need to risk you beatin' me to the draw. You ain't gettin' nothin' from me but a bullet. Say your prayers, Reynolds."

Maggie was almost frantic because Diablo was now standing between her and Berk Barber. If she tried to change locations, Berk might see her, panic, and shoot Hawk. Yet, if she didn't make that attempt and succeed, she had no clear angle on him. Why didn't Hawk realize Diablo was blocking her shot? What was Berk saying to make him look so angry? She'd taken a hasty peek at him through her scope and seen Berk throw something to him as Diablo shifted his position and obstructed her view of him. Could Hawk get to her revolver fast enough to —

Before either Hawk or Maggie could fire their weapons, Diablo stepped backward toward Hawk as Berk's body lurched forward after several arrows struck him forcefully in the back. Ready to fire, Berk's finger jerked on the trigger and he got off one shot as he was thrown off-balance, the bullet barely missing Hawk as it whizzed past his right shoulder.

Hawk's gaze retraced the flight pattern of those arrows, and both he and Maggie sighted the small band of Apaches on a hillside nearby. The group leader lifted his hand, sent Hawk a signal, grasped his mount's reins, and the braves left.

Maggie rushed to Hawk, put down her rifle, and covered his face with kisses. As he hugged her and chuckled, she scolded in lingering anxiety, "You scared years off of my life, Hawk Reynolds! I couldn't get a shot at him because Diablo got in my line of fire. I was afraid he would either sight me changing positions or there wasn't time to do so."

"I know, but it would have aroused his suspicions if I'd told Diablo to move aside. He must have thought I could beat him to the draw because he refused to give me a fair fight. I'm fine, love, so relax."

"What did he toss to you?"

Hawk showed her the locket, and related what Berk had told him.

"So it was Berk with Pete that day, not Ben. As bad as my stepbrother was, Hawk, I'm glad he wasn't involved."

"So am I, for your sake, and for your mother's and Mr. Carver's. Since Ben was innocent of that crime, we don't need to mention it to them later. It's over, Maggie, our work together and my quest for justice. Or it will be as soon as Pete and Slim are hanged. Now, my parents and brother can rest in peace, and I can have peace of mind and heart. I want you to have my mother's locket," he said as he turned her around to fasten it.

Maggie lifted the gold circle, opened it again, and gazed at the two pictures. "She was so beautiful and he so handsome, Hawk; and so is Stone. You and your brother favored each other greatly, and you resemble both of your parents."

"You sure it doesn't bother you I'm part Cheyenne?"

Maggie embraced him as she vowed, "Never. As we've seen today, Indians can be friends if we allow it. After we reach home, you can tell me all about your family."

"First, we have to visit Tucson and clear up matters there. And we have to file our reports and resign our jobs. Then we'll head for our ranch. But for now, wife of mine, let's see if we can make Socorro before dark; a hot meal, bath, and soft bed is what we need."

"That sounds too tempting to pass up, so let's get moving."

"First, I want to remove and hide those arrows. I wouldn't want anybody finding Berk's body and misunderstanding his killing."

Since Maggie knew Indian bands, tribes, and warriors could be identified by the markings on arrows, she concurred with Hawk's precaution. "Are we going to bury him or take his body into town?" she asked.

"This is one time I think it's best to let a man stay where he's fallen and let Nature have her way with him. I don't want the sheriff seeing those kinds of wounds and asking questions I don't want answered."

After his task was finished and they collected their weapons, Hawk and Maggie mounted and returned to where Blaze awaited them. They followed the Rio Salado to where it dumped into the Rio Grande, then rode along that river's bank until they reached Socorro shortly after sunset.

They tended their horses and checked into the Windsor Hotel where Maggie had stayed recently under much different circumstances.

They ate a delicious meal downstairs while water was being heated and hauled to a large oval tub in their lovely room.

After they entered it and Hawk locked the door, he suggested Maggie take her bath first. But she smiled seductively and invited him to join her.

"Surely this huge tub is big enough to accommodate both of us. You can scrub my back and I'll scrub yours. That way, we can finish at the same time and go to bed together." She saw Hawk's gaze gleam with excitement.

"I've never bathed with a woman before, nor anybody else except Stone when we were small. Sounds interesting and fun to me, woman."

Maggie noticed an absence of bitterness and anguish at the mention of his deceased brother. She realized he had accepted that tragic loss and dealt with his grief. She was glad he could remember the good times and had found peace, as she had done following her father's death, though she still missed him.

Maggie slowly and provocatively removed her boots and garments as Hawk watched her with a passion-filled gaze. She stepped into the warm water and asked, "Need any help, partner?"

Hawk stripped fast and joined her, with her at one end and him at the other. For a minute, he only gazed at her, admiring her beauty and congratulating himself for snaring her as his wife. "You're so enchanting, Maggie Reynolds, that you almost steal my breath and wits. Mercy, you're tempting and I'm the luckiest man alive."

"I'm the fortunate one, Hawk; I have the man I love with me forever." Maggie moved toward him and took a position across his lap, her knees touching the tub's bottom and her legs folded back toward their feet. "You are the one who's irresistible, ex-marshal Reynolds. I love you so much I fear my heart will burst with joy."

Hawk's hands cupped her shoulders; then he leisurely roved them down her arms to cover hers on his chest. He lifted the one with the wedding band and kissed its palm. "I love you, woman, with all I am."

Maggie leaned forward to seal their mouths in a long, deep, and heady kiss. She felt the stirring in his loins against hers. She yearned to unite their bodies, but wanted to build up enough anticipation to drive them both wild first. She took a cloth, lathered it, and slowly washed his torso savoring the sight and feel of his virile physique. She now knew that his chest was hairless due to his Indian heritage. She gazed at his midnight hair, brown eyes, and bronzed skin, and surmised they were precious gifts from his mother and her Cheyenne bloodline. She dipped the cloth and drizzled water over his sleek flesh to rinse away the soap, a fragrant brand of the hotel's.

Hawk playfully stole the cloth from her to perform that same task on her satiny skin. He noticed how her breathing quickened and her eyes glowed as he swirled the cloth around her breasts and stroked her nipples with it. He grinned and she smiled as those peaks grew taut, standing at attention like little rosy brown summits covered by melting snow. He rinsed off the lather, chuckling as bubbles slid down her stomach and either swam away in the water or cuddled close to her waist. He bent forward and kissed each inviting point. He dropped the cloth into the water, put his hands on her back, and drew her closer so he could kiss and suckle them.

Maggie arched toward him, allowing her head to drift backward. She closed her eyes and absorbed those blissful sensations. Her fingers played in his ebony hair and danced along the nape of his neck and over his shoulders.

They stroked and caressed and kissed until both were aflame with fiery need. Maggie lifted herself slightly when Hawk grasped his erection and thrust it into her. She lowered herself and he arched upward for deeper penetration until every inch was within her. They hugged tightly and kissed feverishly as their hips remained still for a while as they used hands and lips to tantalize and pleasure each other.

Then they began a rocking pattern which thrilled both. Nothing and no one entered their thoughts as they sealed their vows of love.

Soon, they worked as one in a near mindless frenzy, so great was their hunger for each other. A promise of sweet rapture coiled steadily within them as they rode closer toward the brink of ecstasy.

At last, they were rewarded with mind-soaring climaxes. Even so, Hawk remained ensheathed within her and she refused to release him. The love, satisfaction, and tranquility that encompassed them were wondrously bonding. They kissed with tenderness and joy, and lightly caressed each other's wet flesh.

"You seize me like a wild wind, Maggie, and carry me away to places I've never even dreamed existed. I love you with all of my heart."

"I love *you* with all of my heart. From the first moment I saw you in Yuma, I knew you were the man for me, and I was right."

"So was I, because that same crazy thought crossed my mind."

"Crazy?" she teased and took a playful nibble at his chin.

He chuckled as he gently tugged on a lock of her damp hair. "Sheer loco at that point in time, remember?"

"Yes, but we couldn't battle destiny; we were fated for each other as surely as the sun shines when it rises."

They kissed tenderly as they completed their baths, dried off, and went to bed to cuddle, deciding the tub and water could be removed tomorrow.

The following morning, Hawk and Maggie sent messages to her boss and his superior. Those telegrams included reports on their successes, their decision to resign immediately and retire into ranching and the fact that they could soon be reached in Tucson.

In Tucson days later, they found Newl Carver making a slow but steady recovery from his wounds. Despite the grim news about Ben's guilt and death, Newl was in amazingly good spirits. His mood partly resulted from having Ben's body arrive yesterday for a proper burial, thanks to Hawk, and the astonishing news that Catherine was pregnant with their child, a baby due in December. He said he accepted the bitter truth, and that he had been blinded by love for his son and his claims of innocence.

"I don't know where Ben went wrong, because I did my best to raise him right. Maybe I'll do a better job with this child. I'm sure going to try."

"You can't blame yourself, Newl," Maggie consoled him. "Sometimes, for reasons we may never know, people go bad. Ben had an adventurous streak in him, so perhaps he got caught up in things beyond his control."

"That's kind of you to say, Maggie, and I appreciate all you did for us. I'm glad you won't be getting into trouble for helping us."

"I'm happy you aren't angry with me because of the way I had to handle that matter with Hawk. I promise you, if we had discovered Ben was innocent, we would have found a way to protect him and clear him."

"I know you would. I'm also glad you won't have to report my foolishness in hiring somebody to rescue Ben from prison. I'd hate to get into trouble and be forced to leave my sweet wife alone in her condition."

"Somehow, thanks to Hawk, everything worked out for the best."

"Yes, it did," Newl replied, "and I'm most grateful to him. He'll make a good husband for you, Maggie girl."

She beamed with love and joy as she concurred.

Catherine straightened her husband's bed covers as she told Maggie and Hawk, "Let's retire to the parlor while Newl naps. We'll talk with him again later after he's awake and rested." She stayed behind for a few minutes to kiss and speak with him before she joined her daughter and son-in-law in the sitting room.

The three chatted for hours as they reminisced on past good times, relished their good fortunes, and Catherine and Hawk got better acquainted.

Three days later as Maggie and Hawk were preparing to leave for Yuma to visit with Abby, astonishing news arrived of an attempted jail-break in Tombstone that had resulted in the deaths of Pete and Slim during a bloody shoot-out. Hawk's superior related in his telegram that the other culprits involved in the train robbery were still awaiting trial but their testimonies weren't needed for convictions, sparing them of a return trip there. The friend of Newl's in Sante Fe who had hidden and supplied Ben had been let off with a stern warning and a fine.

But another surprising event had taken place during their visit. As Maggie helped Catherine pack Ben's clothing and possessions to give to the needy, they found a map revealing the location of the money stolen from the Prescott bank. Hawk surmised that Ben had drawn it in the event his memory failed him before he could collect it. The map was sent to the sheriff in Prescott so the money could be returned to the bank, proving Hawk's daring plan had worked to perfection.

As they boarded the train for Yuma, Maggie smiled and quipped, "It's very kind of you, my wonderful husband, to take me to see my best friend. We won't stay long because I know you're eager to see your grandparents and the ranch; so am I. Matthew and the Mercers will be surprised to learn how Abby bravely assisted the authorities with a difficult case. You're going to love her, Hawk, as much as I do; we're so alike in many ways."

"Are you saying Matthew Lawrence has captured him a wild wind, too?" As Maggie laughed and nodded, Hawk added, "I wonder if she'll be as easy and quick to tame as mine was."

"Am I tamed, my love?" she retorted with a playful grin.

"Nope, and I hope you never change. I love you just the way you are."

"And I love you just the way you are, my beloved husband."

Epilogue

In early September, Maggie stood at the ranch door and watched her husband dismount and tend Diablo after riding the range since noon to check out new fencing with his foreman. She saw the black mustang gallop toward Blaze as the roan headed in his direction; the two horses had made good friends. She watched Hawk cover the short distance between the barn and house and smiled when he sighted her.

Maggie's heart leapt with joy and desire, as it always did when she looked at him. She backed away a few steps to allow him to enter, then surrendered herself eagerly to his welcoming embrace and heady kiss.

After their lips parted, Hawk looked into her softened blue gaze and radiant face. "How can you grow more beautiful every day, woman? You've turned me into a greedy and selfish critter who can't get enough of you and doesn't want to share you with anybody else."

"Not even the little bundle I'm expecting next year?" she jested as she tickled his ribs.

"February is a long way off, so I still have you

all to myself for months. But since that's my son or daughter inside you, I'll share you a little after he or she is born."

"If you wanted to keep me all to yourself, Hawk Reynolds, you shouldn't have created this tiny intrusion while we were in Tombstone or Socorro. I was so distracted by our visits with Mother and Newl and then with Abby and Matthew that I didn't realize Nature was telling me a secret. I wish I could have seen Abby's face when she read that surprising news in my letter. I'm sure it would have matched the one she gave us when we arrived in Yuma with other astonishing news in late May."

"She did appear to be stunned for a while there."

"Wouldn't you be shocked to learn you had not only not broken the law but had aided it? Matthew and her parents were just as amazed to learn what she had done to help us. I'm glad she didn't have to worry about exposure any longer; I'm sure that was a strain on her."

"And it meant she didn't have to keep any secrets from Matthew; at least, not much of one, since she discovered it was a good deed after the fact. Were you surprised when she decided to marry while we were there?"

"Not much. After she witnessed how ecstatically happy we are, she wanted to experience that same feeling as soon as possible. Also, I doubt she could wait any longer to have Matthew all to herself. Remember, I told you we're much alike; we both married in haste, are blissfully happy, and both live on ranches. By now, the way those two looked at each other all the time, I bet she's pregnant, too. This is incredible: Mother and I both carrying babies at the same time, and perhaps Abby, too. I know Mother and Newl will be good parents, and news of their child helped Newl endure Ben's loss so much better."

"Yep, and I'm glad he's fully recovered from those wounds. He was lucky Berk didn't kill him."

"That entire episode seems so long ago."

"It sure does, and I don't want to ever face another one like that. I didn't like having you confronting so many perils, woman, even with me there to protect you with my own life if necessary."

Maggie grasped Hawk's hand and guided him toward the sofa in their sitting room. As she cuddled up to him, her gaze drifted to the two pictures hanging over the mantel nearby: theirs and one of his parents. She fingered the locket around her neck and imagined how much James had loved Marie; and she, him. She wished she could have met Hawk's parents, and wished Hawk could have known her father. Yet, if Jed Malone and his family had been alive, they would never have met.

"What are you thinking about, my love? You're so quiet."

"About how strangely fate works at times," she

replied, and explained her words. She tilted her head to look at him. "Do you ever miss being a marshal and traveling around the country having adventures and facing challenges?"

"Nope. I have all the excitement and challenges I need right here at home. What about you? Do you miss being a legendary detective?"

"Nope, I feel the same way you do. But I'm glad we got to visit with Howard when we went to St. Louis to fetch my possessions."

"Yep, but he was irritated with me for stealing his best agent."

"He was only delighted you were for real after he'd been duped."

"We did do a good job of tricking each other for a while," he jested.

"Yes, we did, but we had trouble keeping up our pretenses for very long. If you recall, you had me wedded and bedded in less than a month."

"I work fast and hard when I see something I want badly. I knew that the first time I heard your voice and saw your face in Wilcox."

"Ah, but you didn't let me see and hear yours until Yuma."

Hawk chuckled in amusement. "I did cheat a little, didn't I?"

"Yes, you did, my sly and devilish husband."

As they kissed and caressed, passions flamed within and between them. Soon they felt as if they were trapped in a roaring blaze.

Maggie leaned away and said in a near breath-less state, "Don't forget, your grandparents are coming for supper."

Hawk glanced at the mantel clock, grinned, and said, "Not for two hours. That's plenty of time for my wild wind to blow over me, right?"

"There's never enough time to satisfy my cravings for you, Hawk Reynolds, but I always enjoy trying to sate them. Two hours it is."

Hawk lifted his laughing wife and carried her into their bedroom as the winds of glorious passion swept them away . . .